ANNA DOWNES

THE
SAFE
PLACE

A Novel

MINOTAUR BOOKS
NEW YORK

First published in the United States by Minotaur Books, an imprint of St. Martin's Publishing Group

THE SAFE PLACE. Copyright © 2020 by Anna Downes. All rights reserved. Printed in the United States of America. For information, address St. Martin's Publishing Group, 120 Broadway, New York, NY 10271.

www.minotaurbooks.com

The Library of Congress Cataloging-in-Publication Data is available upon request.

ISBN 978-1-250-26480-0 (hardcover)
ISBN 978-1-250-26479-4 (ebook)

Our books may be purchased in bulk for promotional, educational, or business use. Please contact your local bookseller or the Macmillan Corporate and Premium Sales Department at 1-800-221-7945, extension 5442, or by email at MacmillanSpecialMarkets@macmillan.com.

First U.S. Edition: 2020

10 9 8 7 6 5 4 3 2 1

For my family

THE
SAFE
PLACE

PROLOGUE

WHEN THE car bypassed the main terminal building and pulled up next to a sign that said PRIVATE JET CENTER, Emily breathed in so fast she almost choked.

"You're kidding me," she said to her driver (her very own *driver*!), who smiled and opened the door for her like she was Cinderella.

A security gate led her through a glass tunnel to a departure lounge so elegant it could have been a hotel lobby. Precisely no one rummaged through her luggage or even asked to see a boarding pass; instead, she was ushered straight out onto the tarmac, where two pilots and a flight attendant greeted her personally with shiny white smiles. The attendant took her passport and led her toward a small plane, sleek and bullet-nosed, with just six passenger windows and a little staircase that dropped from a door in the side.

Emily climbed the stairs into a glossy, leather-lined heaven. Suddenly regretting her choice of comfy flight wear (black leggings, a Ramones T-shirt, and a pair of old Converse sneakers), she stood gawping at the armchairs and full-length sofa, waiting for the crew to realize their mistake and escort her back to the terminal. *We're so sorry,* they would surely say. *We thought you were someone else.* Or she would wake up in her shabby little flat, her lungs full of mold spores, to find that it had all been a dream. *Any minute now,* she thought.

But she was not asked to leave, and the plane did not shimmer and fade. It took off into the sky with no questions asked, and a measly one hour and forty minutes later they were back on the tarmac. This time, though, instead of London's neat network of buildings, Emily was looking at a low, barnlike structure with an unpronounceable name painted in large blue letters across the side.

She made her way off the plane and into the tiny terminal, where her suitcase and passport were waiting for her. The arrivals lounge was small and silent, and totally empty. The only other person in the room was a tall man with a tangle of dusty hair and a jaw full of stubble. Emily put her bag down on the floor and squinted at him. The man stared back with heavy-lidded eyes. From somewhere on the tarmac outside, there came a muffled shout and the slow, intermittent beeping of a vehicle in reverse. She hesitated, waiting for someone else to appear—perhaps a nice silver-haired gentleman with a peaked cap and a handwritten sign. But eventually she had to concede that this towering, glowering stranger was her ride. She gave him a tentative smile.

"Emily?" he said in a low, gruff voice. In a thick French accent, her name sounded more like *Ey-milly.*

She nodded.

"Yves," he said. Then he reached out, grabbed her bag, and strode off toward the exit, leaving her to trot after him like a puppy.

In the parking lot, Yves opened the door of an enormous black SUV, so tall that Emily had to climb up into it like she was mounting a horse. He stowed her bags in the trunk, planted himself in the driver's seat, and reversed out of the parking space without so much as a cough.

As they sped away on a flat stretch of road, Emily attempted conversation from the backseat. "It's nice to finally meet you," she said. "Will we be working together much?" But Yves didn't reply, and seventeen minutes later he still hadn't said a word, so she resigned herself to gazing out of the window in silence.

Road signs flashed by: *Avenue de Cordouan, Boulevard de Pontaillac, Rue des Platanes*. She tried them out, rolling the sounds around in her mouth. *L'Île d'Aunis. Saint-Marc-des-Fontaines. Beaulieu-les-Marais*. They tasted like poetry.

Green fields were punctuated by yellow sunflowers and rust-red roofs. White stone walls ran over hills striped with neat rows of grapevines. She saw farmhouses, rivers, and tall spindly trees; pointed spires, crumbling churches, and, in the far distance, a thin blue stripe of ocean.

Gradually, the roads became narrower and the trees became thicker. Then, with no warning at all, Yves swung the car onto a dirt track. Leaves brushed the sides of the car like fingers, and branches reached out to one another overhead, forming a tunnel of green. The bonnet dipped low as the track sloped downhill, giving the impression that they were burrowing deep into the earth.

They drove through increasingly dense woodland for what felt like hours. Twigs tapped at the windows and snapped under the tires, and Emily tried to remember if the Frenchman had produced any actual evidence that he was who he said he was. Kicking herself, she realized that she hadn't thought to verify his identity; she'd just followed him to his car and strapped herself in.

Her breath became shallow. She watched the man who called himself Yves. His eyes were locked on the road, his jaw clenched tight as he navigated the potholes. Furtively, she checked her phone: no service.

It became dark inside the car as the canopy grew thicker and daylight gave up trying to break through. Emily wondered how much farther they would, or *could*, drive; surely they would hit the ocean at some point? She twisted in her seat to search for signs of civilization, but the view through the back window was even less reassuring than the one in front. The land looked as if it had never seen a fence, let alone roads or buildings. They were in the middle of nowhere.

Finally, just as she began to weigh up the pros and cons of throwing herself from a moving vehicle, they began to slow. Peering through the windshield, Emily spotted rods of black iron up ahead. A gate. As they came closer, she could make out letters in the design.

"*Querencia,*" she read aloud.

They pulled up next to a gleaming security panel and Yves opened his window, reaching through to punch buttons on a small keypad. "*Voilà,*" he said, startling Emily so much that she jumped. "We have arrived."

There was a buzz and a clank, and as the gates slowly parted, Emily's mouth fell open, all thoughts of escape melting away. A wonderland of color and sweet floral smells seemed to spill through the gap like paint: purple petals, emerald leaves, pink blossoms, orange butterflies, all pouring out of a pure blue sky. Even the light seemed different from any she'd seen before.

The SUV lumbered onto a sandy driveway. Rolling down her own window, Emily stuck her head out, eager to absorb as much as possible. Cicadas chirruped steadily from their hiding places, and somewhere to her right she could hear chickens clucking as well as a thin plaintive cry—a sheep, maybe? Pathways snaked off between sprays of lavender, and a hammock swung lazily next to a cluster of tomato plants, each one bursting with bright red fruit. Ahead, through branches and foliage, she glimpsed the sparkle of a pool, and beyond that yet more water, darker and flecked with white.

And then two houses rose out of the flora, one on either side of a sprawling circular lawn: two huge whitewashed castles standing sentinel over a fairy kingdom.

Emily gave a low whistle as the car came to a stop. She could feel it already. This was the kind of place where things could be different, where *she* could be different.

"What *is* this place?" she breathed.

"You like it," said Yves, more a statement than a question. His face was turned away, his expression hidden.

"*Like* it?" She was lost for words. She felt like Dorothy stepping out of her monochrome world into the Technicolor land of Oz—so much so that she half expected munchkins to crawl out from between the flowers and start singing. She shook her head, marveling at the speed with which her life had changed. Rock bottom one minute, and the next minute . . . this.

Tipping her face to the sun, Emily let the breeze trail across her face like a silk scarf.

"I love it," she said, as the gates closed behind her. "I never want to leave."

CHAPTER ONE

EMILY

GOOSE BUMPS spread over Emily's arms like a rash.

"Sorry," said a tall blond woman, who had neglected to introduce herself. "We'll be ready to go in just a tick." She fiddled with her digital camera, adjusting its position on the tripod.

Emily smiled politely. She had auditioned in countless church halls, but this one took cold and drafty to new levels. Echoes bounced off the walls and danced around the room, making it almost impossible to hear what anyone was saying.

A bearded man sitting behind a wooden table stifled a yawn.

"I do apologize," the woman muttered, squinting at the camera. "This won't take a moment. . . . Aha! There we go, all sorted. I hope this doesn't make you feel too uncomfortable, Emily, but we're recording all our auditions today. It helps us when we're having our casting discussions later on. Just ignore it if you can."

Emily nodded. Under her skirt, sweat trickled down her thighs.

"Right, so we'll start recording. Just give your name and agent to the camera, then we'll get straight into the scene."

Emily closed her eyes and took a breath, letting it out slowly. *Just breathe.*

The bearded man picked something out of his teeth. She'd recognized him as soon as she walked in, but he seemed smaller in real life, and less handsome. One spindly leg lay draped across the other, the angles of the knee joint sticking out through his trousers, and his arms were folded across his chest in an attitude of utter indifference.

"Take your time. Whenever you're ready," the blond woman said, sneaking a glance at her watch.

Emily swallowed. *Breathe. Come on. You can do this.*

She gave a small nod. *Ready.*

"Okay," said the woman. "Off you go."

"Excuse me. Ex-*cuse* me, can I get past?"

Emily elbowed her way through the slow pedestrian traffic. Pushing past a couple taking selfies, she tripped over the wheels of a pram and smacked her wrist against a lamppost. She kicked the post and swore loudly, twice. The owner of the pram flinched and steered her baby away.

Emily pressed her sleeve to her eyes. Despite weeks of preparation, the audition had been a complete balls-up. All the lines she'd thought were safely committed to memory had somehow evaporated, leaving only a screaming inner monologue of fear and self-doubt: *I can't do this I don't know the lines I can't do this they hate me I can't feel my legs I can't do this.* She'd coughed, stammered, and sweated her way through the whole thing and only just escaped without vomiting. Why did that keep happening? What was wrong with her?

Also, she'd been an absolute idiot to think that Carnaby Street would be a shortcut; she should have known that the lunchtime crowds would be out in full force. *Stupid, stupid, stupid, can't get anything right.* She checked the time on her phone and sped up, squeezing past street performers and buskers until finally she broke free of the crush and scurried down the last few streets to the office.

Gasping for breath, she pushed through the revolving door

and into the lobby. A signal light went on above the nearest elevator and she ran for it, arriving just in time to collide with a tall man emerging from between the silver doors.

"Sorry," she mumbled, her face full of starched lapel.

"No harm done," said the man.

He held the elevator open for her and she rushed inside, looking up at the last minute to realize she'd just crashed into the company's managing director. "Shit," she said as he turned and walked away, then clapped her hand over her mouth. "I mean, good afternoon, Mr. Denny!" Cringing, she jammed her finger repeatedly against the button for the fifth floor until the doors slid shut.

Checking her appearance in the mirrored walls, she realized she looked insane—her hair stuck out in clumps, her top lip glistened with sweat, and her eyes were ringed with smudged mascara. But, she supposed, running all the way from Soho to Mayfair would do that.

When the doors *pinged* open again, Emily scuttled across gleaming tiles with her head bent low and dived behind the reception desk. Glancing around, she rattled pens and flapped paper in a pantomime of important activity. *Just arrived? No, not me, I've been here for hours.* Fortunately, no one seemed to be paying any notice. She pulled out the collar of her shirt and blew downward, trying to dry the excess moisture underneath.

"Sweaty, flushed, out of breath. Somebody get laid on their lunch break, did they?"

She whirled around to see a lacquered head poking out, spy-like, from behind a newspaper. *Urgh. David.* The HR manager of Proem Partners sat on a low sofa with his legs crossed, his eyebrows raised in a matronly expression of disapproval. *Busted.*

Emily decided to brazen it out. "Well, why not?" she said, smiling. "It is hump day."

David simpered. "You're late," he said, tapping his watch. "Again."

"I know, I'm sorry. I lost track of time."

"Audition, was it?"

"Um. Yes. Sorry I didn't tell anyone; it was kind of a last-minute thing."

"I see. Well, we can't keep Spielberg waiting, now, can we?" He made a show of neatly folding his newspaper. Then he stood and smoothed the creases out of his expensive shirt, his eyes roaming a little south of Emily's face. "So how did it go? Are they gonna make you a star?"

"It went great, thanks," she lied. "Fingers crossed."

"I'll watch this space, then."

"Yeah." There was an awkward pause. Emily stacked letters and notepads into useless piles. David flashed her a creepy smile. Why was he hanging around? Didn't he have anything better to do than stare down her top? "Right, well, I'd better crack on," she said. "Make up for all that lost time."

"Oh, sure, absolutely." But David didn't move. He tapped his fingers on the desk. "Actually, Emily?"

"Yes?"

"Can I have a quick word? Meeting room one?" The look he gave her was both patronizing and shifty, and it made Emily's heart thump. She knew that look. She'd seen it many times before on other similarly officious faces.

"Sure, of course," she said, standing up too fast and sending her office chair spinning into the back wall. She followed David into the meeting room, hoping against hope that this "quick word" was not what it appeared to be.

It was exactly what it appeared to be.

Fired, she thought, when Dave had finished talking. She couldn't say it out loud. No matter how many times it happened, it never got any less humiliating. "But . . . ," she stammered. *No, no, no, I can't lose this job.* Her frozen thoughts suddenly began to thaw and came pouring out of her mouth. "I'm really sorry. It'll never happen again. I'm actually a super-punctual person. I can prove it. I can do better, I promise. I just need one more chance."

David shrugged, fake sympathy spreading over his ferrety face like oil. "You know I like you, Emily, but it's not my decision to make. If it were, you'd have a job for life."

"Okay, well, whose decision is it? Maybe you could talk to them for me?" *Don't beg,* she told herself. *Surely you're above begging for a shitty temp job?* But the words kept coming. "Maybe I could do something else, something with less responsibility. There must be other things that need doing?"

"Come now, you don't need us. Good-looking girl like you?" David reached out as if to ruffle her hair but thankfully seemed to change his mind at the last minute. "I'm sure Hollywood is just falling over itself."

Emily felt her cheeks burn. Proem was the only thing keeping her afloat. Bookings for temp jobs had been slow lately, and corporate videos and play readings didn't pay much.

When the ordeal finally came to an end, David patting her shoulder like a headmaster sending her back to class, she returned to the mercifully empty reception area and the desk that was no longer hers. Behind her, the meeting-room door clicked shut and David's busy footsteps faded away into the recesses of the building. A funereal silence settled like snow.

Well . . . fuck. What the hell was she going to do now? The upside of losing her job, of course, was that she would no longer have to pretend to care about filing and making new clients feel welcome. But then again, the rent was due, she was deep into her overdraft, and it wasn't likely that she'd get another temp gig straightaway. Jamie at the temp agency had mentioned only a few days ago that they were struggling to find enough work for everyone, and getting fired wasn't exactly going to propel her to the top of the list.

She lifted her head and glared at the computer screen. The phone rang but she ignored it. Nope, there was no other option: she'd just have to cook up a good sob story, phone Jamie, and throw herself on his mercy.

* * *

There was no reason to stay until the end of the day, but the mid-afternoon rush made it impossible to leave. Every time Emily went to pack up her things, someone would approach the desk and issue instructions so forcefully that she found herself unable to explain that technically she no longer worked there. Then a female client arrived for a meeting with a four-year-old in tow and dumped him at Emily's feet like luggage, so then she *really* couldn't go. The poor little boy looked so forlorn that she ended up playing hide-and-seek among the potted plants while simultaneously directing calls and signing for packages.

After a while she began to feel sad. As she watched the well-dressed human traffic flowing steadily through the foyer, she wondered what it *would* be like to have a job for life. Decent money, security, colleagues, Friday-night drinks. It all sounded so *liberating*.

Emily realized then how much she'd enjoyed her six weeks at Proem. She didn't exactly fit in, of course, but people had started to say hi to her in the coffee room, and she'd even been sent a fun little questionnaire for the in-house "newsletter," whatever that was. "Get to Know Your Team," the email had said, with a note explaining that her answers would be posted the following week along with her photograph. It had felt nice to be included.

She looked for more excuses to hang around. Buoyed by the attentions of the abandoned little boy, she found increasingly elaborate ways to entertain him: Twenty Questions, magic tricks, a treasure hunt. She swept the floor. The photocopier was beeping; the paper tray was jammed. The coffee machine needed cleaning, the cushions straightening. She wanted to leave the place looking perfect. Maybe someone would realize what a great employee she'd been and call her back. But when the office activity began to wind down and the boy's mother finally appeared to reclaim her shrieking, writhing child (Emily had pumped him full of sugary bribes), she knew it was finally time to go.

Picking up her bag, she took a last look around. Somewhere

in a parallel universe, maybe she belonged in a place like this. Maybe there was a version of her walking around in a Stella McCartney outfit and carrying a briefcase.

But back in the elevator, she studied her reflection once more. *On second thought,* she decided, *probably not.*

CHAPTER TWO

SCOTT

THE FAT nib of the pen was too blunt to penetrate his skin, but Scott Denny was giving it his best shot. He forced it into the center of his palm, turning it slowly like a screw, first one way and then the other, grinding the metal against his flesh.

It was painful but not nearly enough. He cast his eyes over his meticulously ordered desk, searching for something that might do the job properly. There wasn't a lot to work with. His phone obviously wouldn't do much damage. Neither would the metal prongs of the charger, not even if he pressed really hard. He could maybe crush his fingers with one of the heavy granite statuettes. Or smash the ornate picture frame and use the glass to carve lines into his arm. If he had a stapler handy, he could slam it repeatedly into his thigh.

Too messy, though. Too loud. Too conspicuous.

On the other side of his desk, her slender frame perched delicately on a Danish cherrywood swivel chair, his executive assistant, Verity, blathered on. Her immaculately manicured nails tapped an irregular beat on the keyboard of her laptop as she made updates to his schedule.

"You've got the managing exec of Alkira-Dunn coming in with her lawyer tomorrow at eight thirty, and after that you've got a conference call with the rep for Truss and Boulder. He's hoping we'll finance a buyout. I've already talked to him; he doesn't have a business plan and we're a bit unclear on competitors, so we need to look at that tonight. And then if you need to run models you've got some time before your lunch meeting. Now, you need to tell me what you want me to do about . . ."

She droned on and on.

And under the table, *grind, grind, grind.*

He really should stop. It was going to leave one hell of a mark.

The sky outside, dissected into squares by bronze-mullioned windows, was dishwater gray. Where had the afternoon gone? In just a few hours, the streetlights would start flickering on: a neat line of fire stretching along Grosvenor Street all the way to Hyde Park, a procession of torches lighting the way home for all but the likes of him, the night owls for whom the days were not defined by the rising and setting of the sun but by the open and close of global trade.

Scott suddenly registered silence. He looked up. Verity had paused mid drivel and was giving him an odd look.

"What?" he said.

"Yesterday's start-up. I need to know if you want me to go ahead and contact their director."

Scott tried to recall the previous day and drew a blank.

"Everything okay?" Verity's doll-like face was rumpled with concern.

"Fine." He smiled thinly. "Just a few issues at home. Nothing major. Yes, set up a meeting. What else?"

Verity gave him a sideways look and returned to her screen, unconvinced but keen to press on.

Grind, grind, grind.

Beside him on his desk, Scott's phone lit up displaying yet another new message. There was now a neat little queue of them.

Please talk to me . . .

Last night I thought . . .

We need you, don't . . .

I swear if you . . .

I fucking hate you . . .

Selfish thoughtless cowardly bastard . . .

Grind, grind, grind.

He nodded along with whatever Verity was saying, his thoughts drifting further and further away. Images darted birdlike through his mind, swooping and flashing their colors at him. He saw an orange sun peeking through feathery fronds of pampas grass. A wet footprint evaporating on hot polished travertine.

Then a pillow, soft and plump. A delicate finger, pointing.

And stars. A thick blanket of stars across a clear, black sky.

He fought the urge to slap himself. His eyes wandered, seeking an anchor. Through the glass wall of his office he could see the worker bees buzzing from room to room at a time-lapsed pace. Clients came and went. Junior staff members leaned in doorways clutching dainty cups of espresso. And over in reception, a large potted fig tree wobbled as a fully grown woman tried to wedge herself behind it.

He narrowed his eyes. Was he seeing things? No. His receptionist really was hiding behind a potted plant. Suddenly, a small boy jumped out from under the desk and hopped up and down, pointing with glee at the ill-concealed blond. She clutched at her chest as if shot, then fell to the ground in a heap. The boy laughed and sat on her head.

Scott removed the pen from his hand.

He watched, entranced, as the receptionist negotiated her way out from under the boy and staved off a second attack with some sort of trick. The child gazed up at her as she produced a small object from behind his ear, and for the first time in a long while, Scott smiled.

There was a soft knock at the door, and both he and Verity turned to see David Mahoney's smarmy little face peeping around the door. "Sorry to interrupt," David said, "but I just wanted to let you know that it's done. I told her."

Scott blinked. "What?"

"The temp on reception. I fired her. As . . . as we discussed." David's eyes slid to Verity, who shrugged.

"Oh." Scott glanced back toward reception. The young woman was now galloping around and flapping her arms like wings. "Yes. Good. Thank you."

David pressed his hand to his heart and pretended to faint. "Oh god, don't do that to me. For a minute there I thought I'd made a mistake."

"No. No mistake."

"Thank heaven for that." He let out a high-pitched laugh. "I was worried *I'd* be out the door next!"

Scott stared at him.

"Okay, well, she ought to be packing up her things as we speak."

"No rush," Scott murmured. Down the hall, the receptionist was wrapping what looked like a stack of cookies in a napkin. She pressed them into the little boy's hand.

David backed away with an almost courtly bow and the door clicked shut after him. There was a brief pause, during which Verity raised a penciled eyebrow. "Dare I ask what she did to offend you?"

Scott said nothing, and Verity went back to her laptop. She knew better than to push him. She resumed her meaningless stream of facts and figures.

And underneath it, a small unpleasant sound.

Tap tap tap.

Scott frowned. It was coming from under the table. A soft, wet rhythm, somewhere near his feet.

Tap tap tap.

Peering down, he saw several tiny dark splashes of blood on the polished concrete. *Well, would you look at that,* he almost said. Clearly, you should never underestimate a blunt instrument.

CHAPTER THREE

EMILY

A FTER HEADING out of the main lobby and onto the street, Emily circled around the back of the building and turned left toward the small Tesco Metro near the Tube station. She was starving, and the cupboards at home were pretty much bare. A mental rummage through her fridge turned up a small hardened block of cheese, a jar of curry paste, tomato sauce, and a carrot. Not even Jamie Oliver could make a meal out of that.

She checked her phone as she walked. No missed calls, no new emails; just a text from her acting agent, Lara, reminding Emily of the times of both the following day's audition and the routine admin meeting they'd scheduled for an hour beforehand. Emily tapped out a response: Yay! See you tomorrow! and quickened her step. At least getting fired meant that she wouldn't have to sneak out of work again. Actually, maybe it was a sign. Destiny or something. Maybe she was supposed to get fired so that she could go to this audition. After all, the universe worked in strange and mysterious ways.

In the supermarket, Emily found herself humming along to the tinny background music as she browsed the aisles, her basket dangling from her elbow. She picked up milk, eggs, cereal, onions, tomatoes, and chicken, and on a cheerful whim she threw in some smoked salmon and an avocado. By the time she reached the self-service checkout, she'd also acquired a block of the good chocolate and a four-pack of Bacardi Breezers, because why not?

Unfortunately, the display on the card reader soon told her why not. Card declined, insufficient funds.

Emily frowned. Impossible. She definitely had money in that account; she hadn't been paid yet, but the rent wasn't due until next week.

A Tesco employee hovered nearby. "Do you need some help?"

"No, no." Emily grinned. "All good, just used the wrong card, that's all. I won't be a sec."

She pulled her phone out of her bag and brought up her banking app. Her account details appeared. *Shit.* The rent came out this week, not next week. It had bounced, which meant she had yet again hit her overdraft limit and would have to apply for her third extension in as many months. She would be laughed out of the bank.

"You sure you don't need help?" asked the shop assistant again.

"Yes, fine, no problem." Emily went to pull out her credit card and remembered that it had been canceled due to irregular payments. *No, no, no.* She briefly considered running out of the shop without paying but thought better of it.

Blushing, she beckoned the Tesco lady over. "Actually, I do have a bit of a problem. This is so embarrassing, but I've left my card at home. I must have picked up my old one by mistake. So annoying—they look exactly the same!"

The woman peered at her over the top of her glasses. She was nobody's fool. "You can go home and get it," she said. "We'll keep your shopping here until you get back."

"Well, no. I live quite far away so that's not really . . . Look, can I just take a couple of things and leave the rest?"

Nobody's Fool rolled her eyes. Without saying a word, she pushed a couple of buttons on the screen and swiped her staff clearance card, erasing Emily's shopping list and bringing up the start page once more.

"Thanks. Sorry." Emily paid for the Breezers, milk, and eggs, and watched as her extravagances were taken away.

Outside on the street, she bit her nails. Her pay would come in next week, but it would only just cover the missed rent, so there would be nothing left for food or travel. Or bills. She thought of the overdue electricity reminder taped to the fridge.

Things were not looking good. Nobody's Fool was right; she needed help.

Rather than get straight on the Tube, Emily took the side streets off Piccadilly Circus and Trafalgar Square down to the river. The smoggy London air was far from fresh, but it beat the vacuum of the underground and she needed a clear head.

On the Golden Jubilee Bridge, she placed her shopping bag at her feet and pulled her phone out of her pocket. Underneath, the Thames slid by, brown and soupy. Her thumb hovered over her mother's number. Did she really have the nerve to call? Was she that desperate?

"I have had *enough*!" Juliet had shrieked during Emily's last visit. "You can't keep doing this! You can't just disappear for months on end, no phone calls, no emails, nothing, and then show up out of nowhere asking for *money*." Afterward, the two of them had sat in stunned silence, neither knowing how to bridge the gap. Juliet, as always, was the first to try. "I'm sorry for raising my voice," she said, her face drawn. "But your father and I worry so much about you, and we're afraid that . . . Look, it would just be lovely to hear from you because you'd like to say hello, and not just because you want something."

That had been Emily's cue to be gracious, conciliatory. Instead she chose the lowest road. "I'm sorry I'm such a massive *disappointment* to you guys," she said, "but you were the ones who adopted a kid from fuck knows where. If you wanted perfection then maybe you should've left me where I was."

Juliet had recoiled as if slapped. "That is not fair, Emily. And you know it."

Emily did know it, but there was a spark of truth in what she'd said. Plus, she always got a kick out of seeing her saintly mother snap. *What, no jolly silver lining for me? Oh, how sad.* This time, though, the look on Juliet's face had been somewhat less satisfying.

After a few moments, Emily replaced the phone in her bag. The river stretched out beneath her, full and fat. Lazy waves licked the cold stone walls and slapped the undersides of party boats, and Emily had a fleeting urge to throw herself in. Life just felt . . . too big. She was supposedly an adult, but for some reason she struggled to deal with, well, anything really. She didn't understand her rental agreements. Tax returns were like cryptic crosswords to her. Conversations about mortgages and small-business loans (very rare in her life, but they did crop up occasionally) might as well have been in Urdu for all the sense they made to her. She seemed to spend most of her days feeling baffled and overwhelmed. Which, she mused, perhaps explained why she now found herself broke and unemployed, standing alone on a bridge with only half her shopping.

Sighing heavily, she picked up her bag and turned away from the water, heading instead for home.

As usual, the door of Emily's building got stuck on the bulging carpet, and she was forced to squeeze her body sideways through the gap. Her cardigan snagged on the latch, which pulled a small hole in the weave. "Crap," she muttered, trying unsuccessfully to shove the door shut again. She gave it a kick. The doorknob fell off.

She trudged up the stairs, brushing a film of dust off the bannister with her sleeve. Inside the flat, the ever-present smell of curry, courtesy of the Indian restaurant below, was today enriched by an acrid tang of burned toast. Spencer must be cooking.

She poked her head into the kitchen, expecting to find her flatmate in his favorite spot at the table, bent over a packet of tobacco and some rolling papers. He wasn't, but the evidence suggested he'd only just left. An ashtray full of roll-up stubs smoldered on the table, and a thin haze of smoke hung in the air. A tub of margarine sat lidless and sweaty next to greasy plates and, in the corner, takeout boxes spilled from the bin.

Curling her lip in disgust, Emily returned the margarine to the fridge, opened a window, and then picked her way over to the countertop to search for a clean glass—one that didn't have a small pool of alcohol at the bottom. Something caught her eye as she rummaged. Among the debris was an oil-spattered note.

Guess what, it said in Spencer's lazy scrawl, *rent bounced again, landlord lost his shit. We've got four weeks.*

Emily sat at the table and cradled her head in both hands. She racked her brains, running through a mental list of friends who might have a spare room or even a sofa she could crash on for a few weeks but, surprisingly, she came up with nothing.

How is that even possible? I have friends, don't I?

She did, but many of them had thrown in the towel and moved away from London to get married and have kids. Now they were all scattered across the country, moving on with their lives, sending invitations to events that made absolutely no sense to her. Tupperware parties. Gender-reveal parties. She had no idea what these things even meant. Whenever she'd made the effort to visit, she'd found that she had nothing to say, nothing to contribute. It was as if they'd all flown off to the moon and left her behind.

Of the friends who had stuck around, she could only think of two who might have had space for her, but Louise had sublet her room while she was away on tour and Rhea's father had just died, so the time probably wasn't the right time to ask for favors. That, and Rhea's place was like a drug den. The last time Emily had stayed over she'd woken up in the living room at 8 A.M., hungover as fuck, surrounded by bearded men and bong smoke. She hadn't the courage to ask who they were or where they'd come from, so she'd fronted it out, sitting up and pretending everything was normal. The TV had been on, spitting out news story after gruesome news story, the men all staring with glassy eyes at grim accounts of domestic violence and mass shootings, child abuse and murders, and she'd sat and watched with them for over half an hour before she'd felt brave enough to stand up and leave the room.

And then Rhea had appeared, gray-faced and groggy, insisting that Emily come with her to her niece's second birthday party. "Please, Em," she'd pleaded, "I can't face it on my own." So, off they'd trudged to a clean white house in Putney where cake-faced kids literally ran rings around them. Emily had never felt so dirty in all her life. That was three years ago, and she hadn't been back to Rhea's house since.

Of course, there were her parents, but the thought of moving back in with Juliet and Peter, even temporarily, almost made her retch. There was another option there, but it was only marginally less horrendous. Over the past five or six years, Emily had called her mother countless times and asked to borrow money; always Juliet and never Peter, who told anyone who would listen that kids these days would only learn self-sufficiency when they were thrown into the churning waters of adulthood with no life jacket. Juliet, on the other hand, always caved, but would it be different this time?

Emily hadn't spoken to either parent since her last visit, so naturally a repeat performance would go down like a shit sandwich. But what was the alternative? Live in a box on the street? She was fairly certain that her mother would rather part with some cash than see her sleep in a doorway. Eighty percent certain, anyway. Maybe seventy-five.

Emily looked at her phone. Her mouth was bone dry.

Just do it.

She picked it up and pressed the call button.

Juliet picked up after six long rings. "Hello, Emily? Is that you?"

"Yes, it's me. Hi."

"Darling, hello! I'm so glad you called! Listen, let me just . . . hang on, I can't quite . . ."

"Hello? Are you there?" There was a lot of noise in the background, clinking and laughter and music.

"Hold on," Juliet was saying, "I'm just . . ." There was a squeak and a bang, and the chatter was instantly muffled. "Ah, that's better! Sorry, I'm in a restaurant. You know the one on the corner where the old bank used to be? They've done it up. It's very nice, the food is superb."

"That's nice." Emily took a breath. "Listen, I just wanted to apologize for, you know, the thing at your house. The way we left things . . . I've been feeling bad."

"Oh. Well. Thank you, darling, I appreciate that." Juliet paused. "How about we just forget it happened, okay?"

"Are you sure?"

"Absolutely."

"Okay. So, we're good?"

"Yes, sweetheart, we're good."

"Cool." Emily picked at a dry smear of egg yolk on the tabletop. "So . . . how've you been?"

Juliet chuckled. "I'm just fine." She made it sound like a question, her tone playful.

She's being weird, Emily thought, instantly on her guard. "And Peter?"

"Yes, your father is also fine. He's here, actually. Your grandparents and Auntie Cath, too. Do you want to say hello?"

"Oh, no, I don't want to disturb." A pang of guilt curdled into bitterness. *How cozy, a quiet family dinner without the black sheep, just the way you like it.* "Look," she said, pressing on. "This is going to sound bad, but please hear me out because I'm, uh, dealing with a bit of a situation here."

"Are you alright?"

"Well, I'm not dying or anything. But things are a bit difficult. I'm in a bit of trouble."

"You're making me nervous." Juliet snickered. "You're not pregnant, are you? I only ask because I *know* you're not calling about money."

"I told you it would sound bad."

"Emily—"

"And I wouldn't ask unless it was an emergency."

"Emily, stop." Juliet's tone had changed completely. "Are you about to ask me for more money? Yes or no."

Emily swallowed. There was no way around it. "Kind of. Yes. But please believe me when I say I'm desperate."

There was a sigh, followed by a short cluck of a sound that could have been a laugh or a sob.

Emily listened resolutely to the muted clink and buzz of the restaurant, steeling herself for a lecture. "Oh, come on," she said, breaking the silence. "It can't be that much of a shock." She didn't mean to sound sulky, but that's how it came out.

When it came, Juliet's voice was thick. "I'm not shocked. Not one bit. I just thought . . ."

"What? What did you think?"

A sniff and a rustle of tissue.

"I just thought you might be calling to wish me a happy birthday."

Oh. Fuck.

"Juliet, I—"

There was a soft click and the line went dead.

CHAPTER FOUR

SCOTT

FOR SCOTT, every working day began with an early morning ritual. He arrived at the office before sunrise and wandered from room to room, trailing his fingers lovingly over the curves and corners of his kingdom. Soft leather, polished timber, frosted glass, and black steel: he caressed it all, making a silent inventory of every detail. He knew the building as intimately as he knew his own skin. He'd overseen the entire renovation process, from knocking down the first wall to repositioning the electrical outlets; he remembered every single purchase, every decision, every placement. This space was his brainchild, his vision, his literal dream come true.

Years ago, just after graduation and before landing his first job with an investment bank, Scott had fallen asleep on a train from London to Bristol and woken up knowing exactly what he was going to do with his career. With a clear and burning certainty, he knew that one day he would launch his own fund, one with an emphasis on the development and mentorship of emerging companies, and that he would build the perfect corporate palace in which to house it. He could see the pure beauty that would be his offices, the devilish expense hidden beneath dazzling simplicity. He'd nursed his dream and worked relentlessly until it came to life. That was his way. That was how he'd been as a child, as a teenager, and as a young adult, always dreaming and planning and working, pulling thoughts out of his head and making them real.

Somehow, he'd managed to orchestrate his married life in the same way, dreaming up the perfect girl to be his perfect wife and only barely believing his good luck when Nina showed up behind the counter of his local coffee shop. He'd never seen anything more beautiful in his life. She was a miracle, the very image of what he wanted: a mysterious stranger from a far-off land with a face as fresh as ocean spray. It was love at first sight. With her, he knew, he would build something pure, something unbreakable. And sure enough, as if by magic, their perfect life had materialized before their eyes.

In fact, for a long time it seemed he only had to think of what he wanted and, lo, it would appear. Even Nina couldn't dispute his ability to make special things happen. She used to say he was like a glassblower, somehow able to coax shape and color from dry, dusty sand.

A warm glow spread over Scott's shoulder, and he turned to see the sun breaking free of the London skyline. Its buttery rays came bouncing through the glass walls of the mezzanine, lighting up the meeting rooms as if from the inside and transforming the whole office into a glittering prism. He tried to smile. In the past, his offices had always made him happy, but lately he'd found himself stroking the surfaces not with pleasure but with melancholy, as if he were saying goodbye. As if the mere touch of his finger could turn his dreams into dust and his glass back into sand.

Shrinking away from the light, he looked down over the balcony. The mezzanine was one of his favorite features, not least because it provided a bird's-eye view of reception. It was from here that he liked to watch his staff arrive for work. Verity was always first, her long hair swishing behind her like a cape. Then his most senior associates appeared, usually followed by a few of the younger, hungrier junior team members. His second-in-command would show up at some point. And then, over the past six weeks, almost always red-faced and out of breath, Emily the receptionist had brought up the rear.

Initially, Emily had caught his attention because there'd been something familiar about her, something Scott couldn't put his finger on. But she'd held it because she was fascinatingly different. Wide-eyed and often late, she couldn't have been further from the highly experienced temps they usually hired. She'd stared at the switchboard as if she'd never seen anything so complicated in her life and greeted everyone who walked through the door like they were a guest at a surprise party without ever stopping to check who anyone was (he once saw her show a courier through to the boardroom). With her panic-stricken responses to most requests, she made for an amusing distraction from his clogged in-box and buzzing phone.

Every day he'd watched her fumble around on the desk, dropping the headset and misplacing paperwork. He watched her eat lunch on her own, compulsively checking her phone with visible disappointment. He watched her watching the team, especially the girls: she followed them with hungry eyes, imitating their show-pony walks and bouncy hairstyles, aping their outfits with high-street knockoffs, desperate for them to notice her. And as he watched, an idea had taken shape, or the seed of one, at least—and not an especially viable one at that. But as the days rolled by and Nina's messages became increasingly frantic, the seed grew, until one day he decided to conduct a few tests.

First, he ran a Google search. He discovered Emily was an actress, though not a successful one. She'd grown up in a village in Derbyshire. Her social-media accounts revealed limited activity—just a few pictures of the same two or three friends hanging out at cheap venues and free events. No boyfriend. No family photos.

He made a few phone calls, dug a little deeper.

He asked Verity to relay a few random requests, assign some

tasks that he knew Emily had already completed, just to see if she would do them again. She did. He asked her to go outside at a specific time every day for a week and take a photograph of the building at the end of the block. She went. He emailed her the password for an absent junior's desktop computer and instructed her to access a file marked PRIVATE. She raised no objections. She was so eager to please that she complied with every order without hesitation.

He then found a Jungian personality quiz online, the type often used for career assessment, and pasted it into an email, tailoring it with a few "fun" questions of his own. Anticipating that Emily would enjoy the special attention, he invented a story about a company newsletter and an initiative to spotlight individual members of the team. Naturally, she took the bait. Her answers were most illuminating.

He even followed her home one night, shadowing her all the way to Deptford, where he'd watched her wrestle with the door to a depressing little flat above a curry house.

And then something amazing had happened. He'd made a call to a former colleague, cashing in on a long-standing debt of thanks. Three days later, that former colleague made good on his word and delivered a thick orange envelope to Scott's desk, the contents of which almost stopped Scott's heart. He'd never been one to believe in fate but here, it seemed, was a certain kind of proof. The heavens, the gods, *whatever*: something had conspired to lead that girl here, to Proem, to him. It could be no coincidence. Everything was too spookily, flawlessly aligned.

That very afternoon, the idea went from tiny seed to fully formed plan. He called in a few more favors, made a few arrangements. Placed some ducks in a neat little row. And then, about a week later, he instructed David Mahoney to terminate Emily's employment.

Of course, he'd had moments of doubt. Moments when he'd questioned his own judgment. But then, as he'd watched Emily play hide-and-seek in reception with the little boy, the final piece fell into place. She was the right choice; he was sure of it.

Soon, he would call Yves. Start the preparations. There was just one thing left to do.

In his pocket, his phone vibrated once. Twice. Three times. Probably Nina again. Fortunately, he'd had the good sense to deal with yesterday's barrage of messages before he'd gone to sleep. They'd spoken at midnight, her anguished whispers traveling the distance between them like a thread-thin beam of light, arcing back and forth over land and sea, bouncing off stars and satellites. He used to see their connection like that: an unbreakable line from his heart to hers, holding them together no matter how far apart they might be. Not anymore.

"Please," she'd begged yet again. "You can't imagine what it's like. I'm so alone."

He'd murmured his support, told her what she wanted to hear.

"If I just had someone to talk to, I . . ." She stopped. Switched tack. "When are you coming? When?"

For a few sweet moments he'd allowed himself to remember what it was like before. He thought about how it felt to laugh with her, to hold her and feel her hair tangled around his fingers. He remembered the day they met, and euphoria rose in his heart like a ghost from a grave. He conjured the smell of her perfumed skin and the warmth of her body, and after they hung up he'd felt, briefly, like he could breathe again. But inevitably, the feeling hadn't lasted long. Within a couple of hours, he was back to jittery, agitated, and semiviolent.

Downstairs, the rumble of the elevator signaled the start of the day. The doors opened and Verity stepped out, her heels clicking across the polished concrete.

Scott cracked his knuckles and rolled back his shoulders. He pulled his phone from his pocket, determined to dismiss Nina's latest communications and forget about her for at least the next few hours. But the missed call wasn't from his wife.

Scott checked the number. The caller had left a voicemail message. Hitting the button, he lifted the phone to his ear.

"Scott. It's Tom. Tom Stanhope?" The voice was eager, confident. "Sorry it's early. Just wanted to tell you that I spoke to Damien and the job's going ahead. Everything's moving surprisingly quickly, actually, which is great. We leave next month. So, I just wanted to call and say how much I appreciate you setting it all up. You've changed my life, man. And that thing we spoke about?" The man's voice became hushed, as if he'd just ducked into a quiet room. "It's getting sorted today. Ten o'clock. So, yeah, I hope it helps you out. Anyway, give me a call later. And thanks again."

Scott deleted the message and slid the phone back into his pocket.

"Scott?" Verity's voice rang out from somewhere below. "Are you up there?"

"Yep," he called back. "Coming down."

Taking a deep breath, he threw one last glance at the empty reception desk before making his way back down the stairs, sliding his palm over the bronze stair rail as he went.

By 9:15, Scott was already exhausted. The breakfast meeting was not going well. Sweeping his aching eyes around the table, he tried to pay attention to the conversation. Verity was on a roll, engaging their investors with her usual flair, but Scott couldn't keep up. The restaurant was too loud. He felt distracted and devoid of ideas. The conversation with Nina had resulted in a fitful night's sleep; he'd tossed and turned, finally drifting off at maybe 3 A.M. Then two hours later, for reasons he now couldn't quite fathom, he'd forced himself out of bed and into the gym.

Underneath the table, he balled his hand into a fist and winced. Gouging a hole in his palm with a pen had not been a great move. He'd cleaned and dressed the wound, but it was still throbbing. When Verity had asked about the bandage he'd told her he'd burned it on the oven. She seemed to buy it.

Someone nudged him.

"Sorry," he said, clearing his throat. "What was that?"

"I said, congratulations on the latest IPO," said the investor to Scott's left, an Italian man with hair plugs and a frozen Botoxed forehead. "Impressive. I don't mind telling you that a few of us had our doubts about that one, but once again, you did it." He tapped Scott gently on the arm. "I tell you something now, Scott Denny: I will always invest with you. Whatever it is, I'm in."

"I appreciate your faith in me."

"Oh, I have faith. You know why? Because you, my friend, are ruthless." The Italian held aloft his macchiato in a silent toast. "They told me in the beginning that you were ruthless, and that's exactly what you are."

Scott nodded, accepting the compliment with what he hoped passed for grace. Yes, he was ruthless. But he had good reason to be.

He clenched his jaw and shifted in his seat. He was in no mood to celebrate. Actually, that was an understatement. Suddenly, he was in no mood to drink, eat, talk, think, or suffer any company whatsoever.

Verity said something to him from across the table. He smiled, but inside him a storm was gathering.

"Another piccolo, Mr. Denny?" The maître d' hovered at his elbow.

Scott dismissed him with a small shake of his head. He felt unwell. A hot rage was building behind his eyes, and the urge to unburden himself right there in the restaurant, to vomit his secrets all over the white linen tablecloth, became almost uncontrollable.

Checking his watch, he placed his napkin on the table and pushed his chair back. "Gentlemen, I hope you'll excuse me," he said to the table. "But I have another meeting to attend."

From the corner of his eye, he saw Verity's head snap up. She mouthed something at him. *What meeting?*

"I'll leave you in Verity's capable hands. Thank you for your time, gentlemen, and I look forward to seeing you again."

Shaking hands with both investors, he turned toward the door, leaving his assistant frantically scrolling through her calendar, looking for an appointment she would never find.

CHAPTER FIVE

EMILY

Feeling somewhat hungover and determined to avoid a discussion with Spencer about their imminent eviction, Emily crept out of the house early and caught the DLR into central London. Curling up against the window, she replayed the phone call with Juliet. There was no getting around it: she'd messed up. Again. She was a terrible person.

She felt the sting of tears and lowered her head, grateful for the unspoken commuter law prohibiting eye contact with fellow passengers. *When did life get so hard? Where did it all go wrong?*

Growing up in Hoxley, she'd always felt different from all the boring nobodies who worked in the village bakery and the butcher's and the post office; she was braver, bolder. *Better.* For years she'd marveled at her parents, astonished that they could stand the boredom. Peter's small dental clinic had been running like clockwork for more than thirty years, the same sequence of events repeating through the week in brain-meltingly dull eight-hour units, and for as long as Emily could remember, Juliet had worked three days a week as a landscaper for a local National Trust site. Filling their weekends with coffee, gardening, and watercolor paints, the two of them were as much a part of the local landscape as the drystone walls threading their way over the Derbyshire hills, and they rarely ventured farther afield than Sheffield, except to take their annual two-week holiday in Tenerife. Her school friends had been the same: no ambition, no imagination. She would listen to them talk about baby names and wedding dresses, and shake her head at them, wondering how they could endure village life, and they would shake their heads right back, equally dumbfounded that she could not.

The look on all their faces when she'd gotten into drama school had been priceless; Emily knew exactly how Cinderella felt when the prince showed up and made the ugly sisters apologize for being bitches. But every Christmas she would return home looking more disheveled, more desperate, and the expressions of astonishment were gradually replaced by confusion. Her grandparents could not fathom why she had not yet been on *EastEnders*. Auntie Cath wanted to know why she wasn't yet friends with Jude Law. Didn't she live in London? Wasn't she an actress? And why didn't she ever have any money?

These were all valid questions to which Emily never had the right answers. Why *didn't* she know more famous people? Why *was* she still living in a shoebox with no central heating? Why *did* she always have holes in her clothes? Every visit home was like one of those lateral-thinking problems they gave you at school, the ones designed to make you look stupid. So eventually she just stopped going.

She pressed her fingertips to her eyes. Maybe London had been a bad idea from the start; maybe she should've stayed in Hoxley. Wedding dresses and watercolors were starting to look less and less like the death sentences she'd always thought them to be.

No. She tossed her head as if to shake the thought free. *No way.* She'd been right to leave. Small-town life would have killed her. She'd have hated the monotony and the repetition and seeing the same faces every day for her entire life. She had always felt different because she *was* different, and not just because she was adopted. This was who she was, this was the life she was meant for, and she would just have to take the rough with the smooth.

Emily sat up, forced her shoulders back, and lifted her chin. Everything was fine. She was going to be okay. More than okay, she was going to be awesome! Yes! She would get that job today. This was her time, dammit. Her star was on the rise. She was living the *dream*!

Shuffling off the train at Bank, Emily caught the Central line to Tottenham Court Road and nursed a small latte in Pret until it was time to meet her agent.

"Darling!" Lara cried as soon as Emily walked through the door, standing up and pulling her into a short, sharp hug. "Aren't you a bit early? What time is it?"

"It's ten, I think."

"Oh. Okay, well, in that case you're right on time. Silly me! How are you, sweetheart? I feel like it's been ages since we caught up. A few weeks at least?"

"Um, maybe five? Or six. I'm not sure," Emily lied. It had been exactly nine weeks and two days since she was last called in for a chat.

"Well, anyway, it's *so* good to see you. You're looking *so* well." Lara ushered her through the open-plan office, weaving through desks and clusters of dripping succulents, until she reached a partitioned meeting area, the back wall of which was plastered with black-and-white headshots, the current success stories most prominently placed (Emily's was at the bottom, half-hidden by a cheese plant). "Come on in, honey. Sit, sit, sit." Lowering herself onto a leather sofa, she crossed her tanned legs and gestured for Emily to join her. "So," she said, a flush of pink creeping up her neck. "I have good news and bad news."

"Everything okay?" Emily asked. Lara seemed a bit flustered.

"Yes, I . . . well, the good news is—drumroll—I'm getting married!" She flexed her wrist and fanned out her fingers, showing off an enormous glittering diamond nestled among lots of other glittering diamonds.

Emily was temporarily blinded as the ring caught the light. "Oh, wow. Congratulations!" she said, blinking.

"Thank you, yes, it's all very exciting. Tom kept me waiting long enough, but we're finally doing it."

Emily rolled her eyes indulgently, as if to say, *You guys!* She knew all about wonderful Tom and his amazing family and their dog and their summer house on the Amalfi coast. A chronic oversharer, Lara offered up odd and borderline inappropriate details in the same way that other people offered refreshments. Emily knew all about Tom's dietary requirements (no gluten, no eggs, and no carbs after 2 P.M.), his secret celebrity crush (Jane Fonda circa 2014), and which side of the bed he slept on (the right; Lara slept on the left because it was nearer the door and she usually got up two or three times in the night on account of her tiny bladder). The few times Emily had tried to share some details of her own, she'd been shut down so fast it was almost funny. Were they friends or weren't they? It was exhausting trying to figure out where the professional line lay; it seemed to move all the time.

"Where are you doing it?" Emily asked politely.

"Um, well, New York actually."

"Oh. That's . . . far."

"Yes. Tom got this fantastic promotion—like, *really* fantastic— so we're sort of moving there."

"Really? Moving to New York?"

"Uh huh." Lara lowered her eyes. "Early next month."

"Next *month*?"

"Yes, I know, it's fast. And, of course, it means I'll have to leave the agency."

"Oh. Okay."

"I'm so sorry it's so last minute. It's all come as a bit of a surprise to me, too, actually," Lara said, with just the merest hint of a frown. "Totally out of the blue. But, you know, it feels right. Tom's been working so hard; he really deserves it. And hopefully, I'll be able to join a new agency over there. After we get the family ball rolling, of course."

Emily nodded, unsure of what to say. Was Lara leaving a good thing or a bad thing? It was the end of an era, she supposed, but maybe her next agent would actually take her calls.

"I'm so sorry," Lara said again, pressing her hands to her face. "Are you very angry?"

"Angry? No, not at all."

"Honestly, I agonized over telling you right before your audition today, but I figured it might give you the fire you need to really nail it this time. I mean, I'm sure it'll be hard at first, finding new representation, but—"

Emily froze. "Wait, what?"

"Inevitably, it'll be a bit of a transitional—"

"Hang on." Emily shook her head. "What new representation? Don't you just pass me on to another agent here?"

"Oh." Lara's hand flew to her mouth. "Oh, darling, I thought I'd been clear."

"Clear about what?"

Lara looked down into her lap. "I . . . Look, there's no easy way to say this. I'm so sorry, but the agency isn't absorbing my client list."

Emily felt her mouth slacken.

"All the agents are at capacity right now." Lara paused and shook her head. Silently, she moved closer and reached out for Emily's hand, squeezing it as though she was dying. "Darling, I'm afraid you're out. I really am so, so sorry."

CHAPTER SIX

SCOTT

FROM THE doorway of a Soho café, Scott watched the windows of a gray building on the opposite side of the street. He checked his watch: 10:17 A.M.

His phone buzzed in his hand. Without breaking his gaze, he answered the call. "Scott Denny."

"Scott!" a voice bellowed. "My man! It's Tom. You got my message?"

"I did." The entrance of the building was still. No one had gone in or come out for over twelve minutes. "And you're welcome. I didn't do much, though. Nothing that you wouldn't have pulled off yourself, given time."

"Are you kidding?" Tom laughed. "I've been trying to get my foot in that particular door for years. I owe you several drinks, mate."

"No need, we're all square." Scott shifted his weight from one foot to the other. The door remained shut, the windows still. "I'm grateful for the returned favor, by the way. I know it's a little unorthodox."

"Nah, it's the least we could do."

"I appreciate it." A shadow crossed one of the windows. It hadn't been difficult to track the agent down. Nor had it been hard to access her personal information. There was a lot of detail available online these days.

"Lara reckons Emma wouldn't have lasted much longer anyway. She wasn't making any money, and it's all about the money, right?" Tom chuckled.

Scott rolled his eyes. He barely knew Tom Stanhope—they'd met just once, at a function several years ago—but it had been laughably easy to convince Tom otherwise. A few names dropped here and a boozy lunch there, and Tom seemed to think they went way back. By the time Scott had offered to tee up the job of a lifetime for him, Tom would've done anything for his "brother from another mother"—including asking his fiancée to drop one of her least successful clients so that Scott could keep his most promising new protégée.

"She was surprised, though."

"Who?"

"Lara. She said she couldn't imagine Emma having a knack for investments."

A flurry of movement across the street caught Scott's eye. The door to the building had opened, and a hunched figure was scurrying out. "Emily," he murmured, following the figure with his eyes.

"Sorry?"

"Her name is Emily." Hanging up, Scott began to move.

CHAPTER SEVEN

EMILY

In a quiet side street, Emily's vision blurred with tears. *Dropped. Cast off. Thrown away.* The very worst thing that could happen to an actor. She knew what it meant: the same thing had happened last year to an old friend from drama school, a poor unassuming Welshman who had immediately disappeared from the London scene never to be seen again. It was like he'd died. No one even talked about him anymore in case the mere mention of his name was enough to bring a plague of obscurity down on the entire West End.

No, come on, hold it together. She dabbed at her face with the sleeves of her cardigan, trying to save her makeup. She had one audition left. There was still hope.

She checked the time on her phone. Fifteen minutes to sort herself out and pull off the performance of a lifetime. *You've got this,* she told herself. Reaching into her bag, she pulled out the pages she'd been emailed. *Just breathe, go over the lines, you'll be okay.*

But the lines danced in front of her eyes, mocking her. The audition was for a chewing-gum advert. *A girl is about to be kissed by her date,* read the summary, *but the foods she's eaten*

at dinner jump out and threaten to ruin everything. A fight en-
sues. The chewing gum wins.

Well, okay, so it wasn't Shakespeare. Emily rolled back her shoulders. *Doesn't matter,* she thought. *I'll still nail it.*

But the last drops of her optimism were leaking away and humiliation was taking over, powering through her body like termites through dead wood. She wasn't even reading for the role of the girl; she would be auditioning to play an onion. A karate-chopping, street-fighting, costume-wearing onion.

What a fucking joke. She crushed the pages of her "script" in her fist. Who had she thought she was kidding? She couldn't make a living like this, with or without an agent. She flashed back to the previous week, when she had been asked, in an airless box of a room, to tackle a makeshift obstacle course in the manner of a "sexy cat." Then another bizarre memory, this one of standing on a chair delivering a monologue while a director lobbed newspapers at her. Another, of singing "Happy Birthday, Mr. President" to a tub of butter.

The tears ran freely now, running down her nose and into her mouth. *I hate myself.* She pushed the words into every corner of her wretched body. Her stupid dream was the only thing that had kept her going, and now it had evaporated before her eyes. What was she going to do now? Where was she going to go? How would she ever get another agent? She had nothing to show anyone—no show reel, no showcase, not even a performance in a shitty advert as an *onion,* for god's sake! No one would ever hire her again. She would have to leave London. She would have to—

"Hey." A voice crashed into her careering train of thought.

Emily recoiled. Wiping her nose on the sleeve of her cardigan, she ducked her head and walked away in the opposite direction.

"Hey," the voice called again.

She kept moving. Probably just some crackhead wanting change.

Lara's words wouldn't leave her alone. *You're on your own.* Her face had been full of pity. *You're out. I'm so sorry.* Shame burned like acid in Emily's gut.

"Hey, wait."

Weaving her way past a group of school kids, she snuck a look back. There was a man in a dark-blue suit just behind her, walking fast. Definitely not a crackhead. *Oh god, it's not one of those charity people, is it?* She sped up. No way was she about to stop and chat to a stranger about the plight of polar bears when her entire life was crashing down around her.

Wiping the mascara tracks from under her eyes, she went to cross the road but tripped as she stepped off the curb, and her script fluttered free of her fingers. The pages came apart and spiraled into the gutter, and Emily, suddenly appalled at the thought that they might fly away, that she might lose her very last chance, cried out and reached for them, stumbling into the path of an oncoming cyclist. The bike swerved, only narrowly avoiding a collision, and Emily gasped, snatching at the paper, desperate now to make it to the audition on time, to prove that she was still worth something after all . . . but it was too late. Sheets of white paper were cartwheeling over the asphalt and disappearing under the wheels of cars.

She stood up, her vision blurred by fresh tears. Behind her, the man called out again.

"Hey, Emily."

Shit, she thought, poised to run. *Please don't be a rapist.* Then her brain caught up with her ears and she froze.

"Emily," the man shouted again, louder this time, and when she turned around she was shocked to see a familiar face.

"Mr. Denny?" she managed.

Suddenly, there was a shout and a squeal of brakes, and her peripheral vision was filled with a huge red shape. More shouting ensued, then the blare of a horn, and Emily covered her ears with her hands, but the noise was deafening and the red shape was getting closer and closer, and the squeal was getting louder and her breath was getting faster and—

The panic hit her before the bus did, a great tidal wave of fear pouring down her throat, flooding her lungs until she could no longer breathe. And then a mad flurry exploded inside her, like the flap of a thousand wings. Something invisible was flattening her ribs, and her hands flew out as if to push a heavy object from her chest.

Oh, great, she thought vaguely as she toppled like a tree. *Here we go again.*

Buildings wobbled and the sky went black as the world turned upside down.

The bus stopped inches from her face—and then, from out of nowhere, Mr. Denny, Emily's ex-boss, was leaping out of the chaos like a handsome human shield, a superhero, a knight with colors flying. Holding up his hand to the driver, he yelled at a few bystanders to give her some space, and she wanted to laugh because it had to be a hallucination. Surely, none of this could be real: this gentle hand on hers, this jacket under her head, this blurry shape with a halo of hair and an outstretched hand, this voice saying, "Don't be scared, Emily. Let me help you."

Surely, all of it was just a beautiful dream.

CHAPTER EIGHT

SCOTT

As HE pulled Emily to her feet and steered her through the door of a nearby pub, Scott felt dizzy with triumph. If his plan had a flaw, it was that there'd been no real reason for Emily to trust him. The bus had fixed that in a matter of seconds.

Fate. It had to be.

Grabbing a handful of napkins and ordering a juice from the bar, Scott settled into his new role of rescuer. Up close, he noticed that Emily was pretty, in a wholesome kind of way. Blond hair, brown eyes, freckled nose . . . there was nothing especially remarkable about her, but all the pieces fit comfortably together. However, the effect was currently marred by blotchy cheeks, bloodshot eyes, and a slimy upper lip.

He waited politely while Emily blew her nose. Flushed and shaking, she babbled incoherently—something about an audition and being late, and all the awful things Lara had said to her. He nodded sympathetically, thanking his lucky stars that his hunch had been right. After just ten minutes of listening to her ramble, he was more convinced than ever that Emily was exactly what he was looking for.

"I'm so sorry," he said, once he could get a word in. "I didn't mean to scare you. I just saw you walk past and wondered if you might need a ride back to work. You seemed upset."

Emily looked at him askance, as he thought she might. "Work?"

"Yes. Work." He laughed. "You know that thing you do for Proem? We give you money in return."

"But . . ." She shook her head. "I don't work for you anymore. I got fired."

Scott put on a show of confusion. "Fired? What do you mean?"

Emily then told him a long and overcomplicated version of how David Mahoney had delivered the news, telling her she was "all out of strikes" and "not Proem material."

Scott appeared duly shocked. "I think there's been some sort of mistake." He chose his moment carefully, waiting until her breathing had returned to normal. He asked if she'd like to be taken to hospital, and when she declined, he offered her a taxi home instead. He then placed his hand gently on her shoulder and told her she was going to be just fine. Everything happened for a reason, he said. Perhaps, he added, they were meant to meet—his only truly sincere words.

Finally, he folded his business card into her palm. Apologizing again for whatever misunderstanding had taken place, he suggested that she give Proem another chance. If she could see a way to forgive and forget, he said, he had another position ready and waiting. She jumped at that, as he knew she would. "Really?" she said, her eyes shining. "Yes. Thank you. I'll take it."

He laughed. "You don't even know what it is yet." He told her he'd like to discuss it further at the office, if she was comfortable with that. "Why don't you come in on Monday so I can explain the role more fully?"

He waited for her response, but the way she looked at him in that moment, the way she cradled his card in her hand like a precious jewel—that was the only answer he needed.

CHAPTER NINE

EMILY

Back in her dull little flat—all the more squalid after the gleaming interior of the Soho pub, all the more dirty after the pure white of Scott's shirt—Emily's heart was still hammering; though how much of that was the residual shock of almost being hit by a bus, she couldn't say. Yes, she was traumatized. Yes, she'd missed her all-important audition, her swan song. But it was more likely that her persistent breathlessness, dizziness, and rapid pulse were in no small part due to Scott Denny.

Ignoring the unspeakable mess in the kitchen (Spencer had obviously upped his filth levels in protest against their eviction), she went straight to her room, where she sat on the bed and seriously considered the possibility that she'd had some kind of encounter with the divine. The hairs on her arms prickled as she thought again of the moment Scott had appeared, his suit jacket flying open like a cape. She never thought she'd be caught dead falling for that white-knight bullshit, but when Scott had deftly pulled her to her feet as if they were dancers, she'd felt something inside her burst.

At the time, his face had shown nothing but polite concern: the kindness of a stranger. But after he'd picked her up and dusted her off, after they'd sat talking in the pub for what felt like forever and Scott had listened so intently, as though he was pressing his ear to her very soul, he said something about destiny, and she knew he'd felt it, too.

And then, as if it wasn't enough that he'd just saved her from certain death, Scott Denny offered her a mysterious new job. No interview, no trial run; just a promise that a position was waiting for her if she wanted it. *Give me a call,* he'd said, flipping a card out of his wallet. *Let's set up a meeting. Shall we say Monday?*

Emily wondered what the job would entail. Not reception again, she guessed. Maybe he would train her up to . . . *hmm.* What was it that they did at Proem again? Stocks and shares? Something like that. Whatever—the point was that she had a new job, which meant money, which meant she no longer needed that loan from her parents. She made a mental note to call Juliet in the morning.

She curled up on the bed, grimacing at the memory of the bus hurtling toward her. She hadn't felt like that for a long time. The pure, blind fear, and the feeling of déjà vu . . . and then that rising weightlessness as she fell, familiar as her own bedsheets. She thought she'd grown out of all that.

She warded her feelings off with an image of Scott. *My hero.* She smiled. In her hand she still held his business card. Could he be real? Perhaps he was a figment of her wishful imagination.

Reaching for her phone, she sent a text. Thank you, thank you, thank you. Seconds later, Scott replied, and his existence was proven.

The weekend was long and painful. *A watched pot never boils,* Emily reminded herself, but the anticipation was too much to bear, and she was soon glued to the pot like a kid to cartoons. But after a while the questions started to creep in. The sheer drama of Scott's appearance and subsequent offer had temporarily erased the anguish of being dropped from Lara's books, but what if he'd reconsidered? Or *forgotten?* What if she showed up at Proem and there was no record of her appointment? What would she do then?

By Monday morning, she was tempted to stay in bed, hidden under the blankets. But after giving herself a stern talking-to, she propelled herself out the door and onto the Tube. Accidentally arriving way ahead of schedule, she dithered on the street corner for as long as she could before finally riding the elevator up to the fifth floor. As she approached the reception desk, her heartbeat seemed so loud she felt sure someone would ask her to turn the volume down.

The woman sitting in Emily's usual place was older than her, and clearly wiser. Emily marveled at the speed and efficiency with which she answered the phone, sent a fax, and filed a contract—all at the same time. "Hi there," said the new (*old*) receptionist. "Do you have an appointment?"

"Um, yes. Yes, I do. I'm Emily? Emily Proudman. I'm here to see Mr. Denny." She hesitated, feeling like a schoolgirl at the headmaster's office. "Scott," she added, and felt better.

The receptionist tapped on her keyboard. There was a nail-biting pause. "Ah, yes," she said, at last. "Eleven thirty?"

"That's right." Emily looked at the clock on the wall. "Sorry, I'm a bit early." The words felt odd coming out of her mouth. She was rarely early for anything—certainly never for work at Proem. *Look at me changing,* she thought happily.

"Take a seat."

On the same velvet couch on which David Mahoney had waited to ambush her, Emily crossed and recrossed her legs, dabbing at her forehead and smoothing her hair. She tugged at her skirt, uncertain about the length. *Be calm,* she told herself. *Be cool.*

She pulled the topmost magazine from a stack on the coffee table and nearly fell off her seat. Scott's dark eyes gazed out from the cover. *Smooth Operator,* read the headline. *Proem Partners founder Scott Denny on innovation, tradition, and creating the perfect workspace.* Emily flicked hurriedly to the main article, where two whole pages were taken up with a photograph of the lobby and its huge LED chandelier.

> Housed within a refurbished Grade 2–listed Edwardian building in Mayfair, Proem is a breakout capital-investment firm focused on both emerging and established companies across a multitude of different industries. They describe themselves as "boutique," but their profit margins and annual turnover indicate that they are anything but.

Another photograph of Scott, now perched casually on the back of a leather sofa, his feet on the seats, elbows resting on his knees. The photographer had caught him mid laugh, and the result was disarming for reasons she didn't quite understand. Scott was undoubtedly good-looking. But the bubbling, kettle-boiling sensation under her ribs was something other than just sexual attraction; it felt *bigger* than that, somehow.

> The wide range of flexible working spaces includes thirty-five workstations, ten offices, seven meeting rooms, and a twenty-seater boardroom with sophisticated AV technology for teleconference, video, and smart-board presentations. By his own admittance, Scott Denny places employee satisfaction at the top of his priority list, so naturally the designs had to include a luxurious breakout area and rooftop terrace.

A group of three analysts, one girl and two guys, wandered out of one of the meeting rooms and crossed the foyer, stopping at the desk to collect a stack of files. Emily smiled and half raised her hand in a greeting.

"Ann-Marie's off sick again," said one of the guys in a loud, bored voice.

"Please, she's not sick," said the girl, tossing blond ringlets over her shoulder. "Any excuse to plant her fat arse on the couch and eat crisps all day."

"Didn't she freak out? Like, have a legit breakdown?"

"Depressed, I heard."

"What does she have to be depressed about?"

"Um, hello? Have you seen her boob job?"

"If anyone made me look like that," said the girl, "I'd fucking sue." The group gathered their files and wandered into the copy room.

Emily dropped her hand back into her lap, wondering whether her dismissal had become common knowledge yet. She couldn't imagine that the office gossips had *not* yet caught wind of it, but then again, maybe she just wasn't worth gossiping about. She bowed her head over the magazine, figuring it was probably best to avoid attention just in case.

> Going into this project, Scott Denny wanted to eschew a traditional office setting in favor of a "warm and welcoming vibe." Inspired by the lofts of New York, an industrial feel is juxtaposed with a "residential" ambiance, creating a textured materiality that brings radiance and depth to the space. Earthy tones and subdued colors provide a peaceful touch, while overscaled artwork and high ceilings create a sense of awe.

Awe. Yes, that was the word. That was what Emily felt when she thought about Scott.

The same loud, bored voice rang out again. Emily looked up. The copy-room door was ajar.

"So, any news on the summer party?"

"I heard we're booking a *restaurant*."

"Ugh, really? So lame."

"We should do the superyacht again. That was *insane*."

"I literally have no memory of that night. Total absinthe blackout."

There was a wave of sniggers.

"So, Scott's not offering up his French mansion this year, then?"

Emily's ears pricked up. She shuffled to the end of the sofa, leaning closer to the open door.

"Dude, let it go," said the female voice, wearily. "It'll never happen. I've been at him for years, but apparently his batshit-crazy wife shuts him down every time."

Emily froze. *Wife?* She put down her magazine. *What wife?*

"I heard she's a bitch," murmured one of the guys.

"Who even *is* she?"

"Is she hot?"

"Can't be that hot if he never sees her."

"I don't know, sounds like the perfect marriage to me."

Emily felt her heart sink. *He's married,* she thought. Then: *Of course he's married. What did you expect?* She leaned a little closer.

"I'm telling you, she's a bitch."

"Cut her some slack. You know what happened, don't you?"

"Well, sure, but that was years ago. And you know what they say; be stronger than your strongest excuse."

"That doesn't even make sense."

"He *hates* her. You can just tell."

Suddenly there was a neat clack of heels. *"Sssh,"* someone hissed. "Kim Kardashian's on the warpath."

Emily jumped back in her seat, scrabbling to pick up the magazine again, and the voices in the copy room fell into a hush as Scott's PA, Verity, strutted into reception like a supermodel president, all spiky stilettos and arched eyebrows. "Make sure that's couriered in the next five minutes," she said to Emily's replacement, dropping a thick black file on the desk. "And please tell those fuckwits that it doesn't take three people to photocopy a contract."

Emily watched from behind her magazine as, one by one, the analysts trickled sheepishly out of the copy room.

"Oh, and Ms. Proudman?" Verity threw a look over her shoulder that was so sharp it made Emily jump. "Scott will see you now."

CHAPTER TEN

SCOTT

SCOTT LAY on the floor of his office, his face pressed against the concrete. While bending down to pick up a dropped piece of paper, his eye had been caught by two dead cockroaches lying on their backs by the skirting board, their legs twitching as a swarm of ants fed on their spindly carcasses. Why two? he wondered. And why so close together? Perhaps there been a duel, or a suicide pact. Maybe these were the Romeo and Juliet of the insect world.

He'd watched the ants for some time and eventually got down on his hands and knees for a closer look. He was struck by both the complexity of the churning mass and the simplicity of the individual task: march, eat, march, eat. Each one of them working as part of a giant superteam to consume and survive. It was hypnotic. Also, the floor felt good. Cool and solid. So, onto the floor he went.

It had been a difficult few days. After a short phase of relative calm, during which Scott had felt comfortable enough to book flights for the upcoming long weekend, the credit account had gone crazy. New charges had started popping up all over the place: three at first, then five more, then another three, the total of which came to £97,556. He'd tried to reach Nina, but his calls and emails had gone unanswered, the only sign of life being one last gigantic charge that had shown up that morning, like the final firework in a pyrotechnic display. There was nothing he could do but watch it all unfold; the only saving grace was that he was not obliged to watch in person. He canceled his flights.

On the floor, the ants continued to swarm over the cock-roaches. A small group succeeded in breaking off a leg and bore it away like a prize. One little guy had lost his way and was missing out on the action, so Scott nudged him back on course with his finger. "Wrong way," he whispered to the ant. "The chow is that way. Go on, off you go. *Bon appétit.*"

"Sorry, are you talking to me?" said a voice.

Scott jumped up. There was a girl in the doorway. No, wait. *The* girl. Emily.

"Hello," she said. "Sorry to disturb you while you were, um . . ."

"No, not at all. I wasn't . . ." Scott brushed himself down. "It's fine. Thank you for coming in." What on earth had he been doing? How could he lose track of the time like that? And how many of his employees had seen him crawling around on the floor? He glanced at his office wall. The smart glass was still transparent, but, mercifully, the corridor beyond was quiet.

"So," he said, crossing to the wall. He hit a switch and the electrochromic glaze immediately rendered the whole thing opaque. "How are you feeling after last week? No broken bones, I take it?"

"Oh, no." She blushed. "I mean, I'm still a bit rattled but, you know . . . fine."

"What happened there, anyway?"

"What do you mean?"

"Well, the bus stopped in time. It never touched you, and yet you went down like a sack of potatoes."

"Oh, yeah." Emily's face went even pinker. "I do that. Faint, I mean. Haven't for a while, but when I was younger I used to get these panic attacks where I'd black out and stuff? Bit weird.

I thought I'd got rid of them, but I guess with all the stress lately . . ." She stopped and shrugged.

Scott sat behind his desk and gestured for her to take the chair opposite. He noticed she was wearing an unusual interpretation of office wear: a floral scoop-necked top tucked into a bright-green high-waisted skirt, thick black tights, and shiny round-toed high heels. She walked as if she'd never worn a pair of heels in her life.

They shared a smile, and there it was again: that vague sense that he knew her or had met her somewhere before.

"Coffee? Tea?" He reached for his desk phone.

"Oh, no, thank you."

"Probably wise. I need to cut back, but nothing else will see me through the day." He pressed a button. "Verity, can I get a long black please? And would you grab me some of those cookies? The chocolate ones? Thanks." He hung up. "This feels like a cookie kind of meeting," he explained with a grin.

Across the table, Emily took a deep, wobbly breath. She seemed nervous, and Scott could sympathize. His own heart was fluttering, his hands were clammy, and his shirt was sticking to his back.

"Right, so let's get down to it." He placed his hands on the desk and laced his fingers together to stop them from shaking. "With regards to the termination of your employment, I'd like to reiterate that the order, so to speak, did not come from me. Personally, I was very happy with your work. You did a wonderful job for us. You were very popular." Emily made a face as if she didn't quite believe him, and she was right not to. At best, most staff members ignored her; at worst, they mocked her for the very same things that had brought her to Scott's attention: she was naive, flaky, inattentive.

Scott carried on. "You may not have seen me much during your time here, but I saw you and I was very impressed. I think it would be a great shame to lose you." For a moment his confidence wavered. It wasn't too late; he could still back out. But then he thought of the orange envelope and the printed pages within, and again the whole situation felt out of his hands. Something had brought Emily to him. The wheels were already in motion, and he couldn't stop them if he tried.

"I'd like you to continue working for me," he said, pressing his shoulders back and sitting up straight. "If that's also what you want, of course. But before we discuss the details, I thought perhaps you could tell me a bit about yourself, given that we were never formally introduced when you started work here."

"Oh. Okay, sure," said Emily. "Though I'm not sure there's much to tell."

There was a sharp rap on the door, and Verity walked in carrying a small black tray. "Lomax meeting in thirty minutes," she said, placing Scott's coffee and cookies in front of him. She cast a sidelong glance at Emily, then swept out of the room as quickly as she had entered it, her perfume swirling behind her like exhaust fumes.

Scott lifted his cup and took a sip. The coffee was scalding. He took several big gulps, relishing the burn in his mouth and down his throat. Placing a cookie on a napkin, he slid it across the desk. "So, tell me. What do you do when you're not temping?"

Emily turned out to be quite a talker. He found her to be sweet and quirky, both witty and unintentionally funny. Her chatter was birdlike, quick and bright, and she threw her thoughts around like paper airplanes. An anecdote here, a little joke there; a step back, then a crazy leap forward. She answered Scott's questions frankly and with little forethought, there clearly being little filtration between what she thought and what she said; it was all out there, even as the thoughts themselves were formed. And then she volunteered an abundance of personal information without even being prompted. Quite predictably, she asked very few questions of him.

As she talked, his theories were confirmed; everything he'd gleaned from his research was proved in just a single conversation. With few solid friendships, no boyfriend, and what seemed to be a fragile relationship with her family, she was isolated and lonely. She was also transient, rarely staying at one address for long. Rather conveniently, she was about to be evicted from her current digs because she'd failed to pay the rent on time (information that she supplied herself, unabashed) and she had no alternative lined up. Her acting career was dead in the water, and the meeting with Lara had left her feeling humiliated and vulnerable, just as he'd hoped it would.

As the personality quiz had suggested, she was a dreamer, a storyteller, a "people person" who lived in the moment. Adventurous but lacking in confidence, she often looked to others for advice before making a decision. She was loyal, compassionate, and most importantly, very, very trusting.

Yes, he thought. *She's the one.*

Twenty minutes later, Emily was still talking. There was a speck of chocolate on her cheek. Scott resisted an urge to reach over and wipe it away with his finger.

He checked his watch. Verity would be tapping on the door again soon. He waited for a lull in Emily's recount of some absurd incident or other (something about an onion?) before interrupting. "Well, it certainly sounds as if you've been through the wringer. Just quickly, I wonder if we might be able to discuss the job."

Emily's hands flew to her face. "Oh god, I've been rambling."

"No, not at all. I'm just a little short on time and want to make sure we've covered as much as possible."

"Yes, of course. Sorry." She stuffed the last of the cookie in her mouth.

"As you may already be aware," said Scott, "I spend a lot of time in Europe. Much of that time is taken up with business, but some is spent at my house in France. I ought to be there more often, to be honest, but I do go whenever possible." He felt his thoughts starting to split and wander. It always happened when he spoke of the estate, as if just talking about it conjured a portal through which he could reach and physically touch the pampas grass. The travertine. The floorboards and the furniture.

The soft, plump pillow . . .

The lone finger pointing up, up, up . . .

Scott took a breath, trying to clear his head. The place was sucking him in. Nina called it her bubble, and he could see why. The shape of the land, the trees overhead, the repetition of circles and curves in the design of the grounds . . . but to him it was something more solid than that, more impermeable. A snow globe. Sometimes, if it had been a long time between visits, he even started to picture the place covered in snow— delicate flakes spinning and floating out of the sky, settling on leaves and petals, piling up in great, fluffy drifts on the window ledges—which was ludicrous, because it almost never snowed there.

He focused. "It's incredibly beautiful. Very remote, but no expense has been spared on setting it up. Everything you could ever wish for . . . it's there." His stomach contracted as his thoughts returned briefly to the bank statement. He cleared his throat. "It's large, though, and difficult to maintain. There are many different features, each requiring a great deal of care, plus two separate houses to manage. My wife has plans to turn one into a guesthouse, so there's a lot of work to be done. And we have a daughter."

Emily erupted in a coughing fit. "God, sorry," she managed. "A daughter? How lovely. How old is she?"

"She just turned six."

Emily was banging on her chest, her eyes watering. "Sorry," she said again. "Wow. Six. That's . . . a nice age."

"Mmm. She has some health issues, though, the management of which can be a bit tricky, so we need to keep her back from school until she's well enough. She needs homeschooling, constant medical attention . . . all in all, my wife is finding it extremely difficult to cope all by herself."

"Of course. It must be very challenging."

"Challenging. Yes." Scott looked at his bandaged hand. "So, she has tasked me with finding her some help. She needs a housekeeper slash au pair slash personal assistant. I'm aware that sounds vague but I—*we*—haven't yet had anyone working at the house in quite this capacity, so the details are a little hazy. You'd probably find that you'd be making many of the rules up as you go along. You'd receive a wage, of course, plus a car, food, and accommodation. Any extra expenses would be covered. And considering your current living situation, I'd be more than happy for you to start immediately."

Emily's mouth had fallen open. "Wow," she said at last. "I don't know what to say. Did you say France?"

"Yes. The midwest coast."

"Wow," she said again.

"Don't feel like you have to make a decision right away. I mean, it would be a big change for you. The job would be flexible in many ways, but the isolation might be difficult. The way my wife lives . . . it's not for everyone." Scott looked Emily square in the eyes and forced himself to smile.

"Okay," said Emily, but her own smile faltered a little. She looked, quite rightly, as though she'd just been handed a briefcase full of cash by a hooded stranger. He could almost see the cogs whirring inside her head.

"Please," he said, "take some time to think about it. We can talk again later in the week." He would call her tomorrow. She would accept, he was sure of it.

"Okay," she said again. "And thanks for having me. Sorry, that sounded weird—for inviting me, I mean. For seeing me. You know what I mean." Blushing hard, she stood up. Scott stood with her, intending to see her out, but halfway to the door she stopped. "Sorry, but can I ask a quick question?"

"Of course, fire away."

"Why me?"

He looked at her, momentarily confused.

"I'm so grateful for the offer, don't get me wrong. It's just . . . it seems a bit random. I get that you want to make amends for accidentally firing me—which you don't have to do, by the way, it's fine—but I don't exactly have much experience with house-keeping. Or with kids. There must be hundreds of professionals to choose from, so why me?"

For a split second, Scott felt his resolve crack. "You're in a fix," he said after a brief but dangerous pause. "You need help."

"Who doesn't?" Emily laughed. "Seriously, though. Why?"

Scott sighed. He had not yet done enough, had not been suf-ficiently convincing. Fleetingly, he considered telling the truth. Walking out from behind his desk, he placed his hands on his hips and flashed his best smile. "Honestly? I don't want to send just anyone. It has to be someone I can trust, someone I know will fit in with my family, but the position needs to be filled immediately and I don't have time to go through the proper channels. The interviews and paperwork would take forever, and formal qualifications aren't necessary anyway. A personal connection is what's important. I think you can offer something we just wouldn't get from an agency. . . ." He trailed off. Not one word was a lie, and yet it wasn't quite the truth either. He laughed to cover his nerves. "I don't know. I guess I just have this feeling about you. Is that so strange?"

Emily looked at him, and a hundred hidden meanings crack-led between them like a current.

There was a knock, and Verity pushed the office door open. "Sorry to interrupt, Scott, but Karen Lomax has been held up and was hoping we might be able to push the meeting back a couple of hours."

Scott frowned. "A couple of hours?"

Verity rolled her eyes. "I know, it's annoying. Do you want me to say no?"

Reflexively, he ran through the rest of the day in his head, rethinking, rescheduling . . . but then he stopped, looked at his watch, glanced at Emily.

"You know what?" he said. "It's fine. Go ahead and tell Karen two thirty, but no more changes." Verity nodded her assent and disappeared again.

Scott returned to his side of the desk. He became aware of a chill at the nape of his neck as beads of moisture soaked into his collar. "Well, Emily," he said, slipping his jacket from the back of his chair. "It seems I have some time to kill. How do you feel about lunch?"

He saw her hesitate: a slight knitting of her brow.

"Purely business, of course," he added. "An opportunity for me to tell you more about the job, and you can ask any questions you might have. Or we could just chat again over the phone later in the week? Whatever you'd prefer. But I'm starving, and my favorite restaurant is right around the corner." He shrugged and spread his hands. "What do you say? They do a mean gelato."

Emily's face softened and a slow smile spread over her face, the corners of her mouth turning up in an expression that was almost impish. And with a sudden bittersweet pang, Scott understood why she seemed so familiar to him. It was so obvious; how had he failed to see it before?

She reminded him of Nina.

It's him. He's here again.

I'm tingling all over as I skip the latte I'd been about to pour and make a piccolo instead. I have it ready before he even makes it to the counter. I push it toward him with a smile, adding a chocolate-chip cookie.

"Thanks," he says with a grin. "How do you always know?"

You never order anything else, I think. "I'm psychic," I tell him, and immediately wish I had thought of something cleverer.

"Oh yeah?" he says, and puts an arm behind his back. "How many fingers am I holding up?"

"Trick question," I say. "None."

He smiles and produces a closed fist. "Unbelievable."

"Not really. You seem like a tricky kind of guy."

The woman waiting for her latte gives me a filthy look. She thinks I'm just a waitress, but what she doesn't know is that under this rust-red apron I'm Wonder Woman. A fighter. A survivor. I flew here, I want to tell her. I strapped a bag to my back like it was a rocket pack. I crossed oceans. I left everything behind. I did it. No help. Just me. I'm invincible.

I turn back to the machine and finish off the woman's coffee. When I turn back to give it to her, he's still standing there, holding his cookie.

"You're still here," I say.

"I am." He looks down and waits for the grumpy latte woman to leave. Then he says, "Listen. I'm starving and I doubt the cookie's going to cut it. What time do you finish?"

"An hour," I say. My face feels hot.

He swallows. "My favorite restaurant is right around the corner. I'm thinking gelato for lunch. Any chance you'd like to join me?"

I look at him in his suit, with his glittering cuff links and unswerving confidence. I bet he glitters on the inside, too. I turn and reach for a cloth, lowering my eyes, pretending to think. Slowly, I wipe the counter. I can feel his eyes on me, sizing me up. I tuck my hair behind my ear and tilt my head, offering a view of my best side.

"Your favorite restaurant. Would that happen to be Bombini?" I say, and his jaw falls open.

"Seriously," he says. "How do you do it?"

I know it because I pass it every day. It has twinkly windows and a chalkboard outside that reads, STRESSED SPELLED BACKWARD IS GELATO. Inside, there's a piano and a woman whose only job is to say hello to people when they walk in. It's the kind of place someone like me could never go to.

Well, perhaps not never. I'm Wonder Woman, I remind myself. I can do anything.

He's still looking at me, staring, studying my every move, and I hesitate. A spasm of fear passes through me, locking my body. What if, what if, what if . . .

But then I shake it off. Wonder Woman wouldn't be afraid.

"Told you," I say. "I'm psychic."

He laughs, and it's such a beautiful sound. I know then that everything will be fine.

CHAPTER ELEVEN

EMILY

EMILY COULDN'T believe her luck. As she followed Scott across Regent Street and into Soho, apparently toward a swanky restaurant, she couldn't stop smiling. Just when she thought she was so far down shit creek that there was no coming back, the universe had thrown her a paddle. No, it had thrown her a *yacht*. She felt like she'd won the lottery, or a game show. *Our top prize tonight, Bob, is a brand new life, complete with car, salary, and a beautiful French castle!*

But could she really just take off and move in with a family she didn't know? What would her parents say? She could call Juliet and ask. *Hey, it's me again; just wondering whether to jack in my career and move to France. What do you think?* Not that it was much of a career, and not that she thought her parents would raise many objections if she did give it up—but for a housekeeping job in a different country? She wasn't ready to hear what they might have to say about that.

But did it really matter what they thought? Her life was shit. Things couldn't get any worse. It wouldn't hurt to hear Scott out. At the very least, it was a free lunch.

The restaurant was beautiful. Tucked away at the end of a Soho lane, almost completely hidden by a wall of ivy, it reminded her of a Christmas grotto in a department store. Fairy lights and candles winked in the windows like promises.

Inside, a tall black-clad woman showed them through to an outdoor terrace where sweet-smelling creepers dangled from an overhead trellis. As Scott pointed to a table in the corner, Emily hung back, tugging at the hem of her skirt. Despite having wrangled with her wardrobe for almost two hours that morning, she'd chosen the wrong outfit. She'd put on weight since she last wore the skirt; the stupid thing was too short and clung in all the wrong places. Totally inappropriate for a business meeting. *Which is what this IS,* she told herself, stubbornly ignoring the skippy little thrill running through her bloodstream.

For some reason, every inch of her wanted to run to the bathroom, check her makeup, practice a few coy smiles in the mirror—her body seemed to be under the misapprehension that this was some kind of *date*—but she had to stay focused. The situation was clear; and besides, who was she kidding? She would have no chance with someone like Scott, even if he wasn't *married*. With a *child*.

But despite all her best efforts, every time their eyes met, Emily's heart leaped painfully into her throat.

Smiling, Scott pulled her chair out for her.

"Thank you," she said, pulling at her skirt again and bending her body in a sort of curtsey. She was already sweating. *Oh, for god's sake, what's wrong with you? Just be normal.* As she sat down, her skirt rode up to the very top of her thighs, and she grabbed desperately at her cloth napkin from the table, intending to lay it out over her exposed lap. But, mortifyingly, her cutlery came with it, and two forks clattered noisily to the ground. Her cheeks burned.

The hostess in the black shirt appeared and bent down to retrieve them with a cheerful smile. "Oops," she said. "Never mind, I'll grab some fresh ones. In the meantime, can I get you any drinks? Wine? Cocktails?"

Scott turned to Emily. "What will you have?"

"Oh, er . . ." Emily's mind went blank. She couldn't think of a single drink. "Umm . . ." *Come on, you order drinks all the time, what do you want?* "I'll have . . ." From one of the other tables, she heard the faint pop of a cork. "Champagne?"

"Great choice," said Scott. "Dom Pérignon, please."

The hostess smiled warmly. "Special occasion?"

Emily laughed so loudly the hostess actually took a small step backward. "No, nothing like that," she said. "This is a *business meeting.*"

"Ah," said the hostess, one eyebrow just fractionally raised. "Of course. I'll leave you to it."

Emily watched her go. *Champagne?* she thought. *Really?*

"So," said Scott, a half smile playing on his lips. "Speaking of business, do you have any questions about the job?"

She nodded, but as he pinned her to her seat with his onyx-black stare, she could only think of one. *What the hell am I doing?*

Two glasses of champagne later, Emily had relaxed. She'd managed to think of some questions about the property itself, and Scott had answered them in detail, telling her all about the ocean, the pool, and the two separate houses. He described the original architectural features—cornices, wall paneling, fireplaces, vaulted ceilings—and actually made them sound interesting. He talked about the grounds. There were vegetable and herb gardens, as well as olive trees and an orchard.

"The whole place seems to have its own little weather system," Scott said. "It's just right for the plants to thrive. We built an art studio last summer, and there's a spot right at the bottom of the property that we've had paved. We call it the sunset point. It sticks right out over the ocean and faces the exact spot where the midsummer sun goes down. If you sit right at the very end with your legs hanging over the edge, it feels like you're hovering in thin air."

Emily held his gaze. There was no getting away from it: Scott was very good-looking. Tall and lean, muscular but not too thick, not like a weight lifter or a gym rat. More like a runner, compact and in proportion. Dark brown hair with a distinguished touch of gray at the temples and a brooding default expression that changed completely when he smiled. His age was difficult to guess; early forties, maybe? She'd barely been aware of him when she worked at Proem; he was just the boss, the big man upstairs. Now, though, she couldn't believe she'd missed him.

Adorably, he showed a little too much of his bottom teeth when he smiled, like a child on a sugar high, and maybe it was just the professional in him, but when she spoke, he made her feel like the most important and interesting person on earth. He really listened. He looked. He laughed. He *saw* her. And his undivided attention was like a drug: now that she'd had a taste of it, she wanted more.

She noticed the contrast of Scott's dark skin against his shirt and the movement of his throat as he swallowed. His collar was impeccably ironed, the top two buttons undone to reveal a scattering of black hairs. *Not too much, not too little,* she thought, and then: *Calm down, woman. You're not supposed to be attracted to him, remember?* If she was, this whole thing—the hush of their conversation, the brush of his knee on hers, the accidental champagne—would all take on a very unsavory tone. But it was okay, because she had a handle on it. He wasn't that hot, anyway. It was probably just the suit.

Scott cleared his throat.

"Well, o-*kay*!" she said, realizing she'd been staring at his chest hair.

He ordered food. Seared scallops. Pasta with diamond-shell clams. Gelato for dessert: sour cherry and sweet vanilla. The most delicious array of flavors she'd ever tasted.

Emboldened, Emily asked him about his life. "I did all the talking this morning. Now it's your turn." She mimicked his director's tone. "Maybe you could tell me a little about *your*self."

Scott hesitated. Then, with downcast eyes, he told her his

story. He'd grown up in the Cotswolds, the younger of two boys. His mother was a dressmaker, and his father, as far as anyone knew, was a successful entrepreneur. Over several years, Terrence Denny had set up multiple companies and made a lot of money, and for many years they'd all lived very comfortably. But it all came crashing down the day bailiffs knocked on the door. Unbeknownst to the family, a serious gambling problem had first raised Terrence up then torn him down. They lost everything. And then he left, taking with him, for some unknown reason, Scott's only brother.

"The shame and grief nearly killed my mother," Scott said, and for one electrifying moment, Emily thought he was going to cry. "I swore I would fight my way to a better life—for both of us. I swore I would do what he couldn't."

Possibly it was the champagne, but for a few raw seconds, everything was different. Time slowed down. There were no walls between them, no hidden agendas, no other people; just the movement of the air between them and the gentle truth of their hearts.

But the moment dissolved just as quickly as it had arrived, and Scott was back: calm, collected, and totally in control.

"So . . . ," Emily said, changing the subject. "This job. Say I was to accept."

"Hypothetically?"

"Hypothetically, yes. What would happen then?"

"Well," Scott pushed his empty plate to one side. "Hypothetically, I would give you this." He reached down beneath the table. From a black laptop bag, he pulled a slim document.

"What is it?"

He passed it to her. It was a sheaf of printed A4 paper, maybe twelve pages, bound together by a black plastic spine.

"It's a confidentiality agreement. Also known as an NDA." He shrugged. "All our staff sign one. Or, at least, the seniors do."

Emily looked at it, her eyes skimming over the clauses and legal jargon. "Okay . . . what's it for?"

"In this case? Nothing really. We use them all the time at Proem because we share sensitive information between clients and investors, but with you it's more just about keeping local gossip to a minimum." He grinned and leaned toward her, his tone suddenly confessional. "Truth? I cheated a bit when I started renovating the property. I needed to push things through quickly so, you know, I've *occasionally* neglected to obtain the correct planning permissions. It's no big deal, but I really don't need it coming back at me. Also . . ." It was hard to tell, but Scott appeared to be blushing. "God, this is going to sound so pompous, but my public image is growing, and I like to keep a low profile."

Emily giggled. "A low profile?" She snapped her fingers in the air. "Hang on, I *knew* I recognized you from somewhere! Can I please have your autograph, Brad? I just loved you in *Benjamin Button*."

Scott laughed. "Don't take the piss."

"Don't freak out, but I think I see helicopters circling. Must be the paps."

"I'm serious. I don't want people knowing where I live."

Emily smiled. She'd heard of nondisclosure agreements. Celebrities used them all the time. "Fine," she said. "I'll keep your secrets for you."

"You're too kind. So, anyway—hypothetically—after that's signed, I might present you with these." He rummaged in his jacket pocket, pulling out a shiny black credit card and three keys on a silver ring. "This would be your card. You can use it for whatever you like, within reason of course. Your weekly wage will be paid into your account. Or you can use the card to withdraw it in cash, if you prefer."

Tax-free income, Emily thought. *This just gets better and better.*

"These are the keys to the house and your car. This little one is for the front gate, but the security system is electronic so you won't need it. Yves will explain everything when you get there."

"Yves?"

"My man on the ground." That boyish smile again. "A local guy; he's a landscaper. Takes care of the heavy lifting, so to speak. Big stuff, like fences, drainage, plumbing. He does most of it himself, but he has plenty of connections should we need anything outside of his expertise."

Emily took the card and the keys and placed them both on top of the agreement. "And after that? What would happen then?"

"Well, if you had no further questions, I'd tell you that your flight is already booked and you leave on Thursday." Scott sat back, studying her, and Emily understood that she was standing at a crossroads. It was now or never. Yes or no. The red pill or the blue pill.

She looked up at the trellis and the patches of pure blue sky just visible between the creepers. *Housekeeper.* Emily thought about her bathroom and the thick layer of grime that covered the sink and the bathtub. *Au pair.* Sure, she was good with kids but she knew nothing about taking care of them, especially not ones with "health issues." But an all-expenses-paid summer on a luxurious estate by the ocean? She could learn on the job, right?

"You know, Em," Scott said, his voice strangely weary. "The smallest thing can change your life. Just one decision can open so many doors. You can walk through any one of them—or all of them at once—and become a completely different person. And just like that, nothing is ever the same again."

Their eyes locked, and Emily felt like he could see right through to her soul. Her heart flared like a struck match. Maybe she *was* special.

Holding the agreement in her hands, she smiled. "Have you got a pen?"

CHAPTER TWELVE

SCOTT

IN THE living room of his riverside apartment, Scott stood with his phone pressed to his ear. Nina wasn't picking up. He tried twice more before the line finally clicked and her voice floated through a crackle of static.

"Scott?" He could only just hear her.

"Nina. Are you there?"

The line hissed in reply.

"Nina?"

". . . hear you," she said. She sounded far away, like she was speaking to him from the back of a giant cave.

He waited. "I'm sending someone," he said, eventually.

More hissing. Then: ". . . body out there."

"What?"

Suddenly Nina's voice came hurtling through the earpiece, loud and clear. ". . . watching me. There's somebody watching the house."

A tremor pulsed through Scott's body, quick and sharp, leaving him prickling all over. He drew in a breath and let it out slowly. "Nina—"

"In the woods. I can hear them."

"Nina, listen. There's no one in the woods."

The static was back. Her voice dropped out.

He waited. "Can you hear me?"

"Yes," she said, faintly.

"Did you hear what I said? I'm sending someone."

"You're what?"

"Sending someone. To you. She arrives on Thursday." There was a pop, then a soft howl, like the wind blowing. "Yves will meet her at the airport and bring her to you."

"You're . . ." Nina faded away again.

"Where are you? Are you outside?" Scott pictured her standing on the lawn, holding the phone in one white-knuckled hand. Her brow would be knotted, her eyes wide. "Go back inside, Nina, there's no one in the woods."

"Scott? Did you just say someone's coming here?"

"Yes, but not now. Thursday."

"Thursday? Who? Who's coming?"

"A housekeeper."

"A housekeeper," Nina echoed, her voice faint.

"Or a gardener. A babysitter. A general dogsbody. She can be whatever you want." He wandered over to the window and looked down. Outside, a heavy rain lashed at tall buildings and pummeled the road. He listened to the water pouring off the eaves outside and pictured himself out there among the raindrops, free-falling through the air, twisting and turning, riding the currents, and then, *SMASH*. Hitting the ground and bursting into a billion wet pieces.

"She?"

"Yes. Her name's Emily." *Emily, Emily, Emily.* His thoughts were full of her. He cringed as he remembered how much he'd shared with her over lunch. His upbringing, his father . . . why had he done that? He needed to be more careful.

Nina said something, but the line crackled again and he didn't quite catch it. "Nina? Are you still there?" Scott walked into the kitchen and leaned on the kitchen island, resting his elbows on the marble. Huge glass pendants floated above his head like planets. "Nina?"

Silence.

"I'm trying to do the right thing here," he murmured.

Still nothing.

He bit his thumbnail, pulling the jagged edge between his teeth; it tore but got stuck at the side. He persisted and the nail came loose, blood blooming underneath.

"I know you want me to be there." His voice was barely more than a whisper. "But we both know I can't."

There was a rustle, and suddenly the line was so clear he could hear every little sound she made. He heard her lips part and her tongue move; he heard the ragged rise and fall of her breath. She was crying.

"Thank you," she breathed. "Thank you."

Scott closed his eyes. Sliding his elbows over the swirling marble, he pressed his forehead into his hands and let her gratitude wash over him. *That's right, Nina,* he thought. *You win. Again.*

But he knew he was wrong. No one could win.

They would all lose. Every one of them.

My husband stumbles backward, trying to catch the pancake, and I laugh, determined not to spoil our last few moments. I want to send him off in a good mood.

"Ha! Got it!" He teases the pancake onto my plate, where it folds into a messy heap. Frowning, he prods it back into shape.

I watch him closely. He's just as handsome as the day we met. I love the way his tongue pokes out the side of his mouth whenever he concentrates, like it's coaching from the sidelines. It really should have its own little hat and whistle.

"Your breakfast is served, *madame,*" he says in a faux-French accent, presenting the plate with a flourish. Smiling, I grab half a lemon and squeeze the juice over the pancake, adding sugar and then a handful of grated cheese, patting it all down and rolling it up into a cigar shape. He makes a face as I pick it up and sink my teeth into it. It is bliss.

"Gross," he says, spreading peanut butter on a piece of toast. "And you call yourself a chef."

"Nope," I say. "Haven't qualified yet."

"And you never will if you keep making stuff like that. You're abusing our unborn child, you know. It's probably retching in there as we speak."

"No, this is what it wants. It told me," I say through a mouthful of lemon and cheese. "*Crêpe Suzette au fromage.* All the rage in Paris."

"Is it now? I'll have to look out for that when I get there."

I swallow and make a sad face. "Do you really have to leave us? What if the baby comes while you're away?"

"It's only three nights. And that baby isn't going anywhere. Not yet. It's very happy in there. It told me." He walks around the kitchen island and leans over to kiss me.

"Yuck!" I say, instantly nauseous. "Don't come near me with your peanut-butter breath, you'll make me vomit!"

"You can stomach lemon, sugar, and cheese, but peanut butter makes you feel sick?" He laughs and nuzzles my neck. "You're a crazy lady."

I bat him away, but not too hard. Funny thing is, I've never felt so sane. Pregnancy seems to have leveled me out and balanced my hormones instead of stirring them up. I can't remember ever feeling so clearheaded and full of energy, which is a huge relief as I've been planning to come off the medication anyway. I imagine the freedom of not having to take it. I won't have to lie anymore; I won't have to hide the pills.

Rubbing the taut skin of my belly, I imagine the little creature inside, all curled up, floating around like a roly-poly astronaut.

"Okay, my love. My two loves, I should say. Daddy's outta here." He kisses my head and wraps his arms around my shoulders. Then he bends down and presses his lips to my bump. "Be good in there, little swimmer," he says. "No parties while I'm away."

A bubble of panic rises in my chest and pops on my tongue. "Can we come, too?" I plead, only half joking. "Give me five minutes. I'll pack a bag and we can all move to Paris."

He laughs. "You, pack a bag in five minutes? I'd like to see you try. And what is your thing with France, anyway? What's the big draw? Aside from the unusual gastronomic trends, I mean."

"I don't know." I press his hand against my cheek. "I've just always wanted to live there. Go to the markets. Sit at little corner cafés. Maybe one day set up a bed-and-breakfast or something."

"Hmm. Well, let's just have this baby first, hey?" He kisses my nose, my eyebrows, the tips of my fingers. "In the meantime, I've got to go and make some money. I'll call you when I get to the hotel."

I watch as he grabs the handle of his flight bag and wheels it toward the door, sucking up every movement, every inch of him, banking it for later when I'm alone. In a few moments, he will be gone, but right now he is here with me, in this house that we share, in this beautiful dreamlike life we have built together.

In the hallway, he turns back. "Why don't you go to the movies later? Get your nails done? Treat yourself."

I try not to react. He does this sometimes; mocks me. It's like I test. A test I always pass.

With a final smile, he disappears through the door and his absence rushes in. The lock clicks into place and I am left with my steadfast companions: the Liberty wallpaper, the Italian espresso machine. The Armani occasional chair and the floral-print tea tray that cost almost as much as I used to make in a year.

I swallow the empty spaces, pull the silence close. I blow a heartfelt kiss toward the door, sending it skipping after my husband, and marvel at my own bubbling happiness, my phenomenal good luck.

CHAPTER THIRTEEN

EMILY

Q UERENCIA, EMILY thought. *What a beautiful word.*

As the SUV passed through the black iron gates at the end of the long dirt track, she found she could hardly breathe. The colors, the smells, the two gleaming houses . . . a part of her, the part that had worried the whole way from London that Scott's job offer was too good to be true, backed away with its hands in the air.

She stared, enraptured, as Yves steered the car farther onto the property. He pointed at things as they went, naming them in a flat monotone. Tennis court, basketball court, vegetable garden. Quad bikes, tree house, koi pond.

Taking the left fork around the central lawn, he parked in front of the larger of the two houses. "You will find *madame* in the gardens," he said, yanking the hand brake and turning off the engine. He was out of the car before Emily could even respond, stamping away toward a stationary white utility truck half-hidden among the trees. He threw himself inside and the truck pulled away, disappearing back through the gates in a cloud of dust.

Alone, Emily turned in her seat, scanning the empty property. Eventually, she opened her door and stepped down onto soft sand; the whole driveway was covered in it, a fine white powder that squeaked under her feet. There were no signs of life anywhere. No shoes on the porch, no towels slung over chairs, no noise.

She reached into her handbag for the keys Scott had given her in Soho. The emblem on the car key matched that of the SUV. She clicked the lock button and the car made a beeping sound. *Holy shit.* Apparently, this enormous black machine was now hers to drive. Ridiculous, really, considering she'd never driven anything larger than a Ford Kia. Even more ridiculous: Scott hadn't verified that she *could* drive.

Jangling the keys in her hand, Emily turned in circles, wondering in which particular part of the vast gardens she might find *"madame."* Scott had emailed her some information about the property but hadn't included his wife's contact details. She pulled out her phone, wondering if she ought to text Scott, but it still wasn't picking up any service.

Suddenly, there was a flash of movement over near the smaller of the two houses. Emily raised her hand to block the glare of the sun, scanning the front door and the windows. She took a few tentative steps, and there it was again. A streak of color behind a hedge to the left.

Emily began to walk with more purpose. "Hello?" she called.

A short, flapping thing shot into view and tore across a patch of grass, disappearing again behind the house. Emily stared. *A child,* she thought. A small girl with black hair running at full tilt, a too-big yellow hat flopping around on her head.

She waited.

"Hello?" she called, louder this time. "Anybody here?"

There was no answer. *"Madame"* must be inside.

The door of the house stood ajar. She wandered over to the front steps, craning her neck to see inside. It opened onto some kind of sitting room, full of light-toned furniture and Impressionist paintings. Thick magazines and photography books were arranged artfully on low tables next to clusters of candles bearing brand names she'd only ever seen during the occasional fantasy browse in Selfridges, and the air was filled with an exotic, flowery scent.

After a minute of listening to nothing but the ticking of an invisible clock, Emily became aware of a mechanical sound, a thin sort of whirring. She stepped back and looked up. Above the door, a security camera swiveled slowly on its mount, its red light blinking. It came to a rest with its lens pointed straight at her. Another was fixed to the wall above a first-floor window, and peering inside the house again, she noticed a third camera high up in the far corner of the sitting room.

Unsure of what else to do, she edged inside, running her fingers absentmindedly over the surface of a nearby side table. They came away coated with a film of sticky black dust.

Moving farther into the room, Emily turned toward the stairs.

Only then did she see the woman standing motionless in the corner.

Shock pulsed through her body and she stumbled backward into the dusty table, causing a small dish to wobble and fall to the floor. It hit the tiles and cracked into three pieces.

"Oh, no! Oh god, I'm so sorry!" Emily bent down to scrabble for the pieces, her cheeks burning with shame.

The woman stepped forward. "Sorry, I didn't mean to scare you."

"No, no, it was my fault," Emily said, laughing. "I get clumsy when I'm nervous." There was a swish of material, and a sweet, summery scent filled her nose. Emily laughed again, too embarrassed to look up. "Not the best way to make an impression, is it? I haven't even been here five minutes and I'm trashing the place already."

"It's just a dish." Perfect pink fingernails met Emily's own bitten ones as both she and the woman went for the same porcelain splinters.

"I'm always doing things like this." Emily knew she was about to start chattering like a monkey but seemed powerless to stop it. "Well, not specifically this. It's not, like, my *thing*. I don't just go around throwing plates at walls. Although I did once throw a whole tray of food at a wall in a restaurant, but that was an accident. The tray was really heavy, and my foot got caught on someone's bag."

Cradling bits of broken dish in her hands, Emily looked up and saw tanned legs and a white cotton dress, an impossibly small waist, and arms covered with a paint splatter of dark freckles. Bare shoulders flowed into delicate, caramel-colored collarbones. A long neck, slender as a ballerina's, gave way to a sharp jaw and cut-glass cheekbones, topped off with a crop of short blond hair flipped over to one side like a wave.

Emily stood up. The woman's face was pure Helen of Troy. A bud-like mouth opened over straight white teeth. Impossibly long lashes framed a pair of almond eyes.

The woman stared back, conducting her own silent assessment. Just as the moment was becoming uncomfortable, she smiled. "So, you must be Emily," she said. "Thank you so much for agreeing to start at such short notice; we really appreciate it." She moved toward Emily with her arms outstretched. "I'm Nina. It's wonderful to meet you."

The hug came as a surprise, and Emily hesitated before returning it, uncertain how she should interpret the pressure around her shoulders, the unfamiliar fingers at her back. Then, from out of nowhere, she was overcome by a brief, wondrous falling sensation, as if Nina was pulling her over a precipice; a feeling that, as the hug dragged on, gave way to discomfort. Shards of porcelain dug into Emily's palms and strands of hair became caught in her mouth.

And then it felt as though she was no longer being pulled but pushed, as if Nina was pressing her whole weight into her, crushing her, gripping her like she was the only anchor in an endless sea.

And somewhere, just underneath wafts of coconut shampoo and expensive candles, there was a smell. A strange and subtle stink like a piece of meat left out in the sun too long; a sourness that seemed to linger on Emily's skin and in the fibers of her clothes long after Nina pulled away.

CHAPTER FOURTEEN

EMILY

EMILY PLACED the bits of broken dish into Nina's cupped palms, carefully brushing the smaller shards off her own skin. Nina smiled politely and insisted again that there was no need to apologize, but still Emily's cheeks flushed pink with shame. She backed off and hung around by the door while Nina disposed of the pieces.

The house, or what little she could see of it, was more elegant than Emily had imagined. The decor was dainty and feminine. She searched the walls of the sitting room for some sign of Scott, but found none. The only tangible presence was that of the beautiful woman standing in front of her.

Scott's wife was not what she'd pictured, either. She was gorgeous—of course she was—but there was something distinctly odd about Nina, something Emily couldn't put into words. She seemed pleasant, but something didn't quite . . . fit. For starters, it was difficult to connect Scott and his suits and lavish offices with this waiflike person who wafted out into the gardens like a spirit, beckoning for Emily to follow. Scott left an impression so strong it packed an almost physical punch, while Nina moved so lightly over the sand she didn't even seem to leave footprints. Scott was self-assured, but Nina had a twitchy energy; her eyes

darted around like a watchful animal. And Scott was so generous, so warm, whereas this woman seemed sort of detached and
ethereal, like part of her wasn't really present. How could they
possibly be suited?

"Let me give you the tour," Nina said. Emily trailed after
her, trying to guess her age. Early thirties, maybe? Definitely
older, but not by much. As she studied Nina's slender wrists,
her tanned calves, her exquisite shoulder blades, pangs of resentment plucked at her body as she imagined Scott touching
them. She watched with barely concealed envy as Nina's white
dress floated around her like a mist, rising and falling in syn-
chronization with her every step. Her gestures were so graceful
they seemed choreographed. She was the very embodiment of
Querencia itself—breathtaking isolation personified—and as
they walked, Emily felt increasingly gawky and lumbering, like
a baby elephant stamping along behind a swan. Becoming painfully aware of her own cheap clothes, limp hair, and smudged
makeup, the words she'd overheard in the office echoed in her
ears: *Batshit-crazy wife; she's a bitch; he hates her.*

Nina chatted as they went, pointing out the herb garden, the
rose garden, the orchard, and the gym. The design of the place
was impressive, like something out of the Chelsea Flower Show.
The white sandy driveway was like a river, flowing through the
center and around the lawn, splitting off into tributaries that led
to various areas and features, each carefully set out in its own
designated space.

The main lawn itself was circular in shape and about the size of
an Olympic swimming pool. On either side, the two sprawling
houses faced one another like opponents, each trying to outdo
the other. The one in which Emily had found Nina was prettier,
with blue shutters and wisteria-covered walls. But the other was
taller, comprising three stories rather than just two. Its roof was
gray, its walls bare, and the windows were long and narrow. It
even had a tower with a turret.

Beyond the two houses, the driveway narrowed and began to

slope downward, becoming more of a path edged with rhubarb, aloe vera, wild iris, and fuchsia. Tiered rock gardens stepped down toward the sea. Trellises and arbors gave structure to stunning circular beds stuffed with wildflowers. Emily couldn't help but think how much Juliet would approve.

At the bottom of a wide set of stone steps, she found herself looking at a pristine infinity pool surrounded by sun loungers and enormous glass lanterns. A cushioned daybed and a swing seat were positioned in front of a wall of tall fluffy grass, each stem like a giant feather duster, and a Balinese-style pergola cast its shadow over a poolside kitchen. Everything was angled to showcase the spectacular ocean view. *This is insane.* Emily's mouth hung open. *Who lives like this?*

They circled around and walked back up toward the houses, veering off to enter the one with the tower. "This is the guest-house," Nina said, showing Emily the laundry room, the dry-goods store, and the linen press. Neat rows of cabinets lined the walls, and sprays of lavender stood tall in ceramic jugs. Wicker hampers sat on shelves above a huge stone sink. It was all impeccably organized, but the shelves themselves were sagging, the walls shedding paint like dry skin. Emily sniffed. There it was again, that smell, just under the laundry powder and lavender. The same as before, but slightly different. Damp. Mold. Rot.

"You'll notice that there's quite a bit of work to be done," Nina was saying. "We have extensive plans to decorate, but it's a slow burn."

They climbed a timber staircase to a landing that gave way to a maze of hallways and doors. Emily struggled to count the bedrooms, but there seemed to be eight; five on the first floor and three on the second, including one in the tower, which turned out to be the most beautiful bedroom Emily had ever seen. "This is you," Nina said, leading the way inside. "I hope it's okay."

White, bright, and airy, the bedroom had tall windows, floaty curtains, and floorboards set in a herringbone pattern. In one corner stood a huge glass-paneled closet; in another, a dressing table was adorned with a small brass alarm clock and a vase of fat pink peonies. French doors led to a small balcony, on which Nina talked Emily through her duties while waving a hand expansively over the grounds.

Emily's overwhelmed brain failed to catch the specifics, but she understood that she would be helping with the cooking, the cleaning, and the laundry. She would do the grocery shopping and take care of the pool. There was a great deal of gardening to do—weeding, mowing, power-washing, pruning, watering, raking—and the animals needed constant care. There were chickens and goats, plus a few rabbits and a miniature pig called Francis Bacon. Nina also required help with DIY projects: sanding, painting, ripping up carpets, varnishing floors . . . the list of jobs went on and on.

"We'd like to open for business at some point," Nina said. "I'm thinking yoga retreats, a cookery school. Maybe even artist residencies. We have an art studio now, did Scott tell you that? Oh, and you'll be relieved to hear that your indoor chores will be limited strictly to the guesthouse. I'll take care of the family house myself."

From the balcony, Emily could see that the lawn had been mown into a neat spiral, at the center of which stood a tall, thin tree. The branches served as a screen between the houses, offering a degree of privacy for the first-floor windows.

"In fact," Nina continued, "I'd like to make the family house a no-go zone. I hope that doesn't make things awkward, but if this arrangement is going to work we need to respect each other's space, don't you think?"

Emily shrugged and nodded. "Sure," she said. "Although Scott mentioned that you might need me to help look after your daughter?"

"Yes, well, we can discuss all of that later." Nina pushed herself off the balustrade and stepped back through the balcony doors. "Speaking of which, why don't we go and find the little rascal? I'll introduce you."

"Okay, great."

"You'll love her," Nina said as she crossed the room and disappeared into the hallway. "She's such a monkey."

Downstairs, Nina led Emily into a long dining room dominated by a giant stone fireplace. Sculptures towered on side tables, crystal glasses winked in cabinets, and bottle upon dusty bottle of wine lay in tall racks. Textured oil paintings ran along the walls in a long line. Emily shivered. Despite the heat outside, it was cold, and there was an old, fusty smell, like in a closed-down museum.

Nina stood in the middle of the room with her hands on her hips. "Come on out, Strawberry," she said. "There's someone I'd like you to meet."

There was no reply.

"She loves to hide," Nina explained with a grin.

Emily smiled politely.

Nina turned back to the room. "Come on out, honey."

Emily began to feel uneasy. She thought about the health issues that Scott had mentioned. Why hadn't she asked about them? A breeze swept in through the open door and tickled the back of her neck. She looked around the room, in the corners and under the table. No feet poked out from underneath the curtains, no stifled giggle floated out from behind the door. The room was completely empty.

There was a soft creak, and a panel in the back wall swung open. After several seconds, a hand emerged, followed by an arm, followed by a swathe of black hair and a huge straw hat. A pale face peeked out from under the brim.

"There you are," said Nina.

A little girl crawled out from her hiding place and stood up.

"Emily, this is our daughter, Aurelia."

Emily released her breath and realized she'd been bracing herself for something obvious, some kind of abnormality or disability that she'd have to pretend not to see, but Aurelia was just an ordinary little girl. Definitely on the skinny side, though, and with eyes so dark and skin so white that Emily almost made a joke about Wednesday Addams. *Almost.* She waved and received a blank look in return.

"Aurelia, I'd like you to say hello to our new friend. Let's make her feel at home, shall we?" Nina placed a hand on Emily's shoulder. "Welcome to Querencia."

Aurelia led the way to the animal sheds, skipping ahead and darting off the path, vanishing suddenly then reappearing in unexpected places.

"She's been so excited to meet you," said Nina. "She's got a whole list of things she wants to show you, but don't be offended if it takes a while for her to warm up. She's extremely shy."

Trying to think of something to say, Emily watched Aurelia's big hat disappear behind a bush. "She seems . . . very sweet."

Nina grinned proudly. "She is."

As they ambled up toward the gates, Emily wondered if they were perhaps heading off the property, but just before they reached the end of the driveway, Nina slowed down and gestured to a gap in the hedge. A gravel path veered off to the left. "After you," she said.

Ahead, Emily glimpsed several wooden huts and a wire fence.

"Did Scott mention Aurelia's condition?"

Emily nodded. "Kind of. He said she wasn't well." She kicked herself again for forgetting to ask Scott about it. She realized she hadn't asked Scott any questions about his wife, either—not even her name.

"Aurelia was very sick as a baby," Nina said. "She pulled through, thank god, but her immune system was very badly damaged. Among other things, she was left with a serious sun allergy. Even the slightest exposure can bring her out in hives. She gets headaches, nausea, vomiting—sometimes she even passes out." Nina shook her head and sighed. "She needs constant sun protection. Long clothing, hats, sunscreen. Her eyes are incredibly sensitive, too. It's not easy to manage but we do our best."

Emily studied the trees and eventually spotted Aurelia about twenty meters away, her huge hat disappearing behind one of the sheds. Ahead, Emily could make out small shapes moving around within the confines of the wire fencing.

"She also has days where her whole system just shuts down and she can't get out of bed. We're told her body will get stronger as she gets older, but for now we're quite limited. We can't really go anywhere. Some days we can't even leave the house." Nina spread her hands. "Which is why you're here. On my own, I can't focus on either Aurelia or the property as much as I'd like. We're falling behind with homeschooling and the reno jobs are piling up, so a lot of the day-to-day stuff just gets pushed to the side."

"Have you thought about hiring a painter or a decorator?" It was an innocent question, but Emily realized she sounded churlish. "I mean, I'm more than happy to help, but wouldn't it be quicker?"

"It would," Nina said. "But not as much fun. I know it seems like I'm making things hard for myself, but it's good for me to have a project on the go, something that isn't child-related. And a decorator would just take over. I want to do things my way." She bent down to pluck a stray toy from the path: a pink plastic shovel. "Plus, we have to be careful about how many people we have on the property. Aurelia isn't good with strangers."

It occurred to Emily that Nina's accent wasn't English. Not totally, anyway. There were plenty of British sounds, but underneath them was something flat and throaty. Dark "L"s and an inflection at the end of sentences that made her statements seem like questions.

As they got closer to the sheds, the shapes behind the fence came into focus. Chickens—but barely recognizable as such.

White and fluffy with a puff of feathers sprouting from their heads, they looked less like birds and more like balls of cotton wool. Their plumage was so long that it hung over their eyes and spilled over their feet like flared trousers.

"Silkie chooks," Nina explained, pushing open the door of one of the sheds. "Sweetest animals ever."

Chooks. The accent fell into place. *Of course. Australian.*

Emily followed, ducking through the doorway and squeezing past nesting boxes until she emerged into the yard.

"These girls will need checking every morning and every evening," said Nina. "Let them out first thing, grab any eggs, then lock them back inside before you go to bed. The food is kept in the end shed. I'll give you a full rundown of their schedules." She reached down and scooped one of them up, stroking it like a kitten.

Aurelia pushed past them and did likewise, squatting in the dirt and picking up a slightly smaller chicken. She brought it right up to her face and nuzzled at the white fluff.

They moved onto the neighboring enclosures. Four brown-and-white goats rushed around them, bleating and nibbling at Emily's clothes. Two huge floppy-eared bunnies peered up at them with black eyes and twitching noses. In the farthest pen, a very small and sleepy-eyed pig trotted out to greet them. Francis Bacon had black spots, a wrinkly snout, and a snuffly little snort that made Emily weak at the knees. "Oh, my goodness." She laughed, bending down.

"Cute, isn't he?" said Nina. She took a handful of green veggies from a nearby tray and scattered them around Emily's feet. "Here, sit down. Let him come to you."

Emily lowered herself to the dusty ground and Francis edged forward. He sniffed the air and decided she was okay. Trotting over, he snorted into her hand, his front trotters resting on her crossed legs. "He's just gorgeous."

A short distance away, Aurelia stood watching, expression-less.

"Hey," Emily said, sensing an opportunity to make friends. "Am I doing it right?"

Aurelia stared back with eyes as dark and dreamy as her father's. She took a few tentative steps forward.

"I don't know much about pigs. Will he let me hold him, d'you think? Can you show me how to pick him up?"

Aurelia shuffled closer.

From the corner of her eye, Emily saw Nina stiffen. *Relax,* Emily thought, *kids like me.* "I have to be gentle with him, right? And quiet?" Emily lowered her voice to a whisper. "Like this? He probably doesn't like loud noises." She raised a finger to her lips—*"ssssshhhh"*—and reached out to take Aurelia's hand.

And then something weird happened. As Emily's fingertips brushed the bare skin of Aurelia's palm, the kid opened her mouth and shrieked—a single sharp note that sent Francis Bacon and all the surrounding animals scattering in alarm. Simultaneously, Nina charged in, slapping Emily's hand away and sweeping Aurelia back as though out of harm's way.

Emily recoiled, too shocked to speak.

In a far corner of the pigpen, Nina fussed over her daughter, holding her face in her hands and whispering urgently. Emily couldn't hear the words, but they seemed to be pleading, reassuring, placating.

"I'm—I'm so sorry," Emily stammered at last. "I was just . . . I thought . . . Is she okay?"

Nina kissed Aurelia's cheeks and smoothed her hair away from her eyes before retrieving her hat from the dirt. "It's not your fault," she said, throwing Emily a quick smile. "I should've warned you. She doesn't like to be touched."

Standing still with her head bowed, Aurelia was breathing heavily, her hands clenched into balls at her side.

"I'm so sorry," Emily said again, getting to her feet. She felt like the worst, most thoughtless person who had ever lived.

"Really, it's okay. You weren't to know." Nina placed the hat back on Aurelia's head and smiled again. "Look, I'm sure you're tired from your journey. Why don't you head on back to the guesthouse? Grab a shower and make yourself at home. We'll finish up here, won't we, Strawberry?"

But Aurelia did not reply. Under the brim of her hat, the little girl's eyes were screwed shut.

Up in her stunning white bedroom, Emily stood on the bed and waved her phone in the air. When after ten minutes she still hadn't found a signal, she climbed down and contemplated her unpacked bag. Clearly, the job wasn't going to work out. The property was lovely, but Aurelia hated her, and Nina was too perfect, too Stepford. Besides, Emily had already messed up so many times that she was as good as fired. *Again.* Best to just get in there first this time.

"I'm sorry," she said to her suitcase, "I'm not sure this is for me." She shook her head and tried again. "It's been really great meeting you, Nina, but I can't see this working. Would you mind if I called a cab?"

A knock at the door startled her into silence.

"Emily?" a voice said. "Are you in there?"

"Just a minute." Emily quickly unzipped her bag and threw some clothes over the bed so it might look like she'd been busy unpacking. She opened the door to find Nina smiling anxiously on the landing.

"Hi," Nina said. "Um. I just wanted to say . . . I wanted to apologize. This hasn't exactly been the welcome I hoped we'd give you." Nina paused, placing her hands on her hips then crossing her arms. She didn't seem to know what to do with her hands. "We're not used to having people around, and I'm afraid we're a little out of practice."

"Oh, that's okay. I understand," Emily said, even though she didn't.

Nina fell silent again. Her eyes flicked from surface to surface, as if she might find the words she was looking for written on the walls or hanging from the ceiling. "Look, can I be honest with you?" she said at last.

"Sure." Emily sighed. *Here it comes.*

"Having you here is a really big deal for Aurelia and me. We've both been so excited to meet you, but we've also been extremely nervous, and I think it just got the better of us. The better of *me*, anyway. I just . . . I really want you to like us. I know that sounds lame, but it's true."

Despite her misgivings, Emily felt the corners of her mouth twitch upward.

Nina swallowed and looked down at her fingernails. "It might take us a little while to adjust," Nina continued, "but if you give us a second chance, I promise we'll do everything we can to make you feel at home. Starting with lunch." She glanced through the doorway to Emily's unpacked suitcase. "That is, if you'd like to join us?"

Emily couldn't help but smile. Maybe Nina wasn't so bad.

"Lunch sounds great. I'd love to join you." She'd give it a few more days at least.

CHAPTER FIFTEEN

EMILY

EMILY SPENT the next morning exploring Querencia. Nina, in an apparent attempt to show her fun side, had come up with a game: a scavenger hunt with clues and prizes. The first clue had Emily stuck for at least half an hour.

My first is in Facial, my second in Blue
Third and fourth are in Able, my fifth is in You
I have my own kitchen, a place you can bake,
So come on inside for some coffee and cake.

After a search that took her through the orchard and past the gym (an extension tacked onto the back of the family house, with bifold doors that opened onto the patio), Emily found a child's playhouse—a *cubby*, she thought, congratulating herself—complete with painted shutters and a little picket fence. On a table inside, wedged under a child-sized coffee pot and a plastic triangle of "cake," she found another riddle, which led her to an old apple tree bursting with fruit. From there, she discovered the art studio, an enormous tree house, and an actual secret garden with an ivy-covered door, just like in the story.

Nina's hunt took several hours to complete and took Emily all over the property. She walked the entire perimeter, following a huge wall that towered over the estate on the forest side but that became shorter as the ground sloped down toward the ocean. At the wall's lowest and most westerly point, the garden had been sculpted to accommodate a wide paved area and an outdoor lounge setting. *The sunset point.* She peeked over the side to find a grassy verge that gave way to a tumble of treacherous-looking rocks and an uninterrupted sprawl of water.

While Emily explored, she took a couple of snaps on her phone, but it seemed that when photographed, the estate looked ordinary. The firsthand experience was anything but. The light, the sense of space . . . Emily felt like she was on an island floating in the sky.

The final clue of the hunt took her back to the guesthouse, where Nina had made a spectacular lunch. A spread of local cheeses, homemade chutneys, and soft, warm bread sat on a table big enough for twelve. A freshly poured glass of sunset-colored wine waited for Emily next to a vase of delicate white and purple flowers.

After lunch, Emily started work. Her first week, Nina explained, would be spent focusing on the guesthouse (to Emily's enormous relief, there'd been no further mention of looking after Aurelia). Yves, still as terse as the day before, showed up with a huge delivery of paint—twenty-two tins—and together they carried it up the stairs, stacking the tins on the first-floor landing. There seemed to be countless rooms that needed sprucing up, mostly full of furniture covered with dust sheets, plus an open area that, according to Nina, might serve as a second living space. Before they could start sanding and painting, though, they needed to clear everything out and clean up.

When she'd first arrived, Emily had been so dazzled by the beauty of the place that she hadn't realized just what bad shape the property was in. A closer inspection revealed warped shutters, cracked tiles, and rotting wood. Leaf mulch blocked the drains and gutters; weeds overran the vegetables; pavement was dark with moss; and the guesthouse, while beautiful and well-decorated, was damp and dirty. Most of the walls bulged with moisture, and she developed a habit of running her fingers over the chalky ripples every time she passed. Fortunately, the causes of the damp had been identified and the problems fixed, so it was now just a matter of repairing the damage, the worst of which could be found in the north-facing bedrooms.

Emily found herself wondering again why Nina didn't just hire a team of professionals to get the whole thing knocked over, but as she worked she began to understand Nina's enthusiasm for doing things her own way. It was surprising how much she enjoyed chucking on a pair of overalls and getting her hands dirty; there was something extremely satisfying about stripping the rooms right back to their purest state.

It wasn't all fun, though. She learned fast that rubber gloves were a constant necessity. Moldy sandwiches, mildewed linen, rat droppings, and abandoned cups lined with stinking green fur: they all showed up in the first week, almost as if they'd been deliberately planted to catch her unawares. The place was riddled with filth—which, she supposed, explained the strange lingering smell. In fact, on the third day, Emily tracked a particularly foul stench to an antique wardrobe, inside of which she found a dead animal—possibly a large rodent or a small cat; she didn't hang around long enough to find out. She fled squealing from the room and slammed the door, only reentering once Yves had been in there with heavy-duty rubbish bags and a dust mask.

Most of the time, though, she found the work relaxing. It was nice to be busy. She put music on and turned the volume up, sweeping and wiping and washing in time to Lady Gaga and Beyoncé. It was, as Juliet would have said, good for the soul. And she wasn't expected to do everything all by herself: Yves was a constant but silent presence, always hovering somewhere close, working away on something or other. Oddly, he seemed determined to avoid actually speaking to anyone. No matter what was happening around him he remained curiously silent but observant, his eyes sliding sideways like someone watching an argument unfold in a public place. Several times a day, Emily would look up from a task to find him studying her, but he never smiled or said hello. Once or twice she even caught him with his mouth open, as if he might be about to say something, but she could never read his expression and he always turned away at the last minute.

At first, assuming that they were on the same team, she tried to make an effort. She offered him coffee, a sandwich, or a glass of water, but Yves never responded with much more than a grunt, so she stopped trying. Nina seemed to have reached the same conclusion long ago; she never invited him to eat with them, never asked him to stay for a glass of wine, never asked after his wife or kids, and it became increasingly clear that he and Emily were, in fact, on very different teams. While Emily was treated like immediate family, Yves was like the weird second cousin that nobody liked. He came and went as he pleased, rarely spoke, never ate, got the bigger, noisier, dirtier jobs done; and after a while she forgot he was even there.

Meanwhile, Emily felt that she and Nina were developing something of a friendship. Nina often joined her in the guesthouse, donning her own pair of gloves and pretending to retch as they peeled back rotting carpets and delved into the fetid cavities of long-forgotten cupboards. They chatted as they worked, sharing their stories in shy fragments, and gradually they both started to relax. The sun shone and the water glittered and they played loud music through the speakers around the pool. Emily told some anecdotes that made Nina laugh, Nina cracked a few bad jokes, and soon it was as though they'd known each other for years.

Aurelia was never far away, either. When she wasn't resting or napping inside, she sat somewhere nearby with a coloring book or a box of LEGO. Or she might drift past an open door with a feigned air of disinterest, stopping to check what Emily or Nina or Yves might be doing before disappearing again. Sometimes she seemed to be absent for long periods of time, but Emily soon realized that both houses were riddled with secret hidey-holes and crawl spaces. At first she had worried that the scuffling sound in the walls might be rats, but then she'd remembered how Aurelia had wriggled out from behind the panel in the dining-room wall. After that, Emily found lots of other con-cealed cupboards, all containing evidence of recent occupation: a collection of dolls, maybe, or a teddy bear's picnic.

For all their company, though, Emily often felt alone. Not *lonely* as such, but the estate was so huge that sometimes it felt like she might be the only person on it. Every so often, the quiet would be so pure that she could easily imagine that there was no one else for hundreds of miles; that Nina, Aurelia, and Yves had been wiped out along with the rest of civilization, and Emily was the last human being left on the planet. And despite their burgeoning friendship, Nina was keeping certain bound-aries firmly in place.

On her fifth day, for example, Emily couldn't find anyone for what felt like hours. She needed help dismantling and mov-ing a bed frame, but Yves, for once, didn't seem to be hanging around, so she went outside to look for him. After an unsuccess-ful search of the grounds, she gave up and went to the family house.

She circled it twice before plucking up the courage to knock on the front door. Reluctant to go inside (the phrase "no-go zone" kept sounding in her head like a warning siren), she re-turned to the back patio and called out. But there was no answer.

Suddenly overcome by an eerie feeling that she really was all by herself (maybe her new employer had abandoned her, per-haps as part of some bizarre practical joke or initiation ritual), she opened the patio doors and stepped into the kitchen, calling out again. Everything was quiet, without even a rustle or a mur-mur to indicate that anyone was home.

Gazing around the room, she took in the antique cabinetry

and tableware, the stone tiles and huge farmhouse-style sink, thinking how much it looked like a picture in a magazine: totally perfect and untouched. There it was again, though: that weird smell, barely detectable underneath the waft of scented candles, but definitely there. It was slightly stronger in here, too; earthy and meaty, like rotten wood but with an inexplicable sourness. Emily covered her nose.

Suddenly there was a hand on her shoulder and a voice at her back, and Emily jumped about a foot in the air.

"Everything okay?" Nina asked, slipping her arm around Emily's shoulders. Emily laughed and nodded, pressing her hand to her heart in a show of relief, so eager to explain herself that she almost missed the strange look on Nina's face, and the slightly too-tight grip of Nina's hand. In fact, it was only later that night, after they'd all gone to bed, that Emily registered just how quickly she'd been ejected from the kitchen. Nina had not wanted her there; she'd practically frog-marched Emily back out the door, steering her away from the house with the efficiency of a nightclub bouncer.

Memo received, Emily thought as she drifted off to sleep. *"No-go zone" means "no-go zone."*

The baby is placed on my chest and we are covered with warm blankets.

My husband looks at us with tears in his eyes. "A healthy little girl," he says.

I gasp, conscious of my reaction, as if I'm playing a role in a movie. "A girl," I breathe. The baby makes a thin, helpless sound and wriggles against my skin, her face all swollen and scrunched like a cabbage. She's purple and covered in rust-red slime, and her head is elongated like an alien's, but to me she's the most beautiful thing on earth.

Later, a small crib made of clear plastic appears next to my bed. It sits on top of a metal frame with wheels so that I can push it around the room like a pram. At the bottom end, facing outward, is a rectangular piece of card with a picture of a pink teddy bear and a series of numbers and letters.

AURELIA ELOISE DENNY.

7 LBS 8 OZ.

BORN 16 MAY AT 5:18 A.M.

My room is packed with gifts. Vases of fresh flowers crowd almost every available surface, and pink balloons sway beneath the ceiling on the ends of shiny ribbons.

I trace my daughter's tiny eyebrows with my finger, sighing with delight as they wriggle apart and then crawl back toward each other like baby caterpillars.

A cup of tea is thrust under my nose, and I shake my head. No, thank you. I don't want to eat or drink or do anything that involves the use of my hands; they're far too busy holding this warm little bundle tight against my chest. In fact, I tell my husband, they'll be busy doing this for the rest of my life. No cups of tea or coffee or anything else, ever again. I never want to let go.

He sighs. He's angry with me. We had a fight—our first since the birth. Silly, really. A whole lot of fuss over the temperature of the bathwater, the correct way to wash her. It was my fault; I'm not getting enough sleep. I tried to apologize, but it came out wrong.

If only he knew what it was like to be me. Sometimes I wish we could swap bodies so he could feel what I feel.

We curl up under a blanket, just me and her, and I tell our birth story for the seven hundredth time. This is my favorite thing to do now. I uncover an astonishing new detail every time. It's tricky, though: like recalling a dream. No matter how hard I try to articulate the magic, it sounds flat and commonplace. "Hey, world," I want to yell out the windows, to the rooftops, to the sky. "Guess what?! I grew a human being inside my own body, a real human with arms and legs and eyelashes and fingernails! For god's sake, CALL THE PAPERS!" Talk about Wonder Woman.

Even the memory is nebulous, like an echo of a previous life. I remember being in a giant blow-up bath, twisting onto my side and hanging on to the edge, shuddering, convulsing. There was a lot of opening and roaring and ripping and burning, and just so much liquid, and him, always him, with me and next to me and behind me, holding and support-ing me and stepping away when I couldn't bear to be touched and coming back again when I needed him. He dug his thumbs into my lower back for what felt like days on end, never stopping, just pressing and kneading away at the black agony that now seems like a lie. My brain has all but erased the whole thing. If it wasn't for the stains on the living room rug, I might think it never happened.

I kiss my daughter's petal-soft lips and smell her milky breath, and I feel a surge of joy so deep, so powerful, that it threatens to burst the walls of my inadequate heart.

My own body hasn't felt closeness like this for a long time. I'm sure my mother held me like this once, but I don't recall. I remember holding her, though. I remember cradling her head and stroking her hair—but that doesn't count because it was right at the end and it didn't feel nice at all. My arms kept slipping because of all the blood.

No, this is love as I've never known it. I am now com-plete. I am whole.

CHAPTER SIXTEEN

SCOTT

THE MAN sitting next to Scott was a talker.

It was hit or miss in these places. You either managed to sit quietly with your thoughts and sink a scotch or five in peace, or you wound up next to the kind of misery that loved company. Most of the time these guys were harmless; they didn't want you to say anything, they just wanted to talk, and if you could tune out and let the words fade into the background, then everyone was happy. But this particular man seemed intent on extracting a conversation if it killed him.

Scott felt vaguely sorry for him: judging from the misogynistic drivel pouring out of his mouth, his wife had just left him, or he'd found her screwing his brother—something like that. But he was unshaven, unkempt, and about eight bourbons deep, all of which spelled the kind of trouble Scott could do without. So he decided to say little, drink a lot, and then make a swift exit.

With the first two objectives firmly under his belt, he was about to put the third into action when the man pointed up at the TV above the bar. "Isn't that the most depressing shit you've ever heard?" he said.

Scott couldn't imagine that it was, but he lifted his head

anyway. There was a news story on, something about a corpse found in a forest. The images were of a muddy riverbank, a taped-off crime scene, and a white van.

"Hey, barman. Turn that up?" the man called. He turned to Scott. "That's gotta be the fucking worst, am I right?"

The volume increased. Words tumbled from a reporter's mouth. *Tragedy. Community. Dead. Buried. Woods.*

"I said, am I right?" the man persevered.

"You're right," Scott said, watching the screen. "What happened?"

"Some backpacker. Missing for weeks. They just found her."

A photograph flashed up of a young woman. Big grin, sandy hair, brown eyes. She was standing on a paved driveway and holding a basketball.

"Imagine getting that call." The man bowed his head and, to Scott's horror, began to cry. His big shoulders shook, and wet sounds came out of his mouth.

Scott turned back to the TV screen. The young woman returned his stare.

"Just puts shit into perspective, you know?" said the man through his tears.

Scott watched him from the corner of his eye. Then he dropped a few notes onto the bar and slid off his stool, heading for the daylight.

Outside, he pulled his phone from his pocket.

Nina answered on the seventh ring. "Not a good time, Scott."

"Should I call back?" There was a faint crackle of static, but otherwise the line was clear. She must be inside somewhere.

"No, it's okay. Can't be long, though. Dinnertime."

In the background, Scott heard kitchen sounds: a gush of running water and the clank of pans. "How are things going?" he asked.

"Fine."

There was a long pause. She wasn't going to make it easy for him, but when had she ever? "Is there a problem?"

"No."

He sighed. "Look, I'm sorry. I know it's been a while between visits."

"Five weeks."

Scott was aware how long it had been. He'd meant to go. He'd booked flights every weekend but always canceled them at the last minute. He'd called countless times, but that was never enough. "Listen," he said, his throat tight. "I just wanted to say that . . . well, I saw something on the news."

The sound of running water stopped. Scott pictured his wife by the sink, soap suds dripping off her hands. Her hair was probably falling in front of her face, as usual. If he was there with her, he would brush it away and tuck it behind her ear.

"What did you see?"

Dead. Buried. Woods. "It's not important. It just made me think. I could make some changes to my schedule. Spend a bit more time with you. Potentially a week in France every month."

Nina sighed heavily. "Right. Okay."

There was a long pause. Scott tipped his head back and looked up at the gray sky. "So, any issues this week?"

"No, not at all. Everything's going quite well."

Scott's mood lifted a little. "That's great. And Aurelia?"

Another pause. "A little better. Out of bed and in the garden every day this week."

Scott hesitated. "Every day? Is that a good idea?"

Nina's silence was loaded.

"Okay, fine. Sorry." Scott knew that when it came to Aurelia, it was better not to push.

The water started up again. "I have to go." Nina's voice was muffled. He guessed she had tucked the phone between her ear and her shoulder to free up both her hands.

"Okay. I'll leave you to it."

"See you soon."

He really should let her go. "Nina?"
There was a faint crackle of static. "Yes?"
"I'll come next weekend. I promise."
"Sure. Whatever you say."
I love you, he almost said, but the line was already dead.

CHAPTER SEVENTEEN

EMILY

EMILY OPENED her eyes. All around her, shards of light blinked and shifted, and tiny bubbles tickled her skin as they rose toward the surface. Stretching her limbs out like a starfish, she allowed her body to rise with them until she bobbed quietly back into the early evening air.

The clouds were turning pink as she climbed out of the pool and crossed to the outdoor shower, where the smell of shampoo mixed with the seaweedy breeze. Beyond the pool, the ocean spread its own shade of blue and melted into the sky.

"Emily," a voice called. "Dinner's ready!"

She squeezed the water from her hair. "Coming!"

"Sebastien has settled in well, don't you think?" said Nina.

"I do," Emily said, nodding as she bent down to pick up a few stray cups and saucers from the driveway, the forgotten remnants of an impromptu tea party. "He seems very happy."

They were returning from the sheds after tucking the animals in for the night; Aurelia usually liked to help but it had been a long day and, despite a great deal of protesting, Nina had insisted on an early bedtime. The chickens were all in their coop, the rabbits in their hutch, and the goats in their shed, the door firmly locked and bolted several times. (While they looked docile enough, the goats were secret prison-breaking masterminds. Emily had no idea how they did it, but after a few ridiculous Keystone Cop chases around the property, she'd decided that no security measures were too drastic.)

Sebastien the pony, the latest addition to the ever-expanding farmyard, had arrived just days before, and he appeared to like his new house very much—as well he should. Yves had built all the animal shelters, and he'd done a particularly good job with the new stable. The addition to Emily's jobs list of mucking out horse poo was not a welcome one, but she'd managed quite well today, and Sebastien really was gorgeous. She'd never been much of an animal lover before, but Nina was converting her.

Emily waved her hand back and forth in front of her face as they walked, trying to generate a breeze. The day had been sticky and soupy, and the evening brought little relief. The charcuterie, bread, and salad they'd eaten for dinner sat uncomfortably in her gut, as if the air had followed it down and sat on it.

They parted ways at the family house, Nina disappearing inside to fetch a chilled bottle of something while Emily headed around the side to the back patio. As per their emerging routine, they would fill their glasses, curl up in the hanging chairs, and watch the night roll in.

"So," said Nina, stepping out through the patio doors, an ice bucket in her hands. "How are you doing? Have you had a gutful of the isolation yet?"

Emily resisted a smile. Soft though it was, Nina's Australian accent still caught her by surprise, the lazy drawl so at odds with her delicate looks. "No, the opposite," she said. "It's weird, I thought I'd find it hard, but it's actually been good to get away from everything."

"You don't miss Facebook?"

"God, no."

"Me neither. The lack of privacy scares me. In fact, I'd prefer not to have any photos of the estate on social media, if that's not too much to ask? As I'm sure Scott explained, discretion is really important to us."

"Oh, of course. I wouldn't post anything anyway. I've never been a fan of social media. Too overwhelming." That wasn't strictly true. Emily would have gladly devoted more time and energy to her accounts if she'd thought she could make anything of them, but she never had anything to show or say, and the bursting profiles of her successful drama-school mates were too much to bear.

That being said, the total loss of connectivity hadn't been easy at first. Querencia was a communications dead zone. She'd checked her phone reflexively in those first few days, frustrated by the lack of reception. She'd even wandered through the gate and out into the woods several times to see if that might help, but it never did. And then on her first drive out to the nearest market she discovered that, in order to pick up any mobile service whatsoever, she would have to drive a good thirty or forty minutes inland, and even then she might only get one bar, maybe two. There was Wi-Fi, apparently, and Nina had given her the code, but for some reason her phone couldn't find the network. Nina had said she'd get Yves to have a look but hadn't mentioned it again, and amid all the work and the food and the wine, Emily kept forgetting to remind her.

After a while, the urgency faded away. Within just a few days, Emily had felt different. Happier. Less anxious. And after a few weeks, she was barely thinking about her phone at all. She knew she could probably ask to use Nina's computer (there'd have to be one in the family house, or how would Nina manage Aurelia's homeschooling?), but the lines had been clearly drawn—*that's your house; this is mine*—and that was fine by Emily. She decided that the summer would be a much-needed digital detox. There was no one she wanted to communicate with, anyway.

"What about your family?" Nina asked, as if reading Emily's thoughts. "Your friends? Aren't you missing home?"

Pressing the cool wineglass glass to her cheek, Emily wrinkled her nose.

Nina laughed. "That bad, huh?"

"No," Emily said, thinking of Hoxley's narrow roads, dreary high street, and soggy playing field. "It's just . . . small. Boring. Your average country village."

"Sounds rather idyllic to me."

"Ugh." Emily scoffed. "Try living there." Growing up, the inertia had been paralyzing. The world had loomed, huge and exciting, but her parents never wanted to go anywhere or do anything new.

"Well," said Nina. "I'm glad you're not homesick. But life here can be pretty small and boring, too." She looked out across the grounds. "I hope you'd tell me if you're finding it too difficult."

"Oh, no." Emily leaned back, resting her head against a cushion. "I could never be bored *here*. It's so beautiful. And there's always something to do." She thought of the countless boxes of books she'd discovered in one room ("for the library," Nina had explained) and the movie projector she'd found in another.

"You're not wrong there," said Nina. "Speaking of which, we should get started on those bathrooms tomorrow."

They swung gently on their hanging chairs, sipping their wine and discussing paintbrushes, cornices, and skirting boards before settling into a comfortable silence. Overhead, thick purple clouds were gathering, slowly obliterating the stars. Bats swooped among the trees as the last of the light left the sky, and somewhere in the distance, a fork of lightning tripped down to earth.

Emily counted four Mississippis before she heard the soft boom of thunder; according to schoolyard science, the storm was less than a mile away. Sighing happily, she studied the horizon, waiting for more flashes of lightning. *So this is what perfection feels like,* she thought.

And then a long, terrified howl cut through the evening air, so loud and so disorientating that it took Emily a few seconds to react.

"Oh my fucking god, what is *that*?" she yelled, sitting bolt upright.

Beside her, Nina leaped to her feet, spilling wine over her dress.

The scream got louder. It was horrific, jagged and raw and full of pain. Suddenly it broke off, leaving an empty silence that had Emily's ears ringing.

"What the . . . ?"

Then it was back, with increased ferocity. It was coming from the house. A slideshow of horrific scenarios ran through her head: someone had broken in and Aurelia was being butchered; she'd fallen down the stairs and broken her back; she'd been bitten by a snake.

"Goddamn these bloody storms," Nina said with a tut, apparently not sharing Emily's concerns. She set down her wineglass and hurried toward the house. She opened one of the patio doors and disappeared inside, reappearing again almost instantly with a tea towel pressed to her dripping-wet dress. "It's okay," she called from the doorway, straining to be heard over the noise. "It's just a night terror. She's had them for years."

"Night terror?"

"One of the many reasons I'm glad we don't have neighbors. They've been much better lately, but we still get the odd doozy, usually during a thunderstorm. She hates the noise."

Somehow, the screeching seemed to intensify, and Nina flinched. She dropped the tea towel on the floor and flashed Emily a nervous smile. "Don't worry, she's fine. It sounds a lot worse than it is. Sorry, I'd better go and . . ." She gestured in the general direction of the clamor and dashed off. A second later she was back, sticking her head through the doorway. "Don't worry about the glasses and stuff, I'll get them later." Then she was gone again.

Emily stood with her hand pressed to her chest. A few minutes later the cries died down, and a lullaby floated gently through an open window.

* * *

Emily walked back to the guesthouse as the first few raindrops began to fall, her heart still hammering against her ribs.

That scream . . . She'd never heard anything like it, and yet it was oddly familiar. She could physically feel the sound in her own throat, scraping her vocal cords raw. She put it down to empathy. She'd been a somewhat difficult child herself—the temperamental owner, as Juliet liked to remind her, of a "right set of lungs"—and although the term "night terror" was never used, she'd definitely had a few bad dreams. She had vague memories of waking in the night drenched in sweat with her parents' arms wrapped around her.

The thought of her parents sent a stab of guilt into her gut. The last few weeks at Querencia had been like living in a parallel universe; nothing else existed, nothing mattered except sunshine and good food and great wine and whether or not the pool chemicals were correctly balanced. And Nina had turned out to be such enjoyable company that Emily hadn't once called home.

She pushed her toes through the sand as she walked, enjoying the splash of rain on her skin. So much had changed in almost a month. Strange to think that she'd very nearly jumped ship on her first day—but that had been her own fault. She could see that now. She hadn't realized the extent to which the Proem office gossip had clouded her judgment, nor to which her meeting with Scott had affected her.

Scott. A little shiver ran around the rim of her pelvis, like an ice-cold spoon stirring a hot cup of tea. Wincing, she remembered how much she'd drunk when they had lunch that day. He must have thought she was an idiot. Hypnotized by his Colgate smile and nice suit, she'd stared and giggled and flipped her hair too much. And despite telling herself over and over again that she was not to confuse the situation, the situation had most definitely been confused.

Thankfully, though, nothing inappropriate had happened. When they left the restaurant, Scott had walked her to the Tube, where they shook hands in an ironic, flirty kind of way, and for a second Emily had felt a weird kind of instability, a shift in the atmosphere. But then they both said goodbye and walked away in opposite directions. (Her thoughts on the journey home, however, had been *very* inappropriate—and during the days that followed, they had transmuted into an almost full-blown obsession, so that by the time she climbed on board his private jet she was wondering whether their first romantic getaway would be in the Maldives or Bora Bora.)

Regardless, she'd turned up at Querencia feeling sly. But now she could see how silly she'd been; there was nothing between her and Scott, and she wouldn't want there to be. She was no home-wrecker. And despite having initially searched for faults in Nina, willing there to be some justification for her resentment, she'd found none. Nina was absolutely lovely. Well, okay, she had her moments, but she had a lot to cope with, stuck out here on her own with a sick child and no friends or family on hand. Overall, she was funny, thoughtful, engaging, sincere, and wholly undeserving of all that malicious office gossip. In fact, Emily couldn't have been more wrong about Scott and his wife not being suited. They were on the exact same level: the very highest one, where only the very best-looking, most charismatic people could go.

Funny, though, that Nina didn't seem to mention her husband much. He came up in conversation when they were with Aurelia, perhaps with reference to a particular food that he liked or a toy that he'd bought, but otherwise they rarely spoke about him. Emily supposed it must be the distance. It must be hard for a family to be separated as much as the Dennys were, but all that money had to come from somewhere, and Scott certainly wasn't going to make it sitting on a sun lounger in the middle of nowhere.

Luckily, Aurelia had a wonderful mother who literally gave every minute of every day to her daughter's needs. Nina's attention was so firmly fixed that you'd think she was competing in some sort of parenting Olympics. The toys, the clothes, the food, the homeschooling resources (Emily wasn't privy to their classes, but the art studio that seemed to double as a classroom was stuffed to the gills with textbooks and crazy-looking technology), not to mention the close eye she kept on Aurelia's health. Sure, some might say it was a bit *too* close—the phrase *helicopter parent* had popped into Emily's head once or twice—but it couldn't be easy coping with a kid whose medical condition meant that you couldn't go anywhere or do anything.

Nina had told several hair-curling stories about times when they'd tried to venture out. Everything would be going great, and then Aurelia's sunscreen would wash off, or she'd throw a fit and rip off her rash vest, or she'd roll up her sleeves to dig in the sand and five minutes later she'd be covered in blisters. And that would be it, Nina said. Bedbound for days. Not worth it.

And then there were the tantrums. According to Nina, Aurelia "had difficulty expressing herself" (an understatement, in Emily's opinion; the kid never spoke), which meant that tension could build very quickly around the smallest of things, like choosing a dessert or explaining a game. Bigger things like eating out were no longer an option, which was a shame, but Emily could see Nina's point. Four times in the past few days, Aurelia had lost it for no discernible reason.

All in all, Emily could understand why Nina might sometimes seem a little stressed out. She considered sharing some of her own childhood experiences (the nightmares, the panic attacks) in the hope that it might make Nina feel better. *Don't worry,* she might say, *it's not just her; all kids do this.* But she never seemed to have the right words. Not like Nina. Nina always had the right words. Nina was so self-aware, so able to talk about her feelings, so open about the relentless pressure of being a parent, the constant fear of getting it wrong, and the days when she wished it would all stop. She managed to talk almost poetically about her own anxiety and how she dealt with it—namely, by removing herself from an ever-changing, frantic roller coaster of a world; by unplugging herself from the news, the internet, smartphones, and a multitude of ludicrous apps; by practicing mindfulness and stripping from her life anything that she didn't absolutely need (Emily assumed this didn't include material possessions, because there were an awful lot of those). By Nina's own admission, she didn't always get it right, but at least she was trying.

That wasn't how they did things in Emily's family. The Proudman tradition was to sweep every worry under the carpet. They'd ignore every problem and then act surprised when it came back to bite them, surfacing in some ugly, undignified way. Juliet was especially good at denial. "I'm sure it'll all work out," she'd say, or "Try not to worry about it," or "Don't dwell on the negatives; think about the positives!" That made Emily want to throw things at her. What was wrong with admitting when things were shit? Juliet wanted people to think that she was happy all the time, but Emily didn't buy it. Her smile was too brittle.

Thunder rolled over the sky and Emily jumped. She realized she'd been standing in front of the guesthouse, deep in thought, for quite some time, and her clothes were now soaking wet.

She tilted her face to the sky and let the rain wash over her. As the water drip-drip-dripped through the trees, she wondered for the thousandth time when Scott might show up. He said he spent as much time as possible in France, but so far there had been no sign of him. Despite feeling increasingly close to Nina, Emily would have felt awkward asking about him, but he'd make an appearance soon, surely. And when he did, he'd be impressed. He'd see that Emily had slotted seamlessly into his family's life, and that she was doing him proud. With a happy sigh, she pushed open the door of the guesthouse.

Above her head, on a metal mount drilled into the brickwork, a camera whirred softly, its red light winking on and off.

Later that night Emily was woken by a beam of light falling across her pillow. Sitting up, she saw that the curtains hanging over the French windows were not quite closed, and something bright was spilling through the gap. She shuffled over and peered outside. One of the security lights had been triggered, the one mounted just outside her balcony.

And below, at the edge of the lawn, something was moving.

Instinctively, she stepped back and dropped the curtain. A few seconds later, she began to wonder if she'd imagined it. She parted the curtains again, just an inch, and saw a figure walking in slow circles on the grass.

Nina. Head down, arms wrapped tightly around her body, shoulders heaving with what looked like sobs.

Emily felt strangely exposed, as if the walls of the large white house were as thin as the soft linen curtains. And then Nina turned and looked up at the window, so directly that Emily flinched.

At the same moment, the security light flicked off and the lawn was plunged into darkness. Emily waited for her eyes to adjust, waiting to see if Nina was still there. . . .

But everything was still. The lawn was empty. Nina had gone.

We made it. The twelfth month. It hasn't been easy, but we got there, just like all the baby books said we would.

It's a perfect day for a party. The sky is bright, and a gentle breeze chases the falling leaves around the garden. Lilac bunting flutters among the trees, and balloons bounce against each other making a happy, hollow sound.

I fetch the last tray from the kitchen and just manage to get it to the table before a huge sneeze explodes out of my nose. My husband looks over from the barbecue and chuckles. He always makes fun of my sneezes; he says I sound like James Brown. "I feel good," he sings, with a shimmy.

I blow my nose. I am so sick of being sick. "Is this head cold ever going to bugger off and leave us alone, hey, bubba?" I tickle my sweetheart under her chin. She's lying on a picnic rug, her red-rimmed eyes peeping out from under a fleecy blanket.

I'm still not sure about the party. I nearly abandoned the whole idea, but it's her first birthday. We can't just do nothing, and the cake took all day yesterday to bake and all this morning to decorate. I spent hours molding those marzipan roses. I unpack the boxes, laying the items out on the table. Cucumber sandwiches, delicate little cupcakes, and a bowl of fat ripe strawberries—my baby's favorite. Sour-cherry gelato for Mummy and Daddy, a nod to our first date. I called the restaurant myself and begged for the recipe, told them it was the most special of occasions.

"She looks pale," I say to my husband, wondering again if I'm doing the right thing. "Do you think she looks pale? Maybe we should've called it off."

"It's a bit late now," he says, gesturing to all the food. "We can always cut it short. Sing the song, cut the cake, go back to bed."

I nod and stroke my baby girl's face. Her forehead and cheeks are burning. "Oh, sweetie, you have a fever again." I brush a lock of hair away from her eyes. "Hey, can you grab the ibuprofen for me, please? It should be in the nappy bag."

He is quiet. He shakes his head. "I gave her some just now. Hasn't it worked?"

"Doesn't feel like it. It's okay, darling. Mummy will get you some more. . . ." I stop. Her hands are icy cold. Her eyes are half-closed. "Hey, sweetheart," I say, shaking her a little. "Did you see your presents?" I point to a huge pile of shiny bags and colorful packages.

She doesn't move.

I pick a strawberry from the bowl and wave it in front of her face. "Here, darling. Your favorite."

She starts to cry, a strange high-pitched wail that reminds me of cats. My blood freezes in my veins, starts flowing backward. I press my fingers to my daughter's face, feeling around to the back of her neck. I draw back the blanket and reach under her dress. "Are you sure it was ibuprofen you gave her?"

As soon as I say it, I know I've made a mistake. I turn to apologize, but then, almost as if in response to my words, she starts vibrating. At first, I think she's just bucking, trying to jerk my hands off her body, but the shaking doesn't stop. It gets worse. Her little limbs are stiff and juddering. She arches her back and her eyes roll back in her head.

"Oh my god." I try to lift her but can't keep hold.

He's just standing there. He doesn't know what to do. "Can she . . . is she breathing?"

I hear a choking sound. It's me. "Do something!" I hear myself yell, my own voice unrecognizable. "What did you do? What did you give her?"

Before I know what I'm doing, I'm slapping his hands away and wrapping my arms around my limp baby girl, cradling her like a newborn, and even though I can feel the convulsions subsiding, my gut burns with a horrible instinct, and all I can think of is the car, the hospital, the fastest way out, and then I'm running, I'm running, running, running, running, running.

CHAPTER EIGHTEEN

EMILY

STRIPS OF garlic peel stuck to Emily's hands like flakes of skin and became wedged under her fingernails. She grunted with frustration as she picked at the clove, gouging holes in the flesh and reducing it to a pulpy mess.

"Here, like this," said Nina, coming up behind her. She demonstrated how to top and tail each clove, then crush it with the heel of a knife so its papery skin slipped off like a jacket. She then picked up a different knife and chopped an onion at superhuman speed.

"Wow," Emily breathed.

Nina laughed. "It's just an onion, Em."

Blushing, Emily looked away. A bird hopped onto the end of the countertop to steal a crumb, chirping its thanks before taking off again. The fully equipped poolside kitchen was by far one of Querencia's best features, at least in Emily's opinion; the simple fact that they could cook and eat lunch outside then slide straight into the water felt like one of the greatest luxuries possible.

She crossed to the barbecue, holding up her hand to shield her eyes from the reflections bouncing off the surface of the pool. A whole fish lay sizzling on the grill. She prodded it with a spatula. "So am I turning this now?"

"You can try," Nina said, "but not with that. Use this instead." She took a carving fork from the utensil rack and showed her how to insert the tines through the grate to gently lever the fish off. "If it's ready, it'll lift right up. If it's not, it'll stick."

"How do you know all this stuff?" Emily marveled at anyone who could do so much as bake a potato. She seemed to ruin every dish she attempted.

"Actually, I trained for a little while. At a culinary school. I've forgotten a lot of it, but the basics were heavily drilled in."

"That's so cool. You should totally start a cookery school. People would fall over themselves to come and learn here. Or maybe you could open up a restaurant? Like, as part of the guesthouse."

"Maybe," Nina said with a smile that didn't quite reach her eyes. She looked tired, and for the tenth time that day, Emily wondered if she ought to mention having seen her in the garden during the night, if only to ask if she was okay. But, for reasons she couldn't quite articulate, Emily felt weird about what she'd seen. She pushed the thought aside. Whatever Nina had been doing down there in the dark last night was nothing to do with her.

Nina turned to her daughter. "Hey, Strawberry, lunch is nearly ready."

Aurelia was playing shops at the long dining-room table, her black hair snaking out in thick wet straps from under her usual straw hat. Spread out over plant pots and dining-room chairs were various items of clothing with handwritten price tags attached. In an attempt to score some brownie points, Emily had donated her entire wardrobe to the cause, a decision she was now regretting. Laid out like that, her dresses and tops looked sad and baggy, especially next to Nina's impeccable contributions. Aurelia didn't seem to mind, though, and had been happily tagging the items for over an hour.

"Is the shop open yet?" Emily called. "Because I have my eye on that hot little red number over there, and I'm prepared to offer a good price." She gestured to a faded sundress she'd picked up in a charity shop a few years ago. "Don't think you can rip me off, either. I'm a mean haggler."

A small snicker escaped from under the hat.

"Here, honey." Nina appeared with a glass of iced tea and two small pills. She placed them on the table next to Aurelia. "Medicine time. And then we're due for more sunscreen, I'm afraid. You've been in the pool again since the last lot."

Obediently, Aurelia reached for the yellow bottle at her elbow and squeezed a few thick dollops into her palm. Quietly, she massaged the cream into her face and neck. When she was finished she turned to Nina, presenting her skin for inspection.

"Good job," said Nina, touching up a few spots. "Almost completely covered. You're getting really good at that now."

Emily felt a pang of pity. All that sun protection would really suck. It probably wasn't so bad in winter, but they looked set to have an especially hot summer. They'd already had a long run of blue skies and high temperatures, and apparently the humidity hadn't even arrived yet.

Nina nudged the pills with her fingers. "Good girl."

Aurelia swallowed the pills with a grimace and then pushed away the iced tea, preferring to get back to work. She gave a little grunt of frustration as the silky sleeves of her princess dress once again got in the way of her pencil.

Emily suppressed a laugh. Aurelia's favorite outfits were not especially practical. Like her mother, she had an exceptional wardrobe: every day she chose from an array of exciting, colorful clothes, many of them covered with Disney characters, or sequins and fairy wings. Several outfits even came with matching crowns and long, shiny gloves. Some items were thick and cozy for cold weather, some light and thin for sunnier days, but everything without exception was long, long, long. True to her word, Nina covered as much of Aurelia's skin as possible, making small concessions only when it was extremely cloudy.

Aurelia even swam in long clothes. Not once had Emily seen

her in a bikini or even a one-piece: it was always long-sleeved rash vests and leggings. Today, for example, she was wearing her full wet suit, her big pink goggles hanging like jewelry around her neck. When she swam, she added a pink swimming cap and the look was complete: baby-alien chic. So cute. It probably didn't *feel* great, though, and Emily often felt sorry for her, because really, the French coast was a strange place to raise a child with a sun allergy. It seemed almost cruel.

Emily put down her knife and wiped her hands on a tea towel. Sauntering around the kitchen bench, she pretended to browse through her own clothes. "Hmm," she said, stopping to check out a green floral skirt she'd bought at a flea market. "I like this. Very stylish. Probably only worth two euros, though."

Aurelia shook her head, her lips pressed tightly together. It had been a shock to discover that Aurelia was not just shy, as Nina put it, but completely mute, and Emily had been wondering for a while whether that was because she *couldn't* speak or because she *wouldn't*.

"Okay, three."

Another head shake.

"Well, I can't possibly pay more than five." Emily produced a note from her pocket and placed it on the table.

Aurelia stood and pushed the note away. Avoiding eye contact as usual, she held up both her hands with her fingers spread.

"Ten?" Throwing up her hands in a show of outrage, Emily turned to Nina. "Can you believe this? I'm being *robbed*!"

Nina was watching from the kitchen sink. Emily gave her a reassuring smile. She hadn't yet won Aurelia over, but she was getting there. The best approach seemed to be through play, but it had to be an activity in which Aurelia was already engaged. She liked to be in control of any given situation and could feel wrong-footed if Emily introduced something new.

"You certainly drive a hard bargain, young lady." Emily stroked her chin, then pulled out another note. "Fine. But only if you throw in these flip-flops, too." She threw the note on the table and took a step back. The other thing she'd learned was not to invade Aurelia's personal space.

Aurelia's face, streaked white with zinc, cracked open, and she laughed out loud, a sweet, full-bellied cackle straight out of a baby-product commercial. Momentarily stunned—*I made her laugh!*—Emily turned to give Nina the thumbs up, and then Aurelia was up and out of her seat, launching herself forward with her head down and her arms spread, throwing her full weight against Emily with the speed and accuracy of a rugby player.

"Whoa!" The impact sent Emily staggering backward into the table. She was so shocked—Aurelia was pawing and nuzzling at her like a dog—that it took her a moment to recognize the attack for what it was: a *hug*. "Oh my goodness." She laughed. "What's all this for?"

"Strawberry, let go, please," Nina murmured from the kitchen.

"No, it's fine!" Emily put her arms around Aurelia and gave her a squeeze. "And there I was thinking you didn't like me!"

"Of course she likes you." Nina frowned as Aurelia tightened her grasp. "Remember, honey, gentle hands."

"It's really okay," said Emily.

But Nina was already hurrying over. "Come on, now, that's enough. Let Emily get back to work." An edge had crept into Nina's voice, and Emily sensed that laughing might not help the situation, but she couldn't help it. After weeks of avoiding any physical contact whatsoever, Aurelia was all but licking her.

Nina fussed at Aurelia's back. "I mean it, Aurelia. Come away now." She spoke firmly, as if her daughter was carrying a loaded weapon. *We have you surrounded. Step. Away. From. The Help.*

But Aurelia held on, her skinny forearms locked like a vice. Emily winced as Nina grabbed at Aurelia's hands, trying to break them apart. "I said, that's enough!" she yelled, and pulled hard. And suddenly it wasn't funny anymore. Nina was furious, and the tussle was becoming awkward. Her efforts to forcibly remove Aurelia were causing them all to lumber around like a three-headed dancing elephant.

Aurelia's grip was now becoming uncomfortable. "Oof," Emily said, as the breath was squeezed from her lungs. Her head began to swim. They lurched again and crashed into the table.

"Aurelia! *Get off!*" Nina gave one more gigantic pull, and they all broke apart with such force that Aurelia flew backward and landed on her bum.

"Well," said Emily, panting. "That was—"

But she didn't get to finish, because at that moment Aurelia lifted her fists to her temples and let out a yell so loud, so ferocious that the air between them seemed to vibrate. Her face went red and her knuckles turned white. Then she scrambled to her feet and ran.

Nina hurried after her.

Emily stared at the half-finished lunch, unsure of how to proceed. She didn't know if either of them would be coming back to eat, but there didn't seem any point in wasting it, so she gently lifted the fish from the grill, the whole thing peeling away neatly in one piece. Placing it on a platter, she covered it to keep it warm, then seasoned the mango salsa and the rice before covering them, too. Next she wiped down all the surfaces and packed away Aurelia's "shop," folding all the clothes and stacking the homemade labels into neat piles.

Feeling terrible about causing another drama, she fussed and straightened and polished until everything looked just right. When it came to Aurelia, even though Nina had urged her several times not to take things like this personally, Emily felt that she was causing more problems than she was alleviating. The noise the kid made was just awful, like nails on a chalkboard—but it was a relief to know she had a voice at all. Whatever caused her muteness, there was nothing wrong with that voice box.

After half an hour or so, Nina came jogging back down the steps, her face flushed. "God, I'm so sorry about that," she said, one hand pressed to her forehead. "I don't know what happened. The medication is supposed to calm her down, not wind her up."

"No, she was fine," Emily said, absentmindedly touching her bruised waist. "Who doesn't like a hug?"

Nina frowned, hands on her hips. Then she shook her head. "Look, I know it must've seemed like I overreacted, but Aurelia doesn't know her own strength. And honestly, it freaked me out. I've never seen her do that before. Not with anyone outside of the family."

"Oh, please. I used to do things like that all the time when I was a kid," said Emily. "I was worse, though. I used to walk up to strangers and ask if I could go home with them. Juliet was mortified."

Nina laughed, the tension draining from her face. "Far out. That's probably how your parents think you ended up here. You just walked up to your boss one day and asked if you could live with him."

"Ha. Probably."

Nina looked like she was about to say something else but stopped, noticing the kitchen. She raised her eyebrows in approval at the spotless sink, the countertop, and the beautifully set table.

"Oh, yeah. Lunch is served." Emily smiled modestly. It was a novelty, this feeling that something she had done, even if it was just putting food on a table, might be worthy of admiration.

"Nice work," Nina said. "I can't wait to taste that salsa. Do you mind if we wait for Aurelia, though? She's just up in her room taking a breather. I'll give her some space, then go get her in a few minutes." Drifting away to the edge of the pool, she dipped her toe in the water.

"You know," she said, after a quiet pause, "despite what just happened, Aurelia's actually been a lot calmer since you've been here. Things have been easier. I've had more time for lessons, exercises, activities, games. She's been loving it."

Emily joined her. "That's good."

"I've been more relaxed, too. Actually, that's probably got a lot to do with it. We spend so much time together that we've become like E.T. and Elliott: one always feels what the other is feeling."

They stood contemplating the horizon. The ocean threw a gentle breeze at them, cool and salty.

Emily stretched her arms to the sky and stifled a yawn. "So what's on after lunch?" she asked. "Shall I head up to the guest-house and crack on with the painting?"

"All good, no hurry," Nina replied, lowering herself gracefully onto a sun lounger. "Why don't you chill for a while?"

Emily didn't need to be asked twice. It was a beautiful day; the last thing she wanted to do was paint. She took the adjacent lounger and lay back, placing her arms above her head and closing her eyes.

The sun shone orange through her eyelids. The sound of her breath made itself at home among the white noise of the ocean, the whisper of the trees, and the gentle slop-tap of the pool filter.

After a while, Emily heard the creak of Nina's lounger and the pad of her feet on the tiles. In the kitchen, the fridge door squeaked and then she was back with a bottle of rosé and two glasses. There was a tinkle and a glug, and a frosty glass was pushed into Emily's hand. "Cheers," Nina said.

They clinked glasses and Emily took a sip. *Best. Job. Ever.*

"Are you close to your mum?" Nina's voice was sleepy.

Emily felt her jaw stiffen. Every time her mother came up in conversation, her whole body tightened up. It was like a tic. She shrugged. "No, not really."

"And why is that?"

"I don't know . . . we're just very different. She doesn't like to talk about things and I'm all over the place. I make her feel uncomfortable."

"Now how could that possibly be true?" Nina said. "She gave birth to you."

"Actually, she didn't. I'm adopted."

"Really?"

Emily took another sip of wine. She could feel Nina looking at her.

"Can I ask at what age?"

"They fostered me when I was two and made it legal when I was eight."

"Do you ever think about them?" Nina asked. "Your birth parents, I mean?"

"Sometimes." Emily usually dodged questions like that. Maybe it was the wine or the heat, or maybe it was just Nina's company, but she was too relaxed to censor herself. "They're dead, though, so it's not like I can go and find them. I wouldn't anyway. They weren't very nice, apparently. Alcoholics. Hit me and stuff."

Nina was quiet.

"It's okay, I don't remember it," Emily continued. "Or at least, I don't think I do. Juliet made me see a child psychologist because they thought for a while that maybe I did."

Nina shifted in her lounger. "Did what? Remember your biological family?"

"Yeah. Or what they did to me, anyway."

"What *did* they do to you?"

Emily swallowed. "I'm not sure, specifically. No one ever said. I think they were all waiting for *me* to tell *them*."

"But how could you possibly remember?" Nina said. "You were so little."

There was a pause. Emily drank more wine. She could see the psychologist's office clearly. Wood-paneled walls covered in pictures drawn by children. A sand tray. A Play-Doh table. A serious-looking woman with short gray hair and red-rimmed glasses: Dr. Forte. After every visit, Juliet would peer intently into Emily's eyes, searching for a sign that she was different, that the doctor had fixed her.

"They told me they thought my body might have retained some memory of the abuse," Emily said. "Like, not the kind of memory we have as adults or older children. Something different. There's a word for it. . . ." She tried to think but her brain felt foggy. The sun was making her drowsy.

They lapsed into silence again. Emily felt as though she should say something else. "It sounds weird but sometimes I wish I did remember. It's like having a blank space inside me."

"Have you asked questions?"

"Yeah, kind of. Juliet told me some stuff when I was younger, but she doesn't like talking about it. Neither do I, to be honest. It's pretty depressing."

"I can understand that."

They sipped their drinks. The wine ran down Emily's throat, glacier-cold.

"Why do you call her Juliet?" Nina asked. "Why not 'Mum'?"

Emily hesitated, remembering the moment she'd decided never to use that word again. She'd been ten years old, a little ball of fury. "Just didn't feel right."

"Does she mind?"

"No." Emily crossed an arm over her stomach. Something was flipping around unpleasantly in there, like a dying fish. "Maybe. I don't know."

"Just a thought," Nina said quietly, "but maybe you should go a little easier on her. No one's perfect. And it sounds like you're a lot better off with her than you would've been otherwise."

"I know. I don't mean to sound ungrateful. I know I'm lucky, it's just . . . it's like I was never enough for her. She always wanted more."

"What do you mean?"

Emily thought about the few times she had seen Juliet cry. Always after hospital appointments or on the phone to doctors, sometimes in strange places like cafés or the supermarket, often behind almost-closed doors at home (Emily remembered pressing her face against the gaps and trying to peer through). Never an outburst; more like a teary stillness followed by a mad tornado of fake happiness: a spontaneous trip to the ice-cream shop or a crazy dash around the adventure playground, Juliet following Emily up ladders and across rope bridges with a shaky smile and sad eyes.

Some part of Emily's brain poked a hole in her boozy stupor. Maybe a little bit of censorship wouldn't go amiss.

"Oh, nothing. Forget it, I'm just being weird." She yawned and turned to look at Nina. There was a thin white scar just next to Nina's eye that Emily hadn't noticed before, a silvery line from her temple down to her jaw. "How about you, anyway? What's your family like?"

Nina laughed softly. "Not much to tell," she said. "Grew up on the Northern Beaches. Do you know Sydney at all?"

"No. Not even a little bit."

"Well, let's just say it's very white bread. Picket fences and bake sales. Mum, Dad, me, my brother. Couple of dogs. Pretty boring, really."

Emily closed her eyes again, feeling as though she might doze off. The Northern Beaches . . . she imagined big houses overlooking the ocean and dads washing their cars out front, families surfing together and having barbecues on the beach. Tall blond mums like Nina and gorgeous sun-kissed children frolicking in the waves. (No wonder the Dennys didn't live there; if poor Aurelia struggled in Europe, she certainly wouldn't last long in Australia.) She could see it all so clearly, could even smell the sausages and the smoke from the grill. . . .

Her eyes snapped open. She really could smell the smoke.

"Hey . . . ," she said, sitting up. She craned her neck to see into the kitchen. "Is something burning?"

"Mmm?"

A breeze pushed past them, bringing with it the dry, acrid stench of charcoal.

"Nina, I think something's burning."

But Nina had already caught the smell. She jumped up, knocking over her glass and spilling the contents. "Bloody hell," she said, breaking into a run. "Not again."

CHAPTER NINETEEN

EMILY

BY THE time they reached the playhouse it was already engulfed in flames.

Just meters away, Aurelia sat cross-legged and open-mouthed, tracing circles on the ground with her finger as the smoke billowed into the sky.

Nina sprinted straight to her. Hooking her hands under her daughter's arms, she dragged her backward and away from the blaze, then, once they'd reached a safe distance, swung her up and over her shoulder. With an intensity Emily had only ever seen on the faces of elite athletes, Nina staggered over the sandy driveway to the family house and deposited Aurelia on the steps. "Stay there!" she yelled, and dashed inside.

Emily knew the command wasn't meant for her, but she obeyed it anyway. She stood rooted to the spot, unable to think of a single thing she could do to help. *It's going to spread,* she thought dimly as the flames rose higher, crackling and spitting at the surrounding dry leaves.

A few seconds later, Nina reemerged from the house brandishing a small fire extinguisher. "I called Yves!" she shouted as she ran back over the sand. "He's on his way."

Yves? Emily thought, surprised. Surely they would need more than just Yves? "What about the fire brigade?" she shouted, but her words were cut off by the guttural roar of the extinguisher.

Pointing it at the playhouse, Nina let loose a stream of white foam until the cylinder was empty. Suds pooled on the ground, but the flames seemed to climb even higher, tearing at the floral curtains and ravaging the little window boxes. The miniature door knocker fell off with a clank, and then the door itself collapsed. The air became thick with heat.

"Get another one!" Nina shouted.

Another one? Another what? Emily's brain had frozen.

"Emily, what the hell are you doing? Guesthouse. Top of the basement stairs. Go!"

Finally, Emily's adrenaline kicked in, and she hurried inside to fetch the second extinguisher while Nina ran for the hose.

Between them, they managed to put out the worst of the fire before Yves hurtled through the gates in his white utility truck. Still, he attacked the remains with a vigor that bordered on comic; he seemed to leap from his car before it even came to a stop and came tearing toward them carrying a huge gray blanket and an extinguisher of his own. *"Bouge! Bouge toi!"* he yelled, throwing the blanket over the burning mess. Then he stalked around with his extinguisher, snarling as he sprayed the foam.

Afterward, they all stood around the charred, soapy mess, their skin shiny with sweat, extinguishers hanging at their sides like guns.

"Who needs the fire brigade?" Emily grinned proudly. "We *are* the fire brigade." She turned to catch Nina's eye, but the smirk soon fell from her face. Nina was bone white, her lips thin and colorless.

Emily looked away, chastened, but not before she caught something pass between Nina and Yves—a look, a pulse. Something obscure and ephemeral, like a flash of reflected light from an unknown source.

Spinning around to where Aurelia was still sitting quietly on the steps of the house, Nina marched over, her limbs stiff with rage. "What did you do?" she spat, grabbing her daughter by the shoulders. "Tell me! Look at me! Why would you do that? Why?" She raised her hand in one furious movement, and Emily held her breath.

But at the last minute, Nina seemed to check herself. She lowered her hand and burst into tears. "Oh, Strawberry, I'm sorry. Are you okay?" She pulled Aurelia into a tight hug. "Are you hurt? What happened? How did you even . . . ?" Releasing her grip, Nina stared into Aurelia's eyes again, her fingers fluttering over her daughter's body like butterflies unsure of where to land. "How many times do I have to tell you, bubba? You mustn't play with fire! Please don't *ever* scare me like that again."

Emily watched as Aurelia melted into her mother and sobbed. Tears streaked down her face, and Nina swept them away with her fingers. As they pressed their heads together, lost in their own private world, Emily experienced a wave of compassion so strong she nearly wept herself. Aurelia's condition was, of course, tough on Aurelia herself, but perhaps even tougher on her mother. The constant hard work, planning, and forethought; all the emotional battles: it was a wonder Nina didn't break down more often. But she kept on going because there was nothing that mattered more to her in the world than her daughter.

Suddenly, Emily felt terrible about not having phoned home yet. Juliet would be losing her shit.

As soon as all the tears had subsided, Emily jogged over. "Hey, Nina?" she said. "Could I possibly use your phone?"

Nina took Aurelia inside to watch a movie and returned a few minutes later with a slim cordless landline phone in her hand.

"What a drama, hey?" she said, with a tight smile. "You okay?"

"Yeah, fine." Emily pressed her fingers against her forehead and felt a gritty sheen of dirt and ash. She needed a shower—a cold one. Possibly it was the effect of standing near a raging bonfire for so long, but it seemed to her as though the heat of the sun had intensified since lunch. Maybe this was the start of the dreaded humidity. "How's Aurelia?"

"She's fine. No harm done, thank god."

They stood facing each other for a moment, Nina tapping the phone thoughtfully against her chin. Behind them, Yves poked at the scorched earth with a shovel, scraping up what was left of the playhouse.

"Look," said Nina, her voice lowered. "About what just happened. I should've said something when you first arrived but, I don't know, I guess I was hoping I wouldn't have to. The thing is, Aurelia can be . . ." She stopped. Took a breath. Started again. "Remember I told you she got sick as a baby?"

Emily nodded.

"Well, there were some . . . aftereffects. Besides her medical condition, I mean." Nina closed her eyes for a moment, and when she opened them again they were bright with tears. "Sometimes she does things that don't make sense. Things that seem . . ." She trailed off.

Emily waited, unsure of what to say.

Wiping a finger under her eye, Nina smiled. "She makes me so mad, but then she looks up at me with those dark eyes of hers. Her father's eyes, really. She looks so much like him, don't you think?"

"The spitting image," Emily said.

"Yeah." Nina's expression was hard to read. "Anyway, she's a good kid. A *wonderful* kid. You see that, don't you?"

Emily nodded, touched by the depth of Nina's emotion. At the center of her sudden homesickness, she noticed a prickle of resentment: if only her parents' love for her could be this strong. Was it a biological thing? Would Emily's birth mother have felt this innate pride, this unqualified adoration? No, of course not. Her birth mother was a violent drunk who'd passed her on like a disease.

Nina took a breath and seemed to change gear. "Look, I hope this isn't too rude of me," she said, "but can I ask who you want to call?"

Emily shrugged. "Just my mum."

"Your mum." Nina smiled and shook her head slightly, as if to dismiss a foolish thought. She held the phone out to Emily. "Of course. Can I ask a favor, though? I'd appreciate it if you didn't mention the fire. I don't want her thinking that you're living with a bunch of derros."

"Derros?"

"Aussieism. You know, unsavory types."

"Oh. Sure, I won't mention it." Emily took the phone.

"Thanks." Nina turned to go back inside. "Oh, and by the way, the phone only works within a certain distance from the base unit, so if you move too far away from the house you might find that the line breaks up a bit."

"Okay. *No worries,*" Emily said in her best Australian accent.

Nina chuckled. "Ah, we'll make an Aussie of you yet, young sheila."

Emily grinned and turned away, dialing her parents' number as she walked. Would they even be home? What day was it, anyway? It was so easy to lose track of time at Querencia; every day felt like the weekend. She lifted the phone to her ear and waited for the ringing, but the phone was silent. She pressed the green call button and listened again. Nothing. Walking back to the house, she tried dialing one more time, but still the phone remained dead.

Nina was over near the front door, hunched over a potted rose bush.

"Uh, Nina?"

"Not home, huh?" Nina asked, fingering a leaf speckled with dark, moldy spots.

"No—well, I don't know. I don't think the phone's working."

Nina stood up, plucking off the spotted leaf as she did so. "Really? That's weird. Can I see?" Emily offered the phone and

Nina took it, pressing it to her ear. She pushed a few buttons and listened again. "Bloody hell." She sighed. "Looks like the line's gone again. We've had some problems, but I thought they were all fixed. Sorry, hon, I'll have to get Yves onto it again."

Emily shrugged, trying to mask her disappointment. "It's okay."

"I'll let him know. Maybe he can look at it before he leaves." Nina held out the rose leaf. "In the meantime, would you mind giving that bush a spray with the fungicide? And clear the dead leaves out? The last thing we need is a spread of black spot."

Emily nodded, but as she made her way around the back of the house to the potting shed, she couldn't help but wonder: if the line was dead, how had Nina managed to call Yves to tell him about the fire?

Convulsion. Infection. Coma.

They're just words. They can't physically touch me; they don't exist except in the brief form of sound waves. So how can they pierce my heart so efficiently, so brutally?

"The cause is unclear," a doctor says—young and blond and inappropriately pretty. "We're running tests."

Beside me, my husband is nodding, his fingers steepled beneath his chin.

"The seizures are similar to those associated with epilepsy. We've administered antibiotics and anesthetics to stop them, but in the meantime we need to consider all possibilities. Cardiac disorders, neurological conditions, abnormal intracranial development. Of course, the most likely explanation is a strain of meningitis."

My chest feels tight. I want to hit her for lying, for being stupid and making what is clearly a huge mistake. "Meningitis?" I say. "It's not possible. She's fully up-to-date with all her vaccinations."

"I'm sure she is. And nine times out of ten vaccines give excellent protection."

Nine times out of ten. I don't understand. "But I'm so careful about hygiene; I always keep a close eye on her."

"Of course," says the doctor. "But these bacteria are actually very common. Lots of people naturally carry them in their throats and noses without ever becoming ill. It's just that the immune systems of babies and young children are more vulnerable. Has Aurelia had a cold recently? Any flu-like symptoms?"

The head cold. The sneezes and the sniffles, the headaches and the shivers. My baby's head resting in my lap. Endless repeats of *Peppa Pig* and *In the Night Garden.* Pins and needles run up and down my arms.

"Did we do this?" my husband says, looking at me. "Could one of us have been a carrier?"

"Oh, well, I don't think it's helpful to—"

"Tell me. In theory?"

"Look, obviously we couldn't confirm anything without tests, but yes, it's possible," says the doctor. "The bacteria are usually spread by close, prolonged contact with nose and throat secretions; so, sneezing and coughing. Kissing."

My husband is looking at me. My throat is closing up.

"But let's not forget that this is not a diagnosis. There are some anomalies here. I'm simply explaining the likeliest cause, as I see it."

They are both looking at me. They are looking, and they are testing me.

"Perhaps your wife would like to sit down?"

No. I will not sit down. I will stay very still. I don't trust myself to move. If I move, I will fail the test. I will stamp and spit and break things. I will charge at the doctor and rip her horrible blond hair out by the roots.

I remember running to the car while my husband did nothing. *What did you do,* I yelled, *what did you give her?* But what if it was me? What if I made her sick? What if, what if, what if . . .

"I'm afraid I'm going to have to ask you to take a seat."

Stay still. Just stay . . . very . . . still.

CHAPTER TWENTY

SCOTT

S COTT OPENED the glass doors and, as usual, the smell of mashed potatoes hit him almost palpably in the face. Why mashed potatoes? Scott wondered this at every visit. He was regularly assured that the residents of Lakeview Care Home were treated to a wide variety of meals. Some days there was even a theme—American, Italian, Moroccan. But all Scott ever smelled was mashed potatoes with a faint trace of bleach.

He stepped into the lobby and the door shut behind him, cutting off the distant rumble of trains on their way into the city. The hush rubbed up against him like a cat.

"Good morning, Scott." A bottom-heavy woman lumbered out from the office, her wispy hair sprayed into a cloud around her face. "You're early today."

Signing his name in the visitor book, he greeted her with a nod. "Well, I wouldn't want to be late now, would I?"

The woman chuckled. "No, Kathryn would certainly have something to say about that. Come on, I'll take you through."

They passed through a set of double doors, the locking system giving way with a clunk as the care worker swiped her card and walked down a long hallway lined with framed watercolors and mahogany side tables.

"You'll be glad to hear she's been doing really well. She's even been playing the piano a little."

"Really?" Scott raised his eyebrows, imagining a discordant plunk echoing through the corridors.

He passed a stinking bowl of potpourri. His stomach heaved, but there was nothing left to bring up. He hadn't managed to keep even water down since the early hours of the morning, a disappointing end to what had, on the whole, been an enjoyable evening. Scott never usually had much of an appetite for award ceremonies, but last night he'd done himself proud, smashing through dozens of social exchanges without once wanting to stick a fork in his thigh. When the time came for the final award of the evening, he was riding high on a sea of nudges, winks, and crossed fingers held high in the air. The mistake he made was to look at his phone.

Right before the supermodel presenter pulled the card from its golden envelope, Scott patted his pockets to check he still had his speech. Feeling the outline of his phone, he took it out to switch it to silent mode—the last thing he needed was the thing ringing while he was onstage. As the model held up the card, Scott glanced at the screen and saw a notification: an email. Unable to help himself, he tapped it lightly and skim-read the message. When his name was announced—*And the award goes to . . . Scott Denny and Proem Partners!*—he looked up into the rapturous faces of his team and saw only flames and charcoal.

Aurelia had tried to set the playhouse on fire again.

He'd at least managed to finish his acceptance speech before bolting to the bar and drinking it dry.

They stopped at the end of a hallway, just shy of a wide archway through which Scott could hear the melancholy tinkle of teaspoons on saucers. The care worker turned to face him. "Her speech has been better lately, I must say," she said, smiling brightly. "And her mood swings have been less erratic. She does keep asking for Terrence, though, which can set her off."

Scott nodded, quelling a rising sting of bile.

"Anyway, I'll leave you to it. Feel free to come and have a chat on your way out if you have any questions." She patted Scott on the arm and waddled back down the hallway.

Scott passed through the archway into a café area set up to look like a traditional British tea shop, complete with red table-cloths, bunting, and a chalkboard menu. On a counter, underneath individual glass domes, stood an array of cakes, pieces of which sat untouched in front of a handful of silver-haired "customers." He stepped into the room and approached a table by the window.

"Hello, Mum."

Kathryn Denny turned to look at him. She *did* look better than she had the week before. She had a bit of color in her cheeks, and her milky blue eyes were somewhat more focused.

"You're late," she said, her voice wavering.

"No, Mum. It's ten o' clock. I'm early."

"Don't you play games with me." Kathryn shook a curled finger at him. "I've been waiting here for over an hour."

Scott pulled out a chair and sat down heavily. "Fine. I'm late. I'm sorry."

He ordered a coffee and sipped it gingerly as Kathryn pressed dry pieces of scone to her lips. Her fingers trembled as the crumbs fell off her tongue and into her lap.

Killing time, he made small talk. Kathryn mumbled her replies, her head wobbling gently on her puckered turtle's neck, and Scott began to feel hopeful that they might avoid a scene today. But after several minutes, she stopped midsentence and looked up at him with her eyes narrowed.

"Who are you?" she said, clear as a bell.

Scott sighed and put down his coffee cup. "I'm Scott. I'm your son."

"Son? I don't have a son."

"Yes, Mum, you do."

"No. Terrence and I don't have any children."

"You do."

"Are you calling me a liar?" Kathryn's gray curls danced at her temples.

Scott rolled his eyes. He hated it when she did this.

"Where is Terrence, anyway?" she asked, addressing the room. An elderly man sitting in the opposite corner flinched and mumbled something. "I've been waiting for him for over an hour."

"Terrence isn't coming," Scott said sharply. Usually he played along, but he was in no mood today. "Terrence is gone."

"Gone? Where?"

"He left us. Remember, Mum? He moved to Hong Kong with some other woman."

"What on earth are you talking about?" Kathryn was shaking, her papery hands quivering on the tablecloth.

Scott lowered his voice to a hiss and leaned in, reaching across the table and grabbing his mother's scrawny wrist. "Terrence. Is. Gone. Understand?" He felt his lip curling into a sneer, but he was too far gone to control it. "Terrence lied to us. He pissed all our money away and lost our house, our car, our furniture. He made us live in a filthy shack on the edge of town. You lost all your friends; we had to leave school. And then, when the shame got too much for him, he took Eddie and fucked off to Asia."

"Eddie?" Kathryn's eyes seemed to vibrate. They moved from side to side, betraying the confusion within.

Scott moved his hand from her wrist to her chin. "Terrence"— he paused, holding her still to ensure she could see his face—"is a cunt."

A tear rolled down the side of Kathryn's nose, and her wobbly gaze came to rest on the table. Scott released her and sat back in his chair, looking out of the window. He waited.

After some time, he felt her eyes on him again.

"Scotty, darling," she said cheerfully. "Have you chosen a piece of cake?"

Scott shook his head slowly. "Not yet."

"Let's see." She looked over at the counter. "They have a Victoria sponge, a lemon drizzle, and an apple cake. If you're a good boy, I'll get you a milkshake, too."

"Hmm. Tough choice."

"I'd recommend the apple cake. It's very nice, although it's got nothing on Angelica's. Do you know, my friends have this joke that if it weren't for my housekeeper's apple cake they wouldn't bother coming to visit at all." She winked at him. "At least, I hope it's a joke."

Angelica. Warmth spread through Scott's chest. "I always liked her chocolate mud cake best," he said, remembering how on Friday evenings he would return home from boarding school to the smell of baking and roast chicken. The washing machine would be lazily clanking away, a gentle heartbeat under the hum of the house, and in the study Billie Holiday would be singing the blues. He would dump his bag at the door and head straight for the kitchen, where Angelica's mixing bowl would be waiting for him to lick clean.

"The mud cake? What would you know?" Kathryn chided playfully. "You're always too busy with your projects to eat anything anyway. What is it this week? A spyglass? An underground tunnel? Oh, please tell me it's not another bird hospital. I couldn't stand the mess. All those feathers in the house . . . it was weeks before I found all the carcasses in my shoeboxes." She shook her head fondly. "Honestly, Scotty, did you really think you could nurse them all back to life?"

Scott smiled. This was the only upside of dementia, this time traveling. He remembered his makeshift operating room. Next door's cat was always leaving half-dead sparrows and blue tits on the doorstep, so Scott would sneak over and pick them up before anyone saw. He'd wrap their delicate little bodies in tissue paper and place them in boxes, wherein he would perform surgical procedures using whatever kitchen utensils he could lay his hands on. Unsurprisingly, the birds never lived.

Opposite, Kathryn shivered and looked away.

"Are you cold, Mum?" Scott asked.

When she looked back, Kathryn had shifted again. Her eyes were now cold and suspicious. "Scott?" she said.

"Yes. Hi, Mum."

"What are you doing here?

"Well, I've come to—"

"Where have you been?" Her voice quavered. "Where did you go?"

Scott held out his hand. "It's okay, Mum."

Kathryn looked around the room, her hands beginning to shake again. "Where are they? Did you bring them?"

"Mum—"

"Did you bring them?" she said again.

Scott flicked his gaze to the door, looking for a care worker. Things could, and usually did, escalate very quickly.

Kathryn sucked in her breath and pushed it out through bared teeth like an animal. "Answer me!" She banged her fist on the table, making the cutlery jump. "Did you bring them with you today?"

"No."

"Why not?"

"They—"

"I said, why not?"

"Alright, let's just calm down."

"Where are they?" Kathryn was shouting now. A few residents had appeared in the doorway, drawn to the noise. "What have you done with them? Where is your wife? Where is my granddaughter?"

Scott stood up, sweat pricking his brow. He was suddenly flushed with heat. The walls pressed in on him. He was struggling to breathe. He backed away, his eye on a fire exit in the far corner of the room. Suddenly, there was a flurry of footsteps behind him and another care worker, a man this time, was at his side.

"What did you do to her?" Kathryn screeched, pointing at Scott. "Why can't I see her?"

"Okay, Kathryn, okay, take it easy." The male care worker gestured to two nurses who were hanging back a little way, and they stepped closer.

Kathryn reached for them. "I want to see my granddaughter. I want to see Aurelia," she pleaded. The nurses took hold of Kathryn's forearms, lifting her to her feet and steering her gently but firmly away, past the cake counter and out through a doorway.

Scott stared after them, jumping as the care worker placed a hand on his shoulder. "Are you okay?"

"Fine." He steadied himself on a nearby chair.

"It's hard for them when they lose someone," the man said sympathetically as they walked back toward reception. "They don't understand."

Scott nodded, his mother's anguished cries echoing in his ears. As always, the noise followed him like a stray dog down the corridor, back into the lobby, out the main doors, and all the way back to the city.

CHAPTER TWENTY-ONE

EMILY

A FEW DAYS after the fire, Emily drove to the market. The nearest town lay forty-five minutes' drive south of Querencia. Every Saturday morning, a small central square sprang to life as all the local farmers rolled in with their produce, and going there was by far one of Emily's favorite tasks: she loved browsing the stalls and rubbing shoulders with the townspeople as they shopped and gossiped.

Parking was a nightmare, though. Emily wouldn't have called herself a confident driver at the best of times, but in the enormous SUV she was a straight-up liability. Gripping the steering wheel, she steered the Land Cruiser over the rutted surface of the parking lot, only just making it through the gaps between other vehicles. She found a spot and reverse-parked, concentrating so hard on not clipping the wing mirror of a red hatchback that she didn't notice the old woman from the cheese stall until she'd stuck her face right through the open window. *"Le char est arrivé!"* said the cheese lady, cackling. *The tank has arrived.*

Emily jumped. "Yes," she said. "I mean, *oui. Bonjour, madame.*"

With its tinted windows and noisy exhaust, the Land Cruiser

did indeed resemble a tank, especially among all the rusty little delivery vans. The first time Emily had done a market run, she had stuck out like a bug on a birthday cake even before she'd tried to order anything. Her halting French and wads of cash had turned her into a sideshow. The local farmers and market vendors had all stopped what they were doing, first to chuckle at the sweet English tourist trying to remember the words for eggs and garlic, and then to marvel at the astonishing amount of money she was spending.

After five visits, she now felt like a local hero. The vendors all greeted her by name. They waved and smiled and sometimes even flocked to say hello before she'd even gotten out of the car. *Look,* they all seemed to be saying to one another, *the rich girl is here to shower us with money!* They would fight over her, calling her this way and that, everyone laughing at some joke that Emily only half understood, and she would leave feeling like the Queen on an official visit.

Occasionally someone would politely inquire as to where she was staying or who she worked for, but Emily just smiled and pretended she didn't understand. Even though the purpose of Scott's confidentiality agreement still wasn't wholly clear to her, it loomed large in her mind. Fortunately, Emily's rusty French (picked up during holidays at Eurocamp, studied at school, and abandoned in London) was polishing up nicely, which meant she was able to avoid sticky topics and comment instead on the weather or a display of new produce.

The sun shone down on her bare shoulders as she wandered around the stalls with a list in her hand, breathing in the heady combination of smells: fresh bread, *saucisson*, cheese, seafood, caramel. Silver trays held colorful mountains of *gingembre lamelle, loukoum rose,* and *ail confit.* She handed over crisp banknote after crisp banknote. At the fishmonger's she picked out mussels and prawns, and watched as a burly man with a mustache cut the flesh from a gigantic swordfish, then deftly turned it into fillets. At the greengrocer's, she asked for lemon and chillies, coriander, ginger, onions, mangoes, and peaches. The cheese lady welcomed her back with a kiss on each cheek and handed over neat packets of Brie, Roquefort, and feta.

As Emily reached out to accept a free gift of salted butter, she glimpsed a familiar face through the crowds. Yves, over by the *boucherie*, studying the cuts of beef like he'd never seen meat before, a reusable bag hooked almost daintily over one arm. Emily felt a little sorry for him. Poor guy; he was so awkward and lumbering, like a giant in a playground.

He looked up and then quickly away, and Emily realized he'd seen her but was pretending he hadn't. She grinned—*oh, no, you're not getting away with that*—and waved. "Yves!" she called. "Hi!"

Yves almost jumped out of his skin, his eyes wide and guilty, as if it was against the rules to be caught fraternizing outside of work. She waved again, determined to elicit even the tiniest of social niceties—they were colleagues, after all—but his face remained stony, and eventually he turned away, pushing his way back through the crowd until he was gone.

She shrugged and tucked the butter into her basket. *What a weirdo.* Refusing to let him spoil her mood, she breathed a happy sigh. Who would ever have predicted that one day she would feel at home in France? No one; and yet here she was, wafting around the markets and waving to locals as if she was one herself.

Emily climbed back into *le char* feeling light as a cloud, dizzy with sunshine and not even a little bit guilty that all of this wonderful food was far too much for just three people and would most likely all end up in the bin.

On the way back to Querencia, just before the point at which she would lose her signal again, Emily pulled over and reached into her bag for her phone. The clamor of the market had all but drowned out her homesickness, but a trace remained, niggling at her like a fingerprint on a windowpane.

She hung up and smacked the heel of her hand on the steering wheel. *Every single time.* Just when she managed to get back on her feet they always found a whole new way to knock her back down again. She threw the phone onto the passenger seat.

Three minutes later, she picked it back up again. There was only one person she wanted to speak to right now, only one person who would understand. She opened her messages and texted Scott.

Back at Querencia, Emily hauled the groceries from the car and placed them in the guesthouse kitchen. She separated out the items that Nina had requested specifically for her and Aurelia, and placed them in a large picnic hamper. She carried it over to the family house, taking the path around the side and placing it on the patio table as usual. She was about to walk away when she heard the slide of bifold doors.

"Em? You okay?"

She turned to see Nina emerging from the gym in shorts and a cropped sports top, a towel in one hand and a water bottle in the other, and the sight of her tripped a switch in Emily. She felt her insides crack and slide away like an ice shelf into the ocean. Mortified, she dropped her head and covered her face.

"Oh, honey, what happened?" Nina's hand on her shoulder made it worse somehow, and a small sob shot out of Emily's throat.

Embarrassed, she shook her head and wiped her nose with the back of her hand. "Nothing, sorry. I just talked to my parents." She sniffed. "But it's fine. I'm fine."

Nina opened her mouth to say something but then seemed to change her mind.

Behind them, the kitchen door opened and Aurelia's pale face appeared. "It's okay, Strawberry," Nina said. "Go on back to your book and I'll be with you in a few minutes, okay?"

Aurelia pouted but didn't argue. She disappeared and the door clicked shut.

When Juliet answered, the familiarity of her voice made Emily feel unexpectedly teary. "Emily? Is that you?"

"Yes, it's me. Hello."

"Oh my goodness, where are you?" Her voice was high and edgy.

"I'm in France. My new job, remember?"

"What new job? And hang on—*France?*"

Emily rolled her eyes. *Typical.* They never listened.

"I've been calling and calling," Juliet said, "but your phone is always off. Your father and I have been worried sick, we thought something had happened to you."

"What are you talking about?" Emily's smile wavered a little. "I . . . I told you I would be out of contact for a little while."

"Did you? I don't remember that! When did you call? Did you speak to Peter? It can't have been me; I would've remembered a conversation about moving to *France.*"

"I haven't moved here, not exactly. I'm just—"

"Emily, it's been almost *six weeks* since you were last in touch. We had no idea where you were; anything could've happened to you. We nearly phoned the police. Are you picking up your emails?"

"No, I—look, there's no need to worry, I'm fine. This place is amazing, it—"

"No need to worry? Darling, we've been going out of our minds! And where is 'this place'?"

"I told you, in bloody France!"

"You didn't tell us."

"I did! I'm working for a family. At their house. I told you all about it."

"You didn't."

Emily hesitated. She *had* told them. She remembered calling the morning of her first meeting with Scott.

Oh, no, wait . . . She'd called, but it had gone to voicemail, so she'd decided to try again later rather than leave a message. Which she definitely had done . . . hadn't she?

Oh, shit the bed. Was it possible she had flown off to France without telling her parents?

"Who is this family, anyway?" Juliet said.

Emily decided to plant herself firmly in denial. She'd told her parents exactly where she was going and what she was doing; they just hadn't listened to her, as usual. She adopted a faux-patient tone, as if she was explaining something to a small child. "They're a perfectly nice British family with a house in France. I worked for the guy in London. He's cool."

"*Cool?* Who is this man, Emily? I'm really not comfortable with this."

"For god's sake, I'm fine. Everything's great. You can relax."

"Oh, I can *relax*, can I? My daughter disappears off the face of the planet after telling me she's in trouble, and I can *relax*?"

In the background, Emily could hear her father jumping around, butting in and asking questions. "Yes, yes, it's Emily," Juliet was saying. "*Shh,* Peter, for god's sake, I can't hear her. Emily, your father wants to know what exactly you're doing at this house? What is this job?"

Emily took a deep breath. "Well, I'm doing a lot of things," she said, evenly. "Scott, that's the guy from London, he hired me to help his wife look after the place and—"

"Are you a cleaner? Peter, she's a *cleaner.*"

"I'm not a cleaner."

"Well, what are you then?"

"I'm sort of a"—Emily cast around for a word that described what she was doing for the Denny family: *Personal shopper? Painter/decorator? Companion?*—"a live-in personal assistant."

"A what? What does that even mean? And did you say you're *living* with these people? Listen, Emily, I think you should come home. Right now. I mean it; your father and I are very worried about you. We think you might be—what's that word that Jenny Sanderson used? Peter, what's that word? *Free-falling.*"

"Calm down," said Emily. "I'm not free-falling, I'm actually really happy. I like this job and I'm good at it."

"Good at *what* exactly?"

Emily flinched at the derision in Juliet's voice. Clearly her mother thought she'd run off to join a polygamist cult or something.

"Whatever you're doing over there with these people, darling, I can tell you now it won't help you build a career. I appreciate that you might need a little holiday but come on."

"It's not a holiday, I—"

There was a muffled interjection in the background and Juliet tutted. "Please, Peter, be quiet, I'm talking. Hang on, Emily, let me deal with your father."

There was a rustle as they played tug-of-war with the phone. Then there was a crackle, and Peter was in her ear, his deep Derbyshire accent vibrating through her skull. "Listen to me, Emily. Come home. Your mother is making herself ill with worry."

"Well, that's her own fault."

"Look, love, I don't mind telling you that we were all hoping you might give up that acting lark." Emily covered her face with her free hand. He was warming up to one of his lectures. "It wasn't getting you anywhere; we all knew that. But we sort of hoped that you might move on to bigger and better things."

"But—"

"Listen, you're a bright girl. You could get a good job, make yourself some money, and set yourself up. But you keep mucking around. You're not eighteen anymore, kid. It's time to grow up."

"This *is* a good job! That's what I'm trying to tell you, but you won't listen."

"No, Emily, it's you who won't listen. You haven't listened for years now and look where it's got you."

"Yes," Emily yelled. "Look where it's got me. Happy, relaxed and far away from you people!"

Nina wiped her face with the towel, then steered Emily gently over to a sunny patch of grass next to the vegetable garden. "Sit," she said, lowering herself into a cross-legged position. She patted the ground beside her.

Emily obeyed and found herself talking, not just about the phone call but other things, too. Juliet's special gift for stonewalling. The puzzled, almost fearful expression she wore whenever Emily opened her mouth. The way Peter never quite looked her in the eye, and the disappointment that rose off him like heat from a car hood. She talked about her long-held belief that there was something wrong with her, that her life didn't have a purpose or even a point. She admitted that she often felt furious for no apparent reason, a feeling over which she had no control.

Nina said nothing, just listened.

When Emily was done, a blanket of shame fell over her. She fell silent, wishing she'd kept her mouth shut, willing the ground to swallow her up.

"Okay, here's what I think," Nina said at last, stretching her long legs out in front of her. "You, Emily Proudman, are a beautiful, wonderful, creative, curious human. You're warm and generous and a joy to be around. You're also very intelligent. But you see yourself as a victim."

Emily reached out and picked a daisy from the grass.

"You're looking for someone to blame for your unhappiness—your parents, all those casting directors, anyone. But here's the thing: at this point in your life, everything you surround yourself with is there because *you* chose it to be."

One by one, Emily picked the petals off the daisy's head. *She loves me, she loves me not.*

"You were raised in a privileged country," Nina continued, her elbows resting on her knees, her blond hair falling in front of her eyes. "You're educated, and you've been given economic opportunity. You have the power and the freedom to choose how you live and, more importantly, how you *feel* about how you live. You're *not* a victim. You're in control. You just don't know it yet."

Emily wiped her nose with the back of her hand. "I do," she lied. "I know I can do what I want. It's just . . . I wish my parents could be just a little bit proud of me."

Nina sighed. "Well, that would be nice, but you know what I've learned? If you wait around for other people to approve your decisions, you'll be waiting a long time. Approve them yourself. Be proud of yourself."

Emily reached out and picked another daisy. Each petal came away with a tiny *snick* and fell to the ground.

Nina nudged her with her shoulder. "*I'm* proud of you."

Emily snorted. "Yeah, right. Because running away is so ballsy."

"You didn't run. If anything, you took the first step toward understanding your own power."

"But when everything fell apart, I just bailed. I didn't even tell my parents I was leaving."

Nina stopped. "You didn't?"

"Nope."

Nina made a face as if to say, *Oops*.

"See? Bailed. And now it feels like I can't ever go back."

"Well, okay, maybe that wasn't the smartest move," Nina said, chuckling. "But ask yourself this: would you *want* to go back? Were you happy?"

Emily shook her head slowly, thinking how much easier and nicer her life would be if someone like Nina had adopted her instead of Juliet. If she were Nina's daughter, she would've been encouraged and supported, loved and accepted. Arguments would've been quickly resolved with calm and respectful communication instead of slammed doors and simmering rage. *Agree to disagree,* Juliet always said, her back turned.

"Everything's going to be alright," Nina said, her arm around Emily's shoulders. "So what if your dream didn't quite work out as planned? Just go get a new one."

Emily sniffed. "A new dream?"

"Sure."

"But what if it sucks just as much as the last one did?"

Nina shrugged. "Look around you."

Emily looked. Querencia seemed to stretch on forever. In front of her, the shrubs and flower beds rolled and tumbled down toward the ocean like a waterfall, and behind, a labyrinth of trees stretched back as far as she could see. The air was alive with bees and dragonflies, and golden rays of sunlight hit the walls of both houses so that they appeared to be lit from inside, like lanterns. Emily breathed in and felt the same light fill her rib cage.

"Do you think it sucks?"

Grinning, Emily shook her head. "No."

"Me neither."

Later that evening, after dinner, they carried the movie projector out onto the lawn and tied a bedsheet up between the trees. They all curled up together on a pile of cushions—Emily on one side, Nina on the other, and Aurelia nestled in the middle—and watched an old comedy, *The Money Pit*, about a couple who buy a huge dilapidated mansion only for it to fall apart around them. They ate popcorn and laughed till their bellies hurt as Tom Hanks and Shelley Long suffered mishap after mishap. Doors fell off their hinges, Tom got stuck in a hole in the floor, Shelley got attacked by a raccoon, and the bathtub fell through the ceiling.

Afterward, as Emily climbed the stairs to bed, she thought how right Nina was. She was exactly where she needed to be. She'd made a good choice—a *great* choice—and she would own it, just as she would own every other choice she made from now on.

She washed her face and brushed her teeth, then climbed under the covers and put her phone on charge. Scott hadn't replied to the text she'd sent earlier—at least, not before she'd lost her signal again. But that was probably no bad thing. An odd feeling had crept into her gut immediately after her chat with Nina. The text, innocuous as it had felt at the time, now seemed almost like a betrayal. Maybe it wasn't a good idea to contact Scott behind Nina's back.

In fact, maybe it wasn't a good idea to use her phone at all. What was the point? Look how her conversation with her parents had turned out. Plus, she'd told them too much about her job at Querencia. She wasn't sure exactly what she could and couldn't say, having signed Scott's confidentiality agreement without reading it properly, but the bottom line was that Scott and Nina didn't want her openly discussing details of their life and home with people they didn't know.

Making a decision, she got out of bed and disconnected the phone from its charger. Then she threw it onto the top shelf of the wardrobe and covered it with a pile of clothes.

CHAPTER TWENTY-TWO

SCOTT

IN THE backseat of the car, Scott stared through the windshield at the grubby rear of a bus. The journey back from the care home had been reasonably smooth until now, his driver expertly navigating the side streets to avoid the clogged A roads, but not even the GPS could help them once they reached Hammersmith.

"What's the holdup?" Scott asked. Both his side views were blocked by filthy, rumbling trucks.

His driver tapped on a screen mounted on the dashboard. "Looks like a problem with the Tube. Service suspensions on the Piccadilly, District, and Circle lines."

Scott checked the time. He was running slightly early for his next appointment, so the delay wasn't a problem, but his hangover seemed to be getting worse by the second, and he was still feeling claustrophobic after his visit with his mother. He hadn't spoken his brother's name aloud in many, many years, and it had left a bitter taste in his mouth.

He swallowed thickly and fidgeted in his seat. He could have done without being trapped in a scorching, belching gridlock.

Just then, his phone pinged with a message. The sender's name sent an odd mix of delight and dread tripping through his body.

Hey, it's me. Just on my way back from the market and thought I'd say hi! Sorry I haven't been in touch to let you know how everything's going but you know what it's like—not one bar of service! Also, I'm sure Nina's been filling you in. Anyway, everything's great here! The weather's been amazing. *Il fait du soleil!* We've had a few dramas (I'm guessing you've heard about the fire?) but on the whole we're cruising. TBH I'm feeling a bit low today (parent problems—with all the fuss they're making, anyone would think I'd run off to join ISIS) but maybe it's just the isolation finally getting to me. I'm sure it won't last long! Anyway, I don't really know why I'm writing this or what I'm trying to say but I just wanted to check in and say hi. You have a beautiful home and I'm so honored to be spending time with your family. Can't wait for you to join us and check out the progress on the guesthouse. Yay!

The bus in front inched forward and stopped. Scott's driver turned up the air-conditioning and wiped his forehead with his sleeve.

In the back, Scott reread Emily's words, then reclined in his seat, deep in thought. He quickly checked her social-media pages, but there was no recent activity.

He tapped his fingers on the center console.

So, Emily was feeling down. She was struggling. It was a good sign that she had chosen to contact him—but was it just a single bad day? Nina had told him everything was fine, that she and Emily were getting on famously. But what if Nina was lying?

He pulled up Emily's number and stared at it for several seconds before sliding the phone back into his pocket. Then he took it back out again. As the traffic finally began to move, he dashed off two emails, one to Verity and one to Nina, putting plans in place before he could change his mind.

He would fly out the following weekend. He'd already left it too long.

When Juliet answered, the familiarity of her voice made Emily feel unexpectedly teary. "Emily? Is that you?"

"Yes, it's me. Hello."

"Oh my goodness, where are you?" Her voice was high and edgy.

"I'm in France. My new job, remember?"

"What new job? And hang on—*France?*"

Emily rolled her eyes. *Typical.* They never listened.

"I've been calling and calling," Juliet said, "but your phone is always off. Your father and I have been worried sick, we thought something had happened to you."

"What are you talking about?" Emily's smile wavered a little. "I . . . I told you I would be out of contact for a little while."

"Did you? I don't remember that! When did you call? Did you speak to Peter? It can't have been me; I would've remembered a conversation about moving to *France.*"

"I haven't moved here, not exactly. I'm just—"

"Emily, it's been almost *six weeks* since you were last in touch. We had no idea where you were; anything could've happened to you. We nearly phoned the police. Are you picking up your emails?"

"No, I—look, there's no need to worry, I'm fine. This place is amazing, it—"

"No need to worry? Darling, we've been going out of our minds! And where is 'this place'?"

"I told you, in bloody France!"

"You didn't tell us."

"I did! I'm working for a family. At their house. I told you all about it."

"You didn't."

Emily hesitated. She *had* told them. She remembered calling the morning of her first meeting with Scott.

Oh, no, wait . . . She'd called, but it had gone to voicemail, so she'd decided to try again later rather than leave a message. Which she definitely had done . . . hadn't she?

149

Oh, shit the bed. Was it possible she had flown off to France without telling her parents?

"Who is this family, anyway?" Juliet said.

Emily decided to plant herself firmly in denial. She'd told her parents exactly where she was going and what she was doing; they just hadn't listened to her, as usual. She adopted a faux-patient tone, as if she was explaining something to a small child. "They're a perfectly nice British family with a house in France. I worked for the guy in London. He's cool."

"*Cool?* Who is this man, Emily? I'm really not comfortable with this."

"For god's sake, I'm fine. Everything's great. You can relax."

"Oh, I can *relax*, can I? My daughter disappears off the face of the planet after telling me she's in trouble, and I can *relax*?"

In the background, Emily could hear her father jumping around, butting in and asking questions. "Yes, yes, it's Emily," Juliet was saying. "*Shh*, Peter, for god's sake, I can't hear her. Emily, your father wants to know what exactly you're doing at this house? What is this job?"

Emily took a deep breath. "Well, I'm doing a lot of things," she said, evenly. "Scott, that's the guy from London, he hired me to help his wife look after the place and—"

"Are you a cleaner? Peter, she's a *cleaner.*"

"I'm not a cleaner."

"Well, what are you then?"

"I'm sort of a"—Emily cast around for a word that described what she was doing for the Denny family: *Personal shopper? Painter/decorator? Companion?*—"a live-in personal assistant."

"A what? What does that even mean? And did you say you're *living* with these people? Listen, Emily, I think you should come home. Right now. I mean it; your father and I are very worried about you. We think you might be—what's that word that Jenny Sanderson used? Peter, what's that word? *Free-falling.*"

"Calm down," said Emily. "I'm not free-falling, I'm actually really happy. I like this job and I'm good at it."

"Good at *what* exactly?"

Emily flinched at the derision in Juliet's voice. Clearly her mother thought she'd run off to join a polygamist cult or something.

"Whatever you're doing over there with these people, darling, I can tell you now it won't help you build a career. I appreciate that you might need a little holiday but come on."

"It's not a holiday, I—"

There was a muffled interjection in the background and Juliet tutted. "Please, Peter, be quiet, I'm talking. Hang on, Emily, let me deal with your father."

There was a rustle as they played tug-of-war with the phone. Then there was a crackle, and Peter was in her ear, his deep Derbyshire accent vibrating through her skull. "Listen to me, Emily. Come home. Your mother is making herself ill with worry."

"Well, that's her own fault."

"Look, love, I don't mind telling you that we were all hoping you might give up that acting lark." Emily covered her face with her free hand. He was warming up to one of his lectures. "It wasn't getting you anywhere; we all knew that. But we sort of hoped that you might move on to bigger and better things."

"But—"

"Listen, you're a bright girl. You could get a good job, make yourself some money, and set yourself up. But you keep on mucking around. You're not eighteen anymore, kid. It's time to grow up."

"This *is* a good job! That's what I'm trying to tell you, but you won't listen."

"No, Emily, it's you who won't listen. You haven't listened for years now and look where it's got you."

"Yes," Emily yelled. "Look where it's got me. Happy and relaxed and far away from you people!"

She hung up and smacked the heel of her hand on the steering wheel. *Every single time.* Just when she managed to get back on her feet they always found a whole new way to knock her back down again. She threw the phone onto the passenger seat.

Three minutes later, she picked it back up again. There was only one person she wanted to speak to right now, only one person who would understand. She opened her messages and texted Scott.

Back at Querencia, Emily hauled the groceries from the car and placed them in the guesthouse kitchen. She separated out the items that Nina had requested specifically for her and Aurelia, and placed them in a large picnic hamper. She carried it over to the family house, taking the path around the side and placing it on the patio table as usual. She was about to walk away when she heard the slide of bifold doors.

"Em? You okay?"

She turned to see Nina emerging from the gym in shorts and a cropped sports top, a towel in one hand and a water bottle in the other, and the sight of her tripped a switch in Emily. She felt her insides crack and slide away like an ice shelf into the ocean. Mortified, she dropped her head and covered her face.

"Oh, honey, what happened?" Nina's hand on her shoulder made it worse somehow, and a small sob shot out of Emily's throat.

Embarrassed, she shook her head and wiped her nose with the back of her hand. "Nothing, sorry. I just talked to my parents." She sniffed. "But it's fine. I'm fine."

Nina opened her mouth to say something but then seemed to change her mind.

Behind them, the kitchen door opened and Aurelia's pale face appeared. "It's okay, Strawberry," Nina said. "Go on back to your book and I'll be with you in a few minutes, okay?"

Aurelia pouted but didn't argue. She disappeared and the door clicked shut.

Nina wiped her face with the towel, then steered Emily gently over to a sunny patch of grass next to the vegetable garden. "Sit," she said, lowering herself into a cross-legged position. She patted the ground beside her.

Emily obeyed and found herself talking, not just about the phone call but other things, too. Juliet's special gift for stonewalling. The puzzled, almost fearful expression she wore whenever Emily opened her mouth. The way Peter never quite looked her in the eye, and the disappointment that rose off him like heat from a car hood. She talked about her long-held belief that there was something wrong with her, that her life didn't have a purpose or even a point. She admitted that she often felt furious for no apparent reason, a feeling over which she had no control.

Nina said nothing, just listened.

When Emily was done, a blanket of shame fell over her. She fell silent, wishing she'd kept her mouth shut, willing the ground to swallow her up.

"Okay, here's what I think," Nina said at last, stretching her long legs out in front of her. "You, Emily Proudman, are a beautiful, wonderful, creative, curious human. You're warm and generous and a joy to be around. You're also very intelligent. But you see yourself as a victim."

Emily reached out and picked a daisy from the grass.

"You're looking for someone to blame for your unhappiness— your parents, all those casting directors, anyone. But here's the thing: at this point in your life, everything you surround yourself with is there because *you* chose it to be."

One by one, Emily picked the petals off the daisy's head. *She loves me, she loves me not.*

"You were raised in a privileged country," Nina continued, her elbows resting on her knees, her blond hair falling in front of her eyes. "You're educated, and you've been given economic opportunity. You have the power and the freedom to choose how you live and, more importantly, how you *feel* about how you live. You're *not* a victim. You're in control. You just don't know it yet."

Emily wiped her nose with the back of her hand. "I do," she lied. "I know I can do what I want. It's just . . . I wish my parents could be just a little bit proud of me."

Nina sighed. "Well, that would be nice, but you know what I've learned? If you wait around for other people to approve your decisions, you'll be waiting a long time. Approve them yourself. Be proud of yourself."

Emily reached out and picked another daisy. Each petal came away with a tiny *snick* and fell to the ground.

Nina nudged her with her shoulder. "*I'm* proud of you."

Emily snorted. "Yeah, right. Because running away is so ballsy."

"You didn't run. If anything, you took the first step toward understanding your own power."

"But when everything fell apart, I just bailed. I didn't even tell my parents I was leaving."

Nina stopped. "You didn't?"

"Nope."

Nina made a face as if to say, *Oops.*

"See? Bailed. And now it feels like I can't ever go back."

"Well, okay, maybe that wasn't the smartest move," Nina said, chuckling. "But ask yourself this: would you *want* to go back? Were you happy?"

Emily shook her head slowly, thinking how much easier and nicer her life would be if someone like Nina had adopted her instead of Juliet. If she were Nina's daughter, she would've been encouraged and supported, loved and accepted. Arguments would've been quickly resolved with calm and respectful communication instead of slammed doors and simmering rage. *Agree to disagree,* Juliet always said, her back turned.

"Everything's going to be alright," Nina said, her arm around Emily's shoulders. "So what if your dream didn't quite work out as planned? Just go get a new one."

Emily sniffed. "A new dream?"

"Sure."

"But what if it sucks just as much as the last one did?"

Nina shrugged. "Look around you."

Emily looked. Querencia seemed to stretch on forever. In front of her, the shrubs and flower beds rolled and tumbled down toward the ocean like a waterfall, and behind, a labyrinth of trees stretched back as far as she could see. The air was alive with bees and dragonflies, and golden rays of sunlight hit the walls of both houses so that they appeared to be lit from inside, like lanterns. Emily breathed in and felt the same light fill her rib cage.

"Do you think it sucks?"

Grinning, Emily shook her head. "No."

"Me neither."

Later that evening, after dinner, they carried the movie projector out onto the lawn and tied a bedsheet up between the trees. They all curled up together on a pile of cushions—Emily on one side, Nina on the other, and Aurelia nestled in the middle—and watched an old comedy, *The Money Pit*, about a couple who buy a huge dilapidated mansion only for it to fall apart around them. They ate popcorn and laughed till their bellies hurt as Tom Hanks and Shelley Long suffered mishap after mishap. Doors fell off their hinges, Tom got stuck in a hole in the floor, Shelley got attacked by a raccoon, and the bathtub fell through the ceiling.

Afterward, as Emily climbed the stairs to bed, she thought how right Nina was. She was exactly where she needed to be. She'd made a good choice—a *great* choice—and she would own it, just as she would own every other choice she made from now on.

She washed her face and brushed her teeth, then climbed under the covers and put her phone on charge. Scott hadn't replied to the text she'd sent earlier—at least, not before she'd lost her signal again. But that was probably no bad thing. An odd feeling had crept into her gut immediately after her chat with Nina. The text, innocuous as it had felt at the time, now seemed almost like a betrayal. Maybe it wasn't a good idea to contact Scott behind Nina's back.

In fact, maybe it wasn't a good idea to use her phone at all. What was the point? Look how her conversation with her parents had turned out. Plus, she'd told them too much about her job at Querencia. She wasn't sure exactly what she could and couldn't say, having signed Scott's confidentiality agreement without reading it properly, but the bottom line was that Scott and Nina didn't want her openly discussing details of their life and home with people they didn't know.

Making a decision, she got out of bed and disconnected the phone from its charger. Then she threw it onto the top shelf of the wardrobe and covered it with a pile of clothes.

CHAPTER TWENTY-THREE

EMILY

He's coming," Nina had said one morning, all eyes and teeth. "Next weekend." And just like that, life at Querencia went from zero to sixty.

Almost immediately, Nina began tearing around the house making lists of jobs to be done, furniture to buy, corners to clean. Seemingly overwhelmed by the chaos, she barked out orders like a harried schoolteacher. "This should've been done by now," she said as she charged in and out of bedrooms, her veins bulging. "The place is so filthy. I can't even stand it." When she wasn't on the move, she stood staring into space, one thumb endlessly kneading the base of the other.

Emily watched as garden chairs were folded up with clucks of disgust and thrown onto the lawn. Tables, benches, and mirrors were added to the pile. Towels, pillows, and sheets. Yves came with a truck and took it all away, reappearing the next day with brand-new replacements. As all the new purchases were unpacked and distributed, she wondered what all the fuss was about. Scott didn't seem the type to care whether or not the cushions on the beds were new or not so new. But Nina looked so stressed that Emily decided to keep quiet and do as she was told. Besides, she was dealing with some nerves of her own. *He's coming,* she kept thinking, her stomach flipping somersaults.

On the morning Scott was due to arrive, she found her stress levels rising to match Nina's. She ran around with her heart so high up in her chest she thought it might fly out of her mouth; she vacuumed and polished, made beds and plumped cushions, and when she finally ran out of jobs, she invented more, just to keep busy. She picked flowers and arranged them in vases. She reorganized all the jars and cans in the cupboards. She straightened all the bath towels, lining them up on their rails with painstaking precision, all the while imagining the moment he drove through the gates. She chastised herself over and over for her excitement, but she couldn't help it. Her skin literally tingled with anticipation.

Finally exhausting her list of even the most pointless tasks, she wandered aimlessly, looking for something else to do. She found Nina and Aurelia in the outdoor kitchen making a welcome banner, but they looked so cozy together that it didn't feel right to intrude. She skirted around them, heading instead to the lawn.

She tidied up a game of *boules* that had been left out, taking the balls back to the games room, then picked up a picnic blanket and two pool towels that had been dumped on the grass, intending to take them in to be washed. But then she spotted another towel and a wet bundle of swimwear on the front steps of the family house. Tutting—*honestly, Aurelia, do you never pick anything up?*—she went to get them but hesitated as she reached the door, suddenly overcome with curiosity.

What did it look like, she wondered? Upstairs, the bedrooms—what did they smell like? What kind of sheets did they use? She'd seen so little of Scott's private space, so little evidence of a shared life with Nina. She couldn't even imagine it.

She snuck a backward look toward the pool. Nina and Aurelia were still moving around in the kitchen.

She knew she shouldn't go in, but she'd been at Querencia for six weeks. Weren't things different now? She and Nina had become close friends. She'd earned a measure of trust, hadn't she? Glancing back at the pool kitchen one more time, she opened the front door and poked her head inside.

The sitting room was exactly the same as it had been on the day she first arrived. Pristine vintage furniture, expensive designer decor, and a thin layer of dust. What did they use this room for, anyway? Actual *sitting*? Did Scott ever kick off his shoes in here, put his feet up on the ottoman, and read a book? Did Nina sit beside him, her hand on his thigh?

She took a step farther, suddenly desperate to see more. Shifting the weight of the towels in her arms, she gazed at the staircase. Why not just pop up to the bathroom and check their laundry? That would be a kind thing to do, wouldn't it? Nina had so much to do, surely she'd appreciate the help.

Emily tiptoed across the sitting room and stopped at the foot of the stairs. The whole house was so quiet, her ears rang. She began to climb, pausing midway, holding her breath. She felt like a cat burglar.

On the top step, she looked around, sucking in every detail. Letting her breath out slowly, she realized that she'd expected to find some big secret, some reason why she'd been forbidden to enter, but it was just a house. A mind-blowingly beautiful and meticulously styled house, sure. But still, just a house.

The landing was long and white. Light streamed in through a large west-facing picture window. Looking out, Emily could see the rose garden, the rockeries, the ocean, and the pool; if she leaned over the balustrade, she could just about make out Nina and Aurelia, still bent over their decorations in the outdoor kitchen.

Timber floorboards stretched away to her left, leading to four closed doors, white with ornate silver handles. To her right, two more doors. Carefully placing the pile of wet towels on the floor, she chose one at random and pushed it open.

Inside was a stunning bedroom: ivory-painted floorboards,

a freestanding full-length mirror, and a large chest of drawers. Plump cushions were piled high on a dreamy-looking bed. A huge plant towered in one corner. A guest room, Emily assumed.

She stepped back out onto the landing, shutting the door behind her. Trying the handle of another door, she found herself in another bedroom, much larger than the last. This one had a bigger bed, a gigantic mirrored wardrobe, a chandelier, and a spacious balcony. Another door led to what looked like a walk-in wardrobe. Assuming it was another guest room, she turned to go, but then something caught her eye: a pink strapless sundress draped artfully over the back of an armchair. One of Nina's favorites.

She looked closer. A tattered romance novel sat on the bedside table next to a small pot of moisturizer, and a necklace hung from the bronze sweep of a wall lamp.

Crossing the room, she picked up the sundress—carefully, reverently—and held it against her body. She checked her reflection in the mirror. Maybe if she cut her hair short and lost some weight . . .

Holding her hair up away from her face, she raised her chin. Angled her hips. Lengthened her spine. Then, without really knowing why, she brought the dress to her nose and inhaled deeply. It smelled like Nina—or a fusty, mothballed version of her anyway.

Returning the dress to the chair, she looked around. The silence was thick. If this was Nina's bedroom, then it was also Scott's, but it didn't look like it belonged to a couple. In fact, it didn't seem lived-in at all. The surfaces were dusty, the sheets too crisp. She let her fingers trail over the bedspread, wondering how it would feel to peel it back and climb in. Which side did Scott favor, the left or the right? Was he a tummy sleeper or did he curl up on his side?

Turning away from the bed, she cast a thoughtful eye over the furnishings. Everything was white or beige and immaculately textured. It was picture-perfect . . . and yet there was something odd about it, something she couldn't quite identify. Actually, now that she came to think of it, there was something odd about the whole house.

Shivering, she turned and crept out the door and back to the landing. Emily checked the window. Nina and Aurelia were still down by the pool, but she knew she shouldn't stay much longer.

Just one more room. She tried another door. It opened on a lovely but dirty bathroom. The tiles were gorgeous—white and deep blue, each one patterned differently—but the grouting was gray with mold, the enormous mirror cracked and speckled with age. A gigantic claw-foot bathtub stood in the corner, and Emily stepped closer, curious about how deep it was.

Huh.

The bottom half of the bath was stained a sort of gray-brown color, with a darker watermark running just below the rim. She reached out to brush it with her fingertips, but it was dry. The porcelain looked like it'd been scrubbed, but the stain was there to stay, as if the bath was filled regularly with mud or ink.

Something furry brushed her bare toes and she jumped.

Please not a mouse, please not a mouse.

Looking down, she saw the edge of a towel poking out from under the tub. Light blue with little yellow flowers. She reached for it, thinking that she'd check the laundry hamper and then get out of there, but as she did, the towel shook loose. It was streaked with a red-black substance.

She dropped it as if it had bitten her. *Urgh, what is that?* Then, bending down for a closer look, she gave it a cautious sniff. No smell. No texture. Could it be blood? She didn't think so. The shade was too dark.

Balling up the towel in her hands, she remembered that she was supposed to be looking for more to wash. Pulling two bath sheets from the wicker laundry hamper, she gathered them in her arms and turned to go, but straightened up too quickly and lost her balance. Tripping over the bathroom scale, she stumbled into the wall and smacked her head hard on the corner of a giant cabinet. A cry leaped out of her throat, and she ducked as the wooden door swung open—then froze when she saw what was inside.

The cabinet was stuffed with rows and rows of little bottles and cardboard packets. Thousands upon thousands of prescription pills. Creams and lotions. Cotton-wool pads and syringes wrapped in plastic. Bandages and scissors and vials of syrupy liquid. It was the world's biggest first-aid kit. A fully stocked private pharmacy.

She reached out to touch a tall stack of identical white boxes. The stack wobbled and the boxes gave a soft rattle, like a warning.

Feeling distinctly uneasy, Emily dropped the towels back in the hamper. What was she thinking, sneaking around Nina's bathroom and riffling through her stuff? She hadn't been invited. She had no right.

Get out, she told herself, finally coming to her senses. *You shouldn't be here.*

Convinced she'd been spotted, Emily had returned to the pool kitchen full of excuses and apologies, but Nina was too preoccupied with Aurelia's bad mood and hadn't even noticed her absence. Apparently, their morning had been a little tense; Aurelia had woken up fractious and twitchy, throwing her breakfast at the kitchen wall and slamming doors, all before the sun had fully risen, so Nina had invented a creative project designed to settle her down. The long dining-room table was covered with pens, paper, and assorted craft materials, and a banner hung from the roof of the pergola: five colorful drawings pegged on a line of string, spaced out among big bright letters. WELCOME HOME DADDY.

"I'll take over from here, if you like," Emily offered. Even though she hadn't been discovered, she felt she ought to make up for her indiscretion.

Exhausted and grateful for a break, Nina nodded and disappeared back up to the house to fetch a selection of wines for dinner.

Emily pulled up a chair next to Aurelia and pointed at her picture. "Who's this, then?" The drawing showed a small stick figure in a bright-pink dress. "Is that your mummy?"

Aurelia's head bobbed up and down.

"Beautiful. And who's that?" Next to the stick woman was a stick man with black hair and what looked like a suitcase. "This must be Daddy. Oh, well *done*. It's a very good likeness." Emily clapped enthusiastically.

Aurelia gave her a look that said, *Chill out, it's only a stick figure.*

Emily pressed on, pointing to a pig and a horse floating near the top left of the picture. "And here we have Sebastien and Francis Bacon. Lovely. And this?" There was a third stick person with a thatch of yellow hair and a big red smile.

Aurelia thrust a skinny finger at Emily's chest.

"Is that me? My goodness, I didn't know I was so pretty." Emily gave Aurelia's shoulder a gentle pat, feeling pleased when she didn't flinch. As long as Emily kept her touch light and didn't overdo it, physical contact now seemed to be okay. "It's a wonderful picture, sweetie, but I think you've forgotten someone. Where are *you*?"

A line appeared between Aurelia's dark eyebrows. She pointed to a gray smudge in the right-hand corner.

Emily peered at the smudge. Underneath a mass of gray scribbles was the outline of yet another, smaller stick figure. "Oh dear, you're all crossed out. Did you make a mistake? Never mind, let's try again. I'll help you."

Aurelia huffed and slumped back in her chair.

Emily reached for a new piece of paper, then stopped. She looked back at the smudge. At the top, the lines of crayon were heavier and darker, and just above the faint figure she could almost make out a purple semicircle. At the bottom, underneath the figure, was a full circle drawn in blue. The crayon here had been pressed so hard that the paper had almost torn. Over the top of the smudge, just above the thicker gray lines, were two bright-yellow zigzags.

Aurelia hadn't crossed herself out, Emily realized. It wasn't a smudge. It was a cloud. The scribbles were rain. The blue bit at the bottom was a puddle, and the semicircle was an umbrella. The zigzags were lightning bolts. Aurelia had drawn a storm.

It reminded Emily of something, but she couldn't think what . . . and then a memory came to her, so sharp it almost physically hurt. She was in Dr. Forte's office, chubby and knock-kneed, sitting in front of a round table covered with butcher's paper. Pencils, markers, and small pots of paint sat in front of her. Her hands were covered in black ink.

Great work, Emily. Can you tell me a bit about your picture?

On the paper, a swirl of black lines.

What did you draw?

The walls were white. The windows and doors were open to let in a breeze.

How does it make you feel?

Dr. Forte smiled and raised her hand for a high five. *Swoosh, slap.* Emily's palm came away red and stinging.

A whack on Emily's arm brought her back to the pool, to the kitchen, to the dining-room table. She looked down. Aurelia was staring up at her with a fierce expression.

"Sorry, sweetie." Emily paused. She felt dizzy, disorientated. "Sorry. I was miles away. Here, uh, let's draw something to-gether." Replacing the storm picture with a clean sheet of paper, she pulled the box of crayons closer.

Without taking her eyes from Emily's face, Aurelia snatched up an orange crayon and pressed hard onto the paper.

Emily took a deep breath to ease the chill that had just crawled under her skin. Another memory: Dr. Forte again, but this time Juliet was in the room, too. A hushed conversation was being conducted over her head. *Her suffering is buried in her subconscious,* Dr. Forte was saying, *it's part of her now.* Emily remembered crying that night, sobbing to Juliet that there was something wrong with her, something rotten and defective inside that made her do bad things. But Juliet had held her close and explained about the hidden memories. *It's not your fault,* Juliet said, and stroked Emily's hair until she fell asleep.

Another slap brought her back to the kitchen. Aurelia was glaring again. She stabbed a finger at her new picture. Emily looked down and saw a big square house with blue shutters and a red roof. Above it, a giant butterfly hovered among silver clouds. For some reason, Emily's eyes filled with tears.

"I love it," she said, tracing the outline of the house with her finger. "The shutters are like the ones on your house. Very French. *Très bien.*"

Aurelia looked up sharply. The look on her face was one of recognition mixed with wary enthusiasm, like a student too shy to raise her hand in class.

Emily's heart melted. Nina must have been teaching her some French. "You know what that means, do you? Clever girl. How about this: *tu es très douée.* Do you know what *douée* means?"

Aurelia remained silent, but her anger was gone. Her usual scowl rearranged itself into a small, sweet smile. It was beautiful.

"It means," Emily said, tapping Aurelia on the nose, "you're very talented."

"That's right, she is," said Nina, hurrying back down the steps and into the kitchen, a stack of wine bottles in her arms. "My straight-A student, aren't you, Strawberry? Give it a few years and we'll be fighting off the fancy universities with a stick."

University? Emily looked away. Aurelia was a socially impaired mute with a serious medical condition. It was hard to imagine her surviving a day at primary school, let alone anything beyond.

"You don't think so?" Nina said, catching Emily's expression. She pushed the last of the bottles into the fridge and swung the door shut. "Mark my words, when the time comes, this one will outdo us all. Won't you, bubba? Just as long as you keep up with your medication."

At the sink, Nina filled a glass with water from the tap. Pulling two small white tablets from her pocket, she crossed to the table and placed both the glass and the pills in front of Aurelia. Emily watched as Aurelia placed the tablets on her tongue and washed them down with several gulps of water.

"Good girl. And don't forget your sunscreen." Nina turned back to the kitchen, sweeping a slender wrist across her forehead. Her cheeks were pink and glistening with perspiration. "Right then, Strawberry, chop-chop. Let's get a few more pictures done so we can hang them all up. Emily, what on earth's the matter?"

"What?" Emily looked up and realized she'd been frowning. "Oh, no, nothing. I was just trying to think what else needs doing, but, honestly, the place looks great."

"Great isn't good enough," Nina said, her back turned. "It has to be perfect."

After Nina declared the banner to be finished, she hustled Emily and Aurelia to the guesthouse. Earlier that morning, Yves had delivered about a dozen more parcels—some big, some small—and lots of flat, squashy packets, leaving them in a pile on the steps of the guesthouse. Nina had barely even got them through the door before she started ripping through the tape of each one, tearing at the cardboard, and throwing little polystyrene shapes into the air like confetti. She pulled out new artwork, ornaments, bedding, toys, and lots and lots of new clothes.

"Whoa," said Emily. "It's like Oxford Circus just vomited all over the hallway."

"Come on," said Nina, laughing. "Let's go try it all on."

They dragged all the clothes up to Emily's bedroom and closed all the curtains. Once the sunlight was sufficiently blocked, Nina helped Aurelia take off her long smock dress, and Emily tried not to stare as Aurelia's scrawny body emerged from the material. Her skin was so white that it seemed to glow, her limbs awkward and vulnerable without her protective clothing.

When Nina stepped out of her own clothes it was like looking at the opposite side of the same coin. Long and lithe, Nina was extremely confident and comfortable in her own bronzed skin. Tugging her tank top (her "singlet," she called it) over her head, she tossed it onto the floor with a flick of her wrist, then wriggled out of her denim shorts. She straightened up with no shame or apology—shoulders back, hips forward, back arched—and once again Emily couldn't help but stare. Nina's underwear was made of satin and lace, and hugged her curves and angles in just the right way: no indent, no muffin top, nothing. It was ridiculous. Even her stretch marks were elegant, a faint silvery ladder climbing the sides of her hips, reaching for her implausibly flat belly. Emily almost reached out to stroke them.

"What do you think of this?" Nina asked, dropping a floaty blue dress over her shoulders.

Emily had to place her hand over her mouth to stop her jaw from dropping all the way to the floor. "Yeah, it's great. I like it," she said haltingly.

"I'm not sure," Nina said, standing in front of the full-length mirror and biting her lip. "Do you think it's a bit much?"

For what, the Oscars? "No, I think it's amazing."

"But d'you reckon Scott will like it? I mean, it's not like I can wear it out anywhere."

"Scott will love it. He's bonkers if he doesn't."

Nina smiled. *"Bonkers . . . ,"* she said, in an exaggerated Northern accent. She turned back to check her reflection in the mirror and blew a nervous breath through pursed lips. "Yes," she murmured. "He'll like it."

Emily looked from Nina's reflection to her own and felt a little queasy. It was like peering into a dark hole after staring at the sun.

In the middle of the room, Aurelia twirled in a long candy-striped sundress, a half smile on her lips and her arms in the air, her skinny wrists emerging from the fabric like flower stamens from their petals. No longer grumpy and agitated, she looked like a stoned hippie at a music festival, oblivious to everything around her. The pills had clearly worked.

"Emily."

"Hmm?" Emily glanced up to find Nina regarding her quizzically

"What's up with you today? You're so serious."

"Am I?" Emily shook her head. "Sorry, I—"

"Here, try these on," Nina said, throwing a couple of dresses at her. "They ought to fit just fine."

They didn't, of course, and Emily felt stupid and frumpy, standing there in her Marks & Spencer knickers while Nina yanked and pulled and tweaked, trying to force the black silky gown to accommodate Emily's vastly different body shape.

"Hmm," said Nina, eventually admitting defeat. Then she clicked her fingers. "Wait here; I have just the thing." She slipped out of the room, leaving Emily and Aurelia alone among the boxes.

An uncomfortable hush fell between them.

"Well." Emily looked around her bedroom and tried to think of something to say. "This is a big old mess."

In response, Aurelia bent low and picked up an armful of tissue paper. Throwing it into the air, she rotated slowly as it floated down around her like snowflakes. Emily pulled more paper out of more boxes and hurled it into the air, kicking it as it came down, then stamping through the piles as if through mounds of autumn leaves. Aurelia laughed, so Emily found some polystyrene packing peanuts and sprinkled them over her own head. Aurelia watched the peanuts fall with glassy eyes. She began to sway again.

Emily frowned. "Hey."

Aurelia was staring past her.

"Hey . . ." Emily stepped closer. "Are you okay?"

Slowly, Aurelia rocked back and forth.

"My goodness," said a voice from the corner.

Emily spun around. Nina was standing in the doorway with her hand on her hip, surveying the mess with irritation. Emily felt strangely abashed, but then Nina grinned. "Look at you two," she said, shaking her head. "My girls. Like kids in a candy store." Crossing the room, she held out a swathe of material, offering it to Emily.

"Wow," Emily breathed. The dress was beautiful, a deep olive green with a full skirt and thin spaghetti straps. She lifted her arms as Nina raised it ceremoniously over her head, and the silk flowed over her body like warm milk from a jug. Surprisingly, it fit.

Aurelia briefly stopped swaying. Her eyes were locked on the green dress. Slowly, she wandered over and swished the skirt a few times with her hands before resuming her swirling stoned-hippie dance.

Nina stood back, an unreadable look on her face. "It's yours," she said.

"What? No." Emily had glimpsed the label. It must have cost a fortune.

Nina shrugged. "I've never even worn it."

"You can't give away something like this. It'd look so much better on you, anyway."

Nina shook her head and lightly brushed the straps with her fingertips. "No," she said eventually. "I've changed too much."

Gazing past Nina at her own reflection in the mirror, Emily saw a different person. The green silk had transformed her into someone new. She pushed out her chest and arched her back. She smiled, and the new person smiled back.

And next to her, spinning and drifting like a paper bag caught in a light breeze, Aurelia smiled, too.

We sit on plastic chairs, our bodies curled like parentheses around the cot. She is a princess trapped in a forest of thorns. Wires hang all around like vines, and evil-looking machinery towers over her little body. I hate them. I want to rip them all away, hack them down and break whatever evil spell has been cast so I can carry my baby away to safety.

Instead, I massage my neck with my free hand. I've been sitting at the same awkward angle for hours. I could have moved, but in the absence of any other helpful course of action, sitting has taken on a symbolic significance. It's my penance, the only way to pay my dues—or a fraction of them, at least. No moving, no eating, no washing, nothing. Just this constant vigil.

Finally, when I can stand the pain no longer, I shift in my chair and a wave of nausea almost knocks me down.

On the other side of the cot, my husband twitches. Reaches into his pocket. Looks at his phone.

"What?" I ask.

"Nothing. Just work. They're on their way to the awards."

The awards. Such a big deal just a few days ago, but now I can barely remember the details. Some big industry accolade. His company was nominated for the first time. He's been looking forward to the ceremony for months. I was supposed to go with him. He bought me a dress. Olive-green silk with a cinched waist and a long, flowing skirt. I picture it hanging limply in the closet at home.

His phone buzzes again. He stands up and walks across the room. Puts it on a table in a corner. Walks back. Sits down again.

Don't look so fucking sad, I want to say. *There'll be other awards.* When this is all over and our baby is better, there will be more parties, more events, more silky dresses. We could even bring her along, when she's a little older. She'd love that. She could sit on my lap and cheer.

Parties and dresses . . . what's wrong with me? I want to punch my own face. I feel so guilty, so disgusted with myself.

I stroke my daughter's achingly soft cheek, her little nose, her hot forehead. I trace the curve of her ear and smooth the velvety place where her hairline begins. I press my lips to her temple and gaze into her eyes, studying the extraordinary shapes and patterns of her iris. All children are unique, blah blah blah, but I know that my baby is special beyond compare. The proof is everywhere: in the lift and wave of her hair, her sweet-as-honey skin, and the unspeakable beauty of her eyes. Both are a deep chocolatey brown with honeyed swirls and nicks of gold, and the right eye holds a little surprise. Northwest of the pupil, there's a spot of pure blue like a single rock pool left behind by the tide. I noticed it when she was about six months old, once the standard newborn gray-blue had started to change. It was like a stamp, a seal—confirmation that she was different.

An icy horror sticks its fingers in my belly. I can't lose her. My precious miracle. They said it would never happen. I will never forget those clammy hands on my body, prodding and pressing in a different hospital room far, far away. They said I was broken. But they were wrong.

I see the car again. The tree. The twisted metal. My memories are razor-sharp diamonds. They cut me and make me bleed. But I'm also grateful for them. I hold them close. I'm thankful for everything that happened because it led me here. It led me to her.

I let my head fall against the metal frame of the cot and silently repeat my vow. The promise I've made to her every single day since she was born.

I promise I will always love you

I will always protect you.

I will do anything to keep you safe.

And I will never, ever let you go.

CHAPTER TWENTY-FOUR

SCOTT

Scott spent the entire flight dreading his arrival at Querencia. He worried about how Nina would greet him, how she might speak to him. He worried about how much Aurelia might have changed, and what new challenges she might present. Most of all, he worried about Emily. He felt sure Nina would have told him if anything had gone wrong; but then again, Nina was unpredictable.

He reassured himself that he'd know as soon as he saw her, that he'd read her like a book. And he did, though not immediately. The formal reception threw him off.

As the car rolled through the gates, Scott leaned forward, staring slack-jawed at the three smiling figures in cocktail gowns standing on the front steps of the family house. He almost laughed—was this a setup, or a performance of some sort?—but the sound snagged in his throat. He blinked, unsure of what he was seeing. There was Nina, his wife, all sharp angles and ice-blond hair, pure Hollywood in a strapless blue gown. But next to her, like a ghost, stood the old Nina, the girl he'd fallen in love with. She was soft, joyful, and full of life, wearing the olive-green dress he'd bought her all those years before, the dress he'd never seen her in. The memory strangled him.

But then the old Nina vanished and in her place was Emily, his sweet-vanilla employee, his one good choice. But she was different somehow: there was something in the spread of her shoulders, the length of her spine. Scott narrowed his eyes as the car pulled up. He craned his neck; he needed to see her face, read her expression. As his eyes finally met hers through the windshield, she lit up like a flare. Her smile was genuine, and Scott felt his joints come undone with relief.

Only then did he let his gaze drop to the smallest of the group. As always, Aurelia's dark eyes were serious under her straw hat, her mouth a thin scratch at the bottom of her face. But there were subtle changes in her, too. Her skin was brighter, healthier, and Scott realized that she must have been outside a great deal more than Nina had let on.

He got out of the car, and the trio seemed to move as one, gliding down the steps to greet him. Contrary to his expectations, Nina put on a very convincing show. Smiling, she led him straight to the poolside for dinner, where a crude welcome banner swayed in the breeze. The table was set with candles in tall glass jars. The shrubs and pampas grasses were shot through with gold as the sun sank toward the ocean, and the pool glittered with silver ripples. If all of that wasn't enchanting enough, she slipped a hand in his and their fingers interlaced. Instinctively, he gave her fingers a squeeze, but quickly jolted himself awake. He mustn't slide into the fantasy. It was important to stay alert.

Both Nina and Emily fussed over him, pouring drinks and asking him the usual surface questions. How was his flight? How had his week been? Was he enjoying his meal? Would he like any more wine? They interacted comfortably, like old friends, and Scott let their chatter wash over him as he studied each of their faces. He had no idea what Nina was really thinking, but Emily was an open book: she was doing that nervous twittering bird thing again, talking nonstop and hopping from subject to subject. However, as dusk drew in and the wine flowed, she seemed to relax.

He watched her leaning back in her chair with her tanned legs crossed and her head tipped back, wineglass dangling from a floppy wrist. She was filled with a boldness he hadn't yet seen. He was mesmerized by her mouth, the way her lips parted and rejoined, then stretched wide as she laughed. She and Nina seemed to be laughing a great deal. Scott struggled to remember the last time he'd made Nina laugh like that.

Shifting uncomfortably in his chair, he reached across the table and plucked a toothpick from a small dish, folding it into his palm.

From the other side of the table, Aurelia eyeballed him from behind a vase of lavender. He ignored her, cocking his head at Nina instead, hoping he would catch her eye and she'd let him in on the joke. Candlelight flickered over his wife's delicate features, exaggerating her cheekbones. She was smiling, but he could see through it. Scott knew what her happiness looked like, and it wasn't this.

Without once taking his eyes from his wife's face, he took the toothpick between the thumb and forefinger of his right hand and quietly, secretly, inserted it under the middle fingernail of his left.

CHAPTER TWENTY-FIVE

EMILY

Aₜₜ... After DINNER, Scott, Nina, and Aurelia all went up to the
house together for a bedtime story, leaving Emily alone at
the table. She sipped prosecco while she waited for them to come
back, crossing and recrossing her legs and enjoying the feel of
the green silk on her freshly shaved skin. She felt amazing: dizzy
and starry-eyed and fuzzy at the edges. So, so happy.

"Well, I have to say, I've never seen the place looking so
good," said Scott, sauntering back down the steps and returning to his seat. Nina came floating after him with a strangely
vacant look on her face. "You girls have been working hard."
He reached for the open bottle in the ice bucket and poured
himself a glass.

Emily blushed, the prosecco popping on her tongue. "There's
still so much to do," she said, turning to Nina with a grin. "And
some days we make pretty slow progress, don't we?"

"Don't be fooled by all this *we* stuff. I haven't done much at
all," Nina said, sitting down with her legs folded neatly underneath her. "Emily is a machine."

Emily beamed. She *had* been working hard. The hedges were
neater, the flowers brighter, and the grass greener. The driveway was spotless (she'd painstakingly raked the sand herself

that very afternoon until not one petal or leaf remained), and both houses were glowing. Since arriving she'd not only been busy with the interior of the guesthouse, she'd also washed the mold from the brickwork, repainted the shutters, and put out new window boxes. The windowpanes sparkled, the steps were swept, and all the new additions artfully arranged in all the right places: a crisp doormat here, a bronze lantern there. On the lawn, a croquet set and brand-new outdoor furniture setting— white with mint-green cushions—now stood under strings of fairy lights. The whole place was now ready for its close-up.

Scott raised his glass. "Well, then. Here's to you, Emily."

"Oh, well," Emily stammered, her cheeks warm. "Obviously it's not *all* me. Yves has been working hard, too. I could never have installed that lighting system by myself, or dug the trench for all the wires."

Scott paused. "Lighting system?" he asked, glancing at Nina. "Yves didn't mention anything about that on the way down."

Nina shrugged. "It's just a few uplighters. The grounds are so dark at night."

"How many?" Scott's expression was polite, interested, but Emily detected a change in his voice.

"Oh, I can't remember." Nina's eyes dropped to her lap.

"No, really. How many?"

Nina didn't reply.

Emily looked at her, then back at Scott. "Fourteen, wasn't it?" she prompted, proud of what they'd achieved. "Don't worry, we were very thorough."

Scott raised an eyebrow.

"It looks so good," Emily said. "You'll see."

His black eyes sent a shiver of pleasure up her spine. She let her fingers drift over the folds of her dress, the seat of her chair, the wooden tabletop. She picked up a spoon and ran the curved metal over her forearms, her chin, her lips. Everything felt incredible.

She paid close attention to Nina, noting the way she swept

her hand through her hair, the way she bit her lip when she was listening to someone. She copied her, trying the same movements out on her own body. She stole looks at Scott, telling herself not to gawk, but she'd now had far too much to drink and was admiring them both openly. They didn't seem to mind; they were probably used to people staring. They were like movie stars: stunning but in a weird blurry way, like an optical illusion. They behaved like movie stars, too. It was like they were acting in a series of rapidly changing scenes: dark and brooding one minute, joyful the next. Emily thought of what she'd heard back at Proem: *he hates her; you can just tell*. Well, that certainly wasn't the impression Emily was getting. They couldn't keep their eyes off each other.

There *was* something slightly off, though, especially in Nina's body language. At any given moment, she might be leaning toward Scott with her arms wrapped around herself; or beaming at him while angling her hips away, closing herself off. Emily had learned to analyze physicality in acting class, and there were some very mixed messages being thrown around.

She watched them watching her watching them, wondering if the feeling in her belly was admiration or jealousy. Probably a little of both, she decided. Resting her head on the back of the chair, she stretched her legs out under the table and stared at the fire in the brazier. Sparks rose from the flames like paper lanterns, and for some reason she was reminded of something she'd seen at a museum once: a short film narrated in a slick, booming voice about the uncharted vastness of the universe and the comparative insignificance of planet Earth. It said that the sun would one day die, and then so would all of human life, and Emily had felt sick with fear at the smallness and the hugeness and the futility of it all. Sitting there at the table, that same sense of hugeness returned, except the fear was replaced with hope and joy, and a conviction that the very opposite was true: that everything mattered.

She closed her eyes, breathing in the magic.

Somewhere close by, a voice whispered in the dark. She heard the scrape of a chair on the flagstones, the brush of bare toes on the floor. Something lightly skimmed her shoulders—*fingertips*—and under the table, a foot nudged against hers.

CHAPTER TWENTY-SIX

SCOTT

I N THE morning, Scott woke up alone. He didn't remember going to bed, but there he was, naked and twisted in the sheets. Nina was nowhere to be seen, and there was no evidence to suggest she'd even slept there.

Shivering, he rolled away from the sweaty imprint his body had made in the mattress. Peeling the damp sheets off his skin as he went, he swung his legs over the edge of the bed. There were sounds coming from outside: laughter, and the clink of plates. He checked the time and was surprised to find that it was already past ten.

He showered, dressed, and made his way downstairs. In the kitchen, he was greeted by the smell of coffee and a table laden with food. There was a freshly baked baguette, butter, home-made jam, swirls of pastry, granola, and a rainbow of fresh fruit. Under an upturned dish, he found several rashers of bacon and two poached eggs, still warm. He ate standing up, listening out for the voices he'd heard earlier, but there was no sign of the girls.

When after half an hour they still hadn't appeared, he went looking for them, ambling around both houses and through the gardens; opening and shutting doors; peeping around corners and over hedges. He could hear them. They were nearby but, it seemed, invisible. He became irritated, convinced they were watching him from some little hidey-hole and sniggering at his confusion. But finally, after hearing a squeal coming from the very bottom of the property, he knew just where to look.

Just beyond the low wall that separated Querencia from the cliffs, there was a spot where the rocks sloped and flattened out, the layers of stone reaching like fingers for the creeping tide. A narrow track led down to a precarious wooden walkway on stilts, at the end of which was an ancient fishing hut. It was sun-bleached and rather wonky, the weather having warped the timber long ago, but the *carrelet* was one of Scott's favorite places to while away an hour or two. Nina hated it, though— the way the shack swayed over the water made her seasick—so he was both amazed and delighted when, as he climbed over the wall and made his way down the walkway, he found his wife leaning over the railing and pointing at the ocean with a huge smile on her face.

Next to her, Emily and Aurelia bounced up and down with glee as they pressed the button that lowered the pulley-operated net. The rusty mechanism screeched as it got going, masking the sound of Scott's steps, enabling him to creep up behind Nina and wrap his arms around her waist, lifting her off the ground. Her laughter bounced off the rocks and skipped into a bluebird sky, joining the seagulls whirling overhead.

They stayed for hours, the four of them taking turns to lower the net. They caught shrimp, river herring, bass, and even a lamprey eel, all of which they threw back at Aurelia's wordless insistence. Then Emily pulled lunch from a wicker hamper: cold meats, cheeses, and another baguette, and a chilled bottle of Sancerre.

Croquet followed, rowdy and hilarious, on the lawn between the houses. Emily was adorable, all knees and elbows and completely incapable of hitting the ball in the right direction.

After that, they all jumped in the pool, and Emily led them in a series of games and races. Marco Polo, inflatable relays, noodle jousting, sharks and minnows. Scott was taken aback, first by how well Aurelia could swim (she could barely float the last time he'd been in the water with her), and then by how much he enjoyed himself. It felt good to let go and get competitive, to splash and shout and cheer like an idiot, to flick the water from his hair and feel his body grow weak with laughter.

He felt young again, the atmosphere charged with a powerful energy reminiscent of school camps and teenage parties. He found himself touching Nina often, laying an arm over her shoulders or a hand on her neck, flicking a glance at Emily to see if she was watching. She always was.

By six thirty that afternoon, Scott had changed his mind about Nina. Maybe she really *was* happy. Maybe his plan was working, the Band-Aid holding. Or maybe it was just the gin. Either way, things were looking up.

He lay in a deck chair, slopping his drink—his third or fourth—around in his glass, listening to the ice cubes clinking merrily together and drifting off into a half snooze. He was vaguely aware of the sleepy smile on his face, his lowered eyelids and wobbling head, but he couldn't muster any degree of self-control. He didn't care enough. Everything was fine. Fine, fine, fine.

Laughter rang out to his left.

"There are all kinds of patterns and pictures in the night sky, Aurelia. Can you think of any?"

"The Plough!"

"Gold star for effort, Em, but how about we let Aurelia answer the next one?"

"Sorry, I'm overexcited!"

"Remember, Aurelia? Orion's Belt? Looks like a saucepan? We'll look for that one first."

The girls were gathered around the patio table, on which sat a huge astronomical telescope. It had turned up earlier, a huge black box sitting on the front doorstep like some alien space-ship, presumably delivered by Yves while they were all in the pool. Ordinarily, Scott would've balked at the sight of yet another needless purchase, but his irritation was tempered by the sight of Nina, Aurelia, and Emily all running up to the box like kids to an ice-cream truck. The telescope, ordered online and tenuously justified by the fact that Aurelia had shown interest in a homeschool astronomy lesson, was sleek, shiny, and apparently extremely complicated. The girls had been deciphering the instruction manual for what felt like hours.

Scott continued to listen as he dozed.

"This is going to be so cool," Emily was saying. "I used to love stargazing when I was a kid. We never had a telescope, though. We just went outside and looked up."

"A long time ago," Nina said, "people used the stars to navigate. Did you know that, Aurelia? By day, sailors would use the position of the sun, but at night they looked at the sky to find their way. Now, of course, they use computers and satellites, but explorers didn't have any of those back then."

"Imagine that, Aurelia," said Emily. "Hundreds of years ago, if I wanted to sail home from here I would've followed the pattern of the stars."

Under the clink and screw of the telescope parts, Nina's voice was steady. "Don't be silly, sweetheart," she said, "you're already home."

CHAPTER TWENTY-SEVEN

EMILY

"TOP UP?"

Emily nodded and moved her glass too quickly, almost shattering the rim against the thick green neck of the bottle. "Shit." A giggle popped out of her mouth like a hiccup. "Too eager."

Scott upended the bottle into her glass. "Another one bites the dust," he said, shaking out the last drops.

They were sitting at the edge of the pool with their feet in the water, so close that their upper arms were touching. The tiles under their skin were still warm from the heat of the day, though the sun had long ago dipped below the horizon. A full pink moon hung spectacularly above their heads. The light was silver, the air like satin, and every now and then, the toes of Emily's left foot would bump up against Scott's right ankle. His musky, woody smell filled her nose.

She sipped the prosecco, knowing that this would be the glass that would tip her over the edge. She hadn't meant to get quite so drunk, not after last night (she'd woken up that morning on top of the sheets, still in the olive-green dress, with a vague memory of stumbling up the driveway clinging onto Nina like a wayward toddler), but the day had been so fun, so perfect, that her resolve to stay sober had crumbled before lunch.

"You sucked at croquet today," Scott said, chuckling.

"That may be true," she replied archly, draining her glass, "but *you* sucked at Marco Polo."

"Are you kidding? I was on fire."

"You didn't catch one person. Even Aurelia was too fast for you."

"I was deliberately holding back. I didn't want to scare anyone with my mad skills."

"Mad skills?"

"Or whatever the kids say these days." He grinned. "I'll get you next time."

"Is that a challenge?" Emily shot back.

He turned and considered her, his eyelids heavy. Then he put down his glass and stood up. "Come on, then. Rematch."

Her heart thumped.

He took his shirt off.

She couldn't help it. She looked up.

He towered above her, one hand resting lightly on his hip, the moonlight bouncing off the contours of his chest. Emily's stomach lurched violently and she looked away, but it was too late. She'd already seen the curve of his pecs and the pattern of dark hair that traveled in a lazy line all the way down to his belly button. She sneaked another peek and glimpsed a deep "V" of muscle disappearing beneath the waistband of his shorts. Something pounded in her body, something other than her heartbeat, and she had to bite the insides of her cheeks to stop herself from giggling.

Nina came sliding silently out of the shadows, startling them both. "Aurelia's asleep," she said, and Emily looked away guiltily. *I was most definitely not staring at your husband's sex lines. Nope. Wasn't me.*

"Going for a swim?" Nina asked.

"Thinking about it," replied Scott. "Her idea," he added, pointing at Emily.

Emily cringed. Maybe it *had* been her idea, but she'd only been joking—she was drunk. She didn't for a second think that he'd actually get up and whip his shirt off. And now, it seemed, he was waiting for her to do the same. *No way,* she thought, grasping the material of her dress as if to stop it from sliding off her body of its own accord. *No one needs to see what's under here.*

But then there was a splash and Nina was gone, nothing but a puddle of blue silk in her place. She popped up in the pool some distance away, her teeth flashing white against a continuation of smooth dark skin, broken only by two triangles of creamy white. Emily didn't know where to look. There was no sign of swimwear or underwear or any kind of wear.

Scott cannonballed into the water, hooting like a lunatic, sending up a spray of silver droplets. "Shush, you'll wake Aurelia," Nina said, but her words were swallowed up by the slap and rush of the water.

And then they both turned expectantly toward Emily, their faces distorted by the underwater lights, and maybe it was the prosecco or the vodka martinis or the adrenaline, but Emily felt her inhibitions fly away into the dark. *Oh, who cares,* she thought, or maybe she said it out loud, because both Scott and Nina laughed. They were both so beautiful, and they made Emily beautiful because she was part of them now, she belonged here in this crazy paradise, and if she was good enough for them, she was good enough for the sweet night air, the twinkling water, and the barefaced moon.

She let her straps fall over her shoulders, and her dress slipped off her body like butter from a hot knife. Cupping her naked boobs in her hands and giving not even one fuck about her plain cotton knickers or her belly fat, she laughed at her own audacity.

"And I'm freeeeeeeee!" she sang as she ran full-pelt toward the pool. "FREE-FALLING!"

She jumped.

For a moment, she hung suspended in the air. The world turned around her. Then she plunged into the water, the surface closing over her head with a snap.

Slippery limbs bumped against her skin.

Oh god. So drunk. So very, very drunk.

She let the water hold her. It carried her to the surface and pushed her up into the violet night where she shut her eyes, afraid of what she might see. She heard them instead: Scott first, then Nina, murmuring in her ear then calling softly from a distance.

"Marco."

"Polo."

They were everywhere and nowhere, all at once.

CHAPTER TWENTY-EIGHT

SCOTT

SCOTT STOOD on the lawn looking up at the tree, unsure of what to do with himself. He felt somewhat better than he had a couple of hours ago, having taken a handful of acetaminophen and not just one but two showers, but his skin still felt grimy and his head still sore. Mystifyingly, he seemed to be the only one with a hangover; both Emily and Nina were bright and energetic, having already smashed through a quarter of their scheduled jobs before he'd even opened his eyes.

"Morning, sleepyhead," Emily had trilled as he'd wandered out of the family house after breakfast, sweeping past him on the driveway with a rake in one hand and a leaf blower in the other. Her cheerfulness had bounced off him like an uncaught ball.

Feeling a bit redundant, he ambled around the garden for a while, eventually finding himself at the shed. He grabbed randomly at the tools, selecting a pair of shears with the intention of making himself useful, but by three o'clock all he'd achieved was a few snips at a hedge and a long and thoughtful contemplation of a vine-covered trellis on the south wall of the guesthouse. He couldn't keep his thoughts straight. What the hell had happened in the pool last night? Had they really all been naked?

190

Had they fallen asleep on the daybed afterward, their heads on each other's shoulders, their legs entwined . . . or had he dreamed that? If it *had* happened, how had he got back to his room? A bus could've driven through the holes in his memory.

Rather than feeling awkward, though, he felt good. Great, in fact. Better than he had in years. Despite the furry tongue and the delicate stomach, he felt light. Buoyant. And *whole*, somehow.

Scott was still standing there staring at the vines, waiting for his brain to catch up with his body, when Aurelia appeared. One minute he was alone, and the next she was there, a little old lady in a long-sleeved dress, barefoot in the grass, arms hanging limply by her sides.

Reflexively, he glanced around for Nina. "Well, hello there, cheeky monkey," he said at last. "What are you up to?"

Aurelia fixed him with a stony look.

There was a slight movement at the kitchen window. Looking up, he saw his wife standing by the sink, staring out at them with a cluster of wineglasses in her hands. She raised her eyebrows at him, then put the glasses down so she could make an emphatic shooing action with her hands. *Go do something with your daughter.*

Scott groaned inwardly, his strange new happiness fading fast. He'd been ambushed. "So," he said to the straw brim of Aurelia's hat. "I hear Mummy bought you a pony."

She continued to stare him down.

Scott snuck a look back at the window. Nina was still watching. "Shall we go and visit him?"

Aurelia contemplated his question like it was a riddle. Then, seemingly unable to find a catch, she turned and set off in the direction of the animal sheds.

Sighing, Scott followed her.

The horse, apparently, was called Sebastien. He was small and brown. He flicked his tail as they approached and turned his head away. *For the love of god,* thought Scott, *a horse? What use is it to anyone?*

Aurelia looked at Scott as if she expected him to do something clever, like leap onto the pony's back and jump the fence.

"Are you, uh, going to feed him?" he asked her.

She shook her head.

"Have you ridden him yet?"

She shook her head.

"Do you want to?"

Head shake.

They stood in silence for a moment. Scott stretched out his hand. "Here, boy," he said.

Sebastien gave Scott a look that said, *Make me,* then wandered off into a corner.

"Well, that was fun," said Scott. "What do you want to do now?"

They walked back toward the house. Scott cast about for an activity. "Wanna play tennis?"

Aurelia shrugged.

"That's the spirit."

On the tennis court, Scott reached into the wooden storage box to retrieve balls and racquets. "Here you go." He passed her a small pink racquet and he took a larger green one. "Alright, Serena Williams. Let's see what you've got."

Aurelia looked at him blankly. Scott gave her a little nudge and she shuffled off to one side of the net. He positioned himself opposite, his mood suddenly lifting as he spun the racquet by its handle and bounced the ball on the asphalt. He loved tennis. He and Eddie used to play when they were young, before they lost the house. It was possible he played with his father, too. He had a hazy memory of Terrence bouncing around in a sweatband and white shorts, but who was to say if that was real or not. He might have just made it up.

Scott served gently to Aurelia. Motionless, she watched as the ball flew past her.

"Okay. That's good, you kept your eye on it. That's tennis one oh one. Now let's see if you can hit it." He served again, and Aurelia swung her racquet limply.

"Great try," Scott said, giving her the thumbs-up. "How about you swing it a little higher this time, and with a bit more force. Like this." He showed her.

He tried to serve so the ball would be easy for Aurelia to reach, but it seemed to sail right through her. She stood still for a moment and then threw the racquet angrily toward the net, her little brows knotted with fury.

"Easy, McEnroe!" Scott laughed. "No need for violence."

But Aurelia didn't even crack a smile. She glared at him, a flush beginning to creep into her cheeks.

"Okay, don't get upset. I'll come and give you a hand." He walked around to her side of the net and reached out to pat her on the head. "Don't worry, you'll soon get the—"

The kick came out of nowhere. Suddenly she was on him, hitting, biting, scratching, grunting, her lips pulled back over bared teeth. A jagged, hate-filled scream tore through Scott's eardrums and rattled his jaw.

"What the . . . ?" He staggered backward, trying to catch hold of her skinny arms, but they were moving so fast and with such fierce intent that he only succeeded in blocking a few blows. She was a tiny hurricane, out of control, spitting and snarling and coming at him again and again. Scott reeled; what should he do? Restrain her? The last time he'd tried that he'd left bruises, and Nina had punished him for months.

"Hey! Stop! Stop it!" he commanded, still backing away, trying to hold her at arm's length, but she pursued him with an animal ferocity, swiping at him with her nails. Her eyes were squeezed shut now, and Scott knew that she couldn't hear him; she'd gone to the dark place. "I'm sorry!" he yelled anyway. "I'm *sorry!*"

He felt twigs and leaves at his back and realized that she'd pushed him into the very corner of the court, right up against the bushes. She opened her eyes and unleashed a deafening wall of sound into his face. Saliva spilled from her mouth and ran down her chin.

He could feel his body collapsing, surrendering to the rage he had summoned and the retribution he deserved. Images swam in front of his eyes: a pillow, soft and plump. A tiny hand, one finger uncurled, pointing directly at him.

"I'm sorry," he repeated, his voice rising in volume to match Aurelia's. *"I'm sorry, I'm sorry, I'm sorry, I'm sorry, I'm sorry, I'M SORRY!"*

CHAPTER TWENTY-NINE

EMILY

"IF YOU'RE going to live in France," Nina said, "you need to know your wine."

Several dusty old bottles stood in a line on the guesthouse dining-room table along with ten sparkling glasses: five for Emily, and five for Nina.

"Let's start with the granddaddy of great reds. Bordeaux. Key grape varieties are merlot, cabernet sauvignon, and cabernet franc, but they're nearly all blends. For example, you might get a wine that's mostly merlot and cab sav, seasoned with some petit verdot or something. Are you with me?"

Emily nodded, totally enchanted—and not just by the wine. Slippery memories of soft skin and glittering water still clung to her like pixie dust. Her recollection was patchy at best—she'd been so drunk—but she knew it had been a *lot* of fun. She'd never been skinny-dipping before. So *wild*. And so silly. She put her hand over her mouth as her brain drip-fed her a series of details: trying to get out of the pool with dignity and failing; scooping up her dress and scurrying behind the daybed; losing her balance and falling in a bush; laughing so hard her stomach hurt.

"The name 'Bordeaux' is misleading, because the vines are

actually dotted all around the region. Sometimes you might buy a bottle that just says 'Bordeaux,' but most of the time you'll see the appellations. See here? Haut-Médoc. And this one: Pauillac. You don't pronounce the 'L's."

Emily gave it a try. *"Poy-ack."*

"Nice. And then there are the classifications, which concern the specific estates."

"Estates?"

"The vineyards themselves. Okay, so let's try one. This is a 2000 Château Pontet-Canet." Nina poured an inch or two into a glass for Emily and then one for herself. "So firstly, let's look at the color. Is it a deep red, or more scarlet? Brownish, or maybe even slightly orangey?"

"Um . . . browny-red?"

"Right. So this is a good clue as to age; the shade of red changes as the wine matures, turning more orange or brown. Next, a small swirl and a sniff. What can you smell?"

Emily stuck her nose into the glass and inhaled, careful to hide the violent roll of her stomach. "Alcohol?" *Hair of the dog,* she reassured herself. *Best hangover cure there is.*

"Yes. But what else?"

Emily tried again. She couldn't smell any fruit; actually, it sort of stank, but she was too embarrassed to say.

"Come on, what do you smell?" Nina said. "You can't get it wrong; it's very subjective."

Emily gave her an apologetic grin. "Honestly? It smells like a barnyard."

Nina laughed. "Well, I'd say more leather and spice, but a lot of these older wines are very complex, and not everyone can pick up on that. Well done. Okay, now, let's take a sip, but not too much. Maybe wash it around the mouth a little. Hold it in your mouth and then spit." She indicated an ice bucket.

They both drank from their glass, and Emily did as she was told, swilling the wine around like it was mouthwash. Her teeth suddenly felt furry, and the barnyard smell became overpowering. She spat into the ice bucket and clacked her tongue against her teeth. "Mmm. It's nice," she lied. "I think I can taste something fruity. Blackberries maybe?" She looked up at Nina for confirmation, but Nina wasn't looking back.

Something outside had caught Nina's attention. Then Emily heard it: a noise—no, a voice. Shouting. The same words over and over again.

"Is that Scott?" Emily said. Nina took a small step toward the door, and a drop of wine ran off her bottom lip, landing on her sundress. Her face was white. "Nina? Are you okay?"

But Nina was already running, tearing through the hallway and out the front door, an indistinct babble of words trailing behind her.

Then through the window, Emily saw them.

To the left of the guesthouse, movement in the trees.

People.

Lots of people, moving in a pack.

Outside, Nina was shouting. "Who are you? Why are you here?"

Standing at her side, Emily peered into the trees. She was able to make out six or seven figures—some men, some women—coming from the direction of the forest, all tramping through the long grass behind the basketball court.

"What are you doing? This is private property, you can't be here!" Nina had hurtled out of the house so fast it had taken a minute for Emily to catch up, but now she was bouncing on the spot, hopping from one foot to another like a boxer.

Emily froze as the people drew closer. Pale and silver-haired, they carried long objects at their sides. Guns? No, too thin. Sticks of some kind.

Emily's body itched to flee. *Run and hide,* it told her, but she couldn't. She was rooted to the spot.

But then she saw that the people were smiling and waving. One of them let out a cheerful holler: *"Ohé!"* They all wore khaki shorts and bandanas and long socks, and the sticks they held were just long poles. Walking sticks. "Nina, it's okay," she said. "I think they're hikers. Probably just lost."

But this didn't seem to comfort Nina. She ran toward the hikers and then backed away again, forward and away, forward and away. She spun in a circle, looking around with wild, rolling eyes. She clawed at her own hair and gasped for breath.

Emily frowned. They were just people. Surely there was nothing to be afraid of.

"*Bonjour,*" called one of the hikers as they drew closer. "*Désolé, nous sommes perdus.*"

"See? Lost," Emily murmured. It felt weird to see and hear strangers on the property after all this time.

The hikers slowed down, coming to a stop several meters away. A man with a gray beard and a red peaked cap edged ahead of the group. "*Nous voulions faire une balade au bord de la mer,*" he said, addressing Emily carefully. "*Nous pensions qu'il était possible d'escalader les rochers, mais . . .*" He trailed off and shrugged helplessly. "*La carte devait être fausse.*"

"What?" Nina hissed, close to tears. "What are you talking about? Emily, what are they saying?"

Emily looked at her, surprised. She'd assumed Nina spoke French. Hadn't she been teaching Aurelia? How had she lived here for so long without learning the language? Emily turned back to the Frenchman. He seemed harmless enough—sweet, even. "I think they're looking for a path," she said. "They thought they could . . . climb around the rocks."

"Liars!" Nina spat, and the hikers flinched.

Emily felt a stab of fear. "Nina, honestly, it's fine. They're just lost."

Tears began to spill down Nina's cheeks, and she whirled around again, searching for something. Scott, probably. *Great idea,* Emily thought. *A little help would be nice.*

She backed away, trying to give Nina some space. "It's alright. I'll deal with them." Turning back to the hikers with what she hoped was a reassuring smile, she summoned her rusty, halting French. "*Pardonnez-moi,*" she said. "*Je comprends. Je vais vous montrer la . . .*" She stopped. What was the French word for "exit"? "*. . . la sortie.*"

The hikers smiled back with relief. "*Ah, merci. Merci bien.*" The bearded man held out his hand. "*Moi, je m'appelle Guillaume, et voici—*"

"GET THE FUCK OUT!" Nina launched herself at them with her fists raised.

The group skittered backward, and someone yelped.

"Alright, come on, hurry up," Emily herded the frightened hikers away like cattle, up the driveway toward the gate, the man mumbling profuse apologies as they went. As soon as they were out of Nina's earshot, Emily whispered "*Je suis désolée. Elle est . . . malade.*" *She is not well.*

The hikers nodded and sped up, their faces white.

CHAPTER THIRTY

SCOTT

From the tennis court, Scott watched everything unfold. At first, he'd been confused, unsure if what he was seeing was real. There'd been so much noise—both he and Aurelia were bawling their lungs raw—and her blows weren't slowing, just getting faster and more frantic, and he thought the onslaught would never end. Then, thank God, he saw Nina sprinting out of the guesthouse, coming to rescue him. He called out, distracting Aurelia sufficiently for him to grab hold of her wrists, then waited, explanation at the ready, for Nina to reach them . . . but his relief vanished fast. Nina was not running in their direction.

When he saw the people in the trees, his blood ran cold. Who were they? How had they got there? But as he watched Nina sprint toward them, ranting and screeching, as he saw Emily dashing after her, a mixture of confusion and fear on her face, he knew he could do nothing but wait it out. Pulling Aurelia with him, he ducked down behind a hedge and silently willed Nina to come to her senses before she blew everything. He kept his lips shut and managed, somehow, to remain still. And, thankfully, so did Aurelia. She sat beside him in a ball, her knees drawn up, her arms wrapped around her bowed head. He placed a hand on her back and applied a degree of pressure.

Only when the unfortunate group had been safely herded off the property did Scott step out from his hiding place, pushing Aurelia in front of him. He knew he looked a state (he could feel the angry red lines rising on his face), but there was nothing to do but play dumb. What scratches? What ripped T-shirt? What bleeding lip?

Nina ignored him and ran straight to Aurelia, sweeping her up and dashing into the house in what seemed like one swift movement.

Emily looked so rattled that he wanted to pull her into a hug and stroke her hair, but instead he cracked a stupid joke and concocted some story about having crawled into a hedge during a game of hide-and-seek. "Look what a mess I'm in," he said. "Damn branches. Sharper than I thought." He could tell she wasn't convinced but didn't have the energy to dig for more. He made his excuses and went inside to look for Nina.

Upstairs, the sounds of a Disney movie spilled onto the landing from behind the bathroom door, accompanied by a cacophony of plops and splashes. He pushed the door open and found Aurelia sitting alone in a bubble bath, an iPad balanced on a nearby stool.

He found Nina standing in their bedroom, her willowy frame silhouetted against the open window.

"I'm sorry," she whispered, without turning around.

Scott gently pushed the door closed. "You could've—"

"Don't say it," Nina said. She bit her nails, her teeth clicking as they met.

Scott waited in silence.

When at last she turned around, her face was ashen. "She likes you."

"What?"

"Emily." Her voice was flat, her eyes cold. "You can sleep with her if you like. If it helps." A breeze slipped in through an open window, blowing a curtain across Nina's face, and for a moment it was as if she had vanished completely.

Scott did not reply. A shudder tumbled through his body. He was Orpheus walking out of the underworld, looking back at Eurydice only to see her shimmer and disappear like seeds in the wind.

I sit alone in a never-changing half-light. Nothing marks the passage of time in here, nothing except shift changes and the distant roll of trolleys—I think it might be evening, though. My girl is sleeping, but that's no real indication. She's been sleeping for days now.

My husband has gone for a walk. He says he needs fresh air; the room smells stale, but I can't imagine where he would go. I can't even remember what's outside the hospital. I can't remember anything at all. I refuse to think about anything except the movement of her chest. Rise. Fall. Rise. Fall.

What is she thinking in there? Is she scared? Can she hear anything? Does she know I'm here with her, that I haven't left her side for more than the couple of frantic seconds it takes to race to the toilet and back?

Yes, she knows. Of course she knows.

Earlier, the doctor came in. "I'm sorry to say," she said with a sad sideways look, "that she's not responding to the antibiotics as we hoped she would." She said some other things, too. Slippery things that didn't quite make sense. One word stuck out, though.

Damage.

Damage, damage, damage, damage.

Weird how that word has followed me around. *Damage control. Damaged goods. Irreparable damage.*

I lift my elbow off the cot frame and stand up, rolling back my shoulders and stretching my arms. I take small steps across the lino as if I am the sick one. I shuffle back and forth from one nothing-colored wall to another, taking small sips of air through sore, cracked lips. I am weak. I am pathetic. I am not Wonder Woman. I never was.

It dimly occurs to me that this might be a good time to go back on my meds, but there's no way to get them. I can't leave and I can't ask my husband; now's not the time for a confession. I glance at the door, wondering where the nurses keep all the drugs. Water, water everywhere, but not a drop to drink.

Something catches my eye, something bright on the table against the back wall.

It's his phone. A stream of texts lights up the screen, messages from people I've never heard of. Jolly, jubilant words. *Congratulations, mate. Warmest wishes. So happy for you. Well deserved.*

I read the little boxes as they appear, unable to understand what there is to be happy about . . . and then I remember the awards. They must have won.

The phone lights up again. And again. And again. I almost feel sad for him, that he's missing his big moment, that he's here in this stale-smelling hospital instead of standing on a stage. But it doesn't matter now. Outside of this room, nothing matters at all.

Later, when all the alarms are going off, and the nurses and doctors are running around, and I can't see my little girl through the wall of people and equipment, and I can't see my husband because he isn't there, he isn't in the room, he's outside sucking in all that fresh fucking air, I focus on the phone. I tether my attention to that little screen in the corner, lighting up and fading away like a Lilliputian lighthouse, bringing happy little words from shiny people laughing and drinking in a red-carpeted room a million miles away.

CHAPTER THIRTY-ONE

EMILY

E MILY WANDERED back to the guesthouse alone.
    She pottered in the kitchen, tidying away the bottles
from the abandoned wine tasting and wiping down the surfaces, but no amount of cleaning could ease her mind. What
had happened back there? Sure, no one liked to have strangers
wandering around in their back garden, but they were hikers,
not axe-murderers. And the way Nina ran outside and started
shouting . . . she'd seemed so ready, almost as if she was *expecting* the intrusion.

Afterward, no one mentioned it. Scott and Nina just made
their excuses and disappeared inside as if nothing unusual had
occurred.

Emily gazed out the window, studying the thick wall of leaves
and branches. She'd assumed there was only one access point
into Querencia, but there must be hidden trails running all
through the woodland. She made a mental note to take her
phone with her on her next shopping trip so she could check out
a map of the area.

She started sweeping out the fireplace but found herself just
staring at the grate. Reading was no more helpful; her mind kept
wandering. Eventually she poured herself a glass of something-

or-other, heated up some leftovers from the night before, and carried it all down to the sunset point.

It was still light and warm outside, but thick black clouds hovered on the horizon. Emily placed her plate carefully on the wall and climbed on beside it, breathing in the view. It felt like years ago that she'd sat in that restaurant in Soho, listening to Scott describing Querencia. Back then she hadn't been able to imagine that such a place even existed, and the reality had totally lived up to his description. Arriving here had been like opening the gates to heaven. She squinted, trying to see the place how she'd seen it on that very first day, but the magic had become the norm, and despite the excitement of Scott's visit, she felt flat. The pixie dust was wearing off. It was bound to happen sooner or later. Nothing stayed perfect forever.

Emily swallowed a mouthful of wine, noting dutifully that it tasted like the end of a pencil. What, exactly, was the root of her discomfort? It wasn't just the thing with the hikers. All weekend, underneath all the sparkle and electricity, there'd been something bugging her. It was something to do with the family house and the weird feeling she got whenever she went in there. It was Aurelia's pills, the bathroom cabinet, and the three of them: Scott, Nina, and Aurelia. Something about the way they all behaved around each other.

It struck her that she hadn't once seen Scott give his daughter a hug. His only displays of affection took the form of the odd pat on the head. It reminded her of the way her own father treated her. For the first time since they'd met, Emily's feelings toward Scott were somewhat less than adoring. Maybe he was ashamed. Maybe that was the real reason he stayed away from Querencia; maybe Aurelia embarrassed him. Suddenly the temper tantrums and nightmares didn't seem so strange.

And of course, they weren't *that* strange. Emily herself had been similar as a child. In fact, the more she thought about it, the more she realized how much she and Aurelia had in common: the nightmares, the outbursts, the slightly off-kilter social behavior—Emily had been through all of that. The more time she spent in Aurelia's company, the more connected to her she felt. What had Nina said? *We're like E.T. and Elliott. One always feels what the other is feeling.* Emily could understand that. Some things about Aurelia seemed to almost physically resonate with her, like the way she responded to touch and sound. The way she cried out in those first few weeks whenever Emily got too close, the way she freaked out during thunderstorms. Even her drawings the other day . . . it was all painfully, bizarrely familiar.

And then, for some reason, Dr. Forte popped into her head again; a startlingly clear image. She was leaning over, her hands outstretched, her lips moving. *Close your eyes, Emily. What do you see?*

Emily shivered and looked out at the ocean. The water was still and flat, scarred with the trails of fishing boats heading home for the night. Slick, spiky rocks appeared and disappeared like sharks' fins as the tide climbed to its highest point. Lightning flashed in the distance.

And somewhere behind her, a twig snapped softly under someone's foot.

Emily whipped around, knocking her fork off the wall and sending it clattering over the rocks.

"Hello?"

Something was moving—a shadow, weaving between the olive trees.

Emily swung her legs back over the wall and stood, her pulse quickening.

The shadow stopped, its edges bleeding into the deepening darkness, and for a second Emily wondered if her mind was playing tricks. But then the shadow spoke.

"Sorry, didn't mean to scare you," said Scott, lumbering into sight.

Emily sagged. "Oh my god, it's you. I wondered what the

hell that was!" She smiled and resisted an urge to flick her hair. "What's up?"

"Oh, you know." He shrugged. "Just came to say hi."

He shuffled closer, and Emily saw that his eyes were blood-shot, the lids pink and swollen. His cheeks were puffy, as if he'd been hit, and the top three buttons of his shirt were undone.

"You look exhausted," she said. "Did you just take a nap?" But as she stepped toward him, she caught a strong whiff of booze.

"Oh dear." She placed her hands on her hips like a school-teacher. "Looks like I missed happy hour."

A crack of thunder leaped out of the darkening sky. Scott blinked and lost his balance.

"Whoops-a-daisy." She laughed. "Maybe you should sit down." He didn't move, and she hesitated. As much as she'd have loved a repeat of whatever had happened the night before, something was different. Gone were the playful flirting and the come-to-bed eyes; this time, Drunk Scott crackled with a dangerous intensity.

Emily wondered if she should take him back to his wife, but Nina would be putting Aurelia to bed and probably wouldn't appreciate her husband crashing around the house and making a mess. Better to take him back to the guesthouse, Emily decided. Make him some coffee.

"Come on, let's get you inside." She went to help him, to take his arm or maybe let him lean on her, but suddenly he grabbed her shoulders and pulled her to him. She swallowed, her cantering heart breaking into a gallop.

Scott was staring at her with a stricken look on his face, his eyes searching hers, his lips quivering with the weight of things unsaid, and suddenly Emily was consumed with a desire she hadn't felt since high school, a burning, racing, dizzying feeling that was part Christmas morning, part fever dream. Her whole body was on fire.

"Hey." His voice cracked and, to Emily's surprise, a tear leaked out of one eye. "Do you believe in ghosts?"

An icy prickle slid down the back of her neck.

And then Scott crumpled, pitching forward so fast that Emily had no time to think. Her body was confused; she held out her arms as if to catch him while also stepping backward to get out of his way, and his momentum propelled them both toward the wall. Her legs bumped up against the stone and she gripped him by the elbows, hanging on as he slumped onto her shoulder. They teetered for a moment, clinging to one another and rocking dangerously over the drop.

Emily managed to stand her ground and regain some balance, but Scott was like an eighty-kilogram rag doll. Looking down at their arms, twisted together like the roots of a tree, she noticed that his skin was covered in what looked like burn marks: little red craters dotting his wrists, his forearms, and the crooks of his elbows.

"You're hurt." The words leaked out of her just as the wind came at them, upsetting their already shaky equilibrium, and suddenly Scott's mouth was on her neck, her cheek, just inches from her lips, and she inhaled sharply, breathing in his clothes, his skin, his hair. The whole world was reduced to the tingle of his stubble against her jaw, the roar of his sweet, sticky breath in her ear—and the moment was so intoxicating that she closed her eyes. She could feel every curve and swell of his body. A desperate need filled her up. Scott was moaning, a spellbindingly low note that called to her, that asked a question that only she could answer. Their lips met. . . .

But then Scott was collapsing again, folding in half, crushing her with his whole weight, toppling to the ground and pulling her with him. She resisted, trying to hold him up.

"Scott . . . I can't . . . I can't breathe."

Lightning flashed, and for a second everything was bright light and stark shadows. But then the night rushed back and Emily was wheezing, struggling under Scott's bulk, choking on his boozy breath, and suddenly she was back there in the street, the bus just inches away, its brakes squealing as white pieces of paper filled the sky like birds, and the panic was rising, filling her up until her ribs splintered under her skin . . . and then she was somewhere else, somewhere unknowable and unseeable but horribly familiar, somewhere dark and lonely and frightening. She bowed her head as she buckled, her legs giving way, her body yielding to the heavy object on top of her. . . .

And then her hands shot out, seeking to push it away. They connected with Scott's chest, and she shoved with everything she had. "*No!*" she yelled, and a bitter cold rushed into the space between their bodies.

Scott dropped to the ground, his hands at his temples, and Emily was instantly filled with regret. She opened her mouth to apologize, but she had no words, no voice: the panic had taken them and wouldn't give them back. She scrabbled at her own throat as if she could tear it open with her fingers.

In front of her, Scott climbed unsteadily to his feet and paused for a second. Then he shrank away and crashed back through the grass toward the family house, so quickly that Emily was left wondering if he'd been there at all. She was alone by the wall with her hands on her heart. Her labored breath got lost in the whip of the wind as the rain came hurtling in from the ocean and thunder boomed like cannon fire.

And from the direction of the house, under the noise of the storm, came the unmistakable sound of a little girl crying.

CHAPTER THIRTY-TWO

SCOTT

Scott stashed his overnight bag in the back of the SUV and climbed into the driver's seat, painfully conscious of Nina and Aurelia watching solemnly from the doorstep. Being careful to keep the sleeves of his shirt from riding up over the scorched surface of his skin, he reached through the car window to wave.

"Bye," he called. "See you soon!"

Neither waved back.

Pulling his arm back inside, he turned the key and the engine rumbled to life. The usual relief washed through him as he pressed his foot against the accelerator and the car began to move over the driveway, carrying him inch by precious inch away from Querencia.

He felt wrecked. Every part of his body hurt. The previous evening was a blur . . . he remembered emptying the contents of the liquor cabinet then scorching himself with the end of the barbecue lighter but had no recollection of anything after that. He'd woken up that morning facedown in Aurelia's playroom.

On the passenger seat next to him, Emily sat with her arms crossed protectively over her body. He wasn't sure why, but he'd felt oddly shy around her all morning. She'd been in his

212

dreams, her face so close he could count her eyelashes. At least, he assumed they were dreams.

He suddenly regretted his decision to have Emily replace Yves as his ride to the airport. Having spotted her scribbled jobs list the day before, he'd known she needed to do a grocery run, so he suggested they kill two birds with one stone. He'd figured the car journey would provide an opportunity to talk. He'd wanted to discuss the weekend and find out what she was thinking. Now, though, he wished he'd kept his mouth shut.

They drove through the gate and over the bumpy dirt track in silence. While Emily pressed buttons on the dashboard, searching in vain for a radio signal, Scott snuck a look at his reflection in the rearview mirror. Along with the rising bruise under his left eye, there were two thin scratches on his right cheek and a big one down the length of his nose. Emily hadn't yet commented. In fact, she'd been uncharacteristically quiet. His unease grew.

They reached the end of the dirt track, the canopy opening up like the roof of a cabriolet, and Scott put his indicator on. A song, some cheesy eighties hit, fought its way through the static. They pulled out onto the main road, and Emily sat back, her head turned to the window. All the markers of normal life began to rush past them—picnic benches, roundabouts, road signs, street lamps—and Scott wondered if they were both thinking the same thing: how shocking it was to find everything just as they left it. In that respect, Scott thought, Querencia was a little like Narnia. You could spend weeks there without ever leaving, months even, and on your return to the real world it seemed that no time had passed at all.

Scott cleared his throat. He had to say something; he had to fix this mess and get Emily back on his side. "So," he said. "That was quite a weekend."

He hesitated, wondering which angle to take. She was definitely spooked, either by Nina's shitshow yesterday or by whatever he'd said or done last night. Or both. Or something else entirely.

They drove on, gliding smoothly down a slip road and joining the traffic on the autoroute. Scott waited, sensing that Emily wanted to say something but couldn't, or wouldn't. At one
point, she opened her mouth, but then seemed to think better
of it.

"Look," he said, "about what happened yesterday—I know
it was a bit weird."

Emily bowed her head. She wasn't going to give him anything. So where to begin? The most important thing, he decided,
was that Emily kept her faith in Nina. Ultimately, she and Nina
had to take care of each other. Maybe he should just tell the
truth, or the best version of it.

"Look, there's something you have to understand about Nina.
She's been through a lot. Her childhood was, uh, difficult."

Emily frowned. "She said it was boring. She said she grew
up on the beach, some rich suburb of Sydney. White bread, she
called it."

"Yeah. That's what she tells people. There's a lot more to it
than that."

Emily fell quiet. Shook her head.

Scott thought for a moment. "Having kids was important to
her, but it was hard for us. We had a lot of issues and there were
many failed attempts. Many procedures. We'd all but given up
hope. So, Aurelia . . . she was a miracle." Signaling right, he
changed lanes. Nina's words echoed in his head: *She likes you.*

"But then Aurelia got sick." He stole another quick look at
Emily. "We got through it, but the experience left its mark, as
I'm sure you can imagine."

She likes you.

"Nina always talked about living in France, somewhere far
away, by the ocean, so when we found Querencia it seemed
ideal. A place where we could start afresh."

She likes you.

"But for a while now, I've worried that the isolation is taking
its toll. My wife has always been sensitive, but lately . . ." He

sighed. "I don't know. I guess we're all human. We all make mistakes; we all overreact. And we all do whatever we can to protect the people we love. Right?"

She likes you.

He stole another look at her. What would a life with her look like? If they had an affair, if they ran away together, would they make each other happy? Would they turn out to be soul mates? He conjured memories of early holidays with Nina, erasing his wife and inserting Emily in her place. Sipping cocktails in a private villa, her head on his shoulder. Her slick body moving against his. Her tongue tracing his lips, her hands in his hair.

But, no. He could never leave. Not ever. A blank, hopeless feeling settled in the pit of his stomach. He gripped the steering wheel with white-knuckled fingers.

"Try not to judge her too harshly, Emily. She loves you." He paused for effect. "We all do." To his immense relief, Emily nodded.

"You're part of this family now," he went on. "You're our missing piece. Whatever problems we've had in the past, you're helping us fix them, and we hope we can help you in return. I'd like to think we can all face our issues together. But we can only do that by accepting each other for who we are, warts and all."

His words hung in the air. Then, from the corner of his eye, he saw Emily brush something from her cheek.

"Warts?" she said, after what felt like a long time. "Gross. I didn't sign up for that."

Scott grinned, and relaxed his grip. He had her.

I can't be sure, but I think I'm in heaven.

I've never seen so many beautiful people. So beautiful and so friendly. I want to ask them what they're doing here, but when I open my mouth, a spider crawls out. I look around but remember that my eyes are shut.

I can hear voices close by. Two people; two beautiful doctors. They're talking to me, asking questions, picking at my skin, peeling it back, trying to see what's inside. But the doctors are trying to trick me. They're pretending to be my husband so that I'll talk to them. So that I will give them information about . . . something. Something important.

But the joke is on them. I won't talk, especially not to him. I hate him. He wasn't there. He left us. He's always leaving us. And he won't swap bodies with me. He refuses to trade places, so he'll never know what it's like to be me. He'll never understand.

The beautiful doctors give up and go away.

My mother is driving me home. We drive down a long stretch of road. I'm small and angry. My mother is yelling. I'm yelling louder. I've had enough. I reach for the door.

My mother yanks the wheel.

There's a tree.

The car explodes. All the pieces break apart and go spinning into the sky. I am flying. And then I am not.

I sit and wait. A twisted lump of metal lies at my feet. Shards of orange glass. I look down and see my mother's swollen, lumpy head in my lap. She looks uncomfortable. I try to move her, but my arms and hands are slippery with blood. She makes a wet sound. "Don't be scared, sweetheart," she says. "Everything's okay. Mummy's here."

I stroke her pulpy face. I'm so sad, and so sorry. Everything is my fault. "Don't worry, Mum. I'll make you better. I'll take care of you."

Bright lights, blue and red, flashing in the distance. A tramping, stamping noise. Leather boots pounding the asphalt.

I look down again. My arms are clean and empty. I am alone.

CHAPTER THIRTY-THREE

EMILY

EMILY DUG the metal weeder into the soil and turned it, trying to get the best hold on what lay beneath. While preparations for Scott's arrival had been underway, the weeds in the bottommost gardens had been left to their own devices, and now they had the run of the place. The roots were thick and stubborn and refused to give way. She frowned while she worked, her forehead bunched with tension.

It had been ten days since Scott flew back to London: ten days of thinking and obsessing over every detail of his visit until she gave herself a migraine. His arrival, the night in the pool, the thing with the hikers, the kiss at the sunset point—what did any of it *mean*?

And the trip to the airport—that hadn't made any sense at all. He'd insisted that she go with him, and she'd assumed that meant he wanted to talk privately, but there'd been no confession of feelings, no explanation, not even an apology. He'd talked about Nina the whole way, and Emily had felt betrayed. How could he just *ignore* the fact that they'd *kissed*? She'd felt confused and furtive. On her return to Querencia, she hadn't been able to look Nina in the eye. But now that she'd had a few days to process things, she decided she hadn't actually done anything wrong. And, quite feasibly, neither had Scott.

As Emily replayed the kiss over and over in her head, it started to look less like a kiss and more like an accident. The more she thought about it, the more she wondered how she could have mistaken it for anything else. Scott had been drunk. He hadn't made a move at all. He'd tripped and fallen on her, and their faces had simply collided.

In the days that followed, she'd romanticized the encounter until it looked in her head like a scene from *Wuthering Heights*. She'd focused on the touch of his lips and ignored the burn marks on his arms. She remembered her excitement but forgot her fear. She'd even blocked out the moment she'd shoved Scott—actually *shoved* him—onto the ground. All of that came back a day or so later, by which time the whole thing didn't seem nearly so romantic.

After much thought, Emily had seen no choice but to try to forget the whole weekend. She couldn't unravel it, and her head hurt when she tried, so she forgave herself and she forgave Scott and she even forgave Nina for scaring those poor lost French people, because clearly they were *all* a bit sensitive and over-tired, and they'd drunk far too much over those three days. She resolved to move on.

But it wasn't that easy. Firstly, the fact that she'd had yet another panic attack, her second in just over three months, was worrying. The encounter with Scott had brought about the same black flurry she'd felt on the day she was almost hit by a bus. It hadn't happened for years, but she'd known it was the same vortex of fear that used to plague her as a child: the bad, rotten thing inside her. After years of therapy, Dr. Forte had declared her to be mentally and emotionally healthy, but Emily had always known that it was still there somewhere, lurking in the background. Now, it seemed, it was back.

Secondly, she couldn't shake the feeling that there was something going on at Querencia, something she didn't know about.

For starters, there was Nina's behavior. *Don't judge her too harshly,* Scott had said in the car, and Emily didn't want to. But she didn't understand. Sure, Nina was overprotective. Fine. But did that explain her reaction to the hikers? And now it seemed that she hadn't been honest about her past, which hurt—especially when Emily had been so open about her own. The ocean, the big houses, the barbecues . . . how much of that was true? And what, exactly, had Scott meant by a "difficult" childhood?

And then there was the medicine cabinet. Emily kept thinking about Aurelia's illness. She'd seen no real evidence of it: no breakouts, no vomiting, no incapacitation—not even a mild fever. She told herself that none of that meant anything; Nina was vigilant, the medication effective. Maybe the sun allergy was only reactive at certain times of the year. But as Nina continued to smear her daughter with thick sunscreen every morning and pump her full of pills, an unpleasant suspicion began to gnaw at Emily's insides.

Lastly, and most importantly, Emily was worried that she'd fallen in love. She couldn't say for sure, but all the signs seemed to point that way. Limited previous experience told her that love was all about electricity (*check*), joy (*check*), longing (*check*), and pain (*check*); also, a reduced appetite and sexy dreams (*check and oh my god check*), all of which were extremely alarming, because what if Scott *had* meant to kiss her that night? What if he'd followed her down to the sunset point because he had feelings for her, too? And what might have happened if she hadn't pushed him away? Would he have laid her down on the grass and pressed his body against hers, maybe run his hands over her skin and lifted her dress . . . ?

But no, no, no, she was heading down the rabbit hole again. She couldn't possibly be in love with Scott; no, that would be unimaginably awful. No. Fifty shades of awkward.

If only she could pick up some bloody signal, she'd go grab her phone and distract herself with the internet. She longed to lose a few hours scrolling through Instagram; maybe she should ask again about the Wi-Fi. But, she reasoned miserably, she'd probably just use it to cyberstalk Scott Denny all afternoon. Not a good idea.

Emily continued to twist the weeder into the earth, ignoring the cramp in her hand and the ache in her lower back. She would not be beaten by a few stubborn roots. Wiping her forehead with her sleeve, she tried again, pulling and pulling until something came loose and she fell backward, landing ungracefully on her bum.

"Ow!" The tool lay in two pieces on the ground; the handle had broken off. *Shit.* Now she'd have to go and find another one.

Sweating, she looked around for Yves. He would have something she could use. Where had he gone? Following the incident with the hikers, Nina had tasked him with fortifying the wall at the bottom of the property, so he'd been hanging around all week, driving Emily mad with his incessant hammering . . . but, of course, when she needed him he was nowhere to be seen.

She looked around. No Nina or Aurelia either. It was eerily quiet.

Peeling off her gardening gloves, she stood up. *This bloody place.* It was too big. Who needed this much space? You could never find anyone. She gave the broken weeder a kick. Fine, whatever, she'd sort it out herself. There'd be something in the toolshed.

Feeling increasingly irritated, she set off back toward the houses, checking left and right as she went. "Hello?" she said. "Nina?" The pool was glassy, the lavender frozen in place. Even the ocean seemed to be holding its breath. She called out again, but there was no reply.

The sheds (tool, animal, bike) stood at the far end of the property, near the front gate. Passing by the family house on her way, Emily glared mutinously at its closed door and flat, mirror-like windows. How ridiculous that she *still* wasn't welcome inside Nina's home! That after two whole months, she *still* hadn't been invited inside. It was stupid. *You're part of this family now,*

Scott had said in the car. *I'd like to think we can all face our issues together.* If only Nina felt the same way. *She loves you. We all do.* Well, Emily loved them, too. She'd have done anything for them. If only Nina would let her in. *Whatever's going on with you,* she might say, *whatever problems you're facing, I won't judge. I'm here for you.* She wondered if—

A small sound suddenly caught her attention.

She stopped. Listened.

The sound was soft and high-pitched. It seemed to be coming from . . . where? Emily pivoted on the spot, straining to hear. It was like a *miaow* but thinner, reedier. More stretched out.

Another noise. A dull scrape this time, coming from somewhere near the family house. Emily took a few steps toward the front door.

There it was again, a muted crash followed by a whimper.

She hurried to the door and tried the handle, but it was locked. She looked up at the second-floor windows. It sounded like crying, but who was it? Nina or Aurelia? The whimper got louder and more strangled—then short, staccato, insistent. It made Emily's heart hurt. She turned to her right and listened again. Running around the side of the house, she rounded the corner, slowing down as she reached the patio. At first, the little courtyard appeared to be empty, but then, over in the corner by the barbecue, something moved.

In the shade of the wooden awning, Aurelia stood hunched and alone.

"Hey, little one," said Emily. "What are you doing out here—"

Aurelia's head snapped up, and Emily gasped. Her face was red and tear-streaked and contorted with pain. With no warning, she bucked sharply and let out a frightened cry. Emily took a step toward her, and Aurelia flinched again, shuffling back against the wall and writhing against the stones. *"Ngh! Nnngh!"* she grunted.

"What's the matter?" Emily cried. Aurelia appeared to be

in agony. Her yelps became even louder, and she thrashed violently. "Okay, okay, okay." Emily ran over and grabbed her by the arms. "Tell me, Aurelia. Tell me what's going on." It was hard to keep hold of her; she kept twisting away. "Sweetie, what's wrong?"

Slowly, Emily became aware of an intermittent buzzing. Aurelia was pulling and tearing at her clothes . . . was there a bee trapped in her dress?

"Okay. Hold still." Aurelia was wearing one of her long smock dresses; the insect could've been anywhere in the folds. Emily grabbed at the material and tried to lift it up and over Aurelia's head, but the kid kept wriggling out of her grasp. "Hold still!" she said again, but Aurelia whipped away from her, and they both spun out into the middle of the patio. "Aurelia! Stop, I have to—"

Aurelia began to shake, and Emily made a snap decision. She yanked at the dress, ripping the seam at the side and splitting it all the way to the hem. Tugging the dress off, she threw it down and stamped on it just to be sure, then she gathered up the material and shook it. Eventually, the crooked corpse of a wasp fell to the floor.

Checking Aurelia over, she found dozens of angry red welts all over her back, stomach, and rib cage. "Oh my god." How many wasp stings could a person handle? "Can you breathe?" Aurelia's breath was coming too thick and too fast, but it was coming. "Open your mouth, sweetie." Neither her throat nor her tongue appeared to be swollen, and rather than turning purple, her face seemed to be very gradually returning to its normal color. No allergic reaction, then, but some serious pain.

"Hang on, I'll be right back." Emily ran inside to the kitchen and ran her hands over the cabinetry, grimacing at the weird musty smell that was still hanging around. She opened and closed low-level cupboards and drawers in search of a glass or a cup, but there seemed to be nothing useful in any of them, just ornaments and decorative bowls—where did Nina keep all the practical stuff? Finally, she discovered a gigantic butler's pantry tucked away behind the back wall. Inside, she found row after gleaming row of glasses, mugs, plates, pots, pans, utensils: everything you could possibly expect to find in a kitchen, plus a few things you wouldn't. Everything looked brand-new.

Filling a glass with water from the tap, she pulled an ice tray from the freezer and wrapped a few cubes in a tea towel. Then she ran back outside, where she gave Aurelia the water and pressed the ice to her welts. *Antihistamine.* That's what they needed. Nina would almost certainly have some in that medicine cabinet of hers.

It was only then that Emily realized that Aurelia was sitting, almost completely naked, right in the full glare of the sun.

She reacted instinctively, hooking her hands under Aurelia's arms and dragging her backward into the shade.

Emily stared, waiting for something terrible to happen.

But nothing did.

When the flagstones became too uncomfortable, Emily suggested to Aurelia that she go inside to lie down. She turned to go, intending to find Nina. (Where was she, anyway? She couldn't be too far away, hadn't she heard all the shouting?) But when Aurelia took her hand and pulled her gently through the door, through the kitchen and down the hallway, Emily followed, curiosity once again getting the better of her.

The hallway was as bright and white as the landing upstairs. She peeked through half-open doors and saw what looked like formal dining, laundry, and powder rooms, all exquisitely furnished. The very last door, the door through which Aurelia was tugging her, opened on a gigantic TV and playroom; actually, private cinema was closer to the truth. The screen mounted on the wall was the biggest Emily had ever seen outside of a movie theater. On the opposite wall, shelves groaned under the weight of textbooks, storybooks, encyclopedias, CDs, and DVDs. Against another wall, neat squares of floating storage units reached for the ceiling, bursting with toys and games. The

remaining wall space was filled with hundreds of framed paintings and drawings, all with Aurelia's name printed neatly across
the top.

There was a teepee in one corner and an easel in another. An
enormous doll's house stood next to a miniature kitchen, and a
large box spilled costumes onto the floor. The ceiling was strung
with bunting and fairy lights.

"Holy crap," Emily said. "This is unbelievable."

Aurelia stood in the middle of it all with a blank expression.
Flopping down on a beanbag, she pointed to the giant screen.

"Yeah, um, I don't know how to work that." Emily grabbed
one of the princess dresses from the dressing-up box. Kneeling
beside Aurelia, she gently helped her into it. "No beasties in this
one, I promise," she said when Aurelia hesitated. She showed
her where to hold the little ice parcel against her skin, then
stood up. "I'm going to find your mummy now, okay?"

Aurelia pressed a palm to her thigh. *Don't go.*

"Oh, sweetie, I have to go get your mum. I shouldn't really
be in here, you know." It had been a long time since the no-
go–zone rule was mentioned, so Emily wasn't exactly sure how
Nina would react, but she didn't want to find out. Being inside
felt like a betrayal, which meant it probably was.

But the pull of Aurelia's doe eyes was too strong, and she
found herself sinking back to the floor. She nestled against the
beanbag and stroked Aurelia's hair, still half expecting the allergic reaction to kick in; what if the kid ballooned up or passed
out or exploded or something? What would she do then? Nina
would go nuts.

Aurelia shuffled and wriggled until she was comfortably nestled in the crook of Emily's arm; then she reached for her hand,
and they laced their fingers together. Emily smiled, catching a
glimpse of what it might have been like to have siblings. Midnight feasts, whispered secrets. *Little sister,* she thought, snug-
gling closer.

"Hey," Emily said softly, after a while. "Can you talk?"

Aurelia, unsurprisingly, did not reply.

"Can you say my name? Can you say *Emily*?"

Nothing. Emily looked down at Aurelia's chalky knees resting against her own. She'd never noticed that Aurelia had so many freckles: a constellation of honey-colored stars.

The minutes crept by, and they fell into a comfortable, drowsy silence. Head to head, hand in hand, they contemplated the ceiling, their chests rising and falling with the same tide-like rhythm, until their eyelids grew heavy and the lights became fireflies, wheeling in the air above them.

Emily woke up. Her mouth was thick with sleep.

She sat up in alarm and looked around. She was still in the playroom, but she was alone. Aurelia had gone.

She pushed herself up on one elbow, her heart pounding. The shadows on the wall had changed, and the light coming in through the window was a golden orange. How long had she been dozing? There was no obvious sign that Nina was back or had been in the room (no noises in the kitchen, no shoes or towel on the playroom floor), but somehow Emily felt watched.

Listening, straining to hear something, anything, she followed the crisscross of lights above her head and the pattern of pictures that dripped down the walls. Dogs and cats. Fairies and witches. Multiplication tables. A poster of the solar system. A drawing of a bear with the words "I love you beary much" written across the bottom.

And in a blinding moment of clarity, she realized what had been bugging her about the house. There were no photos anywhere. Not one. No family snaps, no baby shots, no pictures at the zoo. No messy ice-cream face or birthday candles or first bike ride. Not even a wedding portrait. Nina wasn't big on clutter, but Emily would have thought there'd be at least a few frames scattered around here and there, especially in her bedroom. But except for the framed drawings in this room and the paintings in the sitting room, all the walls were blank. A bare expanse of emptiness.

I touch my cheek with sticky fingers. The powder-pink rug has left an imprint on my skin and fibers on my tongue. I must've been on the floor for some time.

I stretch an arm out. It feels loose and floppy, like a flap of useless skin. Rolling over, I hear the crunch of glass and a splintered wooden frame pokes me in the back.

The room has fallen sideways. The furniture plays tricks on me. Huge paper light shades sprout out of the walls like beanstalks; the cot is hanging from the ceiling. Stuffed toys float on a sloping sea of fuzz.

Seeping toward the toys is a thick spill of blood, a black lake carrying a glass bottle with a message inside. *Be careful,* I call to a small yellow teddy bear. *Don't drown!* I try to save him, but I'm too far away.

I blink, and the blood spill is gone.

CHAPTER THIRTY-FOUR

EMILY

NOTHING HAPPENED after the incident with the wasp. Not a thing. For a second time, Emily made it out of the house apparently unseen, and Aurelia was absolutely fine.

Emily's gnawing suspicion began to bite harder. She found herself watching Aurelia's behavior more closely, and checking regularly on her whereabouts. On the "bad" days, when Aurelia was supposed to be "resting" in the family house, Emily often glimpsed her through partially open windows, running around in the playroom, or jumping on the sitting-room sofas. Once Emily started keeping track, she realized just how many pills Aurelia was taking. There were an awful lot.

But most of the time she seemed okay. A bit spaced out, sure, but fine. And after a few days, Emily decided to turn a blind eye. She wouldn't mention the wasp—not unless Nina mentioned it first—because what would be the point? Okay, so maybe Nina was exaggerating the severity of Aurelia's illness. Maybe the medication wasn't wholly necessary. But Nina's intentions were good; she was just being cautious. And Aurelia had everything she needed. She was loved and cared for, fed and watered. Yes, it would be nice for her to get off the property occasionally, make some friends, but if you had to stay home, then Querencia was the place to do it. And how Nina chose to raise her own child was none of Emily's business.

She didn't dare examine her feelings in any more depth than that. Because, deep down, she knew she didn't *want* it to be her business.

In her quietest moments, lying in the dark at night, Emily thought about confronting Nina, and what that might do to their friendship. She thought about going home to her parents. She thought about Scott. Every day, she thought about him. And suddenly, her new life at Querencia felt like a priceless artifact balanced in the palm of her hand. She didn't want to fumble and drop it.

So Emily pushed her thoughts to the very back of her mind and got on with her jobs. For the next three weeks, she mowed the lawn and fed the animals, mucked out Sebastien and collected the eggs from the chicken shed. She painted more walls, cleaned toilets, fished leaves out of the pool filter, and watered the plants. She helped Nina reorganize the cellar and the games room, making way for more unexpected deliveries: a pinball machine, a vintage jukebox, and astonishingly, a bouncy castle. There were more market visits and supermarket trips. Nina taught Emily how to descale, gut, and bone a fish. They cooked together using ingredients from the garden. Fig and apricot jam. Dauphinoise potatoes. Gazpacho. Homemade pasta topped with a fresh tomato-and-basil sauce. Emily played with Aurelia; they rode the quad bikes, played hide-and-seek, and chased each other around the property with water guns.

And eventually, Emily's doubts loosened and dissolved. Nina would never hurt her daughter; she wasn't hiding anything. And even if she was, Emily was too busy with food and wine to worry about it; too focused on the sun on her skin and the sand between her toes. Life at Querencia returned to normal.

They were down by the pool when it happened, having a pillow fight on the daybed. Surrounded on all four sides by floaty white curtains and fitted with custom-made cushions, the day-bed was the perfect place to relax—or, if you were six years old, to bounce up and down on for hours on end.

It was late afternoon, and Emily had taken a break from peeling and deveining prawns to help Aurelia fix a pair of fairy wings onto the back of her dress. "There you go," she said, patting Aurelia on the back. "A beautiful fairy queen." As she walked away, a pillow hit her between the shoulders, and things escalated from there.

Aurelia's arm was impressive; one shot almost knocked Emily into the pool. "Ooh, you're gonna pay for that one." Emily said, hurling an especially thick cushion as hard as she could. But as soon as it left her hand, she knew she'd gone too far. It hit Aurelia square in the face and sent her flying backward into one of the posts. There was a meaty smack as her head hit the corner, and suddenly there was blood everywhere.

After a moment of paralyzing, gut-churning fear, Emily rushed forward. "Oh my god . . . Aurelia? Are you okay?" She gently rolled Aurelia onto her side and pressed her fingers gingerly to the back of her head, parting her hair to reveal an ugly gash. It was deep but she'd seen worse. Her former roommate, Spencer, had once fallen off a balcony at a party and cut his head so badly you could see the white of his skull.

Aurelia stirred, and more blood gushed from her nose into her mouth. As well as knocking her over, the cushion had whacked her on the nose, opening it like a tap. "Oh my god, oh my god." Emily ran and grabbed a couple of towels from the loungers, pressing one to Aurelia's head, the other to her nose. "I'm so sorry, sweetie," she said.

Aurelia started to wail.

"It's okay," Emily said. "Hey. Look at me—you'll be fine."

Obediently, Aurelia looked up.

Emily froze.

At first, she wasn't sure what she was looking at. Was it a trick of the light? She looked closer. One of Aurelia's eyes had changed color. The left was the usual amber brown, but the right was a pure, bright green.

And then, she saw something else. Sitting on the splayed tendrils of Aurelia's black hair, was a tiny, pearl-like circle. It looked like half of a bubble—transparent, but dark against the white linen.

A contact lens. A colored one.

Placing her hands on Aurelia's cheeks, Emily moved closer. Her pupils were so contracted that each iris was clearly visible. The brown eye was flecked with gold and ringed with a darker hue. The green was pale with a distinct yellow inner ring, like a corona.

Aurelia wears colored contacts? She studied the left iris, searching for the telltale ring against the brown. She looked back and forth, back and forth. But as far as she could tell there *was* no second contact. Both eyes were natural. One brown, one green.

Returning her gaze to the cushion, Emily stretched out a finger to touch the lost lens—but a sudden shriek made her turn. Above them, Nina was flying along the path from the house to the pool. "Aurelia!" she yelled, hurtling down the steps. And then: "Get away from her!"

Emily sat back on her heels and raised her hands in the air like a thief caught in the act. "It's okay. She's okay. She just—"

"I said, *get away*!" Nina threw herself onto the daybed and pulled Aurelia onto her lap. In seconds, her bare arms were covered with blood.

"I'm so sorry," Emily stammered. "It was an accident. She just fell. We were—"

But Nina cut her off. "No, no, no, no, no," she moaned. Tears flowed down her face, her mouth grotesquely distorted.

Emily opened her mouth then shut it again. *It looks worse than it is,* she wanted to say. But Nina was wailing as if Aurelia was dead. "Noooo!" She sobbed. "Please, no."

Emily winced. It was all a bit dramatic. She started to clamber off the bed. "I'll get the keys and bring the car around," she said, but Nina looked up sharply. Her eyes were unsteady, like she'd just woken up.

"No. No. You stay here."

"But—"

"No."

"She needs a hospital, I—"

"I said *no*! No hospital!" Nina turned back to stroke her daughter's matted hair. "She's okay. She'll be okay, won't you, bubba? Mummy will make it better. Mummy will take care of you." Gathering Aurelia in her arms like a bundle of wet washing, she got to her feet.

Emily stood with her. "Are you sure I can't—"

"Just leave us the fuck alone!"

It was like a punch in the gut.

Turning her back, Nina staggered to the steps and disappeared back up the path, leaving Emily alone on the daybed. Stunned, she let her head drop. Blood trickled over the cushions and pooled between her toes. Through her tears, she scoured the white linen, the red splashes, looking for the little half bubble.

But it wasn't there. The contact lens was gone.

CHAPTER THIRTY-FIVE

EMILY

S HAKING, EMILY stripped the covers off the cushions and took them to the laundry room, filling the washing machine with as much detergent as would fit. Taking a sponge and a bucket down to the pool area, she scrubbed every speck of blood off the daybed and its wooden frame. Then she went over the travertine tiles, wiping away even the tiniest of drops.

When she was done, she made her way slowly up to the family house. A trail of blood led up the pool steps and over the driveway; the sand had soaked up the liquid to form little red pellets. She shuddered, unable to stop replaying the scene: Aurelia flying back in slow motion, the sound her head made as it hit the post. Torn flesh under matted black hair, and a dark mass of rising bruises that seemed to cover her entire scalp. It had been bad . . . but not *that* bad. Not enough to warrant keening worthy of an Irish funeral.

And if it *was* that bad, then why refuse to take her to the hospital? If the injury was serious, wouldn't that be the first place you'd go? She thought again about the bathroom cabinet and wondered just how much Nina believed she could handle on her own. Emily had to see if Aurelia was okay, if she could do anything to help.

The blood led to the open door of the family house. There was a smear on the frame, and a series of drops traveled up the stone steps and across the floorboards like a line of ants. She moved farther inside, following the ruby-red bread crumbs to the kitchen. The trail ended, inexplicably, in the butler's pantry.

Emily poked her head in. The pantry was empty, but there were more red dots all over the floor and another smear on the counter, just in front of the microwave.

Emily was about to turn back and look elsewhere when she noticed something odd about the shelves that lined the back wall. They were standing at an angle, as if they didn't quite connect with the adjoining shelves or the countertop. She reached out to touch them, and a whole section wobbled. Then she grabbed the edge and pulled. The shelves swung out in one heavy block.

A door.

And behind the door, stairs, leading down, a fat splash of blood on each one.

What the hell . . . ?

There was a muffled grating noise from somewhere below, and she hesitated, suddenly afraid. What was she doing, creeping around uninvited for a *fourth* time? She was asking for trouble; but there was a low light coming from the bottom of the secret staircase, and Emily wanted so badly to find out what was down there, to get an answer to at least one of her many mounting questions.

Carefully and quietly, she edged her way onto the top step and tiptoed down.

The first thing she noticed was the smell. The faint rotten odor that pervaded the whole house was strong in here, and grew more intense the farther down she went. The air, too, was stuffy and damp.

At the bottom of the staircase was a square of floor space the size of a small lift. It was a dead end; the whole thing had been walled off. At least, that's what it looked like at first, but as Emily's eyes adjusted to the gloom, she realized that the "wall" was made up of cardboard boxes, several stacks of them reaching almost to the ceiling. Looking around, she saw more of them: great piles of boxes, crates, and storage tubs, stretching back into what seemed to be, in fact, quite a large room.

Emily gagged. The smell was awful.

She stared at the nearest box. There seemed to be something written on it, but she couldn't make it out; everything was thrown into shadow by a flat, gray glow coming from somewhere near the back of the room. There was a voice, too. Nina, speaking in a hushed but urgent tone.

Covering her nose and mouth with her hand, Emily inched forward, squeezing through the gaps between the stacks, being careful to stay hidden.

At the far end, beyond all the boxes, was a thick door, standing half-open. The gray light was coming from inside, flickering and changing at short intervals. There were shapes behind the door. Emily squinted. She could just about identify the edge of a chair and the legs of a table or desk. What was this, an office? A warehouse? Maybe Nina was running some sort of packing business from down here.

Suddenly, there was a flash of movement from the doorway, and Emily flattened herself against a crate. Nina appeared, pacing up and down with a phone held against her ear. She was panting like she'd just finished a sprint. Pausing, she pushed the door open a fraction farther and looked out at the boxes. "I can't," she said in a hoarse voice, and Emily jumped, thinking for one pulse-shattering moment that she'd been spotted. But then Nina spoke again. "I did. I cleaned and dressed it." She walked away and her voice faded.

Emily tried to slow her breathing. Where was Aurelia?

A pause, and then Nina was back: "Please, just give him whatever he wants."

Emily felt light-headed. What if Nina saw her? Why hadn't she gone straight back to her room to mind her own business?

Because this is my business. Because there's something weird going on. Because Nina is hiding out in an underground bunker. Because she's lying to me.

"As soon as possible," said Nina. Reaching for the door, she pulled it closed and the room was plunged into darkness.

Quietly, cautiously, Emily felt her way back through the maze of boxes. Then she crept up the staircase and out of the house.

Five minutes later, she stood in the middle of her bedroom, chewing her nails and trying to explain away what she'd seen. *Well, obviously, Nina is a compulsive shopper. The room is just a study, and the weird light was coming from a computer. It's just retail therapy; that's how she gets her kicks. Nothing weird about that.*

Except somewhere down there, Aurelia was bleeding, probably concussed, and nowhere near a hospital. Nina was freaking out. And the room hadn't looked like a study. It had looked more like a dungeon or a laboratory.

Emily stared out the window at the family house. Its lights winked at her through the branches of a tree.

Just after eleven thirty, she heard the faraway whirr of the gate, and a car appeared, gliding down the driveway with its headlights switched off. She moved her head from side to side, but the tree was blocking her view—and then a security light picked out the white of Yves's truck. It came to a stop outside the family house, and for a few moments nothing happened; the car just sat there, its windows dark and impenetrable. Then the driver's door opened with a soft clunk, and Yves got out. He went to the passenger side and pulled open the door.

Yves was not alone. A man got out of the car: short, bald, wearing jeans and a T-shirt. He carried a gym bag with short straps. Yves ushered the man into the house, and the front door closed behind them.

Emily drummed her fingers on the windowsill. After a while,

she left her bedroom and hurried downstairs, switching off the lights so she could peer through the windows undetected.

Exactly twenty-six minutes later, the front door of the family house opened again. Yves stepped out, followed by the bald man with the bag. Emily strained to get a look at his face, but it was dark and they were both moving fast. They scurried to the car with their heads down. The bald man went to the passenger-side door and got in. Yves opened the driver's side, but just as he was about to slide in behind the wheel, he stopped. Emily's heart skipped and scuttered. It was difficult to tell from such a distance, but she could have sworn he was looking right at the guesthouse. At *her*.

Hiding in the shadows of what she had come to think of as her own home, she was suddenly filled with anger—or was it jealousy? She hated that Nina had shared secrets with Yves and not with her. It was like being left out of a game in the schoolyard. *You can't play. We won't let you.*

Yves stood, one foot in the car, one hand up on the top of the door, staring in Emily's direction, his huge frame rigid with tension, and it struck Emily how little she knew him. She'd taken his presence for granted—just the handyman, the landscaper, the "heavy lifting" guy. Harmless. But who was he, really? A stranger. An outsider. She realized then that she'd never known him, and she'd never trusted him.

Without stopping to think, Emily opened the front door and ran out onto the porch, triggering the sensor light. She threw herself into its spotlight, and Yves moved like he'd been poked by a cattle prod. Jerking backward, his hands flew out as if steadying himself. The air between them seemed to solidify. And then he yanked open the car door and was inside before Emily knew what was happening.

"Wait!" she managed. "Stop!" But her voice was drowned out by the engine as Yves turned the car around and drove off toward the gate.

I grip the silver packet between my fingers and push out the pill with my thumb. It looks like a little blue eyeball; not my usual medication but near enough. At least, that's what the website said. Amazing, really, what you can get online these days. I'm surprised anyone goes to the doctor anymore.

I pop the eyeball into my mouth and turn on the tap.

I am drinking directly from the faucet when the doorbell rings—two sharp blasts of the bell. For a few seconds, I can't move. Water drips down my chin. Then I open the bathroom door and cross to the bedroom window. Looking down, I see a delivery van rumbling in the road and a woman standing on my doorstep.

Shaking, I go downstairs and open the front door, just a crack. "Yes?" I say.

The woman is short. She has graying hair and wears a high-visibility jacket. "Where'd you want 'em, love?" she says.

"What?"

"Your shopping. Where'd you want me to put the bags?" She is craning her neck, trying to see past me into the house.

"On the doorstep, please," I say, careful not to open the door any wider.

"You sure? I can bring 'em inside if you like, give you a hand."

"No."

"It's no trouble, love. All part of the service."

"I said no."

The short woman makes a face. "Suit yourself." She puts the bags down and returns to her van.

I look down at the bags. The topmost item peeps out of the nearest one. Cheerful plastic packaging with a picture on the front. Pearly teeth. Dimples. Golden curls. I bend down and reach for the picture, stretching out my fingers until I feel peachy skin, soft as roses. Plump little thighs. Ten tiny toes. This little piggy went to market, this little piggy stayed at home.

"How old's your baby?"

I jump. The delivery woman is back with an electronic signature pad.

"Huh?"

"Your baby." She points at the plastic picture. "How old?"

I can feel her staring at me, at the dressing on my wrists. I pull down my sleeves and look up. Our eyes meet and she flinches. I wonder what she might look like with her head staved in. Like a freshly cut watermelon, I decide, and laugh.

CHAPTER THIRTY-SIX

EMILY

THE NEXT morning, Emily woke to discordant birdsong and a faint wash of light. She lifted her head, her hair sticking uncomfortably to her cheek. Her eyes felt sore and puffy, and her jaw ached, a sure sign that she'd been grinding her teeth.

Heaving herself upright, Emily rubbed her eyes.

Yves and the bald man.

The secret staircase.

Blood in the sand and a pale-green eye.

Had she been dreaming? Despite the heat, she shivered. Dread and nausea burned in her stomach.

Wrapping the top sheet around her body, she crossed to the window and looked out. Querencia lay spread before her, just the same as it always was. There was the lawn, green and ordinary. There were the trees and the flowers and the pool. No sign of anything unusual or sinister. And yet everything seemed different somehow.

Within ten minutes, she was out the door and in the car. There was no real plan, just a burning desire to be away from the property: alone, but among people; just close enough to be sure they were still out there.

As she drove the SUV toward the gates, Emily was seized by

an urge to accelerate so powerful that she almost plowed the car straight through the iron bars without even stopping at the control panel. At the last minute, she pulled up sharply next to the silver keypad and entered the code. She waited, tapping her fingers on the steering wheel, but nothing happened.

Emily frowned. She reached out and pressed the buttons again, more slowly this time. But still the gates remained closed, the mechanism silent. The small red light in the right-hand corner of the keypad, the one that turned green just before the gates opened, wasn't flashing. It wasn't even lit.

She got out of the car and examined the keypad. The digital display panel was blank. Then she looked through the gates at the unit on the other side. No lights anywhere. Even the security cameras, one mounted on either side of the towering wall, were inanimate. The whole system was dead.

She grabbed the bars and rattled them. Locked. A hot swell of alarm rose up in her rib cage. But then she remembered. *These are the keys to the house and your car. This little one is for the front gate, but the security system is electronic so you won't need it.* Scott had been right; it had been so unnecessary she'd forgotten she even had it.

Running back to the car, she yanked the whole bunch out of the ignition. The littlest key slipped into the manual lock at the center of the gate and turned easily. Heaving the gates open, Emily drove through to the other side, taking care to close and lock them after her.

The dirt track was dry. She tapped the accelerator and sped up, sending clouds of dust billowing into the air. Above her head, sunlight searched for a way through the thick canopy, painting everything with an eerie shade of green. Green grass, green stalks, green moss, and layer upon layer of bright-green leaves.

Green. Like Aurelia's eye.

She couldn't get the image out of her head. It was like a sunspot burned into her retina. Thinking about it gave Emily the weirdest feeling. It was sort of like déjà vu: like she'd always known, deep down, but had forgotten.

She frowned and shook her head. *Stop obsessing. You're tired. Just think about something else.* But every time she closed her eyes, she saw it: a ring of light around a small black circle. A pale-green solar eclipse.

Emily drove north for about an hour, finally ending up in a pretty town set in a curved bay. She'd seen it before—she and Yves had passed it on their way from the airport on her first day—but had only properly noticed it during the awkward car ride with Scott; she remembered gazing enviously out the window at all the people drinking coffee and reading papers in the early morning sunshine.

The town had a small sandy beach and a cobbled esplanade lined with shops. Perfect. The emerging plan was to sit at a café, order something chocolatey, and watch the world go by. She also badly needed to digitally *retox*: binge on Wi-Fi. Her head was too noisy, so she would quiet it down by catching up on celebrity gossip, and checking out what her friends had eaten for dinner and where they'd been on holiday. She'd gorge on other people's fake lives, and maybe after that she would take a walk on the beach and eat an ice cream. Then she would feel better.

She reached for her phone—and stopped dead. *Shit.* Yet again, she'd totally forgotten to grab it from the top shelf of the wardrobe. *Never mind,* she thought, quickly adjusting her plan.

She wandered for a while, eventually spotting a cute little building with bright turquoise chairs, mosaic-topped tables, and a sign in the window that read CYBER CAFÉ. Emily approached the counter and asked for a café au lait with a *pain au chocolat*. The waitress took her order and her money, then powered up a dusty old computer sitting in a corner. Emily took a seat and waited for the ancient PC to warm up.

When it arrived, the warm flaky pastry turned out to be exactly what she needed; she could literally feel the stress sliding off her shoulders with every crunchy, oozy bite. Living and working at Querencia had been a dream come true, but it occurred to her that in eleven weeks, she hadn't taken a proper day off; she hadn't felt the need. But now, sitting at the café and gazing out the window at a whole new landscape filled with busy strangers, she realized just how trapped she'd been feeling lately. She should have done this much earlier. Just leaving the estate without telling Nina made her feel light, as if she were made of paper.

Nina.

The past few months had been so intense that Emily had forgotten almost everything about her life before. The estate and its owners had become everything to her. No one had ever made Emily feel even half as welcome as the Dennys had—so unconditionally accepted. What was the saying? *You can't choose your family.* Well, maybe that was true, but if Emily had been asked a month ago to sign a legal document cutting all ties with Juliet and Peter and binding her instead to the Dennys, she would have done it.

But that was then.

Emily leaned back in her chair. The awful asphyxia of the previous evening had eased, and her mind felt released. Away from Querencia, it was easier to lay out all the questions and examine them; specifically, what the hell had been going on last night? Why had Yves shown up? Who was the bald man? What was with the secret basement and all the boxes? And the smell—what was *that* all about?

In fact, here among the little blue tables in the bright daylight, a lot of things were starting to look a bit odd. The absence of Wi-Fi. The broken phone. Even the weekend with Scott. It had been an amazing few days, but how many housekeepers went skinny-dipping with their bosses? She'd become so close to Nina that they now shared a physical intimacy that Emily took for granted . . . but was it weird? Had Scott taken it as some sort of green light? If she tried to explain it to a friend, it might sound like she *had* joined a polygamist cult.

The most important question, though, was this: was Nina really faking Aurelia's illness? People did that sometimes. It had a German-sounding name. Munchausen. That was it. Munchausen by proxy. It seemed a bit far-fetched, though. She tossed the idea around, looking at it from all kinds of angles, but it didn't make sense. Nina was a good person. She would never hurt Aurelia; she was her mother. Then again, that didn't always mean what it should.

Also, if it *was* Munchausen by proxy, then both Scott and Yves were in on it. They were protecting and even *facilitating* it. Why? What did either of them stand to gain?

She sighed and closed her eyes. There it was again. The solar eclipse. The little half bubble. Green, brown, green, brown.

The computer beeped. It was ready. Emily grabbed the mouse and clicked. Seconds later, she was reunited with Google.

With all thoughts of social media sliding away—celebrity gossip could wait—she typed a few words into the search bar.

Google told her that the fancy name for different-colored eyes was heterochromia iridis. Apparently, it was reasonably common, and lots of celebrities had it. Mila Kunis, Kate Bosworth, some baseball player called Max Scherzer. People thought David Bowie had it, but he didn't (his was a paralyzed pupil as a result of getting punched in the face).

Emily skimmed a few medical websites. Heterochromia was usually hereditary, but there were many circumstances under which it might be acquired. It could be the result of an injury, or some kind of growth. Google supplied her with an extensive list of disorders characterized by different colored eyes: Sturge-Weber syndrome, von Recklinghausen disease, Hirschsprung disease, Bloch-Sulzberger syndrome . . . Apparently, tuberculosis and herpes could do it, as could a benign tumor. There was also a thing called Waardenburg syndrome, a genetic condition that could cause deafness and changes in pigmentation, not only in the eyes but also in the skin and hair.

Alarmingly, the use of medicinal eyedrops could change a person's eye color, as could blunt or penetrating trauma, a fact that chilled Emily to the bone.

She flicked through more sites, following links and opening pages until her brain hurt. Eventually, she took her hand off the mouse and ordered another coffee. Pulling at the dry skin on her lips, she stared at the street outside without taking anything in.

In theory, it was possible that Aurelia had one different-colored eye as a result of physical abuse. She could have been hit in the face or pushed into something hard or sharp. But Nina would never do anything like that. Munchausen seemed more likely in comparison. So, maybe Nina had been administering a particular kind of eyedrop as medication for, say, imaginary glaucoma? Hadn't she mentioned on Emily's first day that Aurelia's eyes were sensitive? It would fit right in with all the other fictional symptoms. Hives, vomiting, bed rest for days on end—why not throw in an eye disease, too?

But Nina wouldn't hurt her daughter. Surely she wouldn't.

Emily pressed her hand to her forehead. She was sweating.

Maybe Aurelia did have a medical condition, but Nina was just lying about its true nature. If Aurelia had Waardenburg syndrome, for example, the thing that affects a person's hearing, eyes, skin, and hair, there wouldn't be any real symptoms per se, just physical markers. Emily thought about Aurelia's shyness, her refusal to speak—but there was no other evidence that might suggest that she was even partially deaf.

Hearing, eyes, skin, hair.

Skin. Hair. An image flashed through Emily's mind. Yesterday, when Aurelia hit her head, Emily had checked the damage by parting her hair. She thought she'd seen dark bruising, not just around the wound but all over the scalp—but no one could bruise their entire head, could they?

Her entire head . . . Aurelia's hair was black. The bathtub had been stained, and the towel she'd found stuffed underneath was covered in dark streaky marks.

The truth kicked her in the gut, and she had to fight to keep herself from slipping off her chair: Nina was dying Aurelia's hair.

If Aurelia had Waardenburg's syndrome then, according to Google, she might have a streak of white in her hair, changes in skin pigmentation, and different-colored eyes. Emily had even found a website that mentioned a link between Waardenburg's and "intellectual disability," citing "unprovoked aggressive outbursts" as typical. It made a certain sense. Yes, that had to be it. Aurelia's hair was dyed, her eyes disguised, and her skin kept covered because underneath it all she looked different. She behaved "abnormally." And that just didn't fit in with Nina and Scott's beautiful, flawless existence. Emily had been right: Scott was ashamed of Aurelia. They both were. Nina was embarrassed to have an ugly, weird kid, so she hid her daughter away in a fantasy world where she was free to love her without fear of judgment.

Tear's pricked Emily's eyes. What was wrong with being different? Emily turned back to the PC and scrolled angrily through Google Images. There were loads of cool celebrities with heterochromia, and they were all stunning. *Look!* Mila Kunis? *Gorgeous.* Kate Bosworth? *Dazzling.* What's-his-name, the baseball player? *Ridiculously hot.* Their crystalline eyes only made them more attractive. Jane Seymour, Elizabeth Berkeley, Kiefer Sutherland, Alice Eve.

And . . . a little girl.

Emily stopped scrolling, her index finger hovering over the mouse.

The photograph was familiar. It was different from all the others: not professional at all, and not a red carpet in sight. Slightly blurry and overexposed, it showed a sweet little girl with strawberry-blond hair, a button nose, and gaps between her bright baby teeth. She wore a necklace of yellow plastic around her neck and clutched a My Little Pony in her pudgy hands. In the bottom-left corner, there was a patch of pink rucksack.

Suddenly, Emily found she could no longer breathe. Her skin flushed hot, and her stomach dropped as if she'd just fallen out of a plane.

And then she was pushing her chair back, knocking over her coffee, and racing out of the café as fast as she could, blindly running somewhere, anywhere, it didn't matter. She just had to get as far away from that computer as possible.

At the end of the esplanade, she jumped onto the beach and ran into the water, letting the tide splash over her sandals and up her legs. *No. No. No. This can't . . . it can't . . .* People were looking at her, but she didn't care. Something violent was happening in her chest.

The photograph of the little girl was familiar because she'd seen it before. A sharp, seedy memory came crashing back to her: three years ago, at Rhea's house, lying on the couch with a dry mouth and a headache, looking around to see several random dudes in the room. Beards, bong smoke, and the news on repeat. Everyone hypnotized by endless stories of shootings, child abuse, murder . . . and a kid. A red-haired three-year-old.

Over the sea, a big dark mess of cloud creeped and bulged. A name wriggled in Emily's head like a maggot.

Amandine.

The case had been famous. She remembered it especially clearly because of the stupid birthday thing Rhea had made her go to that same morning. She'd stood in Rhea's sister's back garden with hundreds of toddlers racing around her, just staring into space and thinking about that photo, thinking how inappropriate it was that she'd brought the sadness of it with her to the party along with a potent smell of weed.

A spot of rain landed on her cheek and a gust of wind blew

her hair across her face. The approaching clouds growled with thunder. Another storm was coming.

Emily retched.

L'Enfant d'Orage.

The Storm Child.

That photo had been splashed across every newspaper in Europe. It had traveled the whole world. The girl's eyes were, of course, the focus: one brown, one green.

My husband turns his laptop around so I can see the screen. He shows me a photograph of a house. No, two houses, side by side, with trees, grass, flowers, and a swimming pool.

"This first one has eight bedrooms and four full bathrooms. Just right for guests. It needs work but not too much."

We are standing in the kitchen. I look past the laptop into the living room, at the mirror on the wall, at our reflection in the glass. The perfect couple in their perfect home, heads bent together, discussing real estate over a bottle of pinot.

"I can just see it," he says. "A secluded bed-and-breakfast. We could do most of the renovations ourselves. I'd build your dream kitchen—outside, by the pool, so you could look at the water while you're cooking."

The lilies on the island bench are dying. Their petals are thin and droopy. One flower trembles as if brushed by an invisible finger, then drops onto the countertop. Clumps of orange pollen go skipping across the marble.

He taps the touch pad on his laptop, and the picture changes. "The second house is smaller, just five bedrooms. Very cozy. Just imagine: markets on Saturday mornings, Paris on the long weekends. Just like you always wanted. It could be a fresh start for us. A clean break."

Fresh. Clean. I roll the words around in my head until they come apart and lose their meaning.

"This house will sell quickly, I'm sure. I'll organize the packing. You won't have to lift a finger."

There's a faint ringing in my head: an alarm bell. "No," I hear myself say, a touch too loudly. "I'll do the packing."

"Fine, whatever you prefer. And after that, we'll go on holiday."

My head nods for me. His voice grows faint.

"We'll have everything shipped while we're away so we don't need to come back here. You can go straight from relax mode into new-house mode."

"What?" I say. "I can't hear you."

"How about Nice? Nice is nice."

The edges of my vision begin to cloud. I feel sick. My hands are shaking. It's been too long since my last dose. I turn my back and walk away, heading for the bathroom.

* * *

At first, so many things about the holiday seem like bad omens.

The evening flight out of Gatwick is delayed, which means that by the time we land, the car-rental office has long been closed. We are met instead in the depths of the parking lot by a shady-looking guy with a mustache as patchy as his paperwork, who yawns as he hands over the keys to our Porsche Cayenne. When my husband finds the child seat, he tells the mustached man that there's been a mistake and asks him to remove it. But Mustache Man refuses, claiming he has nowhere to put it, so we are forced to drive to our hotel with an empty toddler seat sitting in the back like a ghost.

We pull up in front of the hotel. The girl on reception is outrageously pregnant. Her belly ripples and twitches as she takes our details and talks us through the facilities.

As I finally start to drift off that night, a baby in the next room begins to cry and doesn't stop. I emerge from the hotel the next morning, cranky and bleary-eyed, to find that the building next door houses a designer boutique that sells toys and clothes and little shoes and lunch boxes.

My husband is horrified, his face becoming increasingly red and angry as the universe sees fit to hurl into our path painful reminder after painful reminder. But I know what to do. I close my eyes and summon my superpowers. I shut down my mind and retreat, leaving my empty body to bob along behind him like a balloon on a string. Nothing can get to me. And nothing does, until the day I am unexpectedly left alone.

And then, all the bad omens start to look like good ones.

* * *

I am pulling back the sheets and climbing into bed when he opens the balcony doors and steps back into the room.

251

"Can I talk to you for a minute?" he says, tapping his phone against the heel of his hand. "That was Verity. There's a problem with one of our exits."

I stare at him.

He sits on the edge of the bed. "Apparently it's not going to go ahead without me. I'm so sorry, but it looks like I'm going to have to pop back to London. Just for a couple of days."

I scratch at my wrists. The scars are almost a year old now, but they still itch.

"You don't have to come, though. I mean, I'm sure you'd rather not. . . ." He trails off.

I nod. I think about going back to London and feel ill.

"We're due to check out on Monday anyway, so it's not cutting the holiday short by much. But it does mean we'll have to scrap the road trip." He takes my hand. "I suggest you take the car back to the airport and hop on a flight to Bordeaux. I'll organize a car from there."

"I want to do the road trip," I hear myself say.

"I'm sorry," he says. "I know it's disappointing."

"No. I mean I'll do it on my own."

"Oh, I don't know." He rakes his hands through his hair, a recently developed habit. "I think I'd be more comfortable if you flew."

"No, I want to."

"Really?"

"Yes. I could do with some time to myself."

He rubs his chin. "It's a long drive. Are you sure you're up to it?"

"Honestly, I'll be fine. I could even do those stops you talked about. I've always wanted to see Marseilles."

He stops. Smiles at me. "God, it's good to hear you talking like this. You haven't taken an interest in anything for so long."

It's true, I haven't. But Wonder Woman is back. And she can do anything.

*   *   *

I wake up to an empty room singing with silence. His suitcase is gone, his side of the bed cold. The balcony door stands ajar, and the curtains billow like wings, an imprint of my dream.

I order room service and eat breakfast on the balcony, chewing eggs without tasting them. I watch as a group of girls in short skirts cross the road. Behind them, a silver-haired couple in matching pastel polo shirts strolls arm in arm. A woman in a tan dress and heels pulls a yappy dog on a leash. Farther down the street, a family emerges from a side street. Five kids in a ragtag procession led by a skinny redhead with a mean face. The redhead stomps toward the pedestrian crossing, yanking on the arm of a scrawny boy, no older than nine, wearing a baseball cap. Two slightly shorter boys—twins?—trail behind, followed by a chunky five- or six-year-old. And at the very back, a smaller girl toddles along in a purple swimsuit.

I focus in on her. I'm five stories up but I can see every detail. She waddles like a duckling, her footsteps flat and irregular. Copper-colored curls bounce around her face as she turns her head from side to side, taking everything in: the traffic, the tourists, the buildings, the shops. She tries to keep up with her siblings but gets distracted, first by a dog and then by something small on the ground. She stops to pick it up, and I feel my body twitch. "Don't pick that up, sweetie," I murmur. "It's yucky." I wince as the little girl pops whatever it is into her mouth.

Ahead, the redheaded woman spins around and throws up her arms in frustration. The twins are fighting. Letting go of the eldest boy, she stalks back to the end of the line and pushes one of them in the back with one hand. Meanwhile, the little girl in the swimsuit has stopped to stare at the souvenir stalls on the other side of the road. Colorful balls and whirling windmills are stacked under red-and-white-striped awnings. She points, mesmerized, and edges toward the curb.

I grip the balcony railing hard.

Blissfully unaware of the cars hurtling by in both directions, the child squats and puts her hands down, steadying herself on the curb. She lowers one plump foot onto the asphalt, and I choke back a terrified sob—and then a man in a Hawaiian shirt bounds to the rescue amid a cacophony of horns. Grabbing the little girl's arm, he hauls her back onto the pavement. I go slack with relief.

The ginger woman, having heard the commotion, is coming back now. Completely ignoring the stranger who has saved her daughter's life, she bends down and, sticking her big red face right up close, yells so loud that the sound carries all the way to my balcony.

Then she draws back her hand and whacks the little girl hard across her legs.

And that's all it takes. I see her anguished little face and feel the sting of the blow on my own skin, and suddenly I'm alive and fizzing, rushing up and out of what feels like a long tunnel, gasping for breath as if I've just been pulled from a watery grave.

* * *

Gripping the handle of my suitcase, I drag it down to the lobby. I pay my bill and request that the valet bring my car around to the street parking spaces.

"I hope you enjoyed your stay with us, madame," said the receptionist. "Stay safe in the storm."

"Storm?"

"*Oui, madame.* There is a storm forecast this morning."

I glance out of the window at the clear blue sky. "Well, there's no sign of it yet. I think I'll head to the beach for one last swim."

"Very good. Will you be leaving your bag with the concierge?"

"No, thank you, I'll take it to the car."

The Porsche is brought to a side street just behind the hotel. After stowing my suitcase in the back, I sling my beach bag over my shoulder and walk across the road to the beach, stopping in at the U Express on the corner for a box of strawberries.

The beach is already busy, surprisingly so for a Monday morning.

255

I pick my spot carefully. I lay on my sun lounger and put on my sunglasses. I just want to watch her. I just want to be close.

With her copper curls and milky skin, she doesn't look exactly like my baby, not at first. She's older than Aurelia was, but even so, there are similarities. The angle at which she cocks her head. The way she tucks her chin into her chest when something catches her attention. The petal-like lower lip, the position of her ears, the way she sticks out her elbows when she walks, like a busy housewife. No time to stop, things to do, places to be.

I pull the strawberries from my bag—Aurelia's favorite. I set the box on my lounger and pick the biggest, juiciest one. I hold it out and press a finger to my lips. *Sssh, it's a secret.* No one sees; most of the surrounding sunbathers have their eyes closed, and the redhead is too busy swiping and scrolling on her phone. The little curly-haired child pads over to me, eyeing the strawberry. I smile, and she edges closer. Finally, she plucks up the courage and swipes it from my palm. Then, spying the box, helps herself to another, then another, stuffing them in her mouth until the juice runs down her chin. At perhaps two and a half, maybe three years old, she is already a practiced thief.

"Come here, strawberry girl," I say, reaching out with a napkin to wipe the evidence off her face—and my heart stops. Her eyes. They're totally different colors, like two gemstones: one tawny gold, and the other the color of shallow seawater.

Aurelia's face comes back to me with an almost physical force; those glittering, complex browns and then that little quarter patch of blue, the little rock pool.

It is overwhelming. It is a sign.

Half an hour later, the redhead sits up. Both her face and shoulders are now a painful shade of orangey-pink. Red Mum, I think with a smile.

I turn back to Strawberry. She is looking more and more like Aurelia. If I squint my eyes in just the right way, I can almost believe it *is* her. She's beautiful, astonishing, and no one is taking a blind bit of notice. Hundreds of special little moments—smiles and frowns and exclamations—are being thrown into the air like bridal bouquets, and I am the only one catching them. Part of me wants to shout at Red Mum. "Put down your drink, woman! Look at what you're missing!" But I don't. I like having Strawberry all to myself.

We play a game of peekaboo together. She gives me gifts of pebbles. I find some old receipts in the back of my purse and she draws pictures on them, passing them to me like love letters. I watch as Red Mum knocks back coffee like shots of tequila, only turning once or twice to check on her daughter.

* * *

By the time lunchtime rolls around, Red Mum is buzzing. She taps her fingers, jiggles her feet, and presses her phone to her ear, making call after unsuccessful call. Muttering under her breath, she glares at the water, then seems to come to a decision. She throws the phone down on her lounger and begins hurling her belongings back into her beach bag, barking in French at her children and slapping frizzy strands of ginger hair out of her eyes.

One by one, four sullen children slouch in from the waves.

I don't move, but inside I'm panicking. I look around for Strawberry but can't see her. I don't want her to leave.

Red Mum's flapping becomes even more frantic. Throwing her bag over her shoulder, she stalks off toward the exit with her phone to her ear. She yells a few more harsh-sounding words over her shoulder, but they're lost on Strawberry's wired, overexcited siblings. They barge past sunbathers and waiters, squawking and squabbling and trying to trip each other up.

I still can't see Strawberry. I sit up. Where is she? And then I hear a giggle and something prods me from underneath. I slide off my lounger and get down on my hands and knees. She's curled up in a ball, a mischievous look on her gorgeous face. "Hey, monkey," I whisper. "You'd better go. They're leaving without you."

Strawberry puts a finger to her lips: *Sssshh.*

"Come on," I say gently. I look from the little girl to her swiftly departing mother and back again. I know I should call out—*Hey! Stop! You've forgotten something!*—but my mouth just won't form the words.

"Come on," I say again to Strawberry, wiping tears from my eyes. I stretch out my hand, but Strawberry shakes her head. Again, she holds her finger to her lips. *Sssshhh.*

And this time I copy her, like a mirror image.

A cold gust of wind ruffles my hair. Surprised, I glance up at the rippling ceiling of blue-striped fabric and see, through the gaps, a billowing mass of purple cloud. Where has that come from? All around me, other people are staring up at the sky in wonder.

Strawberry crawls out from underneath the lounger.

The wind charges again, stronger this time. A few towels are blown onto the ground. In the restaurant area, menus flip off tables and vault away over the deck.

There's a pause and then, like an orchestra, the storm really begins to play. The ocean bulges and delivers an enormous white wave onto the sand, giving the cue for another neat roll of thunder. Then the rain joins in, tapping out a soft introductory rhythm that quickly gets louder and more forceful until fat drops of water are striking a clattering percussion on every available surface.

Strawberry lets out a wail and holds out her arms.

The rain starts to gush in streams off the sides of the umbrellas. People who just moments ago had been lying corpse-like on their loungers are now jumping to their feet and throwing towels over their heads. They hop back through the rows of white furniture, tripping over themselves to get under the roof of the restaurant.

A woman in front of me bundles up her little boy in a towel, covering him from head to toe. She picks him up and hurries away, his little face just visible underneath a fluffy hood. A family rushes past, carrying similarly wrapped children. One of them is wailing like a car alarm. The father catches my eye and flashes me a parent-to-parent grin. Life with kids, hey?

The drumming of the rain becomes a sharp hammer of hard objects as lumps of ice fall from the sky. Strawberry cries out as one strikes her on the shoulder. *"Maman!"* she cries.

I don't even think. I pick her up and hold her tight. "It's okay, little one," I say, pulling her close. "I'll take care of you."

Thunder cracks overhead.

I'll take care of you . . .

I reach down, grab my towel, and throw it over Strawberry's head, copying the woman with the little boy.

I'll take care of you . . .

Strawberry nestles her face against my shoulder . . . and then I'm holding her again, my baby girl, my Aurelia, and I'm running to the car leaving birthday cake and gifts behind, and then I'm in the hospital room, powerless and afraid, reliving the searing, brutal moment her eyes cloud over with fear, the moment she loses hope, the moment she realizes that her mummy can't save her. I see her go limp in the hands of the doctors just as years earlier my own mother had gone limp in my arms. I see her eyes roll back in her head and her skin set like concrete, and I know I have failed her.

Well, I won't fail again.

"It's okay, sweetheart," I say, as the delicate scent of Aurelia's skin fills my nose. "Everything's going to be fine. Mummy's here."

I rush toward the restaurant, my shoulders hunched against the wind. But there's no room; all the space in the restaurant area is taken up by wet, chattering tourists. I try to nudge my way in but no one will move. I run to the stairs.

A purple umbrella lies discarded against the bottom step, and I snatch it off the ground. Shifting Aurelia over onto one hip, I push it open and brace it against the wind.

I rush up and onto the promenade. Lifting the umbrella a little, I glimpse the curb. The hail has stopped and the rain is slowing, but water still churns in the gutters like a river. I check for headlights and flinch as a bright flash of lightning illuminates the road.

Suddenly, there is a terrifying bang: a skull-splitting crack that takes my breath away.

I stagger backward as the crack turns into a roar, and then the whole world burns with a fierce orange light. Aurelia screams, and for one confusing moment I'm sure that a chasm is opening under my feet. I hear loud voices and a ripping, wrenching sound; the ground is shaking—but it does not split and we do not fall. Instead, there's a rush of wind and a strange assault of hot and cold objects against my skin. There are embers everywhere, red-hot sparks shooting and hissing their complaint as they meet the wet concrete.

Turning, I see a raging bonfire just meters from where I stand; a palm tree has been struck by lightning, its split trunk stretching the full width of the road, its leaves crackling with flame. Broken, burning branches litter the ground. I gaze at the fire as it fights with the rain, realizing only too late that Aurelia is transfixed, too, her mouth stretched wide, her face flecked with ash. She is terrified out of her mind.

A voice to my left calls out in English, "Are you okay? Are you hurt?"

I wheel around to find my savior, but a sudden gust of wind blows smoke and ash right in my face and down my throat. I fling the umbrella in front of me, turning it into a shield.

For a moment I am blind. Crying out for the help that no longer seems to be there, I lurch away, stumbling as my foot slips off the curb. The road . . . I'm nearly there. I can do this.

I tighten my grip around my baby's trembling body and press on, losing a sandal in the torrent. "Not far to go now, bubba, hang in there!" I yell as I struggle to the other side. I manage to turn right and keep going until I reach a familiar corner, and then I am on a side street, and then I am next to a car, and it's my car, the rented Porsche.

Fleetingly, I'm struck by a nagging feeling that I'm supposed to do something or go somewhere, but I can't remember what it is and the rain is still coming down, and Aurelia is still screaming, and she's so heavy, she's such a big girl now, and she's soaking, I have to get her inside or she'll get sick. . . .

Still keeping hold of both Aurelia and the umbrella, I wriggle the straps of my sodden beach bag off my shoulder and dig for the keys. I unlock the car, open the back door—and the unwanted child seat greets me like an old friend.

Releasing the umbrella into the wind, I tug the wet towel off my sobbing daughter and hustle her into the seat, taking care to strap her in properly. I toss my bag into the foot well and slam Aurelia's door, leaping around to the other side where I open my own door and throw myself inside.

For a second, I'm not sure where I am.

What's happening? What am I doing? What comes next?

The rain hammers on the roof of the Porsche and flows over the slowly fogging windshield.

Road trip.

Yes. That's right. Now I remember. I'm going on a road trip to a new house. A new life. I will meet my husband there. I will pass through Marseilles. Check out the basilica.

I slide the key into the ignition.

In the backseat, a small whimper.

I feel myself stiffen. A muscle twitches in my cheek.

"Maman?"

My body locks up. I can't turn around.

Aurelia?

Inhale. Exhale.

I close my eyes.

"Hush, darling," I say. "Everything's okay. Mummy's here. Let's take you home, alright?"

I start the engine with trembling fingers and turn on the air. The fog on the windshield evaporates almost instantly.

CHAPTER THIRTY-SEVEN

EMILY

EMILY SAT behind the wheel of the SUV with the engine running, her eyes fixed on the front entrance of a brown building. A set of glass doors slid open and shut, and people went in and out. She chewed her bottom lip, squinting through the rain-spattered windshield.

A man in navy slacks and a light-blue shirt appeared, strolling through the doors toward a car parked at the curb, and Emily sat up straight, her fingers hooked around the door handle. But at the last minute she let go and watched the man drive away, because what was she going to say?

I know where Amandine Tessier is.

She opened her mouth to try the words out, to see what they might sound like, but they caught in her throat like dry crumbs.

"Fuck." Keeling over, she rammed her head against the steering wheel. What the hell did she think she was doing, sitting outside a police station because of something she saw, or thought she'd seen, on the internet? She might be wrong. She got things wrong all the time.

This is insane, she told herself. *You're insane.* What kind of crazy person wades into the ocean, then jumps, dripping wet, into her car only to drive in circles for over an hour, muttering to herself? She'd considered stopping and asking someone for help, but she couldn't bear the thought of actually speaking to someone, a stranger, a *French* stranger, who wouldn't understand what the hell she was talking about. They might think she was drunk or mad; they might call the police to come and arrest *her*, carry *her* off to a padded cell as if *she* was the one who had done something wrong.

Emily couldn't catch her breath. What if the police did arrest her? What if they assumed she was a coconspirator? What if they put her in a cell and called her parents—or worse, called Nina, who would hide all the evidence and bluff her way out of it, and then what would happen?

But no, no one was getting arrested because she'd probably just made a mistake. That girl in the photo wasn't Aurelia. No. She'd just been cooped up for too long. She'd taken all the weird stuff that had been happening lately and written herself a little play.

Oh god, I just want to go home, she thought, desperate for the feel of Juliet's arms around her. Her parents would help. They'd tell her the right thing to do. Emily put one hand on the keys and the other on the gear stick, ready to drive immediately to the nearest airport or, better still, all the way north to Calais, where a sturdy ferry would carry her away over miles of rough gray sea.

But she couldn't go anywhere. Her passport was sitting in a drawer in her bedroom at Querencia.

So, just go talk to the police, she told herself, switching the engine off. She should just walk in there and tell them what she suspected. Surely they could send a car and take a look around? They could make up an excuse—a "routine check" or something. They wouldn't find anything anyway, just a normal family minding their own business.

But if Scott and Nina *had* done something terrible, if that really was Amandine Tessier and she was being held against her will . . . well, then Emily would have done the right thing. Aurelia—no, *Amandine*—would be returned to her rightful family, and Nina would . . .

Go to jail.

Suddenly the full implications hit home. *Oh god, Nina, what have you done?* And Scott . . . he'd be convicted, too. Everything he'd worked his whole life to build, everything he'd managed to do, to be, to have: he would lose it all, and he would die in prison because he wouldn't be able to handle the shame. They'd find him swinging from a noose tied to a light fixture in some squalid little room.

Emily sobbed as the rain outside began to pour. She couldn't do it. She couldn't betray them; these beautiful, wonderful people who had picked her up and taken her in, who had cared for her like she belonged to them. They were good, they were kind, they were her new home, she *loved* them—

BANG BANG BANG. A blurry shape hammered on the passenger window. Someone was standing on the pavement, wiping the water off the glass with a black sleeve and peering inside. Emily jumped back in her seat.

"*Allo, ca va?*" called a woman's voice.

Tell them. Tell them now.

"*Ca va?*" the police officer said again.

Tell them.

Emily turned back to the windshield, wavering. And then she saw something. A white utility truck. Just ahead, idling on the corner with its lights on. In the driver's seat, a dark, hulking shape.

She sat up straight.

"*Madame? Puis-je vous aider?*"

Emily turned the key in the ignition. Fumbling with the gear stick, she threw the SUV into gear and pulled out sharply into the road, leaving the police officer standing openmouthed in the rain.

CHAPTER THIRTY-EIGHT

EMILY

E MILY DROVE back to Querencia in a state of panic, talking to herself, arguing with her conscience, veering off the road, and turning the car around only to switch directions again moments later.

Calm down, she told herself. *Think.*

She'd been convinced that the dark shape sitting in the white truck had been Yves, that he'd followed her there. But that was ridiculous . . . wasn't it? She thought about the day she'd seen him at the market. Had he followed her then, too? How many other times had he tailed her on a shopping trip? Every time? Had she never been alone?

Don't be stupid, this isn't a spy movie. No one's "tailing" you, no one's "after" you. Scott and Nina would never threaten or hurt her, she told herself. But instead of conviction, she felt only uncertainty.

Kicking herself, she considered making another U-turn. She should've told the police. *Coward.*

But it wasn't really cowardice; neither was it fear. It wasn't even the confidentiality agreement she'd signed in London, the purpose of which she was only now beginning to understand.

No, the reason she hadn't gone into that police station was that she couldn't be sure there was anything to tell.

If only she could talk to Scott. He would explain everything. She thought again of her phone, sitting uselessly in the wardrobe.

Unable to bear the clamor of her thoughts any longer, she switched on the local radio and focused on the French, partially translating idiotic conversations about dogs and the state of the roads. Drawing huge, deep breaths into her belly, she took mindful note of her surroundings and relaxed her muscles one by one. She dropped her shoulders and lowered the windows. She visualized her anxiety as a balloon drifting away into the sky, and by the time she reached the turn off for Querencia, her eyes were dry, the rain had eased, and she was convinced she was being irrational. Melodramatic. Paranoid.

The photograph she'd seen on Google couldn't possibly have been Aurelia. What a silly, *silly* idea. She must've been mad, sitting outside that police station. What had she been thinking? She and Nina would laugh about it later.

You did what? Nina would say.

I know, Emily would reply. *How crazy am I?*

So crazy!

The craziest!

She was still chuckling as she reached the gates, but her smile died when she remembered having to manually unlock the gates that morning. Silently regarding the keypad, she saw that the red light was blinking once more. Warily, she punched in the code.

Emily blinked as the mechanism immediately hummed into action. The gates took forever to open. The hinges creaked loudly, and the black letters warped as the metal swung away. Inching the car over the sand, she parked in her usual spot in front of the guesthouse. Perhaps it was the weather, but both houses looked dirtier than they had that morning.

She got out and paused, listening for any sound that might

tell her where Nina was. Almost exactly as she'd done on her first day, she turned in circles, taking in the neat spiral of the lawn and the paths leading away through the grounds. Other than the sound of softly dripping water, everything was quiet.

They were probably inside, Emily decided. Maybe it was time for a shower. She'd be able to think more clearly after that. She climbed onto the porch of the guesthouse and slipped off her sandals. Pushing open the door, she switched on the hallway light.

"Oh, holy *shit*!"

Just inside the doorway, Nina stood with her hands on her hips. "Well, hey there," she said with a smile. "You're back."

Emily gaped. Her handbag slipped off her shoulder and hit the floor with a thud. "Hi," she said, too loudly.

Nina tilted her head. "You worried us this morning, motoring off like that. We thought there might have been some kind of emergency."

"Oh. No. I just . . . went out." *She really is tall,* Emily thought. *And fit. She could probably run quite far and quite fast.*

"Where did you go?"

Emily searched Nina's face for . . . anything. Guilt. Panic. A big red "K" for "Kidnapper." Then it dawned on her that she hadn't thought to come up with a cover story. "I, er, went to the, er, supermarket," she stammered. "I checked the storeroom and we were a bit low on, y'know, stuff. And I was up early anyway so I thought . . ." She trailed off, realizing only too late how flimsy the lie was. There were no bags in the back of the car, no shopping, no receipt.

Nina's eyes flickered to the door as if reading her thoughts. "Great idea," she said, inching forward. "Can I help you unload?"

"Oh, well, no, because it was closed. The supermarket, I mean. I don't know why."

She found herself shaking. *Come on, Emily. You're an actress, aren't you? So, ACT.*

Taking a breath, she met Nina's unblinking stare and held it. "There was a fire engine outside. They weren't letting people in, so I went for a coffee, had a look around a nearby town. I hope you don't mind. It's been a while since I got off the property."

"Oh, sure, it's good to get out." Nina nodded. "Just let me know next time, okay?"

"Okay."

There was a pause, during which it occurred to Emily that Nina might be toying with her. Maybe Nina knew exactly where she'd been. Maybe that *had* been Yves outside the police station.

"Hey, listen." Nina touched Emily on the elbow. "I meant to have a chat with you about yesterday."

"Yesterday?"

"Aurelia's accident?"

Emily clapped a hand to her mouth. She'd completely forgotten. "Oh my god, Aurelia. How is she? Is she okay?"

"She's fine. Just a scratch, really." Nina gave a cheerful shrug. "You know how these head wounds can gush. No, I just wanted to say, I'm sorry for losing my temper. It was totally uncalled for. I'd had a shocker of a day, and when I saw all that blood I just lost it."

"That's okay." Emily's voice came out high and wobbly.

"Well, it isn't really. It wasn't your fault."

"Oh . . ." Emily batted the air awkwardly with her hand. "No worries, mate."

They stood for a moment, both wearing their pantomime grins.

"Anyway," said Nina. "Aurelia's waiting for me by the pool. Lunch is almost ready, if you'd like to join us?"

"Yeah, great. I'll just grab a quick shower."

"See you down there."

Nina moved first, stepping around Emily on her way to the door. Just shy of the threshold, she stopped and looked back, just a half turn. "And I meant to ask . . . how did you get out of the gate this morning?"

"Sorry?"

"We had a power cut overnight," Nina said. "The system was down. Wasn't the gate locked?"

"Oh . . ." Without exactly knowing why, Emily blushed. "Yeah. But I have a key."

"Oh, right." Nina nodded, contemplating the wallpaper. "You have a key. Of course." Then, with the tiniest of smiles, she swept out the door and into the daylight.

CHAPTER THIRTY-NINE

SCOTT

"AH, THERE you are," Verity said, her heels tapping on the concrete mezzanine floor. "What are you doing up here?"

"Nothing," Scott replied, tearing his eyes from the vista beyond the roof terrace: gray buildings, flat roofs, and a bulging blanket of cloud. "Just looking. Haven't you gone for lunch yet? Or is it true that you survive on a diet of air and efficiency?"

"Ha ha." Verity came to stand next to him and looked down over the wall. The cars slid up and down the road below. "I just thought I should tell you that Channel 4 called again, wanting to know if you'd changed your mind about being interviewed for that documentary."

Scott snorted.

"That's what I thought you'd say. I also wanted to show you this." She passed him a glossy magazine, the first few pages peeled back. "You're famous, apparently."

Scott's stomach lurched violently. Then he saw the picture. It was of three people standing on a red carpet. Two of them were startlingly beautiful, their arms around each other. The third was stooped, gray-faced, and haggard. *I should have shaved,* he thought, remembering how he'd caught a cab straight from work that day. He'd changed his clothes in the car.

Shrugging, he looked back at the buildings.

Verity shook her head. "Oh, no, you don't get to be all blasé this time." She tapped the photograph with her finger. "This is you."

"I guess so."

"And do you realize who you're standing with?"

Scott knew very well who it was. There probably wasn't anyone on earth who didn't know that woman's face, or the face of her husband.

"What were you *doing* with them?" Verity gushed, her icy demeanor abandoned in the face of real celebrity. "What did you talk about? What are they like? Oh my god, I'm such a huge fan. When the hell was this?"

"Some benefit thing a few weeks back." Scott sighed. He was an idiot. He should never have gone. "Some charity ball."

"Oh yes, she's very into her charities, isn't she? Save the Children, right?"

"Something like that."

"Speaking of which," Verity said, tucking the magazine under her arm and passing him a piece of paper with a flourish.

"What's that?" he asked.

"It's from the Phare Foundation. They're giving you their top honor this year. The Lodestar Award." She smiled. "Congratulations."

Scott looked at the piece of paper.

Verity raised an eyebrow. "It's quite a big deal, you know. Taylor Swift won it last year."

"What did she do?"

"Gave a lot of money to victims of natural disasters."

"Yeah?"

"Uh huh. What did you do?"

"Oh, you know. Something similar."

"For which cause?"

"I forget."

"Interesting, because it says here that you've given 'unprec-

edented amounts of money exclusively to charities and organi-
zations specializing in the protection and welfare of children.'
In total, you've donated over . . ." Verity paused. "Wow. You
kept that quiet."

Scott cracked his knuckles. "Well, you know, the company
has been on a roll. And I already have a boat, so . . ." He went
back to the window, the darkening sky, and all the people scurrying around beneath it like vermin.

"You're a really good man, Scott," Verity said after a while.
He squirmed.

"I mean it," she said, stepping closer to him. "You do so
much to help others, and you never take any credit. You've
helped *me* so much, and you don't even realize it."

"Please," he said, recoiling. He was not a good man. A bit of
money thrown at a few charities would never change that.

"I don't mean to embarrass you, but I don't think I've ever
really thanked you properly."

Scott was suddenly short of breath. He didn't deserve any
thanks. He was a coward, a failure, the oldest cliché in the
book. No better than his fucked-up father.

In his pocket, his phone buzzed.

"You gave me a chance when no one else would," Verity
continued, clearly warming up to a speech. "You helped me get
back on my feet. You saved me."

"Please," Scott said again. "There's no need." He reached
into his pocket. Pins and needles ran up and down his arm. He
stepped away and Verity stiffened.

"What is it?" she said.

He was being ungracious, he knew that, but he couldn't
breathe. He had to get out of the room immediately. His phone
felt like a burning hot ember in his palm, searing through his
flesh.

"Excuse me, I have to, uh . . ." He ran down the stairs and
into his office, shutting the door and flipping the smart-glass
switch. When the wall was fully opaque, he pulled his phone

out. There they were, trapped in a bubble, the words that he'd been so sure he would never see or hear.

She knows.

His heart stopped. His mouth went dry.

Then, another message, quick on the heels of the last.

She's going to tell.

He fumbled with the phone, his palms slippery.

Don't panic, he typed, we'll pay her.

Three dots appeared at the bottom of the screen, which supposedly meant that Nina was typing, but no message appeared. He imagined her in the basement, her fingers hovering over the keypad of the MacBook.

Moving on autopilot, he crossed the room in just three strides and grabbed the whiskey decanter and a crystal tumbler from the middle shelf of the cabinet. He poured a large measure and tossed it back.

When after several minutes she still hadn't responded, he tried again. Sit tight. Don't do anything. I'm coming.

Another pause. Another drink.

No, came Nina's eventual reply. I'm sick of doing things your way. I'll deal with it myself.

Scott felt his body go limp as though suspended in water.

And then, he drew back his arm and hurled his glass at the wall so hard that it shattered into a thousand glittering pieces.

CHAPTER FORTY

EMILY

L UNCH WAS a steaming, glistening Brazilian seafood stew. Down by the pool, Nina bustled about fetching bowls and cutlery from the kitchen, arranging flowers in a vase, and pouring homemade lemonade into a jug. She positioned it all carefully on the table and stepped back to admire the effect. Her face was fixed in a Barbie-doll smile.

"Aurelia squeezed all the lemons herself, didn't you, Strawberry?" Nina said, indicating the lemonade. She poured a glass and held it out to Emily with a trembling hand. The liquid inside slopped gently up the sides.

Oblivious to the tension, Aurelia sat at the table, carefully arranging a selection of figurines around her plate: horses, fairies, witches, and dragons. There were circles under her eyes, but otherwise there was no sign of the previous day's drama; the wound was hidden under her usual floppy straw hat. Emily hoped it had been dressed properly.

"She's not feeling too crash-hot today," Nina said, following Emily's gaze. "Bad night, poor thing." Nina picked up a knife and began to slice a baguette into small rounds. Aurelia looked up as if to say, *Who, me?*

Emily placed her lemonade on the table without taking a sip.

Everything's fine, she told herself. *I was wrong. I made a mistake.* She tried to smile but her mouth kept twisting downward.

"Come on, my darling." Nina stood behind Aurelia, gently nudging her until she was sitting properly at the table. "You need to eat."

Emily sat down opposite. Directly above, the sun beat down on their backs, warming the silverware until it was almost too hot to touch.

I was wrong. Everything is fine.

She stared into her bowl. Prawns poked through the surface of the stew like crooked fingers.

Nina tore a piece of bread into small pieces and placed it at Aurelia's lips. Absorbed in her game, Aurelia opened her mouth and chewed solemnly, tapping Nina on the arm to remind her she needed to feed the toys, too. Nina obliged, passing the bread from fairy to horse to witch.

Emily fixated on Aurelia's hands, each fingernail a tiny pink rose petal. The index finger held a smudge of purple ink, and her left wrist was decorated with several cheerful red stamps that said, GREAT WORK! On her forearms, just visible under the thick smear of sunscreen, were the telltale freckles. And once she started looking she couldn't stop. The roots of Aurelia's hair were covered by the hat, but Emily thought she could detect a slightly unnatural sheen to the ends, a subtle red-purple tinge. She took her memory of the Google image and laid it over Aurelia's solemn little face. It fit perfectly.

No. I'm wrong. I have to be wrong.

But suddenly everything was falling into place so fast that she had to grip the edge of the table to stay upright. Aurelia was not Aurelia. She was Amandine Tessier, a little French girl who had been snatched from the streets of Nice at almost three years old. She had been kept hidden at Querencia for a further three years, spoiled and babied and fiercely loved by a woman who was not her mother. She'd been disguised beyond all recognition, the "medical condition" providing a multitude of excuses to keep her out of sight, out of school, and covered up from head to toe. Both her heart and her mother tongue had been cruelly ripped out and replaced by something unspeakably foreign. The trauma had rendered her mute; she'd been literally scared speechless.

And Nina . . . ironically, Nina was terrified of losing the person she loved the most, tormented daily by the thought that someone might come and take her away.

Emily was suddenly struck by a feeling of displacement so strong that she nearly broke down. She didn't belong here in this place, with these people. She wanted to run home, but she realized she didn't know where that was. For the first time in her life, she desperately wanted her real mother. She wanted the body that had birthed her, her own flesh and blood. Without her, Emily felt small and alone in the world, an astronaut untethered from a spacecraft.

Please make this stop. Please make me forget. Please let's just go back to the way things were.

Under the table, something kicked her foot. She looked up to see Aurelia watching her with wide eyes, holding a horse in her outstretched hand. *Play with me.* Returning Aurelia's gaze, Emily found that she could see the lens now, a very faint circle right at the edge of the right iris, imperceptible unless you were looking for it. And Aurelia's features . . . Emily understood that she'd been completely fooled. There was no resemblance whatsoever to either Nina or Scott. Her nose was too big, her eyes too round.

A deep sense of betrayal sliced through her, sharp and bitter. *They never trusted me,* she thought. *They never once dropped the pretense.*

"Are you okay, Em?" One look at Nina's beautiful face, so full of love and concern, and Emily almost crumbled. "You don't look well."

"Yes, I—I might go and lie down."

"You do that." Nina fixed her with a level stare. "I hope it's not something you ate."

Something tightened in Emily's chest. She looked at Nina. Then she looked down at the stew.

"Can I get you anything?" Nina said, her stare unblinking.

"No, I don't think so." Emily pushed away her untouched bowl and stood up, her chair scraping noisily on the tiles. "I'll just go get some rest."

As she turned to go, she looked up and her eyes met Nina's. They, too, were wet and anguished, full of pain and sadness . . . and something else.

Resolve.

CHAPTER FORTY-ONE

SCOTT

R YANAIR OUGHT *to be sued for cruelty to humans,* Scott thought, writhing and fidgeting in his airline seat. Maybe *he* would sue them.

He gripped his phone, repeatedly tapping the call button, pressing it against his ear again and again, but there was no answer. *Goddammit, Yves, where are you?*

He felt like a battery chicken squeezed into a steel cage with hundreds of stinking, grimy creatures. The seat itself was unbearably narrow and the armrests so thin it was like trying to lay your elbows on scissor blades. The toilets looked to be the same size as the luggage compartments, and there was a smell, too—Scott sniffed the air and made a face—of feet, and microwaved pies. He glanced around at his fellow passengers, at the bickering families and the couples contentedly flipping through the duty-free magazine. None of them seemed to be even half as appalled as he was. In fact, some people actually seemed to be more interested in *him* than in the brutal conditions in which they all found themselves.

Admittedly, he did look a little out of place in his Tom Ford suit, gleaming Rolex, and Ray-Bans, but there hadn't been any time to change. He'd told Verity it was an emergency, but apparently the jet was in the hangar undergoing scheduled maintenance and there were no charters available at such short notice. Worse, there were no full-service flights until the morning, which meant the only way he was going to get to France immediately was via budget airline.

Thankfully, Verity had found him a last-minute ticket. He'd arrived at the check-in desk sweaty, bewildered, and lost without the usual VIP assistance. He'd stood in line at the gate for hours with countless people all carrying plastic bags and those pathetic travel pillows, his body temperature rising with every passing second, and he still hadn't managed to cool down. He thought about taking his jacket off, but it felt like protection somehow, like armor. The sunglasses, too, felt prophylactic: a deterrent to anyone who might feel the need to make small talk.

Come on, come on, come on, come on. What was the hold up? They'd been sitting on the tarmac for an eternity.

At last, the plane crept backward out of the terminal, and a few people let out half-hearted cheers. Scott mentally calculated his arrival time at Querencia. They'd be in the air for one hour and thirty-five minutes. Another fifteen minutes for disembarkation and passport control at the other end. He had no bags, so there'd be no need to hang around at the carousel, but it was looking increasingly likely that he'd have to make his own way from the airport.

As the engines kicked in and the plane shot forward, Scott marveled, not for the first time, at the situation in which he now found himself. He never could fathom how he'd gone from a man who loved and adored his wife to one who feared her. She was still the same woman he'd fallen in love with, the same girl who'd had him floored from the first day they met, but she was also someone else; a stranger, someone who would not hesitate to do the unthinkable.

He'd known she was fragile when he married her, but that had been part of the appeal. She was broken but refined, like those Japanese vases in which cracks became precious when repaired with gold. The reasons behind that fragility, though, were hazy. He'd asked questions while they were dating, but she was an expert at deflection. What little she *had* shared suggested that she'd fled a painful past and was no longer in touch with her family. He could understand that, and chose not to press her for details. It was only once they were engaged and planning a wedding that the truth came out: there *was* no family. She'd been the only child of a single parent, and that parent had tragically passed away. After a string of failed foster-care arrangements, she got her own place and a job, and saved her money. On her twenty-third birthday, she had booked a trip around the world and never looked back.

So, Scott had decided, he would be her everything. She would never be alone again. He dressed her in expensive clothes and put her in expensive cars and *bang,* she was fixed. Mended. Back to normal. *You're welcome, little lady.*

It never occurred to him that there might be more to it than that.

It took him years to face the enormity of what she'd done. He should have gone to the police the minute he arrived at Querencia, the minute he saw that strange little girl. Maybe then it wouldn't have been so bad; maybe she would have got the help she really needed. But it was too late for that now.

Scott writhed in his seat, sweat now pouring off his forehead. He willed the plane to go faster. He removed his sunglasses and wiped his eyes with his sleeve, trying to sit quietly.

"You alright, mate?" a voice said.

Scott opened his eyes.

The man in the seat next to him was peering at Scott through narrowed eyes. "You don't look like you're doing so well. I've got some travel sickness pills if you want one. Or two?"

"I'm fine," said Scott.

"You sure?"

"I said I'm fine."

"Okay, no probs. They're here if you change your mind."

Scott closed his eyes again and tried to focus. Maybe he *was* sick. He did feel like he could easily throw up or pass out. Perhaps he was having a heart attack. Perhaps he would go into cardiac arrest on the plane, and the guy next to him would stand up and call out, *Is there a doctor on board?* and paramedics would greet them on the tarmac, bundle him into an ambulance, and drive him away to a bright room where nurses would fuss and fold him into soft white blankets.

His neighbor leaned forward again. "Sorry to keep on bothering you, mate, but don't I know you from somewhere?"

With a great effort, Scott turned his head. The man was fat and red-faced with piggy eyes, his neck rolls stuffed into a cheap-looking polo shirt. His skin was barnacled with flaking moles.

"Yeah, I do," said the piggy man. "From the telly. What was that show? You were talking about the stock market."

Scott glared at him. *Look at me again, you repulsive piece of shit, and I'll pull your eyeballs out of your head with my bare fucking hands.*

The pig man's smile faded into a frown, and Scott turned away, staring instead through the window at the wispy clouds floating over the approaching French coastline and wondering, were he to rip open the emergency exit door and hurl himself out, how long it would take for him to die.

CHAPTER FORTY-TWO

EMILY

U P IN her bedroom, Emily hauled her suitcase down from the top of the wardrobe. Her stomach churned. The smell of the stew lingered in her sinuses, clinging to the back of her throat like oil.

You're so fucking stupid, she told herself. *And gullible. Blind. Weak. How did it take you so long?*

She started opening drawers and pulling clothes out, then changed her mind. She would take only what she really needed. Pausing midstride, she wondered how she would get to the airport.

Well, obviously I'll drive. I'll just take the car and leave it at the airport.

But what if I can't get a flight straightaway? What if Nina follows me there, or sends Yves to bring me back?

She imagined sprinting through the airport like Jason Bourne, pushing people aside in her haste to get away. She would just have to go to one of the bigger airports, where she would blend in with the crowd, walk up to the desk, and buy a ticket to anywhere in the UK. London, Manchester, Glasgow, whatever was available. She would pay for it with Scott's credit card, the one she used for groceries.

No. *Bad idea.* They'd be able to access the transaction and they might know which airline she'd used. It would have to be cash. She had a bundle of notes stockpiled in her sock drawer; she could stop at an ATM on the way and grab some more. And then, as soon as she was back in England, her parents would protect her. They would tell her what to do.

As the shadows grew long and dusk crept in, Emily paced around her room, waiting for a chance to venture downstairs without risking a run-in with Nina. Feeling more focused with each passing hour, she scurried between the windows, peeping over the sills and around the curtains and ducking out of sight again at the slightest sign of movement. At one point, she even lay flat on the floor and commando-crawled her way to the balcony so she could peer undetected through the gaps in the balustrade.

Below, Nina seemed to be getting on with the day. She and Aurelia had cleared the table and packed away the dishes. Then they'd gone for a swim. Afterward, as they strolled back past the guesthouse, Nina had looked up several times at Emily's window, but she hadn't made any move to come inside.

Only after they'd both finally gone inside the family house did Emily feel secure enough to open her door and tiptoe out onto the landing. Taking care to keep her head down, she hurried down the stairs and into the hallway, casting around for her handbag. It had to be there somewhere. She remembered dropping it earlier.

Where is it, where is it . . . ? She checked on the coatrack, behind the doors, and even on the porch. Had she taken it upstairs with her? No, she'd definitely dropped it right here in the hallway. Eventually she found it in the dining room, hanging from the back of one of the chairs. She rummaged inside; then, failing to find what she was looking for, she pulled out the contents and spread them out over the table.

Her jaw fell open. There, scattered across the glossy oak surface, was her small change purse and a few loose coins, a pot of lip gloss, an old shopping list, a pink plastic ring Aurelia had given her, Scott's credit card . . . and absolutely nothing else.

Back in her room again, she dragged the chair from under the dressing table and wedged it under the door handle.

Nina had taken the car keys. She probably had them strung around her neck like a jailer.

Nope, Emily thought, trying to rouse some bravery. *No way. I won't be trapped here. I'm not some defenseless toddler. You can't abduct me.* So, she couldn't drive out. Fine. No problem. Change of plan. She would walk out instead.

Changing into a pair of denim shorts and a T-shirt, she glanced at the clock. She had about three and a half hours to wait until darkness fell and Nina went to bed. In the meantime, she would pack. *Phone,* she thought, clicking her fingers. *Don't bloody forget that again.* Returning to the wardrobe, she stretched up on her tiptoes and felt around. Then she yanked a few clothes out of the way and felt some more.

With a horrible cold feeling spreading outward from her breastbone, she ran to the chair, sliding it back out from under the door handle. Placing it in front of the wardrobe, she climbed up. The shelf was empty. Her phone was gone.

She jumped down from the chair, hurried to the dressing table, and tugged open the middle left-hand drawer, riffling through old travel documents, receipts, and UK bank cards, already knowing what she would, or would not, find. No passport. That was gone, too.

Emily spun around, clutching her head as if it might fall off. Phone, passport, car keys. Nina had taken them all. She was trapped.

Crossing to the balcony doors, she peeked through the curtains. Outside, the cicadas were starting up. The gently bobbing sun cast an orange glow over the tallest of the pines, lighting them up like birthday candles. Even though the sky was still bright, all the security lights were already on, their fluorescent beams chasing away every creeping shadow. The message was clear: *I see you.*

Resting her forehead against the window frame, Emily let the tears come. "There's no place like home," she whispered. "There's no place like home."

Click. Click. Click.

CHAPTER FORTY-THREE

SCOTT

THE TAXI driver—a tired-looking man of around forty with bags under his eyes and lines around his mouth—had seemed put out when Scott banged on his window and demanded to be taken almost two hours down the coast, even when he was shown a thick wad of cash. Perhaps he was at the end of his shift, thought Scott. Perhaps he needed to get home to his wife and kids. He pictured the cabbie pushing open his front door after a long day of driving, kicking off his shoes, and sinking into a sofa, wrapping his arms around his sweet, dumpy wife. He might crack open a beer and watch an episode of his favorite detective show before climbing the creaking stairs on his way to bed, peeping in through cracked doorways to check on his sleeping children.

Scott's eyes burned a hole in the back of the man's balding head.

The memory came to him as it always did, stealthy and unexpected, like a snake. It slithered over his skin, coiled itself around his heart, and squeezed.

He is driving through the gates of Querencia, his heart swelling with a hope he thought was dead. The houses emerge from the trees, rippling like mirages. They are blinding white, and the air around them smells of summer. He enters the family house and calls out. He is desperate to see his wife. His trip to London has been hampered by worry, but Nina's texts have been positive. Happy, even. Her road trip went well; the basilica was beautiful. He feels triumphant, like he has conquered a mountain.

"Nina?" He climbs the stairs, grinning like an idiot at the floorboards, the beams, the shutters. Querencia is everything he'd dreamed it would be, and more. Here, they will rebuild their lives.

"In here." There is an echo, as if Nina is speaking from within a great cavern.

He reaches the landing. A door at the far end swings open, and there she is in a bright, sun-filled room, looking like an angel.

But she is not alone.

A child sits next to her. A small, copper-haired toddler with angry red cheeks and frightened eyes. A child he has never seen before, surrounded by dolls and toys and books.

He stands frozen in the doorway. Nina and the child both turn to look at him. "It's Daddy!" Nina cries, her joy so infectious that the child beams, too: two shiny white grins. Two matching eager faces.

"Aurelia," she says, "go give your daddy a hug."

Scott tore his eyes away from the cabbie and stared out the window. It was getting dark. He checked his watch. Nearly 8:30 P.M. He sighed and drummed his fingers on the seat, wishing he was wearing sneakers instead of his stiff leather Oxfords. He would be walking a long time.

An hour later, he was squinting through the car's windshield, searching the empty stretch of road for the markers. He wasn't used to spotting the turning; he'd only ever driven this journey by himself once, three years ago. Every other time since then,

Yves had collected him from the airport and dropped him at the door.

An enormous oak tree flashed by, its V-shaped fork black with decay. Then another, the same as the first, but with two huge circular cankers set above a deep trunk crack: two eyes and a nose. In the early days, Scott had thought of this tree as a sentry, watching over his buried treasure. He used to greet it with a silent nod, as if it were a faithful servant. Now, though, it seemed more like the angel of death.

"Stop here," Scott said.

The cabbie jumped, startled. He slowed down and peered into the gloom. *"Mais il n'y a rien ici,"* he said. *There is nothing here.*

"I said stop."

The man indicated right and slowly pulled over to the side of the road. True enough, it appeared as though there was nothing there at all, just the flat black ribbon of road and a wall of trees on either side. But the cabbie was wrong. Everything was here.

Scott threw a bundle of cash onto the front passenger seat and opened his door, gagging immediately on the fug of damp air and the sickeningly familiar scent of pine cones and sea salt.

CHAPTER FORTY-FOUR

EMILY

THE AIR outside was warm, almost greasy with humidity, but the sand on the driveway felt cold under Emily's bare feet. Her handbag bumped against her hip as she walked, the long strap slung across her body like a sash. Her sandals dangled loosely from the fingers of one hand.

After she'd finished crying, she'd become angry again. She would *not* be imprisoned against her will. Nina may have taken her phone and passport, but that wouldn't stop her. One way or another, she would find her way home.

Initially, she'd planned to creep around the very edges of the property like a jewel thief, quietly, stealthily, until she reached the gates. But it hadn't rained for weeks, and the ground beneath the trees was littered with crunchy leaves and clumps of dry grass; Nina would hear her. Plus, it was possible that Nina hadn't gone to bed like her darkened windows seemed to suggest. She might be sitting down there in that secret room, her fingers steepled like a Bond villain's.

No, it was better to walk casually over the driveway and wait for something to happen. The ring of an alarm, perhaps, or the sting of a trip wire at her ankles. If nothing did, great. She would head off toward the gates—which, she realized, might have to be scaled if the system was "down" again. Hopefully it would be morning before Nina noticed that she was gone.

But if she was discovered and Nina tried to stop her . . . well, Emily didn't actually know what she'd do then. Run, probably. Get through the gates and into the woods. Hide, then creep toward the road. After that, she could hitchhike to the nearest police station, or to the British embassy.

Hitchhike? You'll be killed.

Well, then maybe she would walk, taking shelter in bushes when she got tired.

Take shelter in a bush? Who do you think you are, Bear fucking Grylls?

She slowed down as her confidence waned. Out in the open, without the protection of her soft white bedroom, her idea was looking less brave and more stupid. She should probably just go back inside and shut the door, climb under the bedsheets, and deal with all of this in the morning.

Nope. Can't stay here. Got to get out.

As she neared the place where the playhouse once stood, something rustled in the dark. She stopped and scanned the lawn, her lungs shuddering with the effort of keeping quiet, her heart ready to burst. Stepping into the shadow of a nearby tree, she waited. Two minutes . . . three . . . five.

Nothing. Probably just a bird.

Emily looked back at the Land Cruiser, parked in its usual spot by the guesthouse, its metal bulk outlined against a down-lit tree trunk. It looked so solid, so snug. She could be out of here in seconds if she had the keys. She could be anywhere at all in a matter of hours. Nina wouldn't have a hope of catching up to her, not even if she jumped out of bed and gave chase on a quad bike.

Quad bike.

Two fat-wheeled bikes sat in the shed just opposite the animal enclosures. Emily had ridden them a total of twice. She was far from adept, but the bikes had wheels and engines. One of them would easily get her as far as the nearest town, and she wouldn't even have to start the engine straightaway. Providing she could get the gates open, she could walk it a certain distance first.

Emily had no doubt that Nina would have hidden the car keys along with her phone and passport, but the bike keys were kept in a small wooden box in the family house, along with those for the toolsheds and the mechanized pool cover. The box was mounted on the wall just inside the patio doors; she'd seen Nina using it. The gate key was probably in there, too.

Emily glanced up at the windows. It would only take a couple of seconds to sneak in—if the doors were unlocked.

Creeping around the side of the house, she felt a surge of adrenaline. She could do this. She would take a quad bike and ride out of there like a goddamn Son of Anarchy. Or maybe she wouldn't have to; maybe she'd get lucky and the car keys would also be hanging in the wooden box. Either way, she'd be out of there soon.

Flattening her back against the wall like a special-ops agent, she peered around the corner. The back patio was quiet, reminding her, for some reason, of a movie she'd accidentally watched as a kid, the first one that ever gave her nightmares. Some reboot of a Japanese horror; she couldn't think of the name, but it had scared the shit out of her.

Awesome. Japanese horror movies. Just the calming thoughts I need right now.

She moved slowly across the flagstones, taking care to tread lightly, just like they'd taught her at drama school. Heel first, then roll down to the toe. Never stamp on a stage, her movement teacher used to tell her. *For heaven's sake, Emily, do the stage directions say "Enter the Elephant"?* Emily mentally gave her teacher the finger. Tonight, she was the very definition of stealth.

She reached the patio doors and, taking a breath, laid her fingers on the handle. She pushed down.

Locked.

Bollocks.

On the other side of the door, behind the glass, the door key stuck out from the keyhole. Emily looked at it and, still grasping the handle, contemplated the long, dark walk along the dirt track. She saw herself reaching the road and waiting with her arm outstretched, her thumb pointed upward. Headlights might appear in the distance. Maybe a car would pull up next to her, the window sliding slowly down to reveal a sallow-faced man with a rotten smile.

No, thanks. Gotta get those keys.

She could see the box on the wall behind the door, tantalizingly close.

Leaning back, she scanned the outside wall. At the end of the house, one of the windows stood open just a crack. Emily tiptoed over. It was the window to Aurelia's playroom: a large square frame with two outward-swinging panes at either end. The gaps weren't huge, but they were just wide enough to squeeze through.

Before she knew it, she was reaching inside, knocking the metal arm from its hook and opening the left-side pane as far as it would go. There was a bookcase just inside. She wedged her sandals into what little space remained in her handbag, then put both hands on the ledge and jumped, thrusting her hip sideways. Balancing precariously for a few seconds, she pitched her weight forward, one hand on the frame and the other planted firmly on the bookcase. She inched her bum inside and curved her body into a C shape until she was almost horizontal, then bent her knees and wriggled her legs. Eventually, she half rolled, half fell onto the floor.

She sat up, breathing heavily. She was in.

The playroom looked creepy in the half-light. Long shadows loomed, seemingly without objects to cast them, and the pennant flags, so pretty in the daylight, now dripped eerily like stalactites from the ceiling.

Emily edged toward the door, terrified of disturbing even the air around her. In the hallway the staircase glowed white. There was no sound from upstairs; no lights were on.

She turned left through the kitchen and tiptoed to the patio doors. Reaching the box on the wall, she opened up the front with trembling fingers and studied the contents. Disappointment came like a sucker punch to the solar plexus. The key to the bike shed was there, as were the chunky gold ones to the quads themselves, but there were no car keys.

Right. Quad bike it is, then.

Slowly, carefully, she lifted the keys she needed from their hooks and dropped them into the pocket of her shorts. But she made no move to leave, looking instead toward the butler's pantry. She couldn't stop thinking about the car. Also, the quad bikes would be useless if the gates were locked—and they probably were. She needed her keys. Surely they were in that secret room.

But what if Nina is down there? Emily chewed her lip in the semidarkness, wondering how the hell it had come to this: breaking into Nina's house at night, creeping and stealing and plotting to escape.

Her feet moved of their own accord, padding toward the pantry, carrying her to the place where the shelves did not quite meet. She grabbed one and pulled like she'd done the last time, but the unit didn't move. With her heart so palpably in her mouth she could almost taste it, she began to run her hands over the edges, feeling for a latch or a button. Finding nothing, she slid her palms across the undersides of the shelves, checking the corners and the spaces behind the crockery, and then she leaned her shoulder against the whole thing and pushed.

There was a slight give. Nudging harder, she felt the unit depress ever so slightly, then shift back toward her with a faint click.

The door was open.

She stepped onto the top step and peered down. The staircase was much darker than last time. Her breath was loud and jarring in the confined space.

Having carried her to this point, her feet no longer seemed willing to move, so she forced them, one after the other, step by step, down into the darkness until she reached the bottom of the stairs. The boxes looked enormous, their shadows tall and monstrous. The smell seemed stronger than ever. What the hell was in those things?

In a moment of blind panic, Emily began scrabbling at the wall, looking for a light switch, her fingers combing through several cobwebs before finally hitting the edge of a panel. Finding a button, she pressed down, and a fluorescent strip above her head flickered on.

The room was even bigger than she'd first thought. Other than a narrow thoroughfare that ran through the center, every inch was crammed with objects: mostly cardboard boxes, but she could see other things, too, stacked at the edges against the damp brickwork. High chairs, bassinets, cots, and changing tables. Cushions, mattresses, and a rocking horse, all covered with a thick dusting of mildew.

The boxes nearest to her looked new, still shiny with packing tape and little squares of plastic still bearing the delivery slips. Some had little pictures on the sides: toys, bikes, craft supplies, and sports gear. Mountains of brand new furniture.

Emily pushed her way in, past the first few items until she couldn't go any farther. Things were older toward the back. Wooden crates bore the name "Denny" followed by a West London address and the logo of an overseas moving company. Some of the lids were loose. Gingerly, she lifted one and looked inside. Baby clothes, dank and rotten. Inside another, she found old feeding bottles, stained muslin cloths, and a breast pump. Everything was coated in mold.

Emily stared. There was so much stuff; it would take weeks to look through it all, and it was so tightly packed that she'd have to climb up and over the piles. Brown pellets littered the floor.

No wonder it reeked down here, she thought, remembering the dead rodent she'd found in the guesthouse. Anything could have crawled in here and died.

Beyond all the junk, the door to the secret room stood slightly ajar, the eerie flat light once again spilling through the gap.

Emily drove her body toward it, despite the many bizarre and horrifying images running through her brain. What would she find in that room? *Please, God, let it just be empty except for the keys. Please, please, just let me find the keys.*

Reaching the door, she stretched out and pulled it a little way open, noticing its considerable weight and width. A dozen or so cylindrical bolts protruded from the side, ready to slide into matching holes in the jamb. Something cracked nearby, and she jumped back, suddenly convinced that she would find both Nina and Aurelia in there, curled up in a medicated heap or chained to the wall or strapped to laboratory benches or sleeping in coffins or . . .

Silence. She listened for more noises. The house shuffled and ticked around her. The hot-water system hummed.

Get the keys.

Emily peeked cautiously around the door and saw what looked like a small and rather ordinary-looking studio flat, complete with a sofa, kitchenette, and even a toilet and shower tucked away behind a partition. On a desk in the corner was a phone and an Apple laptop.

A phone.

She reached for it with a trembling hand and nearly cried when she heard the dial tone. But as soon as she pressed the first number, an automated voice asked for a four-digit access code. Shocked by the noise, she jerked back as if the phone had bitten her, silencing it with the "off" button. Carefully, she replaced the handset back in the base unit.

Looking back at the kitchenette and mini-bathroom, two words floated up out of her subconscious: *panic room*."

Moving farther inside and around the door, she found that the peculiar gray light came from a wall of small television screens all showing black-and-white images. Surveillance screens.

The cameras. On her first ever day at Querencia, she'd seen them: tiny silver boxes mounted on the outside of the house and in the sitting room, their miniscule lights flashing like a warning. *Stop. Do not enter.* There were others, too, above the gate and on the guesthouse porch. She'd thought them odd at first, but, she'd reasoned, security was important. You could really freak yourself out living somewhere like this. Since then, she hadn't given them much thought. They'd just become part of the furniture.

Fixed onto the adjoining wall, perpendicular to the screens, was an iPad. A control system, Emily guessed. She stared at the screens. The pictures kept changing. She saw the gates and the track, the driveway and the lawn. Then the pool, the animal sheds, and every room in the family house, including a lavish bedroom Emily had not seen before. It had a four-poster bed, an enormous doll's house, and shelves upon shelves of toys. Aurelia's room.

Then she saw the sunset point. The rooms in the guesthouse. Her own bedroom.

Oh shit oh shit oh shit. The cameras were everywhere, hidden in places she would never have looked. Nina had been watching her the whole time.

She flashed back to cracking open doors and drawers. The feel of Nina's crisp white sheets. The claw-foot bath, the towel, the cabinet. And then Scott's arms around her at the sunset point, his lips against hers. Nina must have seen everything.

Quickly, frantically, she searched the screens for Nina's room and found it just before the picture changed again. The bed appeared to be as empty as when she'd last seen it. She pored over every image, scanning every corner.

Then, in Aurelia's room, she saw something lumpy at the foot of the bed. A blanket, and a foot sticking out from underneath. Emily suddenly understood why Nina's room seemed so unlived in. She slept on Aurelia's floor like a guard dog.

The foot twitched, shocking Emily out of her trancelike state. *The keys.*

She turned to the desk and ran her hands over its surface. Feverishly, she opened the drawers underneath, scrabbling through a neatly ordered array of notebooks and pens, receipts and paperclips. *Come on, come on, they have to be here somewhere.* She tried the shelves, the kitchen cabinets, and even the fridge, finding nothing but dust and empty spaces. But then, in a small recessed cupboard above the toilet, Emily found a battered green cashbox. Nestled inside it were her phone and passport. She almost passed out with relief. "Yes!" she hissed, fishing them out and clutching them to her chest—but her joy quickly faded as she realized that there could no longer be any doubt. It was all real.

Suddenly, there was a shift in the air and a small peeling sound, like a plaster being pulled from soft skin.

Emily whipped around.

In the doorway of the panic room, Aurelia stood wide-eyed and spectral in a white nightgown.

Emily stared, immobilized. *The Grudge,* she thought all of a sudden. That was the name of the terrifying Japanese horror movie.

Aurelia tilted her head to the side and frowned.

"Hi, sweetie," Emily whispered, her mouth paper-dry. "What are you doing up?" There was a noise from somewhere above, a short series of delicate clicks and creaks, and her eyes flew to the ceiling. "Why don't you go on back to bed?"

Aurelia's narrow face fell. Beneath the hem of her nightgown, alabaster feet sickled toward each other like crescent moons.

Why her? Emily wondered. *Why take this little girl and not any other? What had she done to deserve any of this?* Impulsively, she reached out, and Aurelia's skinny body slid wordlessly into her waiting arms. Emily stroked her hair, thinking that the jig would be up the second Nina discovered she had gone—and what would happen then? Would Nina just sit at Querencia and wait for the police? No. She'd run. She'd take Aurelia and disappear, maybe forever. She and Scott had enough money; they probably knew people who would hide them or help them. They might even harm Aurelia—who knew how far they would go to avoid prison?

What will happen to you, little sister?

Suddenly, another sound above their heads, louder this time. Emily held her breath, listening.

It was the creak of a floorboard.

Whirling around, Emily checked the surveillance screens. The lump at the bottom of Aurelia's bed had disappeared.

Without even thinking, Emily grabbed hold of Aurelia's hand. "Come on," she whispered, "let's play a game."

CHAPTER FORTY-FIVE

SCOTT

HELL WAS a never-ending dirt track, Scott decided. He trudged along in the pitch dark using the flashlight on his phone to illuminate the snarl of tree roots and leaves beneath his feet, his suit jacket slung over his arm. He'd been walking for hours. Days. Weeks.

Blisters rose on his heels, the hard leather of his shoes whittling away at his skin. He stumbled over ruts and into holes, tripping on the sticky fingers of fallen branches. But nothing around him ever seemed to change. In fact, he seemed to be passing the same tree over and over again. The cicadas sang in a perpetual canon. An owl hooted precisely every thirty seconds (he counted). It was like a looped recording: "relaxing" sounds of nature.

He slowed down and looked behind him. Where was the goddamn gate? The track was long, but surely not this long. Had he taken a wrong turn? Maybe he'd gone the wrong way. Maybe, unbeknownst to him, there were actually dozens of tracks winding through the woodland, all leading to hidden mansions housing stolen children. Perhaps there was a whole community of child abductors out here in the woods. If only they'd known! Nina could have thrown a party.

Scott turned around and retraced his steps, then stopped and turned back. The trees seemed to reach for him, their spindly branches arching and probing. He tried and failed to recall the geography of the area. What else was around, other than Querencia? What were the landmarks? Where was the ocean? Which way was north? He brought his phone close to his face—surely there was a compass on it somewhere?—just in time to see the battery icon: one percent.

"No," Scott breathed.

The screen went black.

"No!" He tapped on it, pressed the power button, banged it on the heel of his hand. Nothing. It was dead.

He looked up. The night pressed in like a bag over his head.

"MotherFUCK!" he yelled.

And somewhere to his left, far away among the trees, someone answered.

Scott whirled around, listening intently. "Hello?" he called.

Silence . . . and then there it was again, louder this time.

In the distance, someone was screaming.

Scott started to run.

CHAPTER FORTY-SIX

EMILY

"A URELIA! *AURELIA!*"

Emily tore across the lawn and down the driveway with Nina's increasingly frantic cries snapping at her heels like wolves. In one hand she clutched the quad-bike keys; in the other she gripped Aurelia's clammy little fingers as hard as she dared.

Aurelia was running, too, but she slowed to a reluctant trot as they neared the sheds, and Emily had to drag her the rest of the way.

When they reached the bike shed, she reached into her pocket. The key felt slippery in her hands, a tiny silver fish.

"Aurelia!" The beam of a flashlight flashed through the trees behind them.

Emily grabbed the padlock. The key slid in easily but wouldn't turn. Emily twisted it one way and then the other, the metal digging into her skin—*come on, come ON!*—but the stupid thing just wouldn't give. Then it slipped out and fell through her fingers. She groped at the ground, raking through the grass, but she couldn't feel it. The key was gone.

Crouching on all fours, she peered through the leaves of a shrub.

Nina was standing in the middle of the lawn, brandishing her flashlight like a sword.

It was dark, but even without the flashlight, it wouldn't take long. The bushes around them were low and thin; just a few more steps and they would be visible.

Emily looked down at the grass, then up at the padlock. There was no time for the bike. "Come on, sweetie, let's go," Emily hissed, turning to Aurelia, but she wasn't listening. She was ashen and sweaty, shaking in her thin nightgown, her eyes clamped shut. Little squeaks escaped her lips.

Emily knew she had to act fast. She tried to think of a way to engage Aurelia's attention, some way to calm her, to make her smile . . .

And then she remembered. Emily grabbed Aurelia's hand. "*Ecoute,*" she whispered, hoping against hope. "*Tout va bien. Je promets.*"

Aurelia went still. She opened her eyes.

Emily held her breath.

"*Aurelia!*" Nina sounded like she was getting closer.

Emily's whole body was telling her to run. Thirty meters of open driveway lay between them and the gate. They would have to break their cover and move fast if they were going to make it through. *Fuck, please let the gate be unlocked, please let the system be on.* She placed her hand on Aurelia's cheek, willing herself to stay calm.

"*Tout va bien,*" Emily said again. The French was clearly helping but her mind had gone blank. "*Je ne te . . . je ne te ferai . . .*"

"*Aurelia!*"

Aurelia blinked and turned her face toward Nina's raspy cries.

"No, look at me, please," Emily begged. "*S'il te plaît, je . . . je besoin que . . .*" *Come on, think of the words.*

Aurelia whimpered and, screwing her eyes shut again, tried to twist her wrist from Emily's grasp.

"*Amandine,*" Emily felt her chin wobble. "Amandine, please. I have to take you home."

Her words had an instant and unexpected effect. Aurelia's eyes snapped open, her little face radiating pure terror. Then she opened her mouth, her lips spreading slowly over her teeth like an animal about to bite, and screamed bloody murder.

Emily set off at a full sprint, dragging Aurelia behind her, thinking of nothing but the gate, of getting through it, of putting as much distance as possible between them and Nina.

The silver keypad flashed in the dark. She was so close; she could nearly reach it—and then she was there, her hands slapping against the metal, her fingers punching at the buttons. But the light was off, the mechanism dead.

Over Aurelia's horrific cries came the sound of heavy footsteps in the distance, pounding the earth, closing in fast.

"Come on!" Emily tried to yank Aurelia away, scanning the walls for a way over, but Aurelia was pulling in the opposite direction and eventually she broke loose, tearing blindly away toward the woman she thought was her mother.

"No! Come back!" But Aurelia was gone. With nothing left to do, Emily dashed away into the bushes to the left. Breaking free of the foliage, she skittered back and forth along the wall, searching for a foothold. After a few seconds she noticed a brick a few meters up, sticking out just slightly farther than the rest—and just meters away, Yves's wheelbarrow stood next to the compost bin. She pushed the bin onto its side and emptied the contents, then hauled them both over to the wall and placed the bin inside the wheelbarrow.

Somewhere behind her, Nina yelled her name.

Taking a run up, Emily threw herself at the shaky structure, climbing it for all she was worth, scraping her bare toes against the stone, reaching for the brick, and pulling her own weight up, up, up, until her hand slapped over the rim of the wall. By some miracle, she managed to haul herself over onto her stomach and swing her leg over to the other side. Straddling the wall, she looked back toward the house.

Illuminated by the security lights, Nina was running toward

her. The flashlight caught Emily in its beam, momentarily
blinding her, but not before she caught sight of Nina's tight,
snarling face—and something shiny in her other hand.

A gun.

Time seemed to buckle and bend.

Emily let out a short bark of disbelief. The thought of kind-
hearted, animal-loving Nina wielding a weapon was hilariously
incongruous, like a machete in the hands of Snow White. Emily's
rational mind told her that this whole crazy situation would
dissolve in a matter of seconds, because it had to, right? Things
like this didn't happen in real life. People you knew—people you
liked—didn't just turn into gun-toting lunatics overnight.

But it was happening. Nina was powering over the sand, her
face full of hatred. And then she slowed her pace and raised her
arm, and suddenly the gun was real, everything was unbearably
real, and Emily's brain clicked into gear. She launched herself
off the wall, and as she did she heard a deafening crack, like a
hammer hitting a sheet of steel.

Hitting the ground hard, she crumpled and rolled into a ball.
Pain shot from her ankle to her hip bone, but she scrambled to
her feet and bolted over the cracked ground, her mind shattering into a million different thoughts: *she shot at me did she get
me am I hurt am I bleeding not fast enough she's coming she
shot at me I'm going to die she's going to kill me is she coming
where the fuck am I going run run run run run run.*

All she could hear was the roar of blood in her ears and her
own ragged breath . . . and then, in the distance, the clunk of
the gate.

She's coming.

Emily kept running. Keeping the fading lights of the estate at
her back, she plowed into the undergrowth, searching for the
track. Somewhere ahead—many miles ahead—was the road.

Sticks and stones assaulted her bare toes. A low branch
whacked her in the head, sending her spinning off to her right,
where a clump of spiky thorns raked at her legs. She thrust her

arms out in front of her, trying to feel for obstacles, but more things hurtled out of the dark like spears; branches, nettles, hard mounds of earth, a section of rotting fence. A roaring sound to her left made her stop—*Is that the ocean? I'm going the wrong way*—and change direction, stepping down hard into a hole. Her ankle twisted sharply. Pain blasted through her already injured leg and she cried out for help that she knew wouldn't come.

Somehow she kept going, but she was up to her knees in bracken and there were rustling sounds everywhere.

Then something brushed against her arm, warm and solid. A human body. She shot backward and tried to run, but hands were grabbing at her, grasping her wrists, scratching her arms, and a voice was saying, "Stop, it's okay, stop stop stop, it's me, it's me, I'm here."

Scott. It was Scott. She had no idea how, but there he was, her white knight, her superhero, come to rescue her again. Part of her went loose with relief, while another part, the part that knew better, kept struggling.

Behind them, the rustling, snapping noise continued, getting louder and louder until Nina crashed through the scrub, holding the gun out in front of her. Pulling up short, she narrowed her eyes. "Scott? How did you . . . ?"

Emily wrenched her arms free of Scott's grip and backed away. Nina twitched and aimed the gun. Emily could feel the barrel following her every move. She scanned the darkness. They were in a sort of clearing; thin silver-barked trees hemmed them in like the bars of a cage.

She looked from Scott to Nina and back again, searching their shadowy faces for some shred of reason, but their features were warped and misshapen, glistening with sweat. The three of them stood in a breathless, trembling triangle, each one poised like a sprinter on the starting blocks, waiting.

"What the fuck, Nina," Scott said, at last.

Nina looked at the gun in her hand as if she was surprised to see it.

"Give it to me." His voice was low, rational. "I have this under control."

"Under control?" Nina waved the gun at Emily. "She tried to take my baby!"

Emily looked again at the trees. If she took off, how far would she get?

Nina glanced back in the direction of the house, at the lights glinting through the trees. "I have to get back. Aurelia's all by herself."

"Great idea, Nina," said Scott. "You go on back. I'll take it from here."

But Nina shook her head violently. "No. I have to fix this first." Her eyes darted wildly between Emily and the house.

Emily's rib cage began to heave. Somewhere on the property, she realized, Aurelia was alone. Terrified. Confused. *Little sister.* Was she still outside in the gardens? Or had she gone back to her bedroom, crept under her bed, and jammed her hands over her ears? Suddenly, Emily was filled with something like memory, visceral but indistinct.

Scott inched toward Nina, reaching for the gun. "Leave it to me. Let *me* fix it."

"No." Nina spoke through bared teeth, her eyes bulging. "You're too attached. You think you know her, but you don't. Not like I do. She's sneaky. I've seen her poking around the house."

"She's a housekeeper," Scott said, still creeping forward. "That's what we pay her to do."

"Is that right? Do we also pay her to sit outside police stations?" Nina fixed Emily with an ugly glare. "That's right. I know where you went this morning. Yves followed you."

Scott froze, then turned to Emily. "Is that true?"

Emily felt her insides start to slip and slide. There would be no point in running. No one was around; no one would hear. "I'm sorry," she said, the words spilling unbidden from her mouth. "I'm so sorry I found out. I'm so sorry."

The wind picked up, sending dry leaves flying through the air.

"You're sorry?" said Nina, taking a step away from Scott and out of his reach. "You broke into my house. You tried to steal my child from me. You lured her out of bed in the middle of the night and dragged her off into the woods." Her mouth contorted with disgust. "We trusted you."

"No!" Emily shouted, her frayed nerves starting to snap. "No, you didn't! *I* trusted *you*! I loved you, all of you. And you lied to me." She sobbed and her chest rattled. "How could you do this? How could you take someone else's kid?"

Nina reeled back as if slapped, and the injured look on her face filled Emily with rage. "Oh, drop the act," she said. "I know Aurelia isn't yours. That's not even her name." She turned to Scott. His eyes were down. He couldn't even look at her.

Nina shook her head once. Twice.

"Aren't you going to say anything?" Emily yelled. Little specks of light had started to gather at the edges of her vision. "How did you do it? Did you sneak in through her bedroom window? Snatch her off the street?"

Nina blinked. "You don't know what you're talking about."

"Yes, I do. I'm talking about Amandine fucking Tessier."

"No," Nina whispered, clawing at her chest with her free hand. "You don't know anything about it. You don't understand."

"Tell me, then! Tell me what happened."

"You—"

"Tell me!"

"Stop!" A spray of saliva flew from Nina's mouth. "You'd never understand. You have no idea."

"You have to let her go." Emily moaned as a horrible blackness rose inside her like a filthy tide. "You have to let her go."

Nina stepped forward again, her shoulders shaking.

Scott's voice: "Nina, stop. I'll handle it."

"Do you hear her, Scott?" Nina kept moving. "She's crazy."

"I said, stop."

"This has to be done now, Scott. I have to get back to Aurelia. She needs me."

Emily pulled her arms over her head, bracing herself. It was coming. The flurry. The thousands of wings all beating at once, the awful thing that had never gone away. It was twitching and stirring. Waking up.

"I promised I would protect her." Nina raised the gun.

"So, protect her," Scott said. "If she needs you, go. I swear to you I will take care of this."

Emily dragged in more and more air, dragging everything up and under her clavicles until she thought they might crack. The flurry was overwhelming her, consuming her, transporting her somewhere she'd been before but had left behind, somewhere she'd never wanted to go again. It dragged her back like a rip in the ocean to a place where there were no words, just a terrible asphyxia and unknowable darkness.

Emily's eyes closed then flickered open. Closed. Open. Closed. Open.

"Will you, Scott?"

"I will, I swear."

"Because if you don't—"

"I know."

"There's no other way."

"I know."

She saw Nina let go of the gun. Pass it to Scott. Turn and walk away.

Scott, standing motionless. The gun in his hand.

Nina, looking back. Just once.

The tremble of Scott's shoulders. The dead look in his eyes.

The gun.

The gun.

The gun.

Everything tipped. Emily thrashed, trapped once again under a heavy object. She tried to push it away but couldn't. Bright green and orange spots appeared in front of her eyes and she was dropping, and the ground became the sky and the sky became the ground, and the earth came rushing up to meet her like the surface of an icy lake . . .

. . . and at the very same moment, a firecracker went off right near her ear—no, not a firecracker, another *gunshot*—accompanied by the sound of splintering wood. Pain exploded in every part of her body. She began to scream.

Her head hit the forest floor with a sickening smack and everything went dark.

Briefly, she came to.

A light among the trees. Pain. Pressure in her back.

"Stay down," said a voice. "Don't move."

The sweep of headlights over dead leaves.

Silence. Footsteps. Voices.

"Is she . . ."

"Yes."

"I brought the car. And a shovel."

"Where's Yves?"

"I don't know. Can't get hold of him, not since he called this morning."

"Fine. Don't call him, don't text him. Leave him out of this."

Hands slid under her arms, dragging her backward. She was lifted into the air. Placed gently on a bed of leather.

Then the slam of a door, a jangle of keys, and the growl of an engine.

CHAPTER FORTY-SEVEN

SCOTT

About halfway back along the track, Scott found an area that was just about clear and flat enough to accommodate the SUV. He veered off, steering the car through the trees and bushes until he reached a small clearing.

Looking out of the windshield, Scott imagined a ring of blue tape, mounds of freshly dug earth, and a swarm of anonymous figures in white hazmat suits. He bit down on his lip and tasted blood. What the fuck was happening? Why was he parked in the woods in the middle of the night with a body on the backseat? Why had his wife, her face unrecognizable, given him a *shovel*?

Behind him, Emily lay still. Her face was slack and smooth like a child's, mouth parted, lips askew, and Scott fought a sudden flood of memories. Squeaky linoleum floors, starched sheets, and those stiff white blankets with holes in them. The beep of machinery and the clatter of a clipboard falling to the ground. Then the bare walls and stripped floors of Querencia, all their belongings stuffed into crates and left to rot in the basement.

Another memory slithered close, clear and sharp. *He is creeping across the landing in the predawn light, thinking of those crates, about what they contain; the whisper-soft things that no longer smell of her. In a pink bedroom, he picks his way carefully over toys and stands at the foot of the bed. A small hand peeps out from the covers, one delicate finger pointing, accusingly, at him—and at the pillow he is holding in his sweaty, shaking hands. He lifts the pillow. You're not her, he thinks, moving closer, raising the pillow higher, holding it over the bed. You'll never be her . . .*

At the very last minute, though, he crumbles. The pillow falls to the floor, and the pointing finger disappears back under the blanket as its owner rolls over, sighing in her sleep.

Scott collapsed over the steering wheel, his mouth stretched wide in a silent scream.

CHAPTER FORTY-EIGHT

EMILY

OPENING HER eyes, Emily saw familiar upholstery and tinted windows. She was on the backseat of the SUV, lying supine with a rolled-up picnic blanket under her knees. Outside, it was still dark.

In small stages and with difficulty, she hauled herself up onto one elbow.

Scott was sitting in the front seat.

She pressed her fingers to the back of her head and they came away wet. "Have I been shot?" Her voice came out gravelly, as if it hadn't been used for years. Her own words startled her. *Shot? Who's been shot?*

Scott coughed and rubbed his eyes. "No. I aimed high. Up into the trees. You fainted again, hit your head on a rock. Bashed yourself up pretty badly, too, when you were running."

Emily struggled to sit up. Her head throbbed. She touched her left shoulder and felt raw, bloody flesh.

"That looks nasty," Scott said. Their eyes met in the rearview mirror. "Your ankle is swollen, too."

Emily lifted her foot. It was thick and puffy. "What happened? Where's Nina?"

"Back at the house. Don't worry, it's just us."

315

Just us. She couldn't focus. A chill was spreading through her bones. Feeling around at the back of her head again, she found a squelchy, matted lump. She dimly recalled being dragged backward. Instinctively, her hand went to the car door, and her fingers closed around the handle.

"It isn't locked," Scott said, watching her in the mirror.

Emily pulled and sure enough, the door cracked open, ushering in the damp smell of fallen leaves. It took her straight back to Hoxley and the field behind the train station where she'd had her first kiss: fifteen years old, bottle of cider in one hand and the lank hair of some boy tangled in the other. *Home. My real home.* She thought of her parents worrying and waiting for her to call.

"Everything's going to be okay," Scott said as Emily began to cry. "Come on, let's get some fresh air. I'm suffocating in here."

Slowly, warily, they both climbed out of the car and faced one another. Leaves crunched under their feet. Scott stood with his hands shoved in his pockets and his head hung low, like a schoolboy in detention.

"I don't know where to start," he said.

Emily wiped her eyes with the back of her hand. She couldn't speak. An unbearable tension had seized her body and locked her jaw tight.

Scott looked at the ground, the sky, the hood of the car. "That day we drove to the airport? I was telling the truth. We did have a daughter, and her name was Aurelia. And she did get sick. But she didn't survive." He blew out his breath slowly. "Our daughter's death changed everything. It shattered Nina, and . . . well, it's hard to explain if you don't . . . ." He searched the air for the right words.

Emily shivered, feeling vulnerable in her shorts and thin T-shirt. "How long has she been . . . like that?"

Scott shrugged. "I honestly couldn't tell you. She hid so much from me, and for such a long time. I know that sounds impossible—how could I be so blind, right? But she saw doctors in secret, she lied about her medication . . . I mean, it was bad after the funeral, but I had no idea just *how* bad; at least, not until it was too late.

"You mustn't think badly of her," he continued. "She doesn't remember what happened in Nice, not exactly. She's lived the lie for so long that she's starting to believe it. A lot of the time, she thinks that girl *is* our daughter."

"How have you lived with it? Why didn't you go to the police?"

Scott shrugged. "In the beginning, I panicked. I didn't know what to do. I couldn't turn her in. I just couldn't. So I did nothing. I played along because I was scared. And then one day I realized there was no going back."

"That's not true." Emily was shaking. She wrapped her arms around her body, trying to keep warm. "You can still make it right."

"Oh, yes. Because prison will fix everything."

"But if you turned yourself in, I'm sure that—"

"That we'd be let off the hook because we came clean? That a judge might see what nice people we are and let us off with a slap on the wrist?" Scott leaned in, his neck muscles suddenly straining and stretching like cables. "You have no idea what I would lose. No one can ever know about this. Not *ever*."

The words fell between them, heavy as snow.

"Yves knows," said Emily quietly.

"Yes. Yves knows. But two of his sons are now receiving a private education, and a third is top of the list for a brand new heart, so I doubt he's in any hurry to play the responsible citizen."

"Is that what you'll do with me? Pay me off?"

He considered her for a moment. "You signed an agreement, you know."

A bitter laugh rolled out of Emily's mouth. "You know it wouldn't stand up."

Scott nodded thoughtfully. "Then yes," he said. "I'll pay you."

"And what if I can't be bought?"

Scott's eyes were hard, his jaw set.

Emily looked away. *I don't want your money,* she thought miserably. *It's never been about the money.* She was so cold and shaking so violently that her knees were almost literally knocking. "Why . . . why did you bring me here?"

Scott inhaled sharply. "Seemed like a good idea at the time," he said, the words escaping with the air in his lungs. "Nina needed company. I could see how the isolation was just doing even more damage. All alone out here with her guilt, her fear . . . every day I was scared she'd do something stupid." He looked up at the sky. "Someone needed to be here, to look after her, but it couldn't be me. I couldn't stand to be near her. Near *them.* I was so tired, and I'd already made so many mistakes. I wanted my life back. I thought I could make it work. And I did—for a while."

He put his hands on his knees and bent over. Took a deep breath. Stood up.

"You know, she used to call me twenty, thirty times a day? Crying, making threats. Sometimes she'd beg me to come home. 'Don't work so hard,' she'd say. 'Come and spend time with your *daughter.*'" He spat the word out. "And meanwhile she's spending, spending, spending. Surveillance stuff, security equipment. Fucking *horses.* So I'd take on even more work to keep up. And then she'd call me in the middle of the night, telling me she's about to kill herself. And the cycle would begin again."

Scott dragged his fingers through his hair. When he spoke next, his voice was quiet, as if he'd forgotten Emily was there. "It made me so angry. But I felt sad for her, too. I loved her once. I loved her so much. She used to be so funny, so happy; at least, it seemed that way." He paused and shook his head. "I don't know why, but I thought if I gave her everything she'd ever dreamed of, if I gave her time and space, she might get better. I thought the old Nina might come back and we'd figure this shit out together. But she didn't. She got worse.

"I thought some company might help. A friend. I hired Yves, hoping he would keep an eye on her, help her out here and there. But he soon made it clear he wouldn't be her carer."

Emily stared at him. "Is that what I was supposed to be? Her carer?"

Scott looked down at his feet. "She needed someone who understood her. Who needed her back. When I met you, I knew you'd be perfect for her. I just didn't expect that you'd be perfect for me, too."

When he looked up again, Emily saw nothing but pain. And when he reached out his hands, she took them without thinking. They stood like that for a moment, somber and ceremonial. Emily closed her eyes, willing him to pull her close, imagining her cheek fitting perfectly against the dip of his breastbone. She wanted to hear—no, *feel* his heart beating in time with her own. She would mold herself around him like wax and let the dank chill of the forest fade away.

The forest.

Emily opened her eyes again. A mist was rising through the darkness, a haze of dust and dirt seeping out of the ground. Scott's hands were warm around her own. He squeezed her fingers. So comfortable. So intimate. *And so wrong.*

She pulled away, and it felt like stepping out of water.

"No . . . ," she said. "No. I meant, why did you bring me *here*?" She jerked her chin at the trees, their scraggy branches bleached white by the headlights.

Scott's face folded in on itself. It was a long time before he spoke. "I needed to know," he whispered.

"Know what?"

"*Can* you be bought?"

Emily only half understood what he was asking. Scott's eyes flickered to a point just behind her. She followed his gaze and saw a big, tall, moss-covered trunk. An oak tree.

Leaning against the tree was a shovel.

CHAPTER FORTY-NINE

SCOTT

STRIDING OVER the sandy driveway, Scott's foot got caught in the loops of a hose and he tripped, falling awkwardly onto his knees. He felt his trousers rip; a trivial thing, but it felt like the last straw. He smashed his fist on the ground, then picked up a handful of sand and hurled it into the air with a choked cry. The grains flew back at him, peppering his eyes and nose, sticking to his lips.

The family house rose before him, the light above the door blazing like a beacon. He stood up, every muscle pulsing with pain. Hobbling to the front door, he pushed it open.

The familiar stench of scented candles hit him in the face. Everything was pretty as a picture, neat as a doll's house. The delicate curves and whorls of the table legs, the velvety soft seats—everything just for show, like the setting for a play.

Beyond them, Nina sat at the dining-room table dressed in a silvery knee-length robe. On the table was a glass of red wine and a small cheeseboard. Brie, Comté, Bleu d'Auvergne. Crackers and grapes and quince.

Her mouth twisted with sympathy when she saw him. "Poor baby," she whispered, pushing back her chair.

"Stop," he said, holding up a hand.

She hesitated, then started to speak again, but he cut her off.

"It's done." His hand shook. He'd never known fury like this. "What you wanted. What you told me to do. It's done."

Nina stared back with round eyes. *That's right,* Scott thought. *Take a long, hard look. Do you see what you've done? Do you see who I am now? Who you *are?

And then, like a supernova, the fury faded and he buckled.

Nina ran up and caught him as he began to sob. They both sank to the floor. *"Ssshhh,"* she said, cradling his head in her lap. "Hush now. I've got you. I'm here."

She stroked his hair and dried his eyes, and eventually he gave in. Curling up in surrender, he pressed his face into the fabric of her dress.

"There's nothing to worry about," Nina whispered. "Be thankful. We have everything we've ever wanted."

Her words were a warm scarf on a cold day, and Scott couldn't help but wrap himself in them. She was right. Of course, she was right. There was nothing to worry about. Emily was a minor speed bump, and he had dealt with her accordingly.

And yes, he should be thankful. After all, he and Nina had each other, they had Querencia, and the rest of the world was far, far away. They were invisible. They were a bubble in the ocean, a needle in a haystack. No one could find them, no one could reach them.

They were safe.

CHAPTER FIFTY

EMILY

THE SHUTTLE bus to the airport was warm and inviting after the chill of the dawn. The driver gave Emily a sideways look as she shuffled through the door and swung her tattered bag onto the first seat she found. Slumping down next to it, she let her head fall against the window.

As the bus pulled away, Emily tried not to replay what had just happened. She tried to think happy, normal thoughts, but the forest would not leave her alone. Its grit was under her fingernails, its shadows still tangled in her hair.

When Emily had seen the shovel leaning against the tree, her first thought had been, *This is it. This is how I'm going to die.* She'd squeezed her eyes shut, waiting for the dirty metal edge to connect with her skull . . . but nothing happened. Everything sort of hung for a moment. When she opened her eyes again, Scott's cheeks were wet.

"I'm so sorry," he said. He was sorry for bringing her to France. Sorry for involving her, sorry he hadn't done more to protect her. And sorry for the weight he was about to press on her, for the way it would change her life forever. But, he said, he would make up for every ounce. He would give her whatever she wanted.

As it slowly dawned on her that she wasn't about to die, Emily began to shake uncontrollably. Sinking to her knees, she pressed her palms into the damp earth as if in prayer.

Scott said he would let her go on the condition that she kept their secret. She would have to forget all about Querencia, forget it existed, and never speak of it to anyone, ever. In return, he would give her the kind of wealth she would never otherwise have. Her life would be easy. She'd never have to work another crappy temp job. She'd never have to worry about debt. She wouldn't have to save up to buy a house; he'd buy one for her. She could do anything, be anyone. He would foot the bill.

"It's the right thing to do," he said quietly. "Not just for you, but for Aurelia, too." He hesitated. "For Amandine."

When Emily didn't respond, he began to speak quickly and eloquently, ticking off points on his fingers. Aurelia Denny had a good life, he insisted. She remembered nothing of where she came from, of what had happened; Nina was the only mother she knew, and she had everything a little girl could want. She was well-protected and fiercely loved. She was fed, clothed, and educated. And when the time came, Scott promised, she would also be free. She would not spend the rest of her life held captive at Querencia. One way or the other, he would return Amandine Tessier to the real world—but as rich and privileged Aurelia Denny.

"She'll be recognized," Emily managed.

"No," Scott shot back. "She'll be conditioned to believe in her illness. She'll always keep herself covered up. She'll always wear those contacts."

And for the first time, Emily questioned Scott's sanity. *They're both deluding themselves,* Emily thought. There was no way an adult Aurelia would fail to figure out that her condition was a lie.

Scott must have sensed her doubt. "Consider the alternative," he said. "Short-term, I mean. She'd be taken to some white-walled clinic to be poked and prodded. She'd have to give statements. She'd be ripped from her home for the second time in her short life, separated from her parents and handed her over to strangers—but this time, she would see everything, remember everything. And she would carry it with her for the rest of her life." He wiped his eyes. "Don't do that to her, Emily. Don't do it to Nina. They don't deserve any more pain. I would have thought you of all people would understand that."

Me of all people, Emily thought. *What's that supposed to mean?*

But she wasn't given any further chance to ponder it. Scott had plowed on with his argument and, to be fair, he made a good case. Emily couldn't imagine Aurelia in the arms of anyone else. She couldn't bear the thought of her being led into an unfamiliar house where she would be given strange food, strange clothes, and a strange bed. Who was her birth mother, anyway? What kind of person was she? How would she care for Aurelia? How would she speak to her? In *French,* that's how. Amandine Tessier might have spoken French, but Aurelia Denny had barely heard a word spoken in three years.

Emily shook her head. "Nina will find me."

"No. She won't even look."

No, of course Nina would not look for her. Nina thought she was dead. Nina thought Scott had shot, killed, and buried her in the woods.

Emily spun around and vomited. When she was done, she wiped her mouth and nodded her assent. *Yes. I will keep your secret. Cross my heart and hope to die. Here, let me help you dig a fake grave. Do you have an extra shovel?*

Scott told her to keep the credit card and promised an initial lump sum deposited into her own bank account within the next two to three business days. Providing Emily adhered to the conditions, the rest would follow at regular intervals. He smiled, a well-oiled nod. *A pleasure doing business with you.*

Then he stomped off through the trees to gather a number of large rocks. He threw them into the hole and covered them with a blanket pulled from the back of the Land Cruiser. "In case she gets curious," he explained.

Emily threw up again.

After he filled the hole in, Scott drove her to La Rochelle. Neither of them said a word the entire way.

They pulled up next to a bus shelter near the harbor. A thin line of light was just beginning to appear on the horizon.

"Go to the Sinclair Hotel in Covent Garden," he said. "They'll have a room ready for you." Reaching behind him, he pulled his suit jacket from the backseat and draped it over her shoulders. "Wait for me there. I'll come in a few days. We can talk some more."

Emily tried to picture herself in a hotel suite, but she'd been so immersed in Querencia for so long, so consumed by it, that she couldn't imagine being anywhere else. She thought about her first glimpse of the estate and how happy she'd been, how grateful that life had finally thrown her a bone.

As the first rays of the sun broke over the water, Scott turned to her. "Please," he whispered, "think carefully about everything I've said." The moment felt significant, but Emily had nothing to say. Her fear and rage had dissolved, leaving her feeling hollowed out.

She took one last good look at him, pocketing details like souvenirs. The freckle just above his right eyebrow, the neat cluster of hairs below his lower lip, his fingernails, now bitten and dirty, his eyes, red-rimmed with fatigue.

Finally, she opened the door and stepped onto the pavement. Tugging Scott's jacket around her bare shoulders, she looked back, and an absurd, babyish thought flew out of her heart: *please don't leave me.*

"I was right," Scott said with a small smile. "You really were perfect. For all of us." Then he pulled the door shut and drove away.

* * *

It was such a relief to be back among familiar surrounding that she nearly kissed the filthy London street. The traffic, the fumes, all the angry people; nothing on earth could've been more welcome.

Hobbling into the lobby of the Sinclair, she ignored all the curious stares and successfully checked in. She didn't last, though. Wrapped in a towel after taking a long, hot shower, she lay on the ridiculously huge bed, bawling into the pillows. Her wails bounced off the textured wallpaper and disappeared in the folds of the curtains. A marble bust of a topless woman observed her with smooth cloudy eyes.

Wait for me. I'll come in a few days.

Emily imagined Scott opening the door and walking in. Champagne, strawberries. Dinner somewhere nice. How long did he plan to hide her at the hotel? Forever?

After two solid hours of crying, Emily got to her feet, blew her nose, and slung her mud-streaked bag over her shoulder. Throwing Scott's jacket onto the bed, she checked out, then made her way to St. Pancras Station, where she caught the first train going north.

The taxi pulled up outside a semidetached sandstone house with a red door, and Emily's bottom lip trembled at the sight of the brightly lit windows. They were home, just as she knew they would be. Wednesday was *Grand Designs* and an early night, regular as clockwork.

She handed Scott's card over and watched as the driver tapped it against the machine. It beeped. *Payment processed.* The cabbie raised his eyebrows. Emily couldn't blame him for being surprised; she'd cleaned up her wounds as best she could but she still looked like hell.

She was crying even before her mother opened the door.

Juliet gasped. "Oh my god, where have you been? How did you get here?" She pulled Emily into a tight embrace. "You should have called!"

At what point should I have called? Emily thought, her old hackles rising like an allergic reaction. *When I was trapped in the car, being shot at in the woods, or digging my own grave?*

"Oh goodness, are you *bleeding*?"

Emily glanced down as Juliet grabbed hold of her lacerated shoulder.

"Let me look at that." Peter appeared from behind Juliet's shoulder, peering through his tortoiseshell bifocals. He took a handkerchief from his pocket—Peter was the only person alive who still used a handkerchief—and dabbed at the wound, making Emily feel about seven years old.

Straightening up, he breathed a heavy, malty sigh. "What's going on, Emmy?"

Emily opened her mouth. *I nearly died,* she almost said. But those words had no place here in this house, in this shrine to the ordinary.

Her parents smelled of milk and cookies. The smell of cinnamon wafted from the kitchen, and Kevin McCloud delivered his final thoughts from the living room.

It doesn't matter, she thought. *None of it matters. I'm home.*

In the days that followed, Juliet treated Emily like a sick patient, and Emily was happy to be mollycoddled. She offered no explanation for her sudden reappearance, but, in true Proudman fashion, no one asked. Juliet and Peter just tiptoed around her and made more tea, and for once in her life, Emily was grateful for their inability to communicate.

She slept a lot: shallow, fitful naps full of sinister dreams. For three nights running, she woke up drenched in sweat, convinced someone was trying to break into the house.

She cried every day. There was an empty, sick feeling under her ribs, like she hadn't eaten for weeks, but which wouldn't go away no matter how much she ate.

She watched a lot of TV. She crawled into bed and vowed never to leave.

After a few days, however, she ventured outside, taking short trips to the local shops, or walks with Juliet to the park. But every time she left the house, she felt sick. She saw Scott everywhere: driving cars, picking up dry cleaning, waiting in line at the butcher's. What would he do when he discovered she was no longer at the Sinclair? Did he already know? He would contact her; she was sure of it. But when? And how?

Three days after she arrived back in England, Emily got a text from an unknown number.

> I'm sorry the hotel didn't work out. However, I understand the need to regroup. I trust this first installment will take the pressure off.

Her stomach flipped. She immediately checked her banking app and saw that an obscene amount of money had been deposited into her checking account. A second text followed a few minutes later.

> Enjoy your visit. Your parents have a beautiful home.

Leaping off her bed, she ran to the window and pressed her face to the glass. She scanned the pavement, the bus stop, the cars, and the bushes, expecting to see a flash of silk tie or a glint of gold watch. But the street was empty.

Without even a second's hesitation, she dialed the unknown number and waited, listening first to a gaping silence and then to a recorded message informing her that the number she had dialed was not available. She tried Scott's usual number, the one she couldn't quite bring herself to delete, but got the same message. Disconnected.

In her first days back, Emily spent a huge amount of time on the internet. She couldn't help it. She Googled Amandine Tessier compulsively, reading every available article and interview she could find. She watched old news reports showing grainy images of a seaside town beset by a storm. The reporters talked about freak weather conditions, explaining how initially police had assumed that Amandine had been swept into the ocean—knocked out by a falling object, perhaps, her little body unheeded in the melee. But then two tourists had come forward claiming they'd seen her. A man who'd been in the private beach area with his children, and a backpacker on the promenade.

"It was her," said the man. "I'm sure of it."

"She was on the road," said the backpacker. "A woman was carrying her. Then the tree came down and almost hit them. I tried to help. There were flames everywhere."

Neither of the witnesses, however, could provide a positive ID for the woman. They hadn't seen her face; she'd been carrying a large umbrella and wearing a hat, but they couldn't agree on what kind, and couldn't even guess at her age.

"She was wearing sunglasses," said the man.

"It was hard to see through all the rain and smoke," said the backpacker.

CCTV footage had been useless. As well as igniting trees, the lightning had knocked out a crucial section of the network, and the surviving cameras were no help. They showed hundreds of hooded figures dashing into doorways and diving into cars with hats and towels thrown over their heads, many of them carrying children.

Nina, it seemed, had been extremely lucky.

Of course, once the word got out that the disappearance was being treated as an abduction, the phone calls came flooding in, all describing sightings of a red-haired child at the beach, at the shops, at the cinema. They reported a man dragging a child, a woman smacking a child, a child all alone, a child crossing the road, getting into a car, eating ice cream, running, screaming, falling, crying. People posted photos of their neighbors online, pointing out that the DuPonts or the Wilsons or the Garcias who just moved in across the road, they had a daughter or a niece or a cousin with heterochromia, could she be Amandine? Several citizen's arrests were made in shopping centers and doctor's surgeries, young mothers detained and interrogated on account of their daughters' different-colored eyes. Police had apparently spent years trying to follow up on all the leads, but astonishingly, no one had seen anything significant.

"If you have any information at all," said a coiffed TV presenter in a colorful studio, "please call the help line."

Emily pored over every blog, support-group forum, and crazy conspiracy website. She watched endless videos of press conferences. Amandine's family, their faces waxen and pinched in the flashing white light. Her siblings, sad and small. She replayed the footage over and over until she knew each video by heart. She watched Nicolette Tessier break down over and over again, weeping into a bouquet of microphones.

Emily clicked on more links. A famous singer, an international star heavily involved with children's charities, had paid the case some lip service, and the Storm Child made global headlines. There were late-night panel-show discussions and social-media debates. But no amount of talk could bring Amandine back, nor could it produce any further clues as to her whereabouts. Her body was never found, and eventually it was decided that the ocean must have claimed her after all.

Emily also spent a lot of time missing Nina. She thought about the way she laughed, the way she spoke. The way she knew exactly what to say when Emily was feeling low. She thought about all the conversations they'd had. Emily had shared her innermost secrets. *They weren't very nice, apparently. Hit me and stuff. I don't remember it.* She'd never told anyone that.

She'd never spoken about her therapy, either, not with anyone other than her parents. *They thought my body might have retained some memory of the abuse. Not the kind of memory we have as adults or older children. Something different. There's a word for it.* That word, she remembered, was "implicit." Dr.

Forte had once tried to explain it. Past experiences recalled subconsciously. Trauma stored and encoded as pictures or physical sensations. Splinters of memories, slicing into the mind. *The body keeps the score,* she'd said.

Emily returned to Google and searched for information on early childhood trauma. She realized that even though there was very little chance Aurelia explicitly remembered that fateful day in Nice, she was reliving her abduction on an almost daily basis. Every time she heard thunder or got caught in the rain or was touched in a particular way, her *body* remembered—and it reacted. Sometimes that reaction took the shape of an emotional outburst; other times it would manifest as a fixation or a phobia. Or a bloody great bonfire. Either way, everything led back to what had happened . . . which posed unsettling questions about Emily's own behavioral patterns. The tantrums, the nightmares, the visits to Dr. Forte's office. The panic attacks. The flurry. The heavy object. It made her wonder: what exactly was *she* reliving? What did *her* body remember?

On the twelfth day after her return to England, Emily woke up filled with a burning sense of purpose. She got up, got dressed, and spent the morning on her parents' computer, downing cup after cup of instant Nescafé. She scribbled notes in a spiral-bound notebook. She made a phone call. Then she grabbed her wallet and caught the bus into the village.

In the supermarket, she filled her basket with cod fillets, jasmine rice, and feta cheese. She bought tomatoes, garlic, zucchini, eggplant, a fat bunch of mint, and the most expensive bottle of wine in the shop. At the self-service checkout, she waved her card over the card reader. This time, unsurprisingly, she had no problem paying.

Then she crossed the road to the bank, where she gave her account details to a cashier whose pinched mouth and downturned eyes made Emily wonder what kind of life she'd led. *What's your story?* she thought as the woman tapped mechanically at her keyboard. *What secrets are you hiding?* Everyone was carrying something, she was beginning to realize. The world was a much darker and more complicated place than she'd ever thought.

"Are you sure you want to close this account, dear?" asked the cashier, doubtfully.

Emily nodded.

"And what would you like to do with the, er, closing balance."

Emily told her.

The cashier blanched. "All of it?"

"All of it. These," Emily slid a piece of paper under the partition, "are the payee details."

The cashier raised her eyebrows and mumbled something about wonders never ceasing.

Other than the odd coin thrown in a jar, Emily had never donated to charity before, and the feeling it gave her was like stepping into a warm bath. She decided to focus on that, rather than on the little voice inside that whispered, *What have you done, you crazy stupid fool?*

The right thing, she told the voice, slamming a mental door in its face.

The representative she'd spoken to on the phone earlier had been comforting. "I wish there were more people like you," he'd said, once he realized she wasn't joking. "On behalf of Missing People UK, I'd like to thank you from the bottom of our hearts."

Leaving the bank, Emily caught sight of her reflection in the huge square windows. She looked taller, somehow. Lighter.

Back in the kitchen, Emily took a pair of scissors from the cutlery drawer. She cut Scott's Amex card into four neat pieces and dropped them into the bin. Then she unpacked her shopping bags on the countertop. She placed all the ingredients in small bowls, laying them out in the exact order that she would need them, just as Nina had taught her. Stepping back, she checked the clock on the wall. Just over an hour until her parents came home from work. *Perfect.* Plenty of time.

She would make a nice dinner. She would open the wine. She would spend time with her parents. After that . . . well, that was where she ran out of ideas. She would have to earn some money at some point. Get a job. Probably not acting, but hopefully something she liked. There was a multitude of possibilities out there, some more achievable than others, but they were there. And she would build a life, all by herself.

But first, before all that could happen, before she could even start cooking, there was something she had to do.

Grabbing her jacket, she slipped out the back door. The sun was still high in the sky but the afternoon heat had eased considerably with the arrival of a chilly northerly breeze. Autumn was on its way, much to the apparent relief of the British public. According to Peter, the summer had been the hottest on European record, with more consecutive sunny days than ever before. Everyone had enjoyed it, he said, for the first couple of weeks; after that they all started wishing for rain again. There was just no pleasing some people.

Emily wandered down the garden path, ducking under the arch of sweet peas, and pushed open the back gate. All the houses on this side of the street backed onto a chattering stream and a public footpath that ran right from the outermost cottage all the way into town. Turning left, she followed the flowing water past rows of neatly tended yards until she reached the "pooh-stick" bridge, a narrow slab of concrete from which she used to conduct stick-race championships with her friends on her way home from school.

Ducking under green metal railings, Emily scrambled down the bank until she reached an old weathered log with a soft spot in the middle where the wood had been worn smooth. She sat down and stretched out her legs. Then she slipped her phone from her jacket pocket and prised off the case. Plucking out the torn piece of paper she'd stuffed inside earlier that morning, she smoothed it out and read over the string of numbers she'd scrawled on the back.

Something in her stomach slipped and slithered as she entered the numbers into the keypad. *This is it,* she thought. Once she pushed that call button, there was no going back. Just one tiny movement and it would all be over.

She thought of Scott. She was ashamed, now, of the way she'd thrown herself at him, embarrassed to admit how badly she'd wanted to be saved, to be chosen. She'd been so blind. She'd seen only what she wanted to see and had made him into something he wasn't. She felt bitter. Betrayed. But a small shred of affection remained.

A slideshow of images flashed, strobe-like, through her head. The way the rising sun had lit his face at the bus stop in La Rochelle. The sound of his voice as she got out of the car. *Think carefully about everything I've said.* The restaurant in London; that boyish smile. *The smallest thing can change your life. And just like that, nothing is ever the same again.* Her own cookie-smeared face reflected in the gleaming surfaces of his office. *I think you can give us something we just wouldn't get from an agency.* And finally, her belly full of ice cream, her heart full of hope, her hand outstretched to accept a key. *I knew you'd be perfect. For all of us.*

He'd left so many clues, so many white flags. She wondered why it had taken her so long to see them.

A bird wheeled in the sky above her head, and she followed its path, wondering what it might it feel like to fly, to jump up in the air right this minute and take off, to soar among the clouds, over hills and roads, beaches and headlands. If she could fly, she would close her eyes and follow the wind. She would let it take her where it wanted. She might travel over a vast ocean and an expanse of trees, over a canopy so thick and swollen that it appeared to be an extension of the sea. If she looked down, she might see pinpricks of light glittering through the canopy like diamonds in a rock. And if she flew closer, she might see a house, and a woman sitting on a paved outcrop, a glass of crisp flax-colored liquid in her hand.

Perhaps a man would step out of the shadows and join her, a man with brown hair and black eyes. He would be carrying a child.

If Emily dipped down low, she might hear the man speak. *I heard her crying,* he might say. *She had a bad dream.* And the woman would reach out, and they would all wrap their arms around each other and press their heads close, the very picture of love. The perfect family.

Emily might then pull back, reluctant to intrude, and circle away into the night sky like Peter Pan. She would ride the currents across yet more trees and water, winding roads and patchwork fields, until she saw bright lights and tall buildings. Spiraling above houses and tower blocks, she might spot another woman, a woman with red hair and unanswered questions, sitting on a different kind of outcrop: a concrete slab overlooking a busy street. This woman would be alone, her arms empty and aching.

Emily looked down at her phone. Her thumb twitched.

Wait. Not yet.

Any minute now, the world would change. Her life and the lives of many others would never be the same again. But right now, everything was deliciously quiet and still, as if someone had hit the pause button.

Just a little longer, she thought. *Just one more minute.*

From somewhere behind her came the tinkle of cutlery and the rattle of plates. An overlap of voices spilled out of an open window, followed by a burst of laughter. The happy sound of safe, cozy homes.

CHAPTER FIFTY-ONE

SCOTT

WHEN THEY came for him, Scott was upstairs in the guesthouse.

He stood in Emily's old room, leaning on the frame of the balcony doors and looking out at the vast stretch of ocean. A murmuration of starlings moved on the horizon, wheeling and swinging in ever-changing patterns, a group of thousands contracting and dilating as one. Transfixed, he watched them with raised arms, mimicking their movement with his hands, his thoughts swirling with them, his feeble brain able to process neither the sheer beauty of Mother Nature nor the huge amount of drugs in his system.

About an hour ago, he'd found a shitload of pills in Nina's bathroom—Valium, he assumed, but they could've been anything—and had thrown a whole handful down his throat.

Scott had suffered for years, but he'd never taken any medication. He drank—good god, he drank—and he'd found creative ways to ease his pain, pink, puckered evidence of which could be found all over his body. But medication had always been off-limits, because it would be confirmation that his mental health was in no better state than Nina's.

But then Emily left him. Or rather, they left each other.

And then he'd had to lie and pretend to his wife that he'd murdered Emily, which was especially awkward because he'd developed some very complicated feelings for his former employee. Emily had made him feel young and exciting, as if he could start his life all over again. She'd reminded him of who he used to be.

But she was gone now, and she'd taken with her any last vestige of hope that he would ever be that person again. He was trapped in this miserable fucking snow globe for the rest of his life, and he could never leave, no matter how hard he tried to break the glass.

Hence the pills. He felt a flush of pleasure as he patted his pocket, feeling the packet he'd stuffed in there for later.

Scott was discovering that he liked Valium a lot, if that's what it was. He felt wonderfully calm and floaty, with a little fizzy buzz running gently through his bloodstream. He was so relaxed, in fact, that he felt his feet leave the floor. He rose into the air and hovered above the balcony, bobbing gently like a balloon.

As he rose higher, his attention returned to the birds. He wondered if he might actually *be* a bird. He was something other than human, anyway. His skin was splitting, peeling back in strips and giving way to black feathers, which grew and rose up like spines, poking through his torn flesh. Scott stared as his arms melted away, transformed into enormous black wings that stretched out behind him, and the flock of birds stopped their swinging and swaying to admire him. Turning as one, they flew toward him, coming to claim him as one of their own.

Scott squinted. The birds really *were* coming. In fact, a really big one had broken away from the flock and was aiming straight for him, growing bigger and bigger and making a peculiar sound, a dreadful thumping and whirring. Scott reached out his hand—*take me away, giant bird*—but a great wind knocked him backward and whipped at his hair, and he understood then that he was wrong. This was no bird.

A voice scratched through a megaphone. Scott looked down from his great height and was surprised to see people swarming all over the property, little black creatures running up and down the paths, devouring the flower beds just like the ants in his office had devoured the cockroaches. He ought to call Yves, tell him to do a pest spray.

But then he remembered that Yves had taken his family and disappeared without a word. Scott had been to his house and found it empty as a mausoleum. *Touché, my friend,* he'd thought as he surveyed the bare floorboards.

Another strange sound; something was wailing. The gates at the top of the driveway had swung open and cars were streaming through, flashing with pretty lights. They stopped outside the family house, and from their doors burst more swarming creatures.

A woman strode into their midst and barked orders, a woman in uniform with short dark hair and thick-rimmed glasses. *The Ant Queen,* Scott thought.

He watched things unfold with a detached curiosity. He saw the Ant Queen talking into her phone. Saw her army of ants swarming in and out of his home, spilling from the front door as if from the mouth of a corpse. Saw them bearing his wife away, carrying her from the house bucking and howling, shaking her beautiful head from side to side, her face red and screwed up like a newborn baby's. Nina was thrashing so violently that the ants were pulled in all directions; they struggled to keep their grip, their cheeks wet with her spit. She screamed, and her teeth flashed white.

"*Aureeeeeliaaaaaaa!*"

Then Aurelia herself appeared, and Scott felt a dull kick in his belly, a sudden drop that made him think of theme parks.

Aurelia fought like she was being taken to the gallows, her little fingers scrabbling and scratching, her feet lashing out at whatever they could find. She cried petrified, hysterical tears and threw back her head, shrieking her terror to the sky.

Nina reached out to the specter of their dead child one last time before the little ant men forced them both apart, wrestling them into separate police cars. They shoved the doors closed as if rolling a stone across a tomb.

And above it all Scott looked on: impassive, invulnerable. Amid the chaos, the Ant Queen's eyes locked onto his winged form, and he felt momentarily stunned, turned inside out by her stare.

The Ant Queen opened her mouth, her palm flat in front of her. *Stop,* she commanded.

As she broke into a run, Scott tore his eyes away, seeking instead the flat majesty of the ocean. He found himself thinking not of his own escape, but of Emily. He could still feel her in his arms, still hear her voice. "Why am I here?" she'd asked. At the time the answer had seemed simple. He'd hired her because he needed help. Because she was a weak, suggestible person who wouldn't ask questions, a lost soul who wanted to be found. He remembered how ecstatic he'd been when he opened that orange envelope in his office. As he read the court transcripts, the welfare report, and the psychologist's profile, he knew he'd hit the jackpot. He'd found the one person in the world who would *understand*, who would connect with his family and see their line of reasoning.

But standing there on the balcony with his arms outstretched, the truth came to him with diamond-hard clarity. He'd had the whole thing back to front from the very beginning. Emily had been the right choice, not because she *would* support them but because she *wouldn't*. She would identify with Aurelia's experience, but she would also abhor it. She would see the nightmare for what it was. And she would end it.

Without even knowing it, he'd hired Emily for *this*. He'd seen her heart and knew she would do what he never could.

Scott felt his toes curl over the edge of something metallic. He looked down and saw his feet balancing on the balustrade—not birdlike at all, not claws, but pale pink and fleshy, like baby mice.

It's over, he thought as he listened to the thump of footsteps on the stairs.

And he was surprised to find that he didn't feel sad. He didn't feel angry or scared or full of regret.

He felt free.

EPILOGUE

Emily found her parents in the garden, sitting on the terrace under the cherry tree, empty dinner plates on the table in front of them. Juliet was reading aloud from a newspaper, the pages tilted toward the glare of a camping lantern; Peter was reclining in his chair, his hands clasped over his stomach.

"You okay, love?" Peter said, regarding her over the top of his glasses. "You look a bit peaky."

Emily took a deep breath, questions swarming in her head. *Here it is,* she thought. *This is the perfect opportunity to ask.*

A full moon was rising early, its pale face just visible through the branches of the tree. She studied her mother's face, her hands, remembering all the times Juliet had tucked her into bed, picked her up when she fell, clapped when she learned something new. Her father's eyes, once bright and blue, had seen her laugh and cry, dance and run, fail and succeed. Now, soft pouches hung beneath them like bruised plums, and his cheeks were mottled with broken capillaries. When had he become so old?

She realized then how selfish she'd been. She'd treated her parents like monsters when in fact they were just a bit annoying, probably no more so than anyone else's mum and dad. It wasn't

341

true that they never listened; Emily had just never given them the chance. Well, that chance was here. It was now.

"You're right," she said, "I'm not feeling great. But you know what might make me feel better?"

"What's that, darling?"

She nearly said it. She was so close. *What happened to me? Where did I come from? Who am I?* But Juliet's tender expression made her think again. Her parents had done their best, and she was okay. There was nothing wrong with her, nothing rotten inside. Sure, she had a few issues, but she'd made it out of the woods, both literally and figuratively, and she could do it again if she had to. She may have been a victim once, but she wasn't anymore. Perhaps some things were better left buried.

Emily smiled. "A nice cup of tea."

"Cracking idea," Peter said, "Pop the kettle on, would you, love?"

Emily walked back toward the house. Just as she reached the back door, Juliet's voice followed her down the garden path. "There are biscuits in the tin, too, darling. Your favorite."

Emily stopped, her fingers resting on the door handle. Somewhere inside her, things were beginning to shift. It was as if, after years of scrabbling around trying to pick up all the patchwork pieces of her life, she finally held them all in her hands. And even though there was no way of knowing yet how they all fit together, she knew that someday they would.

"Thanks, Mum," she called back.

Raising her face to the fading light, Emily watched as violet clouds merged and parted, drifting soundlessly across the sky, revealing a faint splatter of tiny, winking lights.

The stars were coming out.

ACKNOWLEDGMENTS

It is an honor and a privilege to acknowledge my teammates. All you phenomenal people who took a chance on me, who saw the potential in my manuscript, and who have worked so hard and so collaboratively to put it out into the world. Guys, you've changed my life. Because of you, both my book and I are much better versions of ourselves. Huge heartfelt thanks to:

My spectacular agents. Hillary Jacobson (my first yes), whose relentless Graft and unerring faith in me is a daily miracle, and Tara Wynne, whose advice, reassurance, friendship, and sharp elbows mean the world to me. How I lucked out with you two I will never know. Shout out to the wider teams at Curtis Brown Australia and ICM Partners, for all their support. I'm also forever grateful to the very wonderful Katie Greenstreet at C+W, as well as Kate Cooper and the translation rights team at Curtis Brown UK.

My exceptional publishers the world over. At Minotaur Books, Catherine Richards has managed somehow to convince me that she has been standing by my side throughout this entire journey whilst actually remaining thousands of miles away. Catherine, I could not be more grateful for your guidance, generosity, and eagle-eyed editing expertise. Additional thanks to Nettie Finn,

Hector DeJean, Joe Brosnan, Steve Erickson, Kelley Ragland, and the wider team, who have pulled out all the stops to make this book the best it can be.

Over at Affirm Press, I could not do without the extraordinary passion and enthusiasm of Martin Hughes, which truly has to be experienced first-hand to be believed. Both he and Ruby Ashby-Orr have proved to be the rigorous and insightful editors that both I and this book so desperately needed, while Keiran Rogers and Grace Breen continue to amaze me with their warmth and dedication. Big love to the whole gorgeous gang.

At Hodder and Stoughton, Eve Hall has been an invaluable collaborator and a total joy to work with. Eve, I so appreciate all your input and faith in me. Massive gratitude, too, to the whole Hodder team, for all your time and effort (especially Ellie Wheeldon for the audio encouragement!).

I'd like to thank the writing community at large, both at home and abroad; never have I encountered a warmer and more supportive bunch of people. I'm also indebted to my Curtis Brown Creative course-mates/beta readers/international writers group, for all their solidarity and motivation, especially Polly Crosby, Paula Arblaster, Ben Jones, Jo Kavanagh, Carol Barnes-Burrell, Sarah Jane King, Tracy Curzon-Manners, Kristy Gillies and Matt Telfer, who suggested the title.

This list would not be complete without the mention of my former employees, who I won't name but whose stunning house provided the inspiration for *Querencia*. Thank you so much, both of you.

I'd also like to acknowledge my family and friends, the people who have loved and supported not just my best self but my worst, and all the selves in between. I couldn't, and wouldn't want to, do life without you. Extra special thanks to:

Carly, Annabel, Caitlin, and Polly, for always being there.

Everyone who read early drafts and gave valuable feedback, especially Aoife Searles, Sarah Edwards, Sophie Devonshire, my stepmum, Liz, and my stepdad, Charlie.

Beth Vuk, for answering my questions on child psychology, and Abi Campbell, for the medical advice.

My Aussie tribe (you know who you are), especially Candice Boyd, for being a one-woman cheerleading squad and Jackie Lollback, whose kindness and regular willingness to look after my children so I can write is nothing short of mind-blowing.

My former day-job bosses, Richard and Chris, who did not fire me even though I was frequently found to be writing when I should've been working.

My in-laws, Bev and Pete, for all the emergency babysitting.

My mum, Heather, who basically makes my world go round.

My grandparents Jo and Ken, who always told me I could, and apparently always knew I would. My dad, Robert, the original storyteller. And Lu, my sister, best friend, and best whisp. (We are the same.)

My astonishing, clever, hilarious, beautiful children, Jack and Daisy. In blowing my world apart, you forced me to build a bigger, better and much happier one. I love you so much.

And finally, Matt, who is everything to me, and without whom none of this would ever have been possible.

AUTHOR'S NOTE

First of all, thank you from the very bottom of my heart for reading *The Safe Place*. When I was writing it, I worried all the time about getting it right, making it perfect; but then somewhere around the third draft, a close friend said something that really made me think.

"Your book will never be perfect," she said.

"Thanks," I said.

"I haven't finished," she said. "It will never be perfect until it finds its readers."

I was confused. Surely a book only finds readers through publication, and why would anyone publish a flawed piece of work? But I think what my friend meant was this: that even the most brilliant, rigorously edited story is only a half-formed thing until it is read. And then it is completed by the mind of the person who picks it up.

So, I am forever grateful to you, reader, for picking up my book—not because you have made it perfect (perfection, I have since learned, is a myth), but for completing it. I truly hope that you enjoyed it, and if you'd like to get in touch to tell me what you think, I'd love to hear from you. Drop me an email or say hi on social media. There's not much I love more than book chat.

Speaking of which, I'd like to take a minute to explain exactly how *The Safe Place* came to be. Because, in a roundabout sort of way, it completed me.

I grew up surrounded by storytellers of one kind or another. Raised on a diet of drama, I was always a creative kid, and I especially loved to write. But at around age ten, I was bitten hard by the theater bug.

For years, I was single-minded in my pursuit of an acting career. It was everything to me: my identifier. *The girl in the play.* There was nothing I enjoyed more than the rehearsal process and nowhere I felt more at home than on a stage. I worked relentlessly to achieve my dream of acting professionally and achieve it I did. After I graduated from drama school, I found employment in both theater and television—but it was a hard road and, as it turned out, I am not someone who deals well with unpredictability. The unstable nature of the job knocked me sideways and gave rise to extreme levels of anxiety and loneliness. In the end, it all got too much, and my career crumbled. Stripped of what I'd always considered to be my purpose in life, I felt lost and worthless. So, in 2008, I did the sensible thing and I ran away. (Any of this sound familiar?)

I went traveling. I lived on a snowy mountain and swam in the Red Sea. I climbed temples and rode horses. I fell in love with a tall, handsome Australian who would one day become my husband, and together we chased adventure wherever we could.

One of these adventures led us to a job working for an Anglo-American family of four, taking care of their spectacular holiday home on the mid-west coast of France. It couldn't have been more perfect: the work was cruisy, and our employers were warm, funny, and exceptionally generous (we remain friends to this day). I should emphasize that nothing sinister happened while were there, and the characters in this book are in no way based on them, nor on anyone else with whom we came into contact during our stay. But the property was truly extraordinary. Living there gave us a glimpse into another world and its remote location guaranteed absolute privacy. We were more or less completely off the grid. *Anything could happen here,* I remember thinking at the time, *and no one would know.*

Sunshine, freedom, romance . . . running away had worked out pretty well for me. But in the back of my mind, I had begun to wonder how long I could keep it up. What would happen when the traveling inevitably stopped? What would I do? Who would I be? On one level I was having the time of my life, but on another I was scared. In escaping my problems, I'd left so much of myself behind.

Fast forward to 2016, a year that nearly killed me. I was living in Australia with my wonderful husband and raising two beautiful children. We'd built a lovely life in an idyllic coastal setting—but for some reason I was falling apart. At one particularly low ebb, I found myself curled in a ball on the landing outside my youngest child's bedroom, unable to move. My baby was screaming from her cot, as was my toddler in the next room, but I couldn't go to them. I was having a complete mental shutdown because my children wouldn't take a nap. The anxiety, it seemed, was back.

Eventually, I picked myself up off the floor long enough to make an appointment with a psychologist. I saw her for months. Be kind to yourself, she said after every session. Take time out to do the things you love to do. Relax. Rest up. Recharge your oh-so-depleted batteries. But the only thing I wanted to do was work. Not just any work, though; I already had a part-time job and was in no way fulfilled. Instead, I felt adrift. Beyond all the nappies and the breastfeeding, I'd forgotten who I was. I'd run so far away from myself that I couldn't remember how to get back.

I missed telling stories, but I couldn't face acting again. So, I decided to try a different form of creativity: a quiet way to tell stories, on my own, just for myself. It was hard at first. I had no idea what I was doing, and between my job and the kids (my husband worked full-time) I had very little opportunity to learn. I read a few theory books, listened to some podcasts, and felt totally intimidated. I wrote a scene. It was terrible; I threw it away.

And the postnatal anxiety didn't go quietly. I was terribly homesick for my family and friends on the other side of the world, and I fretted endlessly about my kids. I had become obsessed with a news story from a few years earlier—you know the one: a little girl who vanished from a European holiday resort, never to be seen again. I Googled it constantly. I became irrationally afraid that something terrible was going to happen to my children while I wasn't watching, that someone was going to snatch them from under my nose.

But one of the advantages of that early motherhood "Twilight Zone," of being caught between reality and something else, is that the imagination tends to run wild. I wrote another scene, better than the last. And then I wrote another and another. I made use of the rare occasions when my children slept. I got up at 4:30 a.m. I scribbled notes in the back room at work. Within six months, I had 25,000 words of a novel. More important, I was happier. I was sleeping better, was less distracted, more able to cope. Best of all, I enjoyed spending time with my kids again.

At that point, though, I wasn't thinking about the long term; I just loved writing for writing's sake. I loved crafting my characters and hearing their voices in my head. I loved the sense of control and achievement I got when I nailed a scene. It helped me channel my fears and gave my heart the space it needed to expand. I didn't need it to go anywhere because, this time, creativity wasn't everything to me. It just helped.

But then, in 2017, at a literary festival in Sydney, I had what I can only call a "moment." I had booked myself into a writers' workshop led by an editor at a major publishing house. It was just something fun to do, something to keep me motivated, but at the end of the class the editor expressed interest in my work in progress. She said the story had potential. And just like that, something clicked. I knew it was time to get serious. I left that room on a tremendous high, filled with an indescribable energy.

That night I went home to my husband and posed a question: did he think that perhaps, if we shuffled a few things around, we could make time, as a family, for me to give writing a proper go? Like, as if it were a real thing?

"Sure," he said. "I think we can do that, if it's really what you want?"

"Yes," I said. "It is."

Three years later, here we are. It is a real thing. The proof is in your hands. And life is still complicated, because it always is, and I'm still the same person, but I now have something I never had before: a degree of balance.

That, and a book.

And those two things seem so miraculous to me that I'm . . . lost for words.

Well, *almost*.

ABOUT THE AUTHOR

Ona Janzen

ANNA DOWNES was born and raised in Sheffield, UK, but now lives just north of Sydney, Australia, with her husband and two children. She trained at the Royal Academy of Dramatic Art in London and worked as an actress before turning her attention to writing. She was shortlisted for the Sydney Writers Room Short Story Competition (2017) and longlisted for the Margaret River Press Short Story Competition (2018). *The Safe Place* was inspired by Anna's experiences working as a live-in housekeeper on a remote French estate in 2009 and 2010.